THE BEST OF
DEFENDING THE FUTURE

edited by Mike McPhail
and Danielle Ackley-McPhail

eBooks
Stratford, NJ

PUBLISHED BY
eSpec Books LLC
Danielle McPhail, Publisher
PO Box 493,
Stratford, New Jersey 08084
www.especbooks.com

ISBN (print): 978-1-942990-38-3
ISBN (ebook): 978-1-942990-39-0

Art Direction and Production: Mike McPhail, McP Digital Graphics

Copyeditor: Greg Schauer

Interior Design: Sidhe na Daire Multimedia
www.sidhenadaire.com

AUTOGRAPH DUTY ROSTER

Jack McDevitt	Jeff Young
Jeffrey Lyman	Mike McPhail
Lawrence M. Schoen	John G. Hemry
John C. Wright	Robert E. Waters
Andy Remic	Nancy Jane Moore
Danielle Ackley-McPhail	Maria V. Snyder
Charles E. Gannon	Brenda Cooper
Bud Sparhawk	Keith R.A. DeCandido
CJ Henderson	David Sherman
James Chambers	Judi Fleming

Other Defending The Future Titles

Dogs of War

CONTENTS

DEDICATED TO DTF

THE STORY OF WHAT WOULD BECOME THE DEFENDING THE FUTURE SERIES BEGAN IN THE spring of 2005 with a phone call. The wife, Danielle Ackley-McPhail, was off at Lunacon and for the first time I managed to stay home instead of attending the convention. When I answered her call the first thing she said was, "The next person you talk to, say yes!" Little did I know then what was to come...

The person she put on the phone wanted me to be the editor and cover artist for an anthology by a small press named Spyre. I was confused. Up until that moment I had only worked on game manual designs (namely the Alliance Archives MRPG), and wasn't known as a mainstream editor; but I followed my wife's instructions, and agreed.

Eventually the circumstance of why I was chosen came out into the open. CJ Henderson, a man who I grew to respect and love as a friend, and his cohort, Patrick Thomas, were looking for anthology ideas from my wife. They liked several of those she gave them, but the one they wanted to do was *Breach The Hull*. Only they didn't want to do the editing work. My wife mentioned my military science fiction RPG and all the artwork I had done for it, and my fate was sealed.

That was over a decade ago, and in that time I have been pressed hard against the rails, as I pulled through the learning curve of being an editor and dealing with authors and the uncertainty and outright unprofessionalism of numerous small presses.

Where I had made my biggest mistake (beyond say yes), was not approaching this as an editor (do your job, take your pay, and move on). For me it was personal. This had been a chance to work with the authors I had met and sometime sat on panels with at conventions. Some were just acquaintances (or they could at least identify me in a crowd), but many had become my friends.

Whenever I brought someone into a project, I felt responsible for them, after all they were there because of me; this is where thing started to burn me out. Whenever a publisher started to screw up, I would intervene, often to little or no outcome—it wasn't my company, I had no control—so I stopped doing projects.

That is until 2014, when we started our own small press, eSpec Books LLC, of Stratford NJ. For the very first time, *I* had control of the series, and I could and would make a difference.

It had always been planned, that the very last book in the series would be titled, The Best of Defending The Future. Little did I suspect, it would only be the end of the first chapter.

Thank you all.

Mike McPhail
Series Editor

From **BREACH THE HULL**
Book One of the Defending The Future series

Black to Move by Jack McDevitt
Compartment Alpa by Jeffrey Lyman
Thresher by Lawrence M. Schoen
Peter Power Armor by John C. Wright

BLACK TO MOVE

Jack McDevitt

MAYBE IT'S JUST MY IMAGINATION, BUT I'M WORRIED.

The roast beef has no taste, and I'm guzzling my coffee. I'm sitting here watching Turner and Pappas working on the little brick house across the avenue with their hand picks. Jenson and McCarthy are standing over near the lander, arguing about something. And Julie Bremmer is about a block away drawing sketches of the blue towers. Everything is exactly as it was yesterday.

Except me.

In about two hours, I will talk to the Captain. I will try to warn him. Odd, but this is the only place in the city where people seem able to speak in normal tones. Elsewhere, voices are hushed. Subdued. It's like being in a church at midnight. I guess it's the fountain, with its silvery spray drifting back through the late afternoon sun, windblown, cool. The park glades are a refuge against the wide, still avenues and the empty windows. Leaves and grass are bright gold, but otherwise the vegetation is of a generally familiar cast. Through long, graceful branches, the blue towers glitter in the sunlight.

There is perhaps no sound quite so soothing as the slap of water on stone. (Coulter got the fountain working yesterday, using a generator from the lander.) Listening, seated on one of the benches at the fountain's edge, I can feel how close we are, the builders of this colossal city and I. And that thought is no comfort.

It's been a long, dusty, rockbound road from Earth to this park. The old hunt for extraterrestrial intelligence has taken us across a thousand sandy worlds in a quest that became, in time, a search for a blade of grass.

I will remember all my life standing on a beach under red Capella, watching the waves come in. Sky and sea were crystal blue; no gull wheeled through the still air; no strand of green boiled in the surf. It was a beach without a shell.

But here, west of Centauri, after almost two centuries, we have a living world! We looked down, unbelieving, at forests and jungles, and dipped our scoops into a crowded sea. The perpetual bridge game broke up.

On the second day, we saw the City.

A glittering sundisk, it lay in the southern temperate zone, between a mountain chain and the sea. With it came our first mystery: the City was alone. No other habitation existed anywhere on the planet. On the fourth day, Olzsewski gave his opinion that the City was deserted.

We went down and looked.

It appeared remarkably human, and might almost have been a modern terrestrial metropolis. But its inhabitants had put their cars in their garages, locked their homes, and gone for a walk.

Mark Conover, riding overhead in the *Chicago*, speculated that the builders were not native to this world.

They were jointed bipeds, somewhat larger than we are. We can sit in their chairs and those of us who are tall enough to be able to see through their windshields can drive their cars. Our sense of the place was that they'd left the day before we came.

It's a city of domes and minarets. The homes are spacious, with court-yards and gardens, now run to weed. And they were fond of games and sports. We found gymnasiums and parks and pools everywhere. There was a magnificent oceanfront stadium, and every private home seemed filled with playing cards and dice and geometrical puzzles and 81-square checker-boards.

They had apparently not discovered photography; nor, as far as we could determine, were they given to the plastic arts. There were no statues. Even the fountain lacked the usual boys on dolphins or winged women. It was instead a study in wet geometry, a complex of leaning slabs, balanced spheres, and odd-angled pyramids.

Consequently, we'd been there quite a while before we found out what the inhabitants looked like. That happened when we walked into a small home on the north side, and found some charcoal etchings.

Cats, someone said.

Maybe. The following day we came across an art museum and found several hundred watercolors, oils, tapestries, crystals, and so on.

They are felines, without doubt, but the eyes are chilling. The creatures in the paintings have nevertheless a human dimension. They are bundled against storms; they gaze across plowed fields at sunset; they smile benevolently (or pompously) out of portraits. In one particularly striking watercolor, four females cower beneath an angry sky. Between heaving clouds, a pair of full moons illuminate the scene.

This world has no satellite.

Virtually everyone crowded into the museum. It was a day of sighs and grunts and exclamations, but it brought us no closer to an answer to the central question: where had they gone?

"Just as well they're not here," Turner said, standing in front of the watercolor. "This is the only living world anyone has seen. It's one hell of a valuable piece of real estate. Nice of them to give it to us."

I was at the time standing across the gallery in front of a wall-sized oil. It was done in impressionistic style, reminiscent of Degas: a group of the creatures were gathered about a game of chess. Two were seated at the table, hunched over the pieces in the classic pose of the dedicated player. Several more, half in shadow, watched.

Their expressions were remarkably human. If one allowed for the ears and the fangs, the scene might easily have been a New York coffeehouse.

The table was set under a hanging lamp; its hazy illumination fell squarely on the board.

The game was not actually chess, of course. For one thing, the board had 81 squares. There was no queen. Instead, the king was flanked by a pair of pieces that vaguely resembled shields. Stylized hemispheres at the extremes of the position must have been rooks. (Where else but on the flank would one reasonably place a rook?)

The other pieces, too, were familiar. The left-hand Black bishop had been fianchettoed: a one-square angular move onto the long diagonal, from where it would exercise withering power. All four knights had been moved, and their twisted tracks betrayed their identity.

The game was still in its opening stages. White was two pawns up, temporarily. It appeared to be Black's move, and he would, I suspected, seize a White pawn which had strayed deep into what we would consider his queen-side.

I stood before that painting, feeling the stirrings of kinship and affection for these people and wondering what immutable laws of psychology, mathematics, and aesthetics ordained the creation of chess in cultures so distant from each other. I wondered whether the game might not prove a rite of passage of some sort.

I was about to leave when I detected a wrongness somewhere in the painting, as if a piece were misplaced, or the kibitzers were surreptitiously watching me. Whatever it was, I grew conscious of my breathing.

There was nothing.

I backed away, turned, and hurried out of the building.

I'm a symbologist, with a specialty in linguistics. If we ever do actually find someone out here to talk to, I'm the one who will be expected to say hello. That's an honor, I suppose; but I can't get Captain Cook entirely out of my mind.

By the end of the first week, we had not turned up any written material (and, in fact, still haven't) other than a few undecipherable inscriptions on the sides of buildings. They were even more computerized than we are, and we assumed everything went into the data banks, which we also haven't found. The computers themselves are wrecked. Slagged. So, by the way, is the central power core for the City. Another mystery.

Anyhow, I had little to do, so yesterday I went for a walk in the twilight with Jennifer East, a navigator and the pilot of the other lander. She's lovely, with bright hazel eyes, and a quick smile. Her long tawny hair was radiant in the setting sun. The atmosphere here has a moderately high oxygen content, which affects her the way some women are affected by martinis. She clung to my arm, and I was breathlessly aware of her long-legged stride.

We might have been walking through the streets of an idealized, mystical Baghdad: the towers were gold and purple in the failing light. Flights of brightly-colored birds scattered before us. I half-expected to hear the somber cry of a ram's horn, calling the faithful to prayer.

The avenue is lined with delicate, graybarked trees. Their broad, filamented leaves sighed in the wind, which was constant off the western mountains. Out at sea, thunder rumbled.

Behind the trees are the empty homes, no two alike, and other structures that we have not yet begun to analyze. Only the towers exceed three stories. The buildings are all beveled and curved; right angles do not exist. I wonder what the psychologists will make of that.

"I wonder how long they've been gone?" she said. Her eyes were luminous with excitement, directed (I'm sorry to say) at the architecture.

That had been a point of considerable debate. Many of the interiors revealed a degree of dust that suggested it could not have been more than a few weeks since someone had occupied them. But much of the pavement was in a state of disrepair, and on the City's inland side, forest was beginning to push through.

I told her I thought they'd been around quite recently.

"Mark," she said, staying close. "I wonder whether they've really left."

There was nothing you could put in a report, but I agreed that we were transients, that those streets had long run to laughter and song, that they soon would again, and that it would never really be ours.

She squeezed my arm. "It's magnificent."

I envied her; this was her first flight. For most of us, there had been too many broken landscapes, too much desert.

"Olszewski thinks," I said, "that the northern section of the City is almost two thousand years old.... They'd been here a while."

"And they just packed up and left." She steered us out of the center, angling toward the trees, where I think we both felt less conspicuous.

"It's ironic," I said. "No one would have believed first contact would come like this. They've been here since the time of Constantine, and we miss them by a few weeks. Hard to believe, isn't it?"

She frowned. "It's not believable." She touched one of the trees. "Did you know it's the second time?" she asked. I must have looked blank. "Twenty-two years ago the *Berlin* tracked something across the face of Algol and then lost it. Whatever it was, it threw a couple of sharp turns." We walked silently for several minutes, crossed another avenue, and approached the museum. "Algol," she said, "isn't all that far from here."

"UFO stories," I said. "They used to be common."

She shrugged. "It might be that the thing the *Berlin* saw frightened these people off. Or worse."

The museum is wheel-shaped. Heavy, curving panels of tinted glass are ribbed by polished black stone that is probably marble. The grounds are a wild tangle of weed and shrub anchored by overgrown hedge. A few flowering bushes survive out near the perimeter.

I laughed. "You don't suppose the sun is about to nova, do you?"

She smiled and brushed my cheek with a kiss. Jenny is 23 and a graduate of MIT. "It's going to rain," she said.

We walked past a turret. The air was cool.

"They seem to have taken their time about leaving," I said. "There's no evidence of panic or violence. And most of their personal belongings apparently went with them. Whatever happened, they had time to go home and pack."

She looked uneasily at the sky. Gray clouds were gathering in the west. "Why did they destroy the computers? And the power plant? Doesn't that sound like a retreat before an advancing enemy?"

We stood on the rounded stone steps at the entrance, watching the coming storm. Near the horizon, lightning touched the ground. It was delicate, like the trees.

And I knew what had disturbed me about the painting.

Jenny doesn't play chess. So when we stood again before the portrait and I explained, she listened dutifully, and then tried to reassure me. I couldn't blame her.

I have an appointment to meet the Captain in the gallery after dinner. He doesn't play chess either. Like all good captains down through the ages, he is a man of courage and hardheaded common sense, so he will also try to reassure me.

Maybe I'm wrong. I hope so.

But the position in that game: Black is playing the Benko Gambit. It's different in detail, of course; the game is different. But Black is about to clear a lane for the queenside rook. One bishop, at the opposite end of the board, is astride the long diagonal, where its terrible power will combine with that of the rook. And White, after the next move or two, when that advanced pawn comes off, will be desperately exposed.

It's the most advanced of the gambits for Black, still feared after three hundred years—.

And I keep thinking: the inhabitants of the City were surely aware of this world's value. More, they are competitors. They would assume that we would want to take it from them.

"But we wouldn't," Jenny had argued.

"Are you sure? Anyhow, it doesn't matter. The only thing that does matter is what they believe. And they would expect us to act as they would.

"Now, if they knew in advance that we were coming—"

"The *Berlin* sighting—"

"—Might have done it. Warned them we were in the neighborhood. So they withdraw, and give us the world. And, with it, an enigma." Rain had begun sliding down the tinted glass. "They're playing the Benko."

"You mean they might come back here in force and attack?" She was aghast, not at the possibility, which she dismissed; but at the direction my mind had taken.

"No," I said. "Not us. The Benko isn't designed to recover a lost pawn."

I could not look away from the painting. Did I detect a gleam of arrogance in Black's eyes? "No. It doesn't fool around with pawns. The idea is to launch a strike into the heart of the enemy position."

"Earth?" She smiled weakly. "They wouldn't even know where Earth is."

I didn't ask whether she thought we might not go home alone.

One more thing about that painting: there's a shading of light, a chia-roscuro, in the eyes of the onlookers. It's the joy of battle.

I'm scared.

First published in Asimov's, Sept, 1982. Copyright Davis Publications, 1982.

COMPARTMENT ALPHA

Jeffrey Lyman

COMMAND TO ALL AFT GUN BATTERIES." THE XO'S MESSAGE FLASHED ACROSS MY MIND on the ship's neural link. "Alert, five minutes to flares away. Countdown to Operation Slowdown begins now."

Alarms brayed for general quarters across the *Glory*. A five-minute countdown timer ran behind my right eye.

There was a lot of chatter on the neural link and I tuned it out. My nerves were tight enough. The engineers had struggled to keep us elevated in hyperspace his long. We should have fallen out hours ago, but they were milking the batteries for all they were worth. Forty-seven hours and counting, and now we were out of time.

I was the gunnery sergeant in charge of the aft, port gun, nicknamed "Annie". I hadn't left her remote feeds for all of these forty-seven hours. Other avatars came and went, quick as a wink, checking on our pursuit, but I remained at my post. I had stayed awake for longer periods before. With our bodies suspended in the core of the ship we didn't require much downtime from the link, and I needed to keep my eyes on the enemy. Our sister gun-cruisers had died getting us this far.

Square in Annie's sights sat Bandits 1 and 2. The *Aylin* destroyers glowed in the dim, roiling light of hyperspace. They weren't gaining and they weren't falling back; they were biding their time. They knew we would fall out of hyperspace before we reached inhabited space.

It had taken twenty-nine gun-cruisers to bring down four of their destroyers and three of their big carriers, so what could the *Glory* do alone? We had lost *Upsilon* Station, we had lost the Tarish system, and that was only the tip of the *Aylin* incursion. We had to warn Fleet. We had to survive in realspace long enough to launch a message-drone. That was the captain's orders.

Operation Slowdown was a crazy scheme cooked up by the navigators. It relied on the accuracy of the *Aylin* tracking computers. Those computers were waiting for us to drop out of hyperspace. They could calculate the emergence-time for a ship of our mass vs. a ship of their mass and drop in behind us with guns firing. We wouldn't have enough time to launch the message-drone. Unless we could somehow drop into realspace faster than their tracking computers calculated.

The navigators were going to hook us on a heavy gravitational mass, use it as a momentum yoke, and drop into realspace half a second faster than standard. The destroyers should over-shoot us by a kilometer. Then our forward and midship gun-batteries would rake them from behind while the message-drone sped away. The Captain made it clear we were protecting the drone. He didn't mention survival. So I remained at my post, unable to take my eyes off my killers.

"Eight-five seconds," I said to my targeting techs. "Let's push these flares up their noses."

Back in basic training I used to fantasize about being a hero. I figure everybody does at some point. Now at my final battle, my entire contribution would be a bunch of EMP flares.

I masked my fear. There was already a strange combination of calm and fear smoking up the neural link. Some resignation, some eagerness. Battle fever simmered.

My two techs crunched a thousand calculations a second in their heads and fed me preliminary vectors. Augmented humans are better than computers in hyperspace, but I still didn't trust the data. You just can't target in hyperspace. I prayed that one of our shots would come close enough to cloud the *Aylin* tracking computers. Give us a margin of safety.

My two ordnance jockeys limbered up their remote servos beside the breechings of Annie's twin, ten-meter long barrels and unloaded her 150mm warheads. Our only warheads! We had been ordered to ship them to the forward guns since aft guns would not be involved in the final firefight.

I began to elevate Annie's barrels based on the targeting vectors. I could hear echoes of the other gunnery sergeants prepping their crews. Bits of static that must have been nerves. Then the conveyers kicked to life and the steel balls housing the EMP flares rolled up from the armories.

The Gunnery Officer's voice came down from Fire Control. "Aft guns, load flares. You have been allotted twenty each."

I would have shrugged if I were in my body. Twenty flares, thirty flares, it didn't matter. We would send them on their way and then sit idle while the other guns tried to save our asses. I was desperate to shoot something. I didn't want to die with my barrel empty of warheads. Not after the *Mariah*.

The *Mariah* was the reason we escaped into hyperspace. She was behind us, shielding us, when an *Aylin* rocket caught her amidships. The cores of our gun-cruisers are so compartmentalized that we can operate with multiple hull-breaches. The *Mariah's* aft section continued to maneuver and fire long after her forward section had sheered off and exploded. She bought us an extra twenty seconds. This time, my barrels would be empty of all but flares. There would be no heroes at the aft guns.

"Command to Navigation and Propulsion: ninety seconds to reentry." The XO's voice was crisp and calm. The Captain's voice followed immediately. "Good hunting. I'm proud of the way this crew has manned the *Glory*. See you when they wake us up."

It was a joke, but it felt good to hear him say it. They couldn't wake us up until we were back in homeport on Earth and they had offloaded our bodies.

"Here we go," I said to my crew, happy that my voice was calm on the link. Our countdown was at ten seconds and we did have a part to play. A hundred avatars from other departments joined us at the aft feeds to watch. "Final vectors received," I said when my targeting techs sent me their best estimates. "... four...three...two...Releasing."

I cut power to Annie's magnets and the EMP flares rolled serenely down her barrels. You don't waste warheads in hyperspace because you can't aim, but flares had a much wider effect-radius. Eight flares dropped silently away from the four aft guns. Immediately my jockeys loaded new flares and I let them roll, adjusting Annie's barrel.

As the flares fell further behind the ship, they gyrated and twisted in the fluxes of hyperspace. The timers on the first wave went off and they detonated brightly, some near the destroyers and the rest spread across 180 degrees of view. The second wave detonated similarly. Not close enough. All of the guns changed barrel-elevations again, striving for accuracy.

"Mipship guns," the XO's voice came down, "begin rotation forward to Position-Gamma on my mark."

All avatars vanished except those required to be here. Engineering returned to nursing the FTL batteries. Navigation prepared the momentum yoke. The forward and midship gunners sat on their 150mm warheads like chickens on eggs. I continued releasing flares as fast as my servos could load.

"Mark." The XO's voice was accompanied by a neural signal and the four midship guns began rotating forward in unison on their gimbals. If one gun turned off-speed, it would change our center of gravity. The bow-shock would tear us apart. There is no turning in hyperspace.

I ignored the thought and stared down Annie's barrels, watching the flares detonate, praying for a miracle. As the reentry-timer counted down I pulled up a ghost image off the bow feeds. I needed to see the destroyers overshoot us when we dropped into realspace. I needed to be with the forward guns when they fired. If a compartment breached and a gunner's body died, my avatar might be rotated forward to take over a gun.

The XO's voice counted down to reentry. "... eight... seven..."

"See you when they wake us up," I said to my gun crew. We always say it. Superstition. We continued to roll flares down Annie's barrels until the countdown fell to zero. I hoped we had done enough to disorient the *Aylin* tracking computers.

I struggled against something wet and slippery and snake-like. I couldn't breathe. I panicked. I was blind and deaf. Something hard and cold shoved me. I tumbled, flailing. All of the voices on the link, my constant companions for a year, were gone. I was alone in a muffled shell of cottony thoughtsilence.

An electric cable arced below me bright and loud as I spun. I couldn't feel my legs. I hit a wall hard and someone grabbed me. A hand wiped liquid away from my face and I sucked air, coughing violently. Steel groaned and popped.

Where was our neural link? How could the neural link go down? Where were the destroyers?

The hands that held me rotated me. A face loomed in the dim light, inches in front of my eyes. A man with his hair wet and slicked back, wearing a taught skin-suit. He slapped my cheek and I grabbed his wrist.

"Are you awake, Sergeant?" he shouted in my face. My ears roared. "Focus on me, Damn it! We've had Catastrophic Decoupling. Get these people out of their containers. Disconnect yourself and go! Now, Sergeant!"

I gaped at him as he turned to rescue someone who was drowning in a ball of suspension fluid. The fluid that had cushioned our bodies for so long in our containers was clinging to her head in zero-g like a ball. I understood. Catastrophic Decoupling. The *Glory's* main computers had gone down. The link was gone. The failsafes had pumped us with adrenalin to cold-start our bodies, then thrust us out of our containers and into the core of the ship where there was oxygen. We'd practiced Decoupling drills in basic. Most people 'died' in the simulations.

I started yanking quick-releases on the wires and tubes connected to my leg-flanges. My legs ended in metal cuffs at mid-thigh because Fleet removed our legs to make the suspension containers smaller. Smaller containers, larger crew. They would have regrown our legs if we made it home.

I turned away from the man who'd saved me and started down the open, two-meter wide core-tube towards a bulkhead, hauling myself on handholds. Opened containers and gobs of suspension fluid surrounded me. Bodies tumbled and flailed in the dim light, tangled in tethers or caught in pockets of liquid.

The worst part of Decoupling is the disorientation. I couldn't think. My cybernetic implants were down and I felt slow. I hadn't been in my body in a year and I couldn't coordinate my fingers.

I grabbed a twitching woman and wiped slime from her mouth. She didn't inhale, only continued to twitch, so I spun her around and gave her a clumsy Heimlich. She spat and gasped and I left her. I didn't have time for more. Most people die from Decoupling in the first two minutes. Drowning in space. It sounds funny until your first simulation.

I bypassed the next man. His neck was tilted wrong and he was limp. I kept moving; kept wiping and yanking and slapping people. It took two of us to pull one poor bastard out of the tangled mess of his life support wires. Suddenly I was at the bulkhead. I turned, resting my hand on the lagging riveted to the metal surface. I was panting. Maybe a minute had passed.

The tube stretched six or seven meters away from me to another bulkhead. The space was crowded with people staring wild-eyed. There were bodies. Many survivors shook from adrenaline overdose. All of us were coated in fluid and wearing tight skin-suits marked by stripings of rank. All of us had bright, stainless steel leg flanges glistening in the rows of emergency lights that were still flickering and coming to life.

The man who had first rescued me floated at the far bulkhead, and I rotated my body so that both of our heads shared a common 'up'.

"Listen to me," he yelled unnecessarily and all heads swiveled. "I'm Lieutenant Commander Jacobson, and we've undergone Catastrophic Decoupling. This is not a drill, but I don't have to tell you that." I stared at him and realized that he looked just like his avatar, only legless. He was our resident compartment officer.

They randomly divide up personnel between compartments so that no matter how many compartments are breached, any remaining compartment will have a full skeleton compliment.

"By the numbers," the Lt. Commander continued. "Everyone get into your masks. The oxygen in here won't hold out much longer."

I peeled a mask out of a wall socket, not wanting to fight my way back down to my home container. A hose stretched from the mask to CO_2 scrubbers in the wall.

"By the looks of our lights," the Lt. Commander continued, "the ship has lost main power and we're operating on local batteries. We've taken a bad hit. Maybe the destroyers have left us for dead. Maybe they're coming around again."

I could hear rivets groaning and I gripped the lagging tighter. I hate confined spaces and the tube seemed to be getting smaller and smaller. In the consensus reality of the neural-link, the ship seemed huge. Not here.

"Sergeant," he said to me, "what is your name?"

I lifted my mask. "Gunnery Sgt. Kirchov, Sir!" My throat was hoarse from disuse. I was thirsty.

"Glad to have you aboard. What is the status of the compartment adjacent to you?"

I turned to the gauges at my elbow, squinting. "I read 27 Kelvin, zero atmospheres, Sir."

"Then we have had at least one compartment breach, possibly more. The compartment behind me is the FTL drive chamber. It also contains an emergency shuttle that can provide life support if needed. Roll call, starting at the back. If the person next to you is dead, return them to their stasis container."

I was shivering. The temperature was dropping, but maybe it was the adrenaline shot and the dislocation of waking up. I missed Annie. If we were adjacent to the FTL chamber, then we were Compartment Alpha behind the bow. I was a long way from my gun.

In the end we had thirteen living and seven dead. My old drill sergeant would have called that unbelievable luck. None of my gun crew was here, and I hoped they survived somewhere in another compartment. We did have one surviving ordnance jockey and a maintenance tech. The telemetry tech was dead. I shut her eyes before closing her container.

The life support officer worked with the tube engineer to divert what power they could from the emergency systems to improve the CO_2 scrubbers. They initiated a full air change, and the remaining bubbles of suspension fluid were drawn out through drains with a terrible sucking sound.

The communications tech and the electrician's mate got the local network up and running in relatively short order, and I blessed whatever genius had installed a LAN in each compartment. We jacked in through wall ports and suddenly my world was back. Twelve minds swirled around mine. I damped their fear because mine didn't need any help and tried to access external ship-feeds. They didn't respond. We were isolated.

"I haven't heard any secondary explosions," the Lt. Commander said, "but we don't know what happened. Someone's going outside. Mr. Liu," he looked at the hull tech, "you will be my eyes. Who else?"

I volunteered immediately. I had to get out of here. Better to die out on the hull than in here where the walls were closing in. Mr. Liu and I unracked our compartment's two EVA suits

My new jockey, Michael, and maintenance tech, Leona, helped me on with the suit. My leg flanges clicked into place on the suit's cybernetic leg-jacks and suddenly I felt like a whole man again. I could feel my feet.

"Who's your gun," I said to my two new crewmen.

"Lucky number Seven," said Michael. "Midship, starboard. We call her Betty. Veronica's her sister gun on the ventral side."

"Number Two," Leona said. "Forward, port. Clotilde."

"Did either of you get off a shot?" They lowered the helmet over my head.

"No," they both thought to me on the LAN now that the helmet was on. "We caught a split second of realspace and then nothing."

"Good luck," said the Lt. Commander.

I turned and Mr. Liu was floating right behind me, looking calm. Hull techs are born to crawl the outside skin of ships like lice. He clapped me on the shoulder, pushing me down to the deck because I hadn't been holding a handclasp.

"Shall we?" he said.

We shoved chest to chest into the auxiliary hatch and Leona closed the door on us. The only light was the tiny headlamp we carried. Eleven avatars took up residence in our helmets' feeds. I closed my eyes. This tiny space was worse. What if the hatch didn't open? What if I died in here? C'mon, c'mon. Open the hatch.

"Close your glare shield," Mr. Liu said. "We could be next to a star."

I flipped down the shield as the outer hatch opened. Stars drifted by. The *Glory* was rolling. Suddenly, the brilliant rim of a star flared into view. We were close. Our ship was in orbit around the monster. Roiling reds filled the hatch mouth with harsh light and I lowered a second glare shield. Then I pushed out. Hard wires connected to the LAN played out behind me, keeping the avatars connected. Just being outside I began to relax. I checked the suit's O_2 levels. With the rebreather, I had nearly two hours supply.

"Sgt. Kirchov," the Lt. Commander said, "find those destroyers while Mr. Liu checks the hull." I attached myself to outside handholds while Mr. Liu started climbing.

The overwhelming glare of the star made searching difficult, but at last I located one of the destroyers. I had to lower a third shield to focus on her. I could only make out her black silhouette, but she was listing at a much lower orbit that we were. Some of our guns must have gotten a shot off to cripple her that badly. She was on a decaying orbit. The *Glory* rotated away from the star and I saw the second destroyer.

"She's coming back around, Sir," I said.

"Tap into Mr. Liu's feeds," the Lt. Commander said. "She's not going to bother with us."

I switched to Mr. Liu's feeds and stopped aghast. Our communications arrays were gone. All of the dorsal guns were gone. The docking hatch. Our hull was crushed from bow to stern.

I scrambled up the side of the hull, past the hulks of powerless loaders and maintenance 'bots. I needed to see for myself. And I stopped short at Mr. Liu's side, directly on top of our compartment. The only surviving compartment. A rip extended from just a few meters shy of our feet all the way to the aft drive pods. The hull gaped open; the edges of the wound were coated in frozen fire-extinguishing foam. I took another step and looked down through the double hull and shattered hulks of hyperspace batteries into our adjacent compartment. The stasis containers must have flash frozen, but I could see that the failsafes had opened some. Bodies hung partially out, entrained in frozen globules of suspension fluid. Fourteen compartments, two hundred and eighty men and women.

"I wonder if they felt anything," I said.

"What do we do?" Mr. Liu whispered. "The ship is gone. The communications arrays are gone."

"The *Aylin* destroyer must have come out of hyperspace right on top of us," our surviving navigator said in awe over the link. "They didn't overshoot us."

"Write that up in your report," I said. "Sir?" I called to the Lt. Commander, "You are now the ranking officer of the ship."

"Affirmative," the new Captain said. I couldn't feel a lick of his emotions. He was that controlled. It solidified my resolve.

We rotated back around and the second destroyer came into view again. She was slowing down, probably on a rescue mission to her crippled sister below.

"Some of our guns must work, Captain," I said, watching the long, sleek ship drift past. Hundreds of thousands of tons of steel, waiting to be popped.

"I can aim without telemetry at this range. Give me one shot into her main drive section."

There was a long silence. Finally, "How many shots do you think you can get off before they fire back?"

I sent a thought down to Michael. "Can you load quickly without the computers?"

"I placed third in the military games running a loader just from my implants. Never jammed a shell."

"Captain," I said, "they've already scanned us and found that we're cold iron. They must have seen oxygen venting from every compartment. They're done with us. All of their attention is below. I'm sure I could get in four, maybe five shots."

"Sergeant, our former Captain's orders stand. We must get a message back to Fleet. Fire as many shots as you can. Your primary mission is to draw their attention away from the drone."

"But they'll fire back," someone said. "We'll be destroyed."

I could feel horror crackle across the LAN as realization descended. I bowed my head. At least we would go down fighting like the *Mariah*.

"I'm sorry," the Captain said. "Yes, we'll be destroyed. Many of us will die, but not all. I'm sending out the emergency shuttle with the drone. It has limited FTL capabilities, but only six suspension containers. Sergeant?"

"Yes?"

"I need you to stay and man the gun. Select a gun crew to assist you."

"Aye, Aye, Captain," I said slowly. I felt the frightened attention of the avatars turn to me. Damn it. "We'll need more EVA suits."

"Mr. Liu," the Captain said. "Go down into that failed compartment and retrieve their two EVA suits. Bring them here, then return to the next compartment for additional suits. We will suit everybody."

I felt cold. Then hot. I stared at the destroyer. I had memorized her over the past forty-seven hours. There were three gun batteries up the starboard side and three on top. There would be an equal number on the far side. There were many smaller cannons. I had to get through that and strike her fuel cells somehow.

I sent down to Micheal and Leona: "Looks like we're it. Can I count on you?"

Michael answered right away, "I'll be out as soon as I get the EVA suit." Leona took a longer time in answering. "Yes, Sergeant."

In the end I only requested Alex, the electrician's mate, to help Leona jury-rig a gun to temporary batteries. I couldn't command anyone else to die. That left nine people for six seats. The Captain would have to decide.

Our ship rolled away from the destroyer and I sat in the cool darkness and waited. I liked it out here. I wouldn't mind dying out here, watching the cold stars shine. Watching the giant star rotate by. Maybe I should have been a hull tech instead of a gunner.

Three times the destroyer rotated back into view before Michael, Leona, and Alex joined me. They stopped next to the rent hull just as I had and stared in.

"At least they never woke up," Leona said.

"Let's get to Betty," I said. "We've got a lot to do."

"Why can't we use Clotilde?" Leona asked.

"I don't want to use the forward guns. Without attitude control, they'll twist the ship. The midship guns might roll us faster, but we'll stay straight."

We followed handholds along the edge of the torn hull. I tried not to look inside in case I recognized someone. A nimbus of sheered metal around the ship was all that remained of the dorsal guns and primary communications arrays, but Betty and Veronica were still pristine. They still held a 150mm egg in their baskets. Their loading servos still clutched a second egg at ready, waiting for the shot that had never come.

"For our lost crews and for the survivors," I said. They all nodded. "We'll fire every warhead we've got and hope a couple get through. Michael, I bet that star is putting out a lot of interference. The Aylin may not detect our warheads if we don't fire up the rockets. Can you recalibrate the shell firing control for just enough burst to clear the barrel? I want to send them in cold."

"I haven't run a system directly since the military games," he said. He inserted a neural wire from his helmet into the back of the loader.

"Can you do it?"

He saluted. "I can do it, Sergeant."

Leona and Alex began reconfiguring wires, directing battery power into the loaders and into my barrel adjusters.

"Sergeant," the Captain said across the LAN, "what's your estimated firing-time?"

"Rough estimate of fifteen minutes, Captain. How are you doing on suits?"

"We're short one, but that'll be resolved in a minute. We're going to the shuttle now."

I switched to a private band and sent down to him. "Who's staying?"

"I'm staying. And Ensign Earl and Second Lieutenant Savron have volunteered to stay."

"It's a shame we survived the crash and still have to die, Sir. Come on up when the shuttle's out. Enjoy the show with us here."

"Affirmative, Sergeant."

The LAN shut down as the nine people below exited Compartment Alpha for the FTL chamber.

I started moving Betty as soon as Leona got me an ounce of juice. I used the rough bore-site down the barrel. I doubted it had been used since she was first aligned and test fired at the dockyards, but it would serve me. The destroyer was directly above her crippled sister now. Through visual filters I could see that her shields were crackling irregularly. There was interference. And she may have been trying to extend her shields around her sister to lend some protection. A warhead could get through that.

"How we doing on juice?" I asked. I was growing eager.

"If our hands weren't so weak, we'd be done rewiring by now," Leona said. "I need my tech-servos just to work on the tech-servos." Showers of sparks leapt from her torch and out into space.

At the bow, nine people gathered. The shuttle lifted slowly into view, ejected from the *Glory's* nose on spring-jacks. Six people climbed inside. Three crawled in our direction.

"How long 'til sufficient power," I said.

"Two hundred and eleven seconds," Leona said.

I started a countdown. Yellow lights flashed on Michael's loader.

"I have fifteen warheads, Sergeant," he said. "That's it. The rest were distributed for Operation Slowdown."

"Fifteen it is." I laughed and flexed my fingers. I had often pressed simulated buttons to fire Annie. The manual firing buttons on Betty's control arm were the real thing, and they felt real. I could just imagine the recording from the shuttle, sent back to inhabited space. Me, standing at the back of a ten-meter gun, firing manually. This was the stuff of Recruitment Holos.

"The *Glory* will roll out of range in twenty seconds," I said. "I'll commence firing when the target returns to view."

I dropped Betty's barrel as low as it would crank. The initial shots would have to fly directly across the hull, straight past Veronica. The debris field around the ship made me nervous.

I flexed my fingers again. "Are we good?" I said to Michael.

"The rockets have been reprogrammed, Sergeant. You are good to fire."

"Firing in fifteen, fourteen..."

The three castaways from the shuttle took up station behind us and joined into our tiny LAN. I gripped Betty's control arm and grinned. The star came back into view.

"Alpha Mike Foxtrot, Ladies and Gentlemen," I said and fired. As promised, the rocket flared and immediately went dead, flying swiftly and quietly from the end of the barrel. "One away."

I calculated lead-times through the group-LAN and our cumulative cybernetic implants, compensating as the *Glory's* roll grew slowly greater. I fired as fast as I could, adjusting Betty's elevation. Her long barrel rose to ninety-degrees-high as the *Glory* turned, then began dropping again to port. Fifteen warheads leapt out and then we stood in silence. We had done all we could. The rim of the star passed from view and it was dark and cold.

"How long?" Ensign Earl said.

"They aren't moving that fast because we didn't light the rockets."

We rotated back into the harsh light. Both destroyers still sat below us, unaware and unreacting. I couldn't see the warheads; their tiny silhouettes were lost in the glare. We began to rotate away again.

"Strike near the bow," someone shouted.

I whooped when I saw the explosion and the gout of ejecta. I had aimed for her bridge, hoping to incapacitate her. We rotated away and I couldn't see any more.

"Captain to shuttle, light your engines now! Get away from us! Move!"

The shuttle's drive pods sprang to life and the ship nosed up agonizingly slowly. They had to get away. Beside them, the messenger-drone's rockets also flared up and the tiny 'bot sped away.

"What's happening?" Alex said. "Their rockets are faster than ours, right?"

"There's one now." I pointed up. An *Aylin* rocket flew past like a shooting star, speeding into deep space. Interference or not, they couldn't miss us at this distance. Four more rockets flew past in a cluster. I gripped Betty's control arm, my skin crawling. Soon. The shuttle pushed farther and farther away. Another rocket streaked by our drive pods.

Twenty seconds. Forty seconds. Seventy-eight seconds without another *Aylin* rocket. We rolled back into view.

"What the hell happened?" Michael said.

I zoomed my lenses in on the destroyer. "We knocked them into each other," I said, understanding suddenly.

I replayed the recording from the shuttle over and over later.

The healthy destroyer had dropped in extremely close to her crippled sister. My first lucky shot pushed her bow down and they collided. Their autonomous defensive systems kicked in and launched rockets, aimed at our warheads, not at the *Glory*.

My second lucky shot hit near the tail, pushing her farther into her sister. All the rest of my warheads were intercepted. It was the collision that, in the end, destroyed the ships. When the drive pods impacted, dense yellow flames burned at the edge of the star's red.

Now we wait.

The shuttle's been gone two weeks, but only took four people. The rest of us chose to stay here, on the Glory. Trying to get the stasis containers working again so we can sleep until rescue comes.

Alex repaired the conduits bringing power from the radioisotope thermal generators and he's slowly powering up the undamaged batteries. The oxygen generator and CO2 scrubbers are working fine in our compartment, and we have heat. Leona and Mr. Liu have some hull 'bots working, and they're patching the rent hull as best they can. We want the *Glory* in good enough shape for a tow home when rescue comes.

The gyros are spinning again and they stopped our roll. The pilot turned the hull breach away from the star to protect us from the UV radiation.

I keep our guns ready. Michael and I distributed a few warheads to each of them.

And when I'm not helping with the hull repairs or with wiring, I sit on Annie's barrel. I've seen this view a million times through the remote feeds, but this is the first time I've seen it through my own eyes. After the rescue, I may never get another chance. I never get tired of watching the cold stars.

THRESHER

Lawrence M. Schoen

MERCUTIO'S GHOST CHECKED ITS MATH AND MUSED THAT A LIFE OF PIRACY IN THE middle of an interplanetary war was no life for a physician. The math checked; the *Folio*'s outbound course from Varuna would carry it through the Kuiper Belt, with an eye toward creating the appearance of just another trans-Neptunian object, too small for even a MarzCraft with full sensorial to bother noticing. Its piracy piloting done, the doctor portion of the ghost took over and accelerated its time sense several hundred fold. This burned up the larger share of its temporary lifespan, but gave it the next ninety subjective hours to search for a cure for the Captain.

In the war between Erth and Marz, the Old Man had put himself smack in the middle. Only ErthCraft sported ghost crew. Their ships could produce key decisions several orders of magnitude faster than MarzCraft. Only MarzCraft pilots had access to the sensorial that let them see and taste and touch and hear every iota of information within an AU with utter clarity. A sensorial ship could usually see an enemy vessel coming with enough lead time to get away safely. A ghosted vessel almost invariably outgunned an opponent running with real-time targeting. All that fine technology was proprietary, and neither side had both kinds, at least as far as anyone knew. But Captain Book had both the knack and the means to acquire tech through unscrupulous channels, which made him a natural to command a pirateship.

Mercutio's ghost's current medical effort failed, as all its predecessors had. Disappointed but unsurprised, it dilated its time sense back out to human norm. Varuna had receded far behind the *Folio*. The ghost once more reviewed the course Mercutio had prepared to Ixion, then fired off an acknowledgment to the First Mate's ghost lurking elsewhere in the system.

The MarzGov mining ship *Declaration* would soon be leaving Ixion, its holds laden with tholin and other precious heteropolymers not found on either Marz or Erth. The Captain wanted those heteropolymers, and by extension so did Mercutio, which meant his ghost did too. Time then to get to it. The ghost hurtled back through the system arriving at the interface plate that led to its origin, jumped the gap, and merged its memories with its flesh and blood creator.

In his cool bunk, Mercutio, pilot and ship's doctor, blinked and yawned as his ghost roused him from the chill of suspension and dumped the experience of its brief life into his mind. Piracy wasn't his first calling, it wasn't even his second, but circumstance had taken him this way and complaining wouldn't change things. His body warmed to real time and he winced as he reviewed the particulars of another unsuccessful research session. He could only try again; so long as the Captain lived, it was his duty. Mercutio pressed his face firmly against the activation plate, generated a fresh ghost, and unhooked himself from the harness of the ghosterizer. He swung himself out of his bunk and went to check on the Captain.

"Still no luck?" said the speaker grid on Captain Book's cool bunk as the doctor entered the tiny ship's infirmary.

Mercutio stepped within range of the Captain's acuity sensors and nodded. The Old Man's bunk was colder than his own, though not so cold as the crews'. The First Mate had rigged it to chill the Captain's brain, but allow him to remain conscious all the same. "No, Sir, but I've started another run. Meanwhile, I wanted to see how you're doing." More than two dozen ceramo-magnetic diagnostic beads covered the Captain's body, like glowing red eyes that gave the darkened bunk a demonic feel. Each beamed its readings to the infirmary's computer, which in turn displayed a summary to a wall display. Mercutio studied that summary and frowned. Despite the trickling pace of the Old Man's metabolism, the meds he'd administered had already stopped working.

"I have faith in you, son," said Book. "But then, what other choice do I have?"

"You could abort this run, Sir. Tell the First to let me plot us a course out of the Belt. We can run the distance to Erth or Marz on hard shields. You've got letters of marque from both sides. You'll get a parade as a privateer either place."

"What do I need with a parade? And I'm only a privateer because neither side knows I work for the other. We have business to do out here, Mercutio, pirate business. I'll see Erth, sure, but not before we liberate all the Ixion tholin on that MarzCraft."

"You'll never see Erth then, Captain. The thresher will kill you long before then."

"You're sure of that?"

"I am. Even with maximum chill slowing your body, the drugs haven't been able to suppress your reaction to the field. I've already had to amputate your left leg. Another limb could develop Sagan's fasciitis without warning, and only the cool bunk is keeping organ failure at bay. As long as we're in the Belt we can't turn off the thresher without killing everyone. The hard shields aren't enough to protect the ship here."

Book whistled faintly, summoning a glowbug from the communication console and directing it to land on the trio of gold rings hanging from his left ear. "Then you'd best set aside my share of the haul for my funeral costs," he said. "I want to go out in style."

Every ship in space, whether ErthCraft, MarzCraft, or Indy-made, used a thresher. The machine was as ugly and awkward a sight as a lust-crazed bull mounting a groundcar, and about as big, but the field it generated made space travel possible. The thresher pushed a ship out of Probabilistic space, freeing it from the constraints of Euclid, Einstein, and Chaos. As an added bonus it laughed in the face of conservation and boosted velocity without any messy acceleration issues. And all the while the field protected everything within it from radiation and normal matter up to the mass it contained.

Transition back to Probability dumped the gained velocity but otherwise had no effect on inorganics. Usually it didn't affect flesh and blood either. But every now and then, one time in ten billion, a body came back into normal space changed. The *smarties* they called it, and the luckless spacers who got it had the choice to either leave space quickly or die there. You could live, assuming you never stepped inside a thresher field again. Otherwise the disease progressed with lightning speed, killing you in a burst of brilliance as your brain spun off millions of new connections while every organ in your new genius body failed. Smart death, but death all the same.

Mercutio had diagnosed the Captain's condition before they'd gone to ground on Varuna, and immediately put the Old Man in a cool bunk. Then he'd set about using the limited resources of the *Folio* to do what the best medical minds on two worlds hadn't been able to do. He'd failed. The ghosterizer had only let him fail faster and more thoroughly.

Mercutio owed the Captain his life ten times over, and the most he could do for him now was to plan his funeral party.

"That's it then," said Prospero as he and Mercutio sat in the mess. The man fastidiously nibbled the full crust perimeter of a toasted cheese sandwich as he spoke. "We make way near Ixion as planned, liberate the tholin as planned, and leave them Marzies with the final tale of Captain Book."

"And then what?" said Mercutio. He sniffed and frowned, the First Mate had engineered the foodstation to manufacture curds that went beyond pungent and well into stench.

"Then I'll be captain," said Prospero, "and you'll quicken such crew as need it. Those that choose to sign on under me, as they did for Book, can stay and it will be as it has been. Those what don't, can leave the *Folio* with their full shares as expected."

Mercutio sighed. "Then off we go, on another thrilling pirate adventure."

Prospero finished the last of the crusts and smushed the remainder of the sandwich between his hands, rolling it into a tight ball of melted, smelly cheese and toasted bread. He popped it into his mouth as he regarded the pilot. He chewed silently for a full minute, swallowed, and pointed a greasy finger at Mercutio. "What about you? I know we haven't gotten on well, but I'm hoping you'll stay. You're a passable doc and a better pilot, and I'll need both."

"Right now you're still just ship's engineer and first mate," said Mercutio. "The Captain's not dead."

The First nodded. "Not yet, but my ghosts are in the system same as yours, and they talk to one another, usually more than we manage face to face. I know the status of things same as you. We're cruising your camouflaged route through the belt towards Ixion, the thresher's running at full, and if the Captain ain't dead by the time we crack open that MarzShip, it won't be for lack of trying."

Sixty-seven hours and a dozen failed medical simulations later, tumbling along its seemingly haphazard route, the *Folio* fell into position an hour away from where it would cross *Declaration*'s vector and rendezvous with the unsuspecting mining ship. Mercutio informed the Captain, who in turn ordered the First to prepare an assault, who then sent word to Mercutio to quicken a boarding party.

As both pilot and ship's physician, moments like this required Mercutio to be in two places at once, a situation which the ghosterizer made possible. He spun off a pair of them, one to actually pilot the *Folio*, and one to stand ready to relay messages between that spectral pilot and himself as near to instantly as human synapses could manage. Then he went to thaw the crew.

He quickend MacBeth first. While not an officer, the man had seniority among the crew, and at one time or another had beaten each of them senseless as part of some initiation ritual they all seemed to regard as a rite of passage. Mercutio didn't pretend to understand; he'd merely set the bones and provided the necessary stiches. If it contributed to crew loyalty and boosted morale he had no cause to complain. The cool bunks accelerated healing anyway.

MacBeth, like half of the crew, was classic Marz stock, and stood a foot taller than Mercutio. Generations of Marzian eugenics had made him lean, muscled and golden-skinned. The Captain had named him MacBeth, just as he had given all the crew their names. It didn't do for pirates to know one another's birth name. The nominal Scotsman quickened swiftly and with none of the grogginess that the cool bunk often imparted to the Erthborn. The instant his eyes opened he locked Mercutio's gaze and asked, "How soon?"

"Less than an hour. Give me a hand rousing the others."

MacBeth rolled naked from his bunk, and pulled open the storage locker with his gear. He dressed with quiet efficiency while Mercutio moved on to the next cool bunk, and then joined him. Over the next five minutes they revived the others, Horatio, Benedict, Katrina, Antony, and Romeo.

"Look lively you lot," said MacBeth to his men. "Don't be thinking it's only a mining craft and going all soft. We'll be giving them the hard bump this day, same as we'd give any vessel as Captain Book sets his desire upon. Clear?"

"Aye," said Romeo, and Katrina and Antony nodded in time.

"Bump," said Benedict, who'd taken a blow to the head during their last raid and hadn't been quite right since. He grinned and punched his brother, Horatio, in the shoulder.

"Hard bump, aye," said Horatio, and punched him back.

"Anything else we ought to be knowing, doc?" asked MacBeth.

Mercutio shook his head. "It's a big ship, but mostly automated for all that. A MarzCraft, so no ghosts. Three man crew, according to specs. If they've picked us up on their sensorial, they're still thinking we're a small rock that will pass right through them without touching."

Horatio barked with laughter. "Until our thresher bumps theirs."

"Hard bump," said Benedict, and punched him again.

"All right you lot, head for the lock and suit up." MacBeth waved them toward the exit. "Every man carries a grapple, two cables, and a stunner. No one tries anything fancy and we all come back richer than when we woke up. Now move."

They shuffled out, amidst a raucous chorus of "Bump! Bump! Bump!"

Mercutio put a hand on MacBeth's arm, holding him back a moment. "Why 'bump'?" he asked.

"Cuz the good lord won't be delivering them," said MacBeth.

"Huh?"

"I don't know from ghoulies, but you officers are ghosties and we've our share o'long-legged beasties. And space is as dark as any night I know of."

"Huh," repeated Mercutio, finally recognizing the reference. "I've always thought of space as daytime. The sun's always shining."

MacBeth grinned at him. "You think too much, doc," and he turned to follow his men.

The boarding was especially anticlimactic. Trusting to their own thresher field to spare them impact from anything smaller than themselves, *Declaration* didn't clue to the Folio being more than a stray stone until the pirate vessel tumbled within a kilometer and matched vectors. By then it was too late. As the *Folio* drew closer, the two thresher fields merged, pulling the ships together. Mercutio's ghost had used the sensorial on precision settings to line up their locks with perfection. It signaled the First's ghost to begin the swiftly completed raid.

It was over almost before it began. MacBeth and company forced the lock, boarded the ship, rounded up, and efficiently disarmed the trio of personnel by the time Prospero and Mercutio followed them onboard. The doctor set the men to converting *Declaration*'s ward room into a temporary brig, while the First began preparing their prize for transit.

Half an hour later Mercutio joined Prospero on *Declaration*'s bridge. It smelled of sweat and boredom, a result of someone always being at the helm. The First aimed to fix that. He lay on his back, waist deep in the guts of a computer relay, installing a spare ghosterizer to the mining ship's sytems. "We've got quite a haul," he said, the acoustics making his voice reedy.

"You're not usually one to get misty about money," said Mercutio.

"I've never had so much of it from one job. Between the payoff from the heteropolymers, and with what we'll get selling this ship back to MarzGov, I'm thinking maybe it's time to get out of piracy and become a business man."

Mercutio laughed. "Don't go spending your shares quite yet. This job's a long way from done. We can't sell this ship until we've ransomed her crew."

Prospero slid out from the relay, pulled the panel closed, and sat up. "Don't be getting naïve on me, Mercutio. This isn't a military ship like we normally target. There's no ransom to be had for this lot. We'll be spacing the crew before we head out."

Mercutio paled. "Piracy is one thing, but I won't be party to murder."

Prospero smirked. "That's for the Captain to decide now ain't it?"

Mercutio returned to the *Folio* and went straight to the infirmary; Prospero trailed behind chuckling to himself, but stopped when they discovered their Captain had left. His modified cool bunk lay open, his diagnostic beads scattered upon the floor like marbles.

"Where could he have gone?" asked the First, following the doctor into the infirmary and joining the search.

"C'mon," said Mercutio after assuring himself that Captain Book hadn't fallen behind the cool bunk or hidden himself away in a supply cubby. "We'll check his cabin, then yours, then mine. Mind the beads as you go."

"Why would he be in either of our cabins?"

"Why would he have left his cool bunk?" said Mercutio. "It was the only thing keeping him alive."

The Captain's own quarters were empty, everything organized and shipshape as they'd been since he'd gone into the infirmary for treatment. They moved on to the First's cabin, found it less tidy but no less empty. To the doctor's horror and relief, Captain Book proved to be in his cabin, sprawled head-first, half in and half out of the active cool bunk. He'd died there, his body wracked by spasms as opposing muscle groups contracted simultaneously, tearing flesh free from bone as his cortical functions froze. Blood, now dry, had trickled from ears and eyes, and the Old Man had bitten through his tongue as well.

"Well, at least we know why he came here," said Prospero. He sat at the doctor's workstation, and gestured to an active screen. "He was running some kind of bio-medical analysis using your gear."

Mercutio stared at the screen and nodded.

Prospero scowled. "This makes sense to you?"

"Yeah. As soon as he left the cool bunk the smarties kicked in. He was trying to use it to find a cure before it killed him. He must have given up and tried to get back in a bunk to buy himself more time, and didn't make it."

Mercutio glanced at the body and then back to the screen. "It will take me weeks to figure out how close he got."

"Not close enough," said Prospero. He stood, and regarded Mercutio and then Book. "Move his corpse back to the infirmary; chill it for now. Once we've sorted the mining ship, then you can prepare the body for a vacuum burial; I know it's not what he told you he wanted, but he doesn't get a say any more. Now, if you'll excuse me, I've got to go talk to the crew."

"What are you going to tell them?"

Prospero paused, one hand on the door of the cabin. He spoke without looking back. "That Captain Book is dead, and that there's a new Captain. As we discussed." He walked out a different man than he'd entered.

"I think I'm being generous," said Captain Prospero. Two hours had passed and he'd assembled everyone in *Declaration*'s ward room. Mercutio knew the man had already made his decision; this was all for show.

"Your physician's oath won't allow you the expedience of killing our three captives, and I respect that. I think my solution is quite elegant."

"You're taking my shares, in violation of the code," said Mercutio.

"No, I'm giving you your shares, and our late captain's too, and then I'm swapping them back and trading you the *Folio* for them. And I'm throwing in the captives you're so squeamish about. Keep them as crew or keep them in cool bunks until you drop them off, I don't much care.

"Time's change, doctor. The letters of marque are in Book's name, not mine. Sure I could likely get one or both transferred, but there's more wealth and less risk in mining than in pirating. MacBeth and the rest of the crew agree. Not much need for a pilot of your talents, nor a doctor for all that. So it works out well for everyone."

"You're cheating me," said Mercutio, "and you're trying to be rid of me. You've already ripped out half the cool bunks and most of the armaments."

"I need 'em, and you don't," said Prospero. "And as for being rid of you, as Captain I'm within my rights to kill you outright and there's not a man here that doesn't know it."

Mercutio gnawed his lip a moment. "That'd be true," he conceded, "if you were still a pirate and not a miner. But fine, let your last act of piracy be robbing me of my fair shares. I'll take the *Folio*, and chart a course where I can give Captain Book the send off he wanted. And I'll take your prisoners and see they find their way somewheres safe."

"That's it then," said Prospero, "save one last thing. Your word, that you'll not prey upon this ship and crew of innocent miners in the future."

"No bump," said Horatio.

MacBeth eyed the doctor solemnly and nodded, "Aye, no bump," And looked away.

"You've my word on it," said Mercutio. "Give me an escort to get the prisoners over and safely stowed; I'll ungrapple and be gone in under an hour." Without waiting for confirmation he turned and headed to his ship.

The former crew of *Declaration* looked to slip into their new cool bunks almost willingly, given brutal murder was their only alternative. Mercutio sealed them in, and went to his own quarters next. The Old Man had asked not to be jettisoned into space, as was pirate tradition, but to have his remains drowned for all time in the seas beyond Old Britannia. Mercutio had no other plans. After his ship had tumbled away from *Declaration* he slid into his own cool bunk and connected to the ghosterizer to spin off a simulacrum to plot a course for Erth.

The ghost he'd left running in the system greeted him first. "You're not going to believe this," the spectral Mercutio told the original.

"Believe what? Merge and let me know what you're going on about?

"Now where would the fun be in that?" said his ghost, speaking around a grin, and in a deep and familiar voice.

"Captain? I didn't think you had a ghost in the system, not since you took ill."

"Crazy system, having to talk through your ghost," said the Captain. "But he's been very helpful. You know a lot more about medicine than you've let on, son."

"Captain, you do understand that you're dead?"

"Well, we both saw that coming, now didn't we? But never mind me, did you get the heteropolymers?"

"Yes, Sir. Only, well, what with you being dead and all, Prospero named himself captain, and with the rest of the men decided to take the mining ship and give up piracy. It's just me here, Captain. We've no cargo."

"Not a problem, doctor. Between your ghosts and mine, the *Folio* will do fine.

"About that, Sir. I saw your notes, I get what you were trying to do, but even with the smarties hyping your brain there just wasn't time to work out a cure. It would have taken you months at least."

"You might have told me that," chided the ghost. "It would have saved me at least three minutes. But no harm, I had time to get to your cabin and plug in. I'm not an old spirit. I've filled your buffer with a couple dozen fresh ghosts."

Mercutio paused a moment, trying to wrap his head around the notion of his ghost channeling the ghost of his dead captain. "Why? Captain, no offense, but that doesn't change things. You're still dead. Are you planning on haunting me?"

"No, son, I'm planning on finding a cure. My ghosts are copies of me, so they're smartie ghosts."

Mercutio wiped at his eyes, half surprised to find them wet. "Nothing like that has ever been done," he said.

"But even if it doesn't work, well, I just want to say I'm glad to have you back, Captain."

"Of course it will work. All my buffered copies are dialed down as low as their time sense can go. They're more suspended than any cool bunk could slow flesh and bone. When this ghost nears its limit, I'll wake up another and so on. Now if you'll excuse me, I've work to do. I'll let you get caught up and get us bound for Erth. If you have any questions, you know where to find me."

Mercutio nodded to himself as his ghost merged and a flood of wild and ragged medical conversations poured into his memory, more than his conscious mind could process at once. But that wasn't a problem. It would all get sorted out in his unconscious while he slept. His goals as a pirate and a physician had merged as neatly as he had with his ghost. There was medical adventure ahead, a course plotted for the unknown, and treasure the like of which no man, be he doctor or pilot, had ever beheld. He pressed his forehead against the activation plate, generated a replacement ghost to handle navigation, and let the cool bunk take him down into dreamless sleep.

PETER POWER ARMOR

John C. Wright

LET ME TELL YOU A STORY ABOUT A GIRL NAMED ETHNE. I DIDN'T LIKE HER WHEN I FIRST met her, but all that is changed now.

I found the power-armor I used to wear as a child in the wall-space behind my parent's attic, behind a door paneled to look like part of the wainscoting. No dust disturbed this miniature clean-room; no looters had found it here, not in all the years.

The fact that smooth white light filled the room when the silent door opened filled me with a premonition. I stepped inside and saw, (as I had not dared hope) that an umbilicus connected the little suit to sockets in the wall. The energy-box above the socket was stamped with three black triangles in a yellow circle.

Behind me, in the main attic space, I could hear the little brat named Ethne grunt a little high-pitched grunt as she picked up a crow-bar. A moment later there was a shivering crash as she tossed it through one of the living stain-glassed dormer windows. I remembered the day Mother had purchased those windows, grown one molecule at a time by a nano-mathematician artist. Those had been days of sunshine, and even the upper windows no one saw had been works of fine art, charged with life.

You see, Ethne was a naughty, silly girl. It is really not her fault. She was raised to be that way.

"Darling," I said, trying to keep my voice even. "Don't kill the windows. They are special. They were bulletproof, once, back before their cohesion faded. They're antiques, and cannot reproduce. It makes them the last of their kind."

Ethne was bright enough to ask a question: "So what? What makes them special?" It is always good to ask questions.

I said gently: "You see how the old building had their windows facing outward? Not like modern buildings. Remember your school? All the windows only face inside, toward the courtyard. And your dorm is the same way, isn't it? You can tell a lot a about a culture by where they put their windows."

The courtyard-based construction of modern buildings reminds me of European designs. I don't really like Europe.

I heard little Ethne whine to the matron: "Mother Hechler! Mr. Paine is trying to oppress me again!"

It was not my real name. I always introduced myself as Thomas Paine, these days. No one ever caught the reference, not even people my age.

The chestplate of the power-armor was set with large phosphorescent buttons, with little cartoon-character faces to indicate the function options. I hit the Peter Power-Armor Power-on Pumpkin with my thumb. There was a goo-ga flourish of toy trumpet noise, a whisper of servomotors, and the suit stood up.

I know Ethne did not know her parents. I am guessing the age at about seven years old. Her mother, her real mother, had been a lovely, lively, caring woman, smart as a devil and with a sense of humor to match. That sense of humor managed to get her declared an unfit parent.

The father, Geoffrey, had been an environmental engineer. Very bright man. He had written papers, back before the Diebacks, questioning whether the trends showed a General Global Warming or a General Cooling. Those papers had cropped up again after Ethne was born. Geoffrey had been sterilized by the committee in charge of the First Redistribution; they believed in Global Warming. He had been made to vanish by the Second. They believed in Cooling.

And little Ethne was just not as bright as Geoffrey's daughter should have been. I knew the ugly reason why.

The helmet came only about to my waist, even when the armor was upright on its stubby legs. It looked like a miniature King-Arthur's knight, although I remember other attachments could make it look like a deep-sea diver's suit or a fireman. The smart-metal was made of a flex of microscopic interlocking strands, and I saw telescopic segments at the limb-joints and breastplate-seams, enabling the suit to expand to fit a growing child.

I heard, behind and below me, a soggy, heavy noise as the stairs whined under the bulk of Mrs. Hechler's footsteps. I heard her pant. She said, "Ethne!" she was calling up the stairs. Hechler was too inert, it seemed, to make it all the way. "Stop familiarizing with the People's Helpers. You are to call him 'Janitor' or 'Shit-sweeper.' We don't use his name, moppet: it makes them uppity."

Tiny xylophone-notes came from inside the helmet as the suit ran through its systems check. I could see the colors of a puppet-show reflected backward in the faceplate during the warm-up, as big-eyed rabbits and ducks in sailor suits pantomimed out safety messages as each suit function went through its automatic check.

It may seem absurd, but tears came to my eyes when Battery Bunny turned into a skeleton-silhouette surrounded by twinkling lightning-bolts above the words: KEEP FINGERS CLEAR OF THE RECHARGE SOCKET! Battery Bunny had once been a best playmate of mine, since I had had no real, non-virtual friends.

(Billy Worthemer was a real friend of mine. A real flesh and blood boy. Lots of blood. I will tell you about him if I have time. But, after Billy, no, after that I had had no real friends, except for Bunny. Well, maybe one.) Good old loyal bunny. How could I have forgotten him?

I wiped my eyes. At the same time, to cover the xylophone-noise of the suit-check, I was saying loudly: "Matron Hechler! The student-child is destroying property of the state! This may lead to bad habits later!"

Another soggy noise as Hechler climbed another step. She wheezed a moment, then said, "Let her have her fun. This stuff is from the Time of Greed. It's worthless. Go ahead, Ethne."

I heard a dull giggle, and then more smashing.

I twisted and removed the adult-override key from the armor's chestplate, picked up the remote handset from the socket, and thumbed the test button on the microwave relay. The LED lit up. I tapped my fingers on the handset and the little armored suit did a silent little jig of joy. Such elegant controls! Such a well-made machine!

Another button made Mr. Don't-Point-Me come out of his holster. I had forgotten, or I never knew, that the holster had a child-safety relay on it, which made an alarm-noise blatt from the handset. With one thumb I pushed the suppress button on the handset to kill the noise. With the other I reached for the larger, colored controls on the chestplate. I remembered that the Deadly Donkey button armed the lethal rounds. I hit Sleepy Sancho Pancake, and watched as a clip of narcoleptic darts was jacked into the chamber. The little armor twirled the gun on its gauntlet-finger and slid Mr. Don't-Point-Me back into the holster. I had programmed that little flourish in, when I was a child. I had seen Laser Cowboy do it on STV, and I had practiced and practiced in front of a mirror. That was my hand motion.

Hechler had heard the alarm. Her voice came nearer, sounding angry, "What's that noise?"

I said in a loud happy voice, "Ethne! Come quick!"

Ethne, sullenly, "What...?! Is a machine? They're bad for you."

"Never mind," I called out. I heard her little footsteps coming closer. "I'll just keep it all for myself."

Ethne's footsteps sped up. Any adult who cannot outwit a seven-year-old should turn in his license.

I also heard the Matron's voice coming at a lumbering trot. Stairs squealed, and then the attic floorboards protested. "What—what's that light up there!"

I had to get her to come up. I said loudly, "It should be obvious what it is, you soggy old fart! I've found a working light. Don't you have eyes? I must say that I am continually amazed, now that each village and hamlet is divided into work zones and care zones for the communal raising and nurture of children, at the consistently low quality of the substitute parents involved."

Ethne was in the doorway, now. Her eyes grew big and round. I remember days when children often had such looks on their faces, at birthday parties, or at Christmas. Back when we had Christmas.

I took Ethne by the shoulder and guided her toward the armor. My other hand pushed the introduction menu sequence with the handset. The armor turned toward Ethne, evidently recognizing her as having the infrared profile and radar-silhouette of a child. It performed a perfect courtly bow toward her. She watched in awe as it took her hand and bent over it, pretending to kiss it.

And the little brat (her brattyness forgotten, or on hold) actually blushed and looked pleased, a modest princess. She was utterly charmed. I had to smile.

I continued talking the way I used to talk, in a loud voice, "But we cannot have a society where all child-rearing is public, without expecting it to end up in the same state as our public bathrooms. And what kind of low, common, ignorant folk will volunteer to serve as wardens for children not their own, whom they cannot adopt or make their own? Who would be willing to raise a child by rulebook? By committee? I suspect those who cannot get jobs as prison guards..."

But that was enough. Mrs. Hechler was here, red-faced, and angry enough that she had forgotten to use her radio-phone to call Jerry. Jerry, downstairs, was not a Regulator; he was an Infant Proctor, which was something between a Baby Sitter and the Bull. But I think he was packing heat.

Maybe she was too dumb to call him; too dumb to think I was dangerous. Or maybe her phone was broken again.

Her eyes grew round when she saw the lights, the atomic-power symbol on the wall, the brass-and-gold little armored figure. I do not think she recognized what the armor was; I think she thought it was a statue or a toy or something.

A woman raised in her generation, of course, could not understand the kind of folks people of my parent's generation were.

And so she stepped into the room. She did not know what kind of thing Peter was; or what kind of person I am.

Let me explain it to you. I don't know how much room is in the file: I'll try to be brief. But I have to tell you the way it was.

My dad was there the day the rules of war changed. He was about eight years old. He had climbed a tree, and found a little green-and-brown colored aerosol spray-can wedged into the branches, pointing over the sidewalk below. I remember him telling me how bright and sunny the day was, how the sidewalk sparkled, how the people looked so happy, so normal, when they walked by, walking dogs, carrying groceries, herding children, balancing schoolbooks on heads.

Every time someone walked by, the little aerosol can button went down. Activated by a motion sensor. Dad put his hand in front of the nozzle, and felt a wet invisible spray touch his palm. He sniffed it; it was odorless. He wiped the sticky wetness off on the green-and-brown label of the can.

His district was one of the few with a death toll under one hundred. A day or two later, a swarm of self-propelled smart-bullets, maybe launched from a passing crop-duster, maybe mortar-shot off the back of a flatbed truck, swept through the area, and homed in on everything which had been tagged by the invisible radio-active mist.

One of the bullets struck the aerosol can, of course, so that no further tagging was done, and the second and third wave of smart-bullets which came the next day, and the next week, found no targets.

Everyone who walked by on the sidewalk that day—Dad used to tell me their names, they were his neighbors and playmates—was gone.

When I was young, and played with my Dad, he used to pretend to be Captain Hook. His prostethic was actually a complex thing, that could open and close almost like a pair of fingers. But it did look like a hook.

The next generation of smart bullets were even smarter, smaller, and able to fly longer distances. With a shoulder-launched booster, a rifleman could throw a packet of smart bullets over the horizon.

And warfare wasn't warfare any more. No more gathering on battlefields, no more getting into big battleships, and steaming out to meet other battle-ships. No sir. Soldiers traveled in pairs, not in platoons. One rifleman to launch the bullets. He would sit in a tree, or wearing a diving suit and lay on the bottom of a lake or something. His partner, the forward observer, would walk into town with a laser pencil. He would sit on a park bench and pretend to eat a submarine sandwich or something, or smoke a cigarette—which was legal, back then—and point the laser pencil at a passer-by. A bullet from out of the sky would drop down and hit the target. In a crowd, who would hear the noise? Maybe he'd get two or three, he'd pack up his sandwich, walk down the street, find another bench.

You could launch smart bullets from a normal shotgun, or even a lead pipe. Heck, if you dropped one off a tall enough building, it could pick up enough speed for its lifting surfaces to get purchase, reach terminal velocity, and if your target was anywhere below the building, the bullet could angle over. There wouldn't even be the sound of a gunshot. Same thing dropping a boxful from a cropduster.

Those smart bullets were smart. They had memory metal jackets which could act like little tiny fins and ailerons, giving them some ability to correct their course in-flight when diving into the target. Some changed shape as they entered the target, swelling or dilating to change their cross-section. The could slim down their noses right before hitting bullet proof vests, to become armor-penetrating, and flattening their heads when they hit flesh to become dum-dums.

Mom told me her bridesmaid was shot during the wedding. The girl was standing too near an open window, and maybe her gown gave her a silhouette that some dumb smart bullet thought looked like a target. That was back when people still gathered in churches for weddings and stuff. Back when buildings still had open windows.

The pixel resolution on these weapons was not the greatest. Forty-nine times out of fifty they could not tell the difference between a school-child and a lamp-post, a passer-by, a shadow on the wall, a fire hydrant. So you'd have to shoot fifty-one bullets to make sure you hit a target.

Yes, I said a school-child. Target of choice, once the rules of war went away. Why? Well, the point of war is to use violence to terrify the enemy into submission; to break his will to resist. Right? The best place for violence was in a town; that's where the people are. The best place for terror is in a school; that's where the people gather all their children.

All their unarmed, unprotected, beloved, innocent children.

If you were a soldier, there was no point in looking for other soldiers to shoot at. They were all dressed like civilians, like you were, sitting on park benches, eating submarine sandwiches, or pretending to smoke. Or sitting up a tree thirty miles away; or in a diving suit taking a rest on the bottom of a nearby lake, watching for a target-lock. No point in trying to shoot at soldiers. There were none to find.

I know what you're thinking. What about shooting the leaders? Assassinating the captains and colonels and commissars on the other side? Presidents, Premiers, Prime ministers?

Listen, honey, I'm running low on memory, so I'll try to make this quick, but it is complex—everything is tied into everything else. I'm trying to explain what kind of people your folks were, your real folks, and why they made a power- armored suit like this.

When the nature of war changed the nature of government changed. What is a government, anyway, besides a group of people in the business of winning wars and stopping fights, right? Even before when I was born, politicians had been using computer enhanced imagery to make their images on STV look younger, more commanding, more handsome, less fat. Whatever. Guys with squeaky voices were given nice baritones. It was fake, but so what? We never minded if a politician did not write his own speeches, did we? Why should we mind what he really looked like, so long as he did his job?

Well, it was just a small step from cartoon-drawing over real politicians to replacing those politicians entirely with computer-generated talking heads. You see, the world when I was young was not divided into Haves and Have-nots. It was divided into Knowns and Unknowns.

When the nature of government changed, the nature of citizenship changed. The nature of wealth and power changed.

Not everyone was trying to shoot the kids, though. Thank God for that. When everything went away, when everything went bad, there were still some people who kept their heads. After my parents were killed, this family of Amish farmers found me, wandering the fields at night, still carrying my Mom's head. I guess I was out of my mind, a bit. Jeez! How old was I then? Younger than you.

My other real-time, real-life friend was Mr. Eister. He had taught me how to shoot, what to do during incoming-fire drills, how to check food for foreign substances after saying grace. I remember him as a tall man, tall as a mountain it seemed to me, who always wore an odd, old-fashioned wide-brimmed hat. When I was six, I had insisted the mansion-circuits make such a hat like that for me, which I insisted on wearing all the time, even to bed, even to church (we had churches back then.)

The only thing which could get me to take that damn hat off, was Mr. Eister himself, when we were suiting up. I remember arguing with him that my helmet was big enough to allow me to wear the hat beneath it, if I scrunched it up a bit. He had explained...once...that the extra fabric would prevent the helmet cushions from seating properly on my skull. When I hadn't listened he waited patiently till I suited up, then he struck me in the head with his gun-stock, knocking me from my feet and setting my ears ringing.

"English," (he always called me that,) "English, a hard-shot shell would conduct a thousand time more foot-pounds of force that that little tap." He had leaned over me to talk. "The only thing what keeps thy brains from being churned to jam during a fire-fight, lad, is that thy helm here can flex to deflect the shockwave into the exo-skeleton anchor-points. Which it cannot do if thee must wear thy hat; remove it."

Poor Mr. Eister. Someone posted a bounty on the Amish. Didn't like their ways, didn't like their looks, didn't like their farm carts blocking the road. Who knew why? Who gave a reason? I was in my armor when a flock of bullets dropped out of a clear blue sky and stuck the house, spreading jellied gasoline everywhere. I was cool and safe, surrounded by flames. Peter played jump-and-run music, so I could not hear the sound of my new family sizzling and screaming. I jumped and ran. With the Jack Rabbit toggle thrown, I could jump over a church steeple.

How could they get away with shooting at us?

It was the crypto, you see. Encryption. Encryption and digital money. Governments did not bother raising and training armies. You did not need *esprit de corps* and unit cohesion to win a war any more. Governments just put out bounties over the Net, posted the reward and the bag they wanted on a public board in some neutral country. There was always a neutral country willing to carry the board.

The posting? Just a public announcement that decryption keys to a certain amount of digital cash would be sent out to anyone who could anonymously post a 'prediction' of how many people of a certain nation would be killed on a certain day. There was a third party verification system to confirm the kills, also encrypted both ways.

You see, with double-encryption, you could actually pay someone the digital cash, or even leave it laying around at a public bulletin board address, but anyone who picked it up could not spend it without unscrambling it. It was worthless and safe.

Each time someone downloaded a copy of your bag of cash to their personal station, a new unique key and counter-key would be generated automatically.

Let us say a hundred people, or a million, make copies of the scrambled cash. A hundred keys, or a million, are generated. Each personal to the person making the copy.

You send your counter-key back in to the government hiring you, along with whatever proof you want that you've killed the number of people they wanted killed. You sent it in anonymously.

Once they have your unique counter key, they can publicly post the decryption for your unique key. They can shout the decrypt from the roof-tops; it doesn't do anyone any good but you. Unique means that you and only you can unscramble your copy of the cash bundle. Everyone else just has a string of garbled ones and zeros, meaningless and worthless. You have a code which opens a credit line through a numbered Swiss bank account. You never meet your employer; he never meets you. The other party could not even help the police find you even if he wanted to.

And not just governments. Anyone who wanted anyone killed, for any reason or no reason. Someone posted bounties on black children. Someone else posted bounties on Ku Klux Klansmen. A retaliation? Who knew?

Someone else posted bounties on Jews. Someone else picked Witches. Someone else picked Christians. Homosexuals. Smokers. Non-smokers. Heterosexuals. Dog-owners. A zero-population group posted bounties on anyone. Anyone at all.

And it did not need to be one person posting the bounty. I contributed a few bucks myself, when I was in school, to have a certain famous entertainer who annoyed me bumped off. It was only a dollar or two; I meant it as a joke. I was drunk. But people kept adding to the fund. A dollar here, a gold gram there. After about five years, the bounty on the guy was half a million.

Now, I am not a murderer. That guy escaped. You see, that entertainer did not look like he looked in the See-vees. His picture was computer-generated. He was rich. He had friends. He was an Unknown.

Remember what I said about the difference between Knowns and Unknowns? It was the difference between life and death. Unknowns had all their money encrypted, overseas, stored as strings of scrambled numbers. You never met them face to face; you talked over the phone; and the picture and the voice on the phone could be someone, anyone, no one. But it wasn't them.

Remember I said governments changed? They were run by Unknowns. Appointed bureaucrats, some of them; others were just campaign finance contributors.

And taxes? Well, when everyone can hide their assets, there is no way to collect from them.

Tangible assets were different. Governments just seize them. They don't need a reason. They see a house or car they like, they take it. A piece of property, a publicly traded company. In the early days, they had to plant evidence of drug-dealing, or cigarette smoking, unauthorized public prayer, or gun ownership or something. Later, they just claimed the right of Eminent Domain and took what they needed.

How else could they be fed, those governments? How else could they continue?

It didn't bother the Unknowns. They just took out Seizure Insurance and kept most of their assets intangible. The ultra-rich sold or burned their cars after every car trip, and bought new ones before they went out again, just so they would have nothing on the highways to be seized. That was back when we had highways.

So how do you protect your children, in a time like that, with a civilization going to hell? You cannot negotiate with the assassins because no one knows who they are. Your rulers will not protect you. They are anonymous kelpto-crats. The police? Don't make me laugh; everyone I knew kicked a few bucks into the kill-the-pigs kitty every time they got a traffic ticket, or had another car seized. The army? But there is no army. There will never be another army again.

A bullet-proof vest is not thick enough to stop a mid-sized smart bullet. And in order to have plate thick enough to shield your little child's heart and head from the assassins, you must mount it on an articulated exoskeleton.

I hated the stuff when I was young, and I always used to play with my faceplate open, so I could smell the free summer breeze. Billy Worthemer was the same way. Open faceplate. I talked him into doing it too, so he couldn't tell on me.

We were in the courtyard green-area. In a protected zone, with no line-of-sight to any taller buildings.

I remember seeing the targeting platform that painted us, Billy and me. It was just a motion sensor clipped to the collar of a puppy dog, with the sensitivity turned down so that only a body larger than a dog, but smaller than an adult, would set it off. Billy went over to pet the dog. I raced him to it to be the first one there, and picked up the dog.

I remember Peter Power Armor saved my life. I was hit in the shoulder by the round, but the shot did not penetrate. But the ricochet caught Billy in the face. He was turning around to say something to me; maybe to ask me to let him have a turn petting the dog.

I do not remember what happened to his face. I really do not. I remember the whine in my gauntlets when I pulled the innocent little puppy in half. Poor dog. I remember that. I do not remember what Billy looked like. Not at all.

I should erase that last bit. It has nothing to do with what I was saying. I am trying to tell you what your parents and grandparents were like. Are like. You're my granddaughter. It took me so long to find you. But I never gave up.

We are the kind of people who look after our kids. Having power armor for kids seems ridiculous, doesn't it? These days, it does. In the old days, it did not.

Everything you've been told about history is a lie. The People's Jesus did not come back to Earth and marry Mother Gaia, and appoint the First Protector of the Green People. That's not what happened.

The society I was raised in, the nightmare, could not last. The Unknowns could not last. They did not even know each other, did they? How could they help each other?

But what could stop the nightmare? Shut off the Net, you're saying. Cut the cables, arrest the Providers, take an ax to the mainframes, tear up the ground-lines. Easy enough. But who was going to do it? Not the multinationals; all their money was in the Net. Not the Unknowns; the Net was their universe.

In a society where everyone is being shot at, shot at any time and at all times, there are only two things you can do. Either you make sure everyone has a gun or you make sure no one has a gun.

The people West of the Mississippi chose the option number one. The people in the East chose option two.

The reality behind option two, of course, is that 'no one has a gun' actually means, 'no one but the authorities has a gun.' And that means, 'everyone but the authorities shuts up and does what they're told.'

The reality behind option one, of course, is that 'everyone has a gun' actually means, 'If you want me to shut up, tough guy, come over here and make me.'

The two systems are incompatible.

That's what the Second Civil War was really about; it was not about the Sacred Spotted Owl. And when the war got hot enough, and enough transatlantic cables got sabotaged, the Net went down. The Stock Market, all the stock markets, really, and bank records, personal records, everyone's identities, known and unknown, just went away.

The economy just went away.

And when that happened, the civilization's ability to feed the population of the world was cut roughly in half.

And the old-fashioned methods of warfare came back. We had soldiers again. I am not saying whether that was a good thing or a bad thing. They are brave, the soldiers these days; they wear uniforms, they do not hide and slink and sneak like soldiers from my day.

I am not brave. I am not like the soldiers of today. I am one of the old men of the days. My mission was to rescue you. I did it our way.

I was telling you about Peter Power Armor. I was telling you that I knew Mrs. Hechler would not know what it was. She had not lived through my grandfather's time, when fathers took their boys out into the woods to shoot squirrels. Or my father's time, when school uniforms were all woven with bulletproof material. My time I've told you about, the time of the Unknowns. The time of your mother (my daughter.) Her time was even worse; the time of the Diebacks.

Industrial collapse. No more computers, no more smart-bullets. War is more like the old days; men in uniforms who can see each other through the grass, in the trenches, shooting. The bullets aren't smart enough to pick their own targets any more. The nature of war turned back.

Your generation is so lucky. You don't know anything. Lucky, stupid, stupid, lucky fools.

A woman of Mrs. Hechler's generation would not believe any children's toy could be armed.

But Mrs. Hechler knew it was a machine, and machines of any kind were rare these days, and she knew the Correct Thought. "Ethne! Get away from that Satan-metal thing! Green Jesus and Mother Earth hate machines! Don't touch it!"

I said, "Darling Ethne; this is your magic fairy-tale knight-in-shining-armor, come to rescue you. Its yours, yours, all yours, your very own."

"Shut up!" Mrs. Hechler said to me.

I shrugged, putting my hands behind my back. "Oh, come now, you foul-smelling sack of lumpish fat. I am not the one who cannot control a seven-year -old girl. You signed the authorization saying we could explore this deserted old house to see if there was anything we could loot or sell for the communal kitchen. I'm not the one who will catch hell from the District Helpfulness Manager."

That directed her attention back to the child. 'Ethne Cornwall Delaplace! Ward of the State 142! Come here right now! Let go of that thing! It belongs to everyone!"

I said, "You are a princess, raised by trolls, who hate that you come from a high and noble lineage. This gentle knight-errant shall rescue you and take you to a free land across the Mississippi to the West. On your very life, do not let go!"

"Ethne! Come here! Don't make me call for Jerry downstairs!"

I said, "Free, Ethne. Freedom. No more equalization injections because you are smarter than other kids. Freedom."

Ethne smiled at me, looking very beautiful to me for the first time since I met her, just like her mother when she was a little girl.

And she said, "Please, sir. I want to be smart again, like I used to. I want to be free." And that was when I fell in love with her.

I think the mention of the F word did it.

Mrs. Hechler strode forward, huge and ponderous in her wrath. Mrs. Hechler grabbed Ethne by the arm. It was a good grab, swift as a snake, the kind of grip guards should learn to use on prisoners. And I am sure it hurt, because Ethne screamed.

I pointed the handset at the scene, opened the lens, and said carefully into the mic: "Child under attack."

It was amazing how surprised Mrs. Hechler looked when she fell. I had underestimated how loud the shot of the tranquilizer dart would be. I had not expected Jerry, who had been waiting outside, to come up shooting.

Jerry was not licensed as a cop, just as security. A baby-sitter. Regulations said he was not allowed to be armed with anything but a stunner. That hand-cannon he held was no stunner; it was shooting through walls, brick and plaster. Made a hell of a noise. Just like the old days, eh?

I had also underestimated how clever the power-armor's neural net had been programmed. It practically opened up in half and scooped Ethne into itself. Jerry really never stood a chance. It was very noisy and very bloody; not the sort of thing a child should see.

It is too bad you are unconscious. Peter sedated you because you were screaming and putting your hands in front of his gun barrels. I am recording this all through the hand-set into the suit playback for you to hear when you wake up.

Yes, I was wounded in the fire-fight. Wood-shrapnel from where a stray slug hit the door-frame. In my day, our doctors could have saved my leg.

I wish you could see what you looked like when you took off just now. It was lovely. You jumped out the window and over the next house. You should see the Seven-League-Boots program in action; each jet-assisted leap was two hundred yards if it was an inch.

I've already called in the escape over Mrs. Hechler's radio phone. The patrols are headed up north, into the swampland. In a minute, if I am strong enough, I'll send in a report that you were sighted down south, in the hills. All their equipment still runs off the old, old programs. Old as me. And I know the magic words to open the trap-doors and make my voice whatever CO's voice they need to hear.

I am a wizard, a warlock, a fraud, a gray old Prospero from a lost island, who never repented or burned his books or broke his wand. I have cast a spell on you, princess, and befuddled them.

They will not catch you. They will never catch you. I can just imagine the troopers on horseback, those of them who can afford horses, trying to catch you by lantern-light. I was the one who played hide-and-seek with my little friend Battery Bunny when I was eight, in that armor. One touch of the Mr. Frog button turns on the sneeky-peeky lowlight goggles, activates the aqualung, lets you to crawl along a river-bottom at night. The smart-metal is radar-invisible. If those barbarians still have any working radar sets. If they could get the bureaucrats in their organization to release them to the river patrol. Which I doubt. Which I doubt.

And Homer the Homing Pigeon who lives in the helmet is gyroscopically aligned and corrects himself by star-pattern recognition. So you cannot get lost or get turned around. I selected the map-program through the handset. It was the first thing I did before I started recording.

I do not mind going away. I was one of them, darling. An Unknown. That's why my name is not on the records. Dad gave me trapdoors into the computer systems that survived the Netcrash. That's why I was able to find my family. To find you. I am sorry for the things I did and I do not really mind dying. I've tried to make up for it.

What else do I need to say? I am getting sleepy now, and its hard to think.

I am the last of the Unknowns. I could make myself a fake ID. I could travel in the East on forged papers. I could give myself authorization to read the Child Safety and Domestication Bureau records, to unseal sealed files, and depart without a trace.

My magic. Left over from the old days. I wove a cloak of cunning mist and made myself invisible, while I was right in front of their eyes. Who looks at janitors? My papers were in order.

The job as a janitor at the Children's Center I got by hard work and sweat; something rare here. Tricking Mrs. Hechler into violating regulations and going to loot a deserted house in a public-owned area was simply not difficult. All serfs ignore regulations when they can; it's the only way they can live. There are just so many regulations, you see, no one can listen to them all.

Is there anything else I need to tell you, anything else I need to explain?

What they told you about the West is all lies too. We don't shoot each other down in the streets, we don't have gunfights in every bar. We do have bars, but not everyone drinks.

I do not know what went wrong with all the people back East, after the Diebacks. I do not know why they could not rebuild. The Western states are mostly empty desert. How come they got rich? I do not know. Maybe the East-erners did not have the will to resist when the People's Green Church of Mother Life came along. They certainly did not have the means to resist. They did not have anything like Peter.

But those deserts are so beautiful under the starlight. You'll see them soon.

Oh, God, let me stay awake long enough to tell you this.

Darling, I do not know the names of my contacts in the underground railroad. Remember I told you about encryption? You just go to any public phone once you are across the Mississippi, in the wide Western places they've remembered finally what a free country is supposed to be. They've also remembered how to set up a working Net again.

Another Net. Are the bad old days coming back again? I don't know. I'm very tired, and I just don't know. Maybe you can grow up and stop those bad things from happening.

Don't let me forget. Get to the phone. Push the button shaped like Puss-in-Boot. It's the crypto cat. It will turn on the circuit and make the phone call for you. It will call the nice people.

Get to a phone. Peter will know what to do. Trust Peter. He'll take care of you.

Peter loves you; I love you.

Goodbye, God bless, and Godspeed.

You mother is waiting for you in Austin. Your real mother. We got her out of the camps months ago. Her name is Roselinde. She was very pretty when she was your age.

From SO IT BEGINS
Book Two in the Defending The Future series

Junked by Andy Remic
First Line by Danielle Ackley-McPhail
To Spec by Charles E. Gannon
The Glass Box by Bud Sparhawk
Everything's Better With Monkeys by C.J. Henderson

JUNKED
A Combat K Adventure

Andy Remic

THE SLAM CRUISER HOWLED THROUGH THE UPPER ATMOSPHERE OF RYZOR, BUFFETED by an enraged storm. Lightning sparkling from armoured hull shells in crackles. Iron bruise clouds closed around the SLAM like a fist around a pebble, holding it tight for a frozen moment before flinging it down in a violent acceleration...

"We're gonna die," moaned Franco, curled fetal in his CrashCouch, forehead touching his knees, beard rimed with droplets of sweat and vibrating vigorously. He clutched his Kekra quad-barrel machine pistol to his chest, as a mother would a weary child.

"Don't be such a pussy," snarled Pippa, glaring at Franco with cold eyes. The female member of this particular Combat K squad, Pippa was low on empathy and understanding, high on the twin goals of violence and destruction. "You knew we were breaching the storm, dickhead. What did you expect, sunshine?"

"I would have preferred a scanty-clad welcome party of thong-strapped, lap-dancing beauties," said Franco, without any hint of sarcasm. "Either that, or a good pub. Maybe a tastefully decorated brothel." He glanced up, making eye contact with Pippa who was battling the SLAM cruiser's controls. "Hey, actually, now we're on the subject of sex, what about you and I . . ."

"No."

"You don't know what I was going to suggest."

"Yeah I do, Franco. You're a sexual deviant, and I've suffered enough depraved suggestions to last any woman, whore, or gal-slacker a lifetime. Just stay in your couch, focus on the mission, and keep your paws off my arse."

Franco mumbled, and closed his eyes as the SLAM rattled violently, huge shudders juddering corrugated walls, buffeted by Nature. Nature was in a foul mood. She was good and ready for a spot of fisticuffs.

"Coming in fast, Keenan. Bang goes our covert entry."

Keenan reclined, one army boot on the console, drawing on a home-rolled smoke filled with harsh Widow Maker tobacco. He gave a single nod, rubbed weary eyes. "They'll not scan shit in this storm," he drawled on an exhalation of diesel smoke. "Drop us vertical under the Beacon Scanners, an' we'll cruise up the river and go in light. I doubt General Zenab is hard to find; the junks will be treating the bastard like a king."

Combat K were elite, murderous combat squads trained by the Quad-Gal Military specializing in interrogation, infiltration, assassination and detonation. Their original game-plan had been simple: to end The Helix War, which had raged for a thousand years. However, after QGM quelled one conflict, so another had taken its place—in the form of junks, a twisted, hazardous species of deviated aliens, a toxic race intent on polluting the Quad-Gal with their infestation—and wiping out *all* species in the process.

Once believed extinct, the junks had reappeared on Galhari, a quiet fringe planet, with devastating suddenness...in a flood of *millions*. The planet had been taken in hours, and from that foothold the junks began a galaxy-wide conquest which had, in all honesty, gone *bad* for Quad-Gal Military. Recently, a series of freak coincidences led to military intelligence uncovering a source of the junk's expertise: a psychic general, capable of reading minds across the Four Galaxies and uncovering QGM's secret plans. Named Zenab, the general was also rumored to have invented a Nano-Bomb, a microscopic detonation device which could put QGM out of the game for good. Zenab was making it possible for the junks to extend their diseased and toxic empire, and had set up camp in his Nano-Bomb Factory. Now, it was Combat K's mission to take him out . . . before millions more died.

"Tipping in now," said Pippa.

The SLAM's engines quietened and it fell vertical, accelerating through high-altitude rage toward the smash of jungle canopy below. Like a meteorite they plummeted, the ship's computers masking their profile and using a radioactive Doppelganger Shift to pre-empt rogue AI SAMs.

Without incident, the SLAM reached a half klick above the rain-lashed jungle, and engines suddenly roared, energy whumping against trees and blasting a crater fifty metres wide. Every tree in the radius was shredded, instantly. The SLAM levelled out, stabilizers grunting, and settled into the crater. Engines died. Rain played drumbeats on the hull, and Franco uncurled from his CrashCouch and glared at Pippa with a teenage pout. "Not exactly what I'd call smooth," he said.

"Get to shit, Franco. I'd like to see you do better."

"Actually, they don't call me Franco "Ace Pilot" Haggis for nothing, chipmunk."

Keenan placed a hand on Pippa's shoulder, and smiled into her blossoming wrath. Relax, said that smile. Chill. There are more important things than Franco's attitude.

Keenan stood, stretched, and removing his cigarette, which he stubbed into a whirring mechanical ashtray with six metal fingers which took the weed and crushed it into recyclable pulp, said, "Let's tool up."

The ramp hit the blasted jungle crater, and Combat K descended, guns primed, covering one another's arcs of fire with a practiced finesse. Pippa held a PAD computer alongside her D5 shotgun. "All clear," she said, expert eyes reading the scanner.

They stepped into the rain and a cool wind, and were instantly drenched. In one fist Franco carried a small black ball, which appeared to be made from rubber. It gleamed in the rain.

They crossed the crater, climbed slick mud slides, and moved efficiently into the jungle, a well-oiled military machine, with Keenan walking point, Pippa scanning central, and Franco, complaining as usual in a mumbling mutter, bringing up the rear. He had three D5 shotguns on his back, a military porcupine, a Kekra quad-barrel in one fist, and a Bausch & Harris sniper rifle strapped to his pack. As was usual, Franco was terribly over-tooled for the mission—but he wouldn't have it any other way. He'd been in a savage fire-fight once and run out of ammo; it hadn't been a pleasant experience, and Franco spent many long hours, drunk, regaling people with an exaggeration of the tale.

The trees were eerie, silent. The rain danced. A strong aroma of rotting vegetation flooded the jungle like toxic gas.

It was too . . . still. Just too damn lifeless.

The squad halted in a vast swathe of curving jungle. Somewhere they could hear a raging waterfall. Keenan glanced at Pippa. "How far to the contact?"

Pippa smiled at that. Keenan could be so . . . clinical. The contact. The target. The assassination. The taking of a human life, and yeah, OK, that guy was responsible for the deaths of millions according to the unreliable monkeys of QGM military intelligence, but who's to say they were right? Who gave Combat K the right to play God?

"Twenty klicks. Northeast."

"How far to the Blood River?"

"Eight hundred and twenty-seven metres. Give or take."

"Let's move out."

They eased through the enemy jungle. There had been no early ScoutBot Scan infiltrations or WebCloud relays, because QGM wanted to retain the element of surprise. In and out in three hours. A neat excision.

It was immensely dark in the jungle, and muted sounds echoed metallic between trees. The sounds were odd, unlike usual jungle noises. Keenan and Pippa exchanged glances, but continued, heightened senses alert to danger, guns rain-slick and slippery in gloved hands. Permatex WarSuits moderated body temperature and kept the stifling jungle humidity from biting…too much. Franco still mumbled curses as he brought up the rear, expertly scanning their back-trail, and expertly watching Pippa's arse. *I wish,* he thought sourly. *Oh to get my paws on that ripe pair of peaches!* But it would never happen, especially as Franco was currently married to an eight-foot mutated zombie super-soldier, once beautiful, now an abomination of pus. He frowned at the memory. It was a long story, a tale of violence and psychopathic *biohell.*

The river surprised them, despite electronic warnings. It slammed from the darkness, a muted roaring greeting them instantaneously from the gloom. It was lighter here, out from under the tree canopy, and a rime of green moonlight crept from behind bruised copper clouds. Keenan gave Franco a nod, and the small ginger squaddie knelt in the mud by the side of the river.

"Do it."

"Yeah boss."

Franco twisted the small rubber ball, and tossed it into the river on the end of a flexing TitaniumIII cord. The ball gave a *crack* of ignition, and a hiss, and inflated instantly into a special forces covert boat, nicknamed a Rubber Duck, or *Sitting Duck* by the more cynical members of the squads. Pippa and Keenan climbed in, guns tracking dark shorelines overhung with skeletal branches. The air crackled with strange, metallic creaking, not unlike the discharge of energy. Pippa gave a shudder.

"You OK?"

"I feel like we're being watched. The PAD states otherwise, although the thing's playing up—which is unusual. They're normally good for a billion years. Maybe it's the high magnetic field? Maybe we're being dicked with."

"Still no life?"

"No life," said Pippa. "By that, I mean *absolutely* no life. This jungle is deader than a crypt. There's no indigenous life-forms; no birds, no insects. Nothing. I've seen more energy in a corpse."

Franco jumped in and fired stealth engines, a twin-set of Suzuki Whisper MkIVs. He eased the boat out into the strong tug of the river, and turned against the current. They were headed up-river; deeper into the jungle, deeper into nigritude, deeper into the heart of darkness.

Franco stared at the gloom. "I don't suppose there's any brothels up there?" he muttered.

"Don't be an idiot," snapped Pippa.

"Pubs? You reckon?" He sounded feebly hopeful.

"Dickhead."

"What about a casino or two? It's ages since I've had a flutter."

"Mate, the last time you gambled you lost your damn *house.* Haven't you learnt your lesson?"

"'Twas a simple error of reading the cards. I'll do better next time, so I will."

"Well," said Pippa carefully, "I don't see how. After you shot the place up with that K7 shotgun, and dropped a BABE grenade in the manager's office. Fair blew the place to shit. You've been banned from every gambling franchise on The City."

"Rubbish! They know that was only little old me playing toy soldiers." He brightened. "Still. This guy is a king, right? This General Zenab? Showered in gold and jewels by the junks? Treated like royalty?" His eyes went suddenly crafty, as he guided the small submersible through dark channels of foaming river. Rainfall gleamed on his skin, and as green moonlight caught him, he looked quite demonic. Like a devil, sick of sin. Like a twice reanimated corpse. "We might even make a few dollars!" He beamed. "There might be dancing girls in the palace!" He beamed wider, showing his broken tooth from too many drunken bar-brawls.

Pippa slapped his arm. "You're a muppet. You need to focus, Franco, and focus hard. This ain't no game we're playing. Kee? I told you he'd be a damn liability. I told you to choose somebody else."

"Well, charming!" stuttered Franco. "Thanks for your vote of confidence, sweetie."

"We might need his detonation skills," growled Keenan, with a shaded glance. "And you *know* there's nobody better with a Bausch & Harris. I'm hoping we can get this gig finished—*without* getting our hands dirty."

They cruised in silence through obsidian shadows. The jungle closed in as the river narrowed, became yet more violent, raging and pounding around black fists of ancient volcanic rock. Quietly, Pippa said, "Never in a million years."

They stopped in a small bay of calm water for navigation checks. Pippa was jagging the touch-dials of the PAD, and shook her head. "No good, Kee. There's something wrong—either with the PAD, or with the whole damn planet."

"Leave the pad," said Keenan. "We'll use our eyes and ears. Just like the old days on Molkrush Fed."

He glanced up, and there, at the edge of the jungle, perhaps five metres away, stood a squad of junks. Four of them. Heavily armed. For what seemed an eternity the two groups faced one another across the expanse of stagnant water, a platter of stinking glass . . . then hell erupted—

Keenan's Techrim 11mm was out and pumping in his fist and he dived right, over the edge of the boat. Pippa dropped to one knee, D5 in her gloved hands, booms crashing through the jungle. Franco split left, a Kekra quad-barrel machine pistol in each hand slamming bullets at the squad. The junks, tall and powerful wearing basic electronic leather armour, skin pitted like metal, eyes like pools of blood, short, forked silver tongues flickering in silver mouths like liquid metal—they split with equal skill and speed, their MPKs firing volleys of roaring bullets at Combat K. Everything was a deafening bellow of chaos and confusion. The jungle screamed with concussion and bullets, a distillation of confusion, as Keenan pumped rounds into a junk's face and watched him stumble back, blood spewing from destroyed eyes, his face a mash of chewed bone and gristle and flapping cheek skin. Franco, yelling, charged with Kekras roaring. Two bullets *thumped* his WarSuit like hammer blows, knocking the wind from him, slamming his heart with pounding fists but he was on the junk, both guns screaming, aware like the others that junks were insanely tough, hard to kill, real *bastards* to put down. Their eyes were their Achilles' heel; shoot out their eyes and death would follow. Franco was on the junk, both boots slamming the stunned, eye-destroyed face and riding him to the ground to crouch beside the writhing figure. The two remaining junks charged Pippa, her D5 still cracking but they *absorbed* shells in primitive armour and skin and muscle, which rolled like melted wax, reforming, repairing even as it was decimated and Pippa felt panic well in her breast at this seemingly indestructible threat before her...and closing fast. One reached out, took the D5 from her hands and bent it into two discrete parts with a *snap* and scatter of unspent shells. The junk screamed in her face, a toxic blast of poisonous air that made her weak at the knees, ingested toxins attacking her central nervous system as the second junk turned on Franco and fired a volley of MPK rounds...

And Keenan was there, Techrim against the junk's head. "Put her down, shitbag." The junk turned and grinned at him, blood red eyes narrowing as Keenan pulled the trigger and the bullet whined through skull and brain, erupting in a mushroom shower of shards and mashed brain-slop. It rammed a fist into Keenan's chest, slamming him back over the boat in an acceleration of gasping pain and realization that the junk *could still operate with a bullet in the head* . . . the junk turned on Pippa, who smiled a nasty smile, and slammed her knife into one eye with a downward punch. She ripped the blade sideways, cutting out the junk's second blood orb and it screamed, a sudden high-pitched shrill, flopping back in the Duck, thrashing as Pippa hurled the blade to embed in the final junk's armour. It turned from Franco, lying back on the rocks, stunned by bullet blasts in his Permatex. When it glanced at Pippa, Franco reached back and grabbed the first thing which came to hand. His Bausch & Harris sniper rifle, packing high velocity 8.98 medium calibre rounds. At that range, face to face, the weapon was devastating. The rifle gave a *thump* in Franco's gloved fists and the junk's head disintegrated. The body stood for a moment, jiggling, blood a fountain from the jagged neck, then fell flat and dead on the rocks. A thick, evil stench poured from the open neck. An aroma of rotten eternity. The perfume of the junk.

Franco coughed, and looked to Keenan, who struggled from the water clutching his chest. He felt like he'd suffered a heart attack. Felt like he'd died. "Get back on the boat," he wheezed, and they all scrambled aboard.

As they cruised into violent storm waters, wind howling, the heavens pounding their insignificant craft with needles of rain, Pippa gave Keenan and Franco a savage snarl. "We can assume the bastard PAD is well and truly compromised, yeah? We're on our own, boys."

"Just the way we like it," smiled Franco sardonically.

The storm died in a sudden rush of warm air, like a dragon blast. As if in response, or perhaps by coincidence, the river became a flat platter, glass, ice. Pippa, now pilot, slowed their cruise to a halt and they sat for a few moments, rocking, listening, peering at the overhanging edges of uncompromising metallic-stinking jungle.

"Never get out of the boat," muttered Franco.

"What?" snapped Pippa.

"Just something I heard."

"How far?" said Keenan.

"Three klicks. We're getting close. That's why we met that little scouting party. Was it an accident, I wonder, or were the bastards looking for us? Maybe they saw the SLAM come in, thought they'd investigate."

"To all sensors it'd still look like a meteor strike."

"Still," said Pippa. "I'd want to know what came down twenty klicks from *my* base of operations. Especially if this place *is* a Nano-Bomb Factory."

"Let's assume they know we're here," said Keenan, mind ticking. "What would General Zenab do? He can read minds, or so we're told. See through tangled paths of the future. Has he seen his own impending assassination?"

Pippa stared at Keenan. "That isn't even funny."

"Do you see me laughing? OK. So you've got patrols in the jungle, textbook. What about the river? Patrol boats? We've not seen anything here. What else could you use?"

"It's not deep enough for a sub," said Franco, frowning.

"When I went in the river before, this water, it's not normal. I know it's red because of mineral deposits, but it was also full of . . . oil, or something. A lubricant. It wasn't natural."

"Is that why we can smell metal?"

Keenan shrugged. "Not sure. But whatever it is, it may have a purpose. It reminded me of the Terminus5 Shell reactor; remember the bunker? Full of that insane AI bio-wire which ate through your bones and separated a person long-ways out?"

"I remember," said Franco, voice low. "You think they may have AI tech?"

"I always thought the junks low-tech, but . . . we should prepare for anything. This gig stinks like a dead cat."

"You want to ditch the boat?"

"Maybe. I'm considering it."

They paused, and something slopped in the river. They glanced at one another. "I saw something," said Pippa, carefully, hoisting her weapon, nervous now, gun tracking an invisible foe. The river seemed deeper, here, more stable; and yet more threatening at the same time. Like a motionless predator; a hunter waiting to pounce.

Ripples suddenly drifted away from the Rubber Duck, or at least, from something *near* it. Pippa stood, alongside Keenan, and they both aimed weapons at the flat surface.

"I don't like this," moaned Franco.

"Shut up. Pippa, get us out of here."

Pippa nodded, and eased them forward. They moved across the water, still as a lake, green-tinged from the moon. Ripples flowed, slapping shores. The engine purred, near-silent, and Pippa angled toward the shore . . . .

It was this which saved their lives.

The *thing* squirmed across the river, surfacing sideways like a sidewinder serpent, a long, bright silver eel as thick as a man's waist and perhaps thirty or forty feet long. Pippa gasped and Keenan started firing at the creature undulating toward them. Pippa joined him, but their bullets were absorbed with tiny *plops* as it accelerated, a massive eel that crashed into the Rubber Duck with stunning force, sending all three Combat K soldiers flipping into the river . . .

Keenan went under, felt something cold and metallic brush his WarSuit, recoil for an instant, then *slap* him with such force only his armor stopped immediate death through impact. He choked. Everything, all wind and life were knocked from him and yet he forced himself to swim, powerful strokes, toward the shore. He *felt* the eel's approach rather than saw it, and dived, twisting, by some miracle passing under the undulating body of thick muscle. He struck out, under the river, fighting strange currents until he clambered up the shore, dripping, panting, muscles screaming like irate fishmongers. Franco was already there, heaving, hands on knees, looking sorry for himself in a hangdog fashion.

"Where's Pippa?"

Franco stood upright, stared out, watched the mercury eel circle their Rubber Duck and suddenly ensnare it, its whole body flipping from the river to wrap around the boat again and again in huge circles, and with a sudden *pulse* and tug, crushed the boat into a hissing, buckling, pulped oblivion.

Slowly, Franco pulled free his Bausch & Harris. "She's there. See. Pippa, Hey!" He waved. She seemed disorientated in the gloom, in the drizzle of light rain, but focused on his words and struck out toward him. However, the eel also heard Franco and turned, writhing in foam as Franco snarled a curse and aimed down the rifle's sight.

"You'll draw attention to us!" snapped Keenan, hoisting his own guns and casting about for enemy.

"I can't let her *die,*" said Franco.

He fired, a muted *thump* and the bullet disappeared in the eel's mass. Pippa powered on, but the eel moved fast for something so big. It gained swiftly. If it caught her, it would crush her without doubt. Franco breathed deep, and fired off another three shots in quick succession. The thump of bullets echoed off, flesh slaps, muted by the jungle.

"It's going to kill her," said Keenan.

"Not on *my* watch," snapped Franco, and began pumping shot after shot after shot into the silver eel, unaware if his bullets had effect, unaware if this *thing* was something they could *kill*. What was it? AI? A simpConstruct robot? Organic? Or a meld of all three?

"Come on!" urged Keenan.

Franco kept on firing, and the eel suddenly slowed, its sidewinder motion becoming erratic. Pippa reached the shore, but the eel's tail lunged from blood waters and wrapped around her chest. It dragged her back, and both Keenan and Franco leapt forward, guns thundering and howling into the thick silver body which twitched and pulsed. Pippa screamed, hands straining against the metallic surface. Then her fingers slipped inside, as if entering jelly, and came out, shocked, trailing umbilicals of silver eel strand . . .

Franco dropped to his knees on the rocks, in the mud, his eyes locked to Pippa's and reading the pain and suffering there. He pulled a BABE grenade from his belt, gave her a wide grin, pulled the pin and plunged his fist *inside* the eel's apparently semi-solid body. He pulled free his arm, rocked back on heels, and fell to his arse. He watched as there came a muffled *crack*. Ripples shuddered along the length of the eel, and it twitched, every molecule vibrating out of synchronization with every other. Then, the creature was still.

Franco and Keenan dragged Pippa from the strange creature's embrace, Pippa coughing, holding her chest. Without her WarSuit she'd be a mashed pulp, a skin bag of crumbled bones. Even now, the armor was buzzing warnings; it was seriously damaged, and would fail if it took another impact.

"I'd say they know we're here," said Franco.

"Let's move out. The quicker we get this done, the quicker we go home."

"I'm beginning to hate this planet," said Franco, pulling his sulky lip.

Pippa coughed, and stood. She took several deep breaths. She looked annoyed. More than annoyed. She looked ready to *kill*. "Let's go assassinate this bastard," she said, and hoisted her shotgun with a scowl.

They moved like ghosts through the jungle. Up close, the trees were metallic, coated in a sheen of oil. They were not living, not organic, but simple machines designed to imitate life. A machine jungle. An army of sentry steel.

"What kind of freak creates such a place?" said Franco, frowning. It was the waste and pointlessness, more than anything, that offended him.

"Just keep your eye on the PAD."

For the last two klicks they'd evaded nine junk patrols, keeping low and quiet, going to ground at the first hint of enemy activity. But the fact still nagged Combat K—if the enemy knew they were there, on the planet, alertness would be increased. And the enemy may also now have discovered the SLAM cruiser. The last thing a soldier needed after a bad gig was a compromised ride home.

Franco, bringing up the rear, caught Keenan's signal and dropped instantly, silent. He carried the Bausch & Harris, now, in his big pugilist's paws. He was twitchy; on edge. A man on a high wire. A hairline trigger.

Dropping to his belly against the floppy, metallic leaves, Franco commando-crawled forward. They were on a cliff-top overlooking a bowl valley devoid of jungle, although with so many thick creepers it could happily be described as a bowel valley. To the left, the Blood River eased sluggish and wide. Boats were moored there, low-alloy vessels with big guns. Several ornately carved stone buildings squatted at the center of the cleared jungle, lights shone in windows. And yet the whole place looked deserted, especially as this was supposed to be the Nano-Bomb Factory. It felt wrong, and much too small in scale. If this was a Nano-Bomb Factory, would General Zenab really surround himself with a mere handful of junk protectors? If this man really was as richly rewarded, highly prized, and threatening to QGM as they claimed, wouldn't the security be far more aggressive?

"This stinks," said Pippa.

"Like a ten-week dead pig," added Franco.

"Let me think," said Keenan. "Is the PAD still dead?"

"Like a ten-week dead skunk," said Franco.

Keenan held up one fist. "Stop! I need to think. Pippa, is this the target?"

"Yeah."

"It's so wrong."

"I know that, Kee. This ain't no Nano-Bomb Factory."

Keenan bellied down, chin on his hands, and watched the modest activity which surrounded the small stone buildings. The carvings were ancient. Alien archaeology. He shuddered. It always filled him with a desolation, as if humans had only been kicking around the Quad-Gal for a few minutes—which in reality, they had. Aliens, sentient life-species as a matrix, had been around a billion times longer. This simple infancy made humanity feel quite insecure; something they made up for with aggression and a savage empire.

"Maybe," said Keenan, "this bastard is so tough he doesn't need protection. We're looking at this wrong. Maybe Zenab is an ancient alien creature, more powerful than any of us dreamed. After all, we're assuming he's human, because QGM *assumed* he was human. That was never confirmed."

"Shit intel, again," snapped Pippa. "The story of our lives."

"We need to make the best of it," said Keenan. "This is the gig. I'll head in alone; you two cover me, especially Franco with that lethal bastard rifle. OK?"

"I don't like it," said Pippa.

"I didn't ask whether you liked it."

Pippa took his arm, stared into his eyes. And he could read it there, the love the need the want the lust, sexual desire but more than that, a deep and meaningful *connection*.

"Don't go, Kee," she said.

"We need to get this done."

And he was gone, easing down the slope, fingers digging in rock, eyes and senses alert for enemy activity. But the camp, or base, the supposed Nano-Bomb Factory was pretty much deserted. It was a ghost ship.

"He'll be OK," said Franco, grinning, and patting Pippa on the shoulder. "Let's keep him covered."

"If he's not back in ten minutes, I'm going in."

"That isn't what he said."

"It's what *I said*," she hissed, eyes an insane glare.

"OK, OK, don't take it out on poor old Franco."

"Just play with your gun."

Mumbling, Franco checked over his rifle, and tried not to look concerned.

Keenan touched down on moist soil. His eyes raked the jungle perimeter. The stone buildings appeared inviting, warm, homely, and for the first time in a long, *long* time he found himself thinking of home. His old home. Before Galhari, and before the...*murders*. The word sat foul on his tongue, in his brain, like a diseased implant, a toxic augmentation. His wife, Freya, and their children, Rachel and Ally, had been killed. At first, it had been pinned on Pippa and they had hated one another, tried to kill one another—after all, hadn't Pippa been his lover? Hadn't he cast her aside? Hadn't she had *motive* to murder his family? But as days fell into weeks fell into months it had blurred and become apparent that something far more sinister was at work, so complex even Pippa herself wasn't sure if she'd committed the evil deed. One thing was for sure, however. Keenan's family were dead, slaughtered, and sometimes, occasionally, more often now as months flowed like mercury, he longed to join them.

He knew they were waiting.

Keenan descended the final section of rocky slope, boots digging in, searching for targets. But the area was deserted and this worried him more than any waiting army. Keeping a low profile, he crossed the bare ground to the largest of the stone buildings, eyes taking in ancient carvings which passed through several planes of reality. They were deeply alien, twisted, some shifting from sight to scent to aural expression, and dazzling Keenan with a form of sensual confusion. "Alien shit," he muttered. "Bring back Picasso."

He stopped, back to the wall, gun against his cheek, and glanced up to where Franco and Pippa were camouflaged, invisible, their guns trained, protecting him like hot metal guardians. A robot dad. He peered into the building, which was cool and inviting, a staggered tile floor, every inch of the walls lined with rich tapestries hanging ceiling to floor.

Keenan stepped in, sounds muffled by the vibrant needlework. He moved through rooms, realizing the building was much larger than anticipated . . . but there was no bomb-making equipment on show, no advanced circuitry for the design and production of nano technology. It was primitive. Bare. A let-down. A cerebral retard.

He emerged on the edges of a modest room, circular, walls hung with green tapestries which shifted in a breeze. Sliding behind these convenient screens, he observed three figures, three huge junks with rippling muscles and holstered machine guns. Before them stood a child, a girl, six years old with fine blonde hair and blue eyes in a pretty, oval face. She wore a simple white robe, and clutched a low-profile wooden box in both hands. She was talking, words gentle, like whispers on the wind.

Keenan's gaze shifted back to the three junks and he wondered which one was General Zenab . . .

"Hello, Mr Keenan," said the child, turning, head tilting, just as Keenan was deciding which junk to kill first. He froze, aware he'd made no sound, had not compromised his position in the slightest. He relaxed. So. They knew he was coming; and more than that—they knew who he was.

Combat K. QGM. *Shit.*

He stepped from his tapestry-concealed hiding place, grinning wryly. He'd never made a good assassin. *Hell,* he thought, *I'm barely a soldier these days; barely human.* He expected a battle, but the junks failed to present arms. They stood, facing away like automatons, apparently oblivious to his existence. Drones in the hive.

"Come forward," said the little girl.

Keenan moved, D5 shotgun in his gloved hands, ready at a twitch to blow any living creature in half. He was watching the junks, eyes narrowed, senses screaming at him with his tainted alien blood; but he could *feel* no others. The five of them were alone . . .

"Which of you is Zenab?"

"Ahh," said the little girl, eyes sparkling, hands clutching the wooden box so tightly her knuckles were white. "You have come for murder. Assassination. Death. We will be sorry to disappoint you; sorry to send you away."

"So he's not here?"

"Assumptions by Quad-Gal Military are so refreshing." Something about the way she spoke the name made Keenan freeze, boots welded to floor tiles, eyes fixed on her and realizing, an instant too late, that she was more than the sum of her parts, and infinitely more dangerous than her simple image led him to believe . . .

He gazed into that face, and his heart melted, and he knew, knew in a blinding white-hot intensity that this girl this child this pale innocent was the *general* he sought to exterminate. And he knew, knew deep in his soul that he could not kill this person.

That's what it wants you think . . . whispered the dark side of his soul.

No! She's a child, a puppet of the junks; I should kill them, her guards, the scourge which has imprisoned her! I should take her away from this place, this evil, take her away to a better life . . . a life with kindness, and family, a place filled with warmth and love.

She will kill you, Keenan. She will possess you! She is not human . . . she will usurp your flesh.

But that's impossible, he realized. She could not usurp him, or possess him, because he barely lived there himself.

"You are General Zenab." It was not a question.

"So very perceptive." She smiled, with small white teeth. And he knew; understood that her arrogance precluded an awesome power. She was no human, because *Keenan was no longer human,* and the alien blood from an earlier encounter *had* tainted his own blood, own soul, had somehow elevated him, somehow desecrated him, dropped him into another plane of existence.

"I have been sent to—to *kill* you." Keenan's voice was quiet. "But I will give you a choice. I will take you away from this place. Give you another life, a better life." He no longer saw Zenab. He saw Rachel and Ally. Their bloody corpses. It ate him like acid.

"Like you would have done for your girls?"

"Yes." Keenan's voice was strangled, neither human nor animal; an imitation of the organic. And a tidal wave of guilt and shame washed over him, flooded him inside out and he felt his knees go weak, his anger flee, any straggled remnants of hatred were torn and all he wanted, more than anything in this world, in this life, was to save this child . . . as he failed to save his own.

He knelt, and placed his gun on the floor with a *clack.*

"Come with me," he said.

She laughed. "I cannot. You do not understand."

"I understand you are prisoner, forced to use your talents for the junks; to aid their empire, to extend their evil."

She smiled, pretty face wrinkling, and Keenan's heart melted, his soul burned, and he only realised Pippa and Franco were behind him when he saw the barrel of Franco's Bausch & Harris rifle ease past his shoulder . . .

"Don't move, buddy," said Franco.

"What are you *doing?*" snapped Keenan.

"She's a witch, a changer, a junk-spawn. She's *infested, mate.* She's hooked into your brain, and into your spine. She's using you, Kee. She'll kill you. Don't trust her." He grinned, but the smile looked wrong on his face. Twisted. Too much bone. Too much skull.

Keenan frowned, the whole world tumbling down. "Bullshit!" he snapped. "She's a prisoner. We have to rescue her . . . to free her! What's wrong with you, Franco? Can't you see?"

"He's right." Pippa's hand touched Keenan's shoulder, then her gun caressed the side of his head. "Sorry, Kee. It's time to die."

A *feeling* swept over Keenan, nausea, a violent bout of sickness worse than anything ever felt. Like a puzzle solved, everything clicked into place. The *pulse* of alien blood through his veins, the beat of his heart, all melded to show him the truth . . . he ducked as Pippa pulled the trigger, and her bullet whined, entered Franco's skull with a *slap,* blasting his head into ribbons of flesh and curled bone. Brain mushroomed out then paused, like elastic caught at the point of furthest trajectory, and ravelled swiftly back in as the head reformed itself disjointedly and for a moment, the briefest of instants, Keenan saw the face disintegrate into a cloud of particles . . . and rearrange as solid flesh.

Keenan whirled fast and the world kicked into guns and bullets, into action and reaction as Franco and Pippa leapt from a doorway with guns thundering, bullets scything into the fake forms of Franco and Pippa, into their *simulacrums,* created things, imitations of life.

Pippa killed herself with a shotgun blast to the head, and watched her own body curl in on itself, into a shower of silver powder that trickled down between cracks in the floor tiles. Franco had a short, vicious fight with his own head-holed ganger, and shot himself in the stomach, then the throat, and finally the face. He watched himself die, and in dying, so the real Franco was born again.

"Shit," he panted, face bathed in sweat. "They nearly had you, Keenan!"

The three junks attacked, as Combat K attacked. Keenan was kicked out of his shock, grabbing the D5 shotgun and leaping forward, blasting a junk guard in the face with a burst of shells and removing his head. There was a whirlwind of violence which left Combat K crouched on the tiles, surrounded by blood and junk gore, limbs, chunks of flesh, as a cool wind blew through the chamber and they realised the little girl had gone.

"The General's fled," said Pippa. "What the fuck's going on?"

"Nano-technology," snarled Keenan. "And the box she carries. It's the Nano-Bomb Factory. I don't know why we thought it'd be an installation; it's something complex, something small, something incredibly advanced. We have to get it. It's too dangerous to let go."

They ran through corridors, through chambers, all writhing with ancient alien stone-craft. They emerged, saw the little girl sprinting toward the river and a sleek alloy craft.

"She's going to escape," snapped Pippa. "Shoot her! QGM rely on it! Millions rely on it."

Franco lifted his rifle, and caught Keenan's eye. Keenan looked as if he'd been hit by a hammer. How could he shoot his own daughter in the back? *How could he murder his little girl?*

Franco, also, was flooded with doubt. He lowered the gun, long barrel pointing at the churned mud floor. "I can't," he said. "I can't shoot a child in the back. It's just not right!"

"Give me the gun," snarled Pippa, dragging the rifle from Franco's scarred hands. She aimed, and with a crack took the back of the girl's head off. General Zenab toppled to the floor in a tangle of limbs; and did not move.

"I'm just mangled," said Franco. "What the hell actually happened? Why did I just kill myself?"

They moved to the girl, a destroyed form. Even as they watched, a tiny cloud, millions of silver particles, formed into a fist, then dissipated swiftly on the wind.

"Nanobots," said Keenan, mouth twisted in a sour grin. "They imitated you. Imitated the girl. General Zenab doesn't exist; it's an AI construct, a very, very advanced machine."

Pippa stooped, picked up the wooden box. "But we got the Nano-Bomb equipment."

"Yeah. At least we got something."

"We didn't kill her, him . . . *it*, did we?" said Pippa.

"We hurt it," said Keenan. "Whatever the hell it was. And we bought QGM some time."

"So we'll be back?"

Keenan, programming the rejuvenated PAD to bring in the SLAM, nodded. "Yeah Pippa. The war ain't over. We'll be back. For people like us, this kind of shit never ends. The suffering never stops."

Pippa gave a nod, and clutching the small wooden box, waited for exit.

FIRST LINE
An Alliance Archives Adventure

Danielle Ackley-McPhail

"Go! Go! GO!"

The order pinged her transceiver, a sharp reminder of many missions past. Quieter than the barest whisper, hard, taut, and intense, it triggered automatic responses in a battle-honed soldier: a flood of adrenaline, combat awareness drilled in by special ops training and countless field missions, a fierce impulse to bring a weapon to bear.

In one instant, she went from drifting through oblivion, to combat-ready.

She was no longer capable of adrenaline rushes, but the rest of her reflexes were still on the mark. It wasn't supposed to work that way. By all rights, there shouldn't be anything left of Lieutenant Sheila "Trey" Tremaine. Well, nothing capable of such a knee-jerk reaction to the issued order. Now who the hell's cock-up was that?

There were large gaps in her memory, or at least she presumed there were, seeing as the last thing she could recall was dying. She used to be an officer assigned to the 428th Special Ops unit, MOS: demolitions specialist, but when an enemy round took her down, on its way to taking her out, she'd been offered a chance. She remembered that too (before the dying part). The head of the tech division had shown up beside her hospital cot once it was clear she was well on her way to succumbing to her injuries.

Horrible way for a soldier to die, by the way: slowly, in a hospital bed, a burden to the very society you were meant to serve. Feeling worse than useless. It just wasn't right. You either kicked ass and survived to fight another day, or you took a shitload of them down on your way out. That was the way it was supposed to be. For a soldier. Anything else just felt wrong. They'd lost two men saving her should-have-been-dead ass. The only thing worse than waiting to die was staring that guilt in the face the entire time.

"How serious do you take your oath to serve, Lieutenant?" the bureaucrat had solemnly asked.

She'd allowed her gaze to sweep across her broken body before giving him a look as sharp as a knife's edge. Her lip had curled up in a bare approximation of the warning sneer her unit would have recognized before she tore into someone particularly dense. Of course, her clear status of "non-threat" made him oblivious to her reaction at the insult he'd issued. If she'd had any energy left for anything except guilt and dying, she would have shown him how wrong his assessment was.

"Very," she responded, if faintly.

That was when he offered her an approximation of immortality. Okay. Maybe not. But definitely a way to make up for dying the wrong way, and an opportunity to protect her unit in a way she'd never imagined.

"We'd like to neuro-scan your brain," he went on, very matter-of-fact, as if he were discussing the watch schedule, or what was being served in the Mess. "To preserve your expertise and instincts." He went on to explain the great advancements in this process and how they would then be able to imprint the scan-capture onto a neural matrix so that her training and experience would not be lost at her demise, but could be utilized in this time of conflict to ensure others did not fall as she had . . . *blah, blah, blah.*

Manipulative prick.

"Why wait . . . till now?" she managed. After all, she'd been there in that cot quite a while.

There was an uncomfortable silence on the egg-head's part. "The process is terminal."

Well. Okay. So was she, apparently. Not that she hadn't figured that out already. Still, she'd been tempted to say no, just for the piss-poor way he handled the proposal. The idea itself intrigued her, though. The way he explained it, if she agreed, her thought processes would be imprinted on the newest generation of packbot to augment the technical data already hard-wired in, with the intent of mating that automated programming with her learned reflexes and evaluative capabilities. She didn't get all the technical bits; after all, her training was in demolitions, not computers. But really, the only thing she needed to understand was that a part of her would live on to fight those that had taken her out.

Ultimately (clearly), she'd agreed. The clincher, in the end: the mech in question had been requisitioned by the 428th. The guy should have mentioned that to begin with. That was her only real enticement. What did she care about revenge? She'd believed in why they were fighting. That and protecting her men mattered to her more than any petty revenge.

"Will they know it's me?" she managed to ask. The answer was no. "Will *I* know it's me?" Again, no.

"Though urban legends persist to the contrary," the egg-head assured her, "there is no evidence to substantiate the rumors that personality is transferable with this process."

She'd taken his word for it. She'd wanted to believe some part of her would go on, would continue to serve. That didn't mean she wanted to be conscious of it.

Her body had failed just as the final neural pathways were scanned. Trey knew this, because even that the process had captured. Now, she was the next level in advanced warfare. And contrary to all assurances, she was still self-aware.

Trey took stock of her current situation. Besides overall being FUBARed, sensors indicated she was currently being jostled, but the motion spoke more of stealth than open assault. Something close to excitement, leavened by a bit of apprehension went through her. It wasn't supposed to work this way. But what the hell; too late now, right?

There were murmurs going back and forth across her transceiver. Just bits and pieces, mostly sub-vocal sounds rather than words. She understood this, though. Most of the communicating going on between the deployed team was done through gestures and glances. They'd been a team a long time. Who needed words?

Of course, that meant Trey was in the dark. The packbot that housed her was in standby mode. The transceiver was active and ready to receive input, but the cameras that would be her eyes were powered down and she had no access to the subroutines that would power them up. It was like she was tied up and blindfolded.

Not something she was into.

She was used to being in charge, or at least an active participant. The deal she'd made was not quite looking so good at the moment. The waiting, the not knowing, was doing a number on whatever part of her personality had glommed onto the scan.

Finally the forward motion stopped.

Trey felt a jolt as power flooded her system. Data was keyed in, leaving her disoriented. She was, after all, merely a passenger within the robotic interface, a data source that allowed the CPU to interpret scenarios for the handler based on her collective experience. She was a resource with not one whit of control over anything.

Yeah, maybe her deathbed wasn't such a good place to make life-altering decisions. She may have been a demo specialist, and understood the mechanical workings of the packbot, but from the inside she couldn't follow impulse one of the directives being fed into the unit for the pending incursion. This passive-observer mode definitely had the potential of evolving into her own personal hell. At least as a part of the military she'd had the freedom to act within the structure of command. In combat she was used to taking charge, even. Trey was not a passive creature.

She felt better once the internal gyros registered a change in the robotic unit's orientation as its handler drew it from his pack and lobbed it into the crumbling shell of a building.

"Boombot deployed, Sarge," Trey's handler subvocalized into his bone-jack. "Unit transmission at . . . 85 percent optimal." Nothing sounded like it used to, but from the irreverent terminology, Trey figured Coop was the soldier reassigned her demo duties. She hadn't known him so well, beyond an officer's familiarity with those she led, but he'd always been the one to add some hint of humor to every mission. By her reckoning, wisecracks were one more part of his armor, right along with his ballistic mesh. She was finding it comforting, herself.

"Damn . . . we need better than that, soldier," responded whoever had taken over as team leader—Trey couldn't help feeling a bit smug that it had taken two men to replace her . . . at least, until she recalled her new role was "Boombot, " and why.

"Adjust your frequency; no one goes in until that 'bot is transmitting at 95 percent minimum. *I'm* not losing any men to sloppiness."

The implication wasn't lost on Trey. For the briefest instant she had the overwhelming impulse to go "buggy" on the colossal shit. Let him see how "optimal" he could be when things were out of his control and there was pressure from the higher ups to achieve the mission directives *now*.

Hell, he was the one nice and cozy at the fall-back position, while here she was completely *over* the front line. Of course, it was so easy to forget she was only a passenger. Right up until Coop started fiddling with the controller.

Talk about weird. Trey could "feel" as he adjusted the packbot's settings, maneuvering the unit around the crumbled remains of the building, manipulating the camera angles. She heard him murmur about the darkness. It should have served as a warning, but she totally didn't pick up on it. When he triggered the variable-intensity LEDs she would have flinched, if she could have. The sudden light had the intensity of a bomb blast without the fade away. She could visualize her eyes snapping closed. And suddenly, they did. Or at least, there was an abrupt return to total darkness. It was a coincidence, of course, but a welcome one. Well. For her.

Coop swore like a cross between a marine and a twenty-dollar whore.

A flood of data transmitted to the 'bot. Then once again, supernova. Trey reflexively "flinched" and was returned to total darkness. She was in awe as the revelation dawned. Maybe passive observer wasn't her lot after all.

"Military-issue piece of crap! We don't have time for this!"

There was that guilt again. What was relief for her was just a dangerous complication for the squad. But it did demonstrate that perhaps she had some control over her fate. To test the theory, she triggered the circuits that brought the lights up again independent of Coop's efforts, only gradually. Okay, enough experimentation. She had some amount of control. That alone made her just a bit more comfortable in her titanium skin.

Enough. She didn't want Coop scrapping the mission because 'Boombot' was malfunctioning. She "stepped back," releasing control to the handler.

It was odd not having to go to any effort to do her job. She had finally reached the state seasoned soldiers both dreamed of and dreaded: where a combat zone didn't require active thought to evaluate. Of course, she'd had to die to achieve it.

Always a down side, wasn't there?

Between her knowledge and the packbot's superfast processors, analysis of the building interior was instantaneous. The moment the cameras panned across a zone all the potential hot points were identified and assessed, simultaneously scrolling across the unit's micro-display and the handler's monitor.

All threats on the first floor were old activity, already neutralized. As the last lower-level quadrant scan completed, Trey and the packbot approached the staircase. A sensor extended from the 'bot until it connected with the first riser. Next the unit emitted a supersonic peal, followed by a probe shooting out from the front facing, forcefully punching up against the structure. Again, data analysis was instantaneous. The sonic blast revealed nothing but the standard staircase infrastructure. The impact test confirmed the architecture was sound and was not rigged to blow or collapse. With the all-clear given, the handler activated the 'bot's front flipper assembly. Trey was fascinated as the flipper extended up and forward until the belted track grabbed the next tread. She found the sensation odd as the servos engaged and the front of the unit was raised up, followed the flippers up the steps. The monitors continually tracked the stability of the structure as the process repeated, until the 'bot rested soundly on the upper level.

There was nothing there or in the rest of the surrounding buildings. Nothing recent, anyway. Plenty of signs of neutralized ordinance, along with one or two that had clearly been triggered, but by the levels of accumulated dust, signs of animal habitation, the weathering . . . all indications were that the outpost had been abandoned by all parties.

"Echo sector has been cleared for occupation, sir," Coop reported over the comm to his squad leader.

"Our ETA is 0700," was the response. "Have your men set up base operations and then stand down until we arrive."

Trey wanted to protest as the 'bot's systems were again powered down and the unit was returned to Coop's MOLLE pack. She noticed that once the rest of the system was shut off and beyond her reach, her own power source was likewise reduced until she was operating under what felt like brown-out conditions. Apparently, she was in her own version of stand-by.

Part of her railed against the restrictions; she was just getting the feel of her new situation, the freedom and capabilities she had never dreamed would be open to her. But then, the squad leader had no clue she was anything more than a complex data dump. Having to admit that made her seethe. Not that she had a right to. She'd signed on for this tour, after all.

As the outside world went away, she perversely wondered if this was how her laptop had felt each time she'd shut it down. And had it likewise amused itself in the darkness plotting theoretical rebellion?

Was it days or weeks or even longer that her existence went on this way? Trey had no clue. Well . . . she knew the chronological time and date stamp that queued up each time her systems were powered back up, but you know . . . when you spend an eternity in isolation in between those fraught, tedious moments of recon, the relative time bore no connection with a clock or a calendar. Trey, in short, felt ancient. And kind of like she was suspended in purgatory, or maybe limbo.

Before her was another crumbling structure, another potential hotbed of insurgents. It was time to earn her one step further from hell.

As she went about her duties—she no longer thought of herself separate from Boombot, though her identity of Trey was still very real to her—her processors filtered out the background chatter of the waiting squad. There was increasingly too much of it. The men were getting too relaxed the longer they went without encountering opposition. It was making them sloppy.

Already several had to be patched up by the medic after tripping over the remnants of a misfired hydra mine. The plungers had been obscured by the overgrown ground cover, but that was no excuse for the soldiers' blunder. Trey would have torn them a new one for being that sloppy on her watch. Demerits would have been the least of their problems. Fortunate for them, if not the whole squad, the payload had long ago been triggered. Trapped in the can at detonation when the lid malfunctioned, the mine apparently had geysered, rather than blowing out in a radial pattern; otherwise there would have been nothing but a crater as testament to where it used to be. Of course, as cold as the thought was, perhaps it wasn't a good thing the mine had been spent. If the men had gotten more than a gash for their inattention they would have learned their lesson better. Sloppy soldiers often got more than just themselves killed.

Speaking of which, Trey chastised herself for dwelling on the folly of others when she had her own duties to execute.

Nightmares were the worst part of standby mode. Yeah, even that plague of every soldier hadn't been left behind. Kind of hard to wake up from a reoccurring hell when you had no body, no icy sweat to whisk away, no rapid breath to ramp down to a normal speed, nothing physical to distract you from the images you could never forget, or to remind you they weren't happening in real-time.

Trey wished she had enough control to power herself back up. Of course, it wasn't like she could drop and do push-ups until she tumbled into a deep, dreamless sleep, as she would have done in her other life, so what was the point? Though she could imagine how Coop would freak if he'd caught her trying it.

Trey settled for reviewing the data she'd so far gathered in their recon of the sector. Something about the zone was making her uneasy. She caught glimpses in her nightmares, hints of whatever had her "nerves" buzzing, but just as in her flesh-bound dreams, everything was shadowy, more impressions than anything else. Well, except for the blood. And the screams. Shrugging it off, she went back to analyzing the data. Had she been here before? It was so hard to tell, after all, as she already noted, the world was a heck of a lot different through the camera-eye of a 'bot. Whether or not she was covering familiar ground, she was getting a bad feeling the closer they drew to the next sector.

There had to be something in the data and damn if she wouldn't find it. She wasn't about to lead another squad straight into the guns of the enemy.

Hours later she finally recognized what she was looking for. It was 0Dark00 and the squad had been on the move for two hours. They were entering unsecured territory. This was the sector her unit had been heading for that fateful day. The one where good men died retrieving her.

Up until now Coop had reserved her for establishing the all-clear of structures in zones their side had already pacified, cleaning up any parting gifts left by the insurgents. This time when she was powered up she discovered he'd reconfigured her chassis with the explosive ordinance detection kit, increasing her speed and adding more muscle to her manipulator arm. Now she was running point for the squad across uncleared terrain, looking for more aggressive threats along their path. Already, together she and Coop had discovered and disabled half a dozen hydras and discreetly marked and redirected the squad's route around countless claymores. Those that came behind them would have more leisure to decommission the munitions. Their squad wouldn't risk it now. To do so would slow them down at best, and give away their position at worst, should even one mine be mishandled.

"Sarge, copy," Coop subvocalized.

"Acknowledged, report," came the response.

Coop kept it short, as even comm signals could be intercepted, if the enemy cracked the frequency. "Cleared to perimeter, sector Tango; squad heading in. Going comm dark."

"Roger."

The rest of the unit would now follow via the cleared corridor.

Trey was so on edge her lip would be twitching, if she'd still had one. She was surprised she wasn't shooting sparks as it was. She felt charged enough for a full fireworks display. Earlier, while exploring the internal pathway of the packbot, she discovered the protocol that would initiate self-destruct should the unit be compromised. If she could figure out how to trigger that at will, it could come in handy. If nothing else, she'd feel better knowing that, at least in a way, she was armed. She set a portion of her . . . mind to the puzzle as she continued rolling along.

Eventually, she came upon a civilian compound. It had been hit hard, as had many she had seen before. Coop ran her up to the first of the buildings with infrared sensors activated. There were some thermal, but nothing larger than the planet's equivalent of a rat.

She saw no traces of munitions rigged to blow, though there were signs of recent habitation. Local wildlife, perhaps, or squatters displaced by the recent conflict. There was nothing to imply occupation by a military force, though. Trey assessed the risk factor of the building at a level three, and fed the cautionary note to her handler. After careful inspection sent up no additional red flags, she was directed to the next building. Inspection continued in a similar manner through most the compound, bringing her about to the main structure.

By now Trey was twitching like anything, if only on the inside. There was still nothing registering on infrared, but her mics were picking up trace sounds that might be stealth movement . . . or might just be a branch in the wind. She was running all four cameras, though only data from the primary was feeding to the control monitor. It was odd being able to scan forward and still watch over her own shoulder; not as reassuring as it should be, though. After all, it only served to remind her she was out here solo.

As she entered the final building her instincts started grumbling. Flashbacks of her nightmares sprang to the forefront, demanding she back out of the structure, double-time.

With sheer determination and her virtual jaw set, Trey ignored the impulse and powered through to do her duty.

The lower level was clear. More signs of habitation, less clear as to the source. Her unit had rudimentary olfactory sensors Coop never seemed to activate. Chances were he didn't even know they were there. It was a new feature Trey herself had never seen before this model, only recently discovered. She made an executive decision and brought them on-line. Traces of human sweat. Food. Some particles of ordinance components.

Shit.

There were times she definitely hated being right. Her self-preservation instincts were all but standing on her non-existent head screaming. She ignored them once more, rolling up the stairs and turning down the upper corridor in the direction from which the odors were strongest. Trey could feel an internal tug as her actions diverged from those dictated by Coop and the controller, but this was a case where instinct (the combat kind, rather than the self-preservation kind) demanded a different course of action. Her primary camera had a fiber-optic extension for situations where the bulkier unit would not serve. She extended it now as she approached the first doorway. At the same time, she readied the self-destruct protocol. Just in case.

There was time for her to identify a crude munitions lab and roughly fifteen operatives clothed in thermal-dampening suits positioned around the room before a hand shot out and grabbed the extension.

Crap! She tried to backpedal, but as he drew her within range, his other hand brought up a silenced pistol and fired on the camera assembly, shattering the lens.

Before he could do more damage, she aimed a probe at his leg and zapped him with enough current to fry his brain. Her olfactory sensors overloaded on burnt flesh as her manipulator arm came around to drag the corpse out of her way.

The enemy forces were not idle. She transferred optical to her backup camera and assessed the situation. Weapons had been brought to bear and the soldiers were converging. She couldn't handle them all, and the lab and its contingent were a serious threat to her unit and the offensive. Without a second thought, she initiated the self-destruct protocol, ready to die a warrior's death.

There was yelling and a sudden sizzle of sound as Coop lost visual. He breathed a curse and his hands clutching the controller tighter, though it had gone nonfunctional. He was still receiving data from the 'bot. In fact, impossible as it was, the unit somehow seemed to be moving independently. Before he could settle on a plan of action, an image reappeared on his monitor, the angle skewed as it came from a secondary camera. He watched in stunned silence as more than a dozen Dominion soldiers rushed the Boombot.

"We have hostile contact," he called to his men, who scrambled to defensive positions on all sides. Coop turned his attention back to the monitor. He tried once more to pull the 'bot back, but it was no use; the unit still didn't respond to the controls. He watched with a mixture of awe and frustration as it revved forward, grabbing the foremost enemy's rifle hand in what oddly looked like a judo move, snapping it. The soldier dropped his weapon. The corresponding scream echoed oddly, coming both through the 'bot's comlink and more faintly from the building a half a klick away.

"What the . . ." he murmured, startling the unit's sniper, who crouched beside him. Coop stared hard at the words that appeared on his monitor.

<<GO BACK TO HELL, DEMONS!!!>>

The words triggered a memory of many a past mission.

It couldn't be. There was no way. But he'd been assigned to this unit a long time, most of that time in this squad. Under the command of Lieutenant Tremaine . . . His left hand moved away from the 'bot controller to the keyboard, rapidly tapping just four keys . . .

<<T...R...E...Y>>

On the last stroke there was a *pop*, and a fireball engulfed the structure under surveillance.

"No!" Coop yelled, silence no longer an issue. On the monitor, in the camera-view window there was nothing but snow as the comlink with the packbot was severed. He gulped at the final entry in the log window:

<<LtST - initiating self-destruct.>>

His fingers flew over the keyboard, frantically trying to call up the final transmission made by the 'bot, which was programmed to back up its system data prior to self-destruct. As he did so he couldn't help wondering, was he imagining things, or had he just lost his lieutenant . . . for the second time?

"Go! Go! GO!" the squad leader barked into the comm.

The order pinged her transceiver, a sharp reminder of many missions past.She jerked to awareness with a start, her nerves tighter than a well-set tripline. In one instant she went from drifting through oblivion to combat-ready.

There were large gaps in her memory, or at least she presumed there were, seeing as the last thing she could recall was deciding blow up a room full of Demons... and preparing to die...again. *So who the hell's cock-up was this?* she thought, as the 'bot was powered up and tossed through a nearby gaping hole that used to hold a window.

"Treybot deployed, Sarge," Coop subvocalized into his bonejack. "She's transmitting at . . . 99 percent optimal."

TO SPEC

Charles E. Gannon

Mendez, the newest guy in the squad, had been jumpy ever since the worsening weather updates started coming in. The most recent message—that Priestley's replacement wouldn't show up for at least another three hours—just made him more anxious. As Eureka command post signed off, Grim saw Mendez hold his new rifle—a flimsy piece of experimental junk known as the Cochrane XM 1—a bit too tightly. So, in an effort to take the newbie's mind off his anxiety, Grim asked him, "So, what's on the 'other' radio today?"

A tentative grin twitched at the right corner of Mendez's mouth. "It's against regs to listen to—"

"I'm not a snitch, Mendez."

Mendez needed no further encouragement: broad, short, and compact in his pint-sized vacc suit, he made a fast, flat zero-gee hop over to the control panel. Steadying himself on a handhold, he pushed a preset button, jumping the radio over to the Commonwealth Armed Forces frequency.

But instead of plaintively wailing guitars, they heard a painfully jocular deejay working his way through the end of the news. First, Mendez looked like the kid who got coal for Christmas—but then he went rigid as the announcer segued into the weather:

"Hey, here's a CWAF flash from our siblings-in-arms guarding the Big Secret out at Eureka. "Quaff" this one, grunts: they tell us that it's another beautiful February day out at the Mars L-5 point, with the mercury peaking at minus 215 Celsius. There's good visibility despite average dust densities and a continued surge of downstream trash sent by some unknown admirers near Mars. But for everyone out here in the fourth orbit, remember: that huge solar storm-front we've been watching will move on through in just an hour or so. So come on inside before the weather turns and send a shout out to the folks back home. Don't let those 2.1 AU stop you."

Great: now Mendez looked more anxious than ever. Grim reached out a brown, blunt-fingered hand to shut off the radio, reflecting that this might be the right moment to employ some of the conversational and psychological subtlety for which sergeants have always been famous.

Grim looked directly into Mendez's eyes. "What the hell is wrong with you, Mendez?"

Mendez looked gratifyingly startled, then abashed. "Well, sir—"

Grim sighed. "Mendez, don't offend me with that 'sir' crap: I'm not an officer. I work for a living."

"Yes, si—Master Sergeant Grimsby."

Eldridge Grimsby—who was never called anything other than Grim—grunted at the narrow margin by which Mendez had avoided a repetition of the original slur, and nodded for him to continue.

"I don't know, Sarge; it just makes me nervous—guarding the Big Secret they're building on Eureka."

"Why?"

"Well—because it's a secret, I guess. And if it's as important as all the security precautions seem to indicate, that means that someone out there"—he swung an arm at the space beyond the bulkhead—"could have us in their crosshairs now, this very second." When Grim failed to respond in any way, Mendez added, "Sarge, we could die without warning—and without ever knowing what it was we were guarding."

Grim stared at him. "And your point is?"

"Well—that's an awful lot of risk without an awful lot of information."

"Mendez, if the spacesuit you're wearing hasn't tipped you off just yet, you're in the ExoAtmospheric Corps, and we don't get information; we get orders. And bad food and worse pay. What part of this have you failed to understand?"

But Grim could see, from the way that Mendez's gaze wandered away, that his fear wasn't as general as he had made it sound: there was something more specific behind it. And Grim had a pretty good idea what that might be. "Okay, Mendez, spill it. What have you learned about the Big Secret? Why are we more at risk now?"

Mendez folded his hands and stared at them. "Sarge, I was floating watch outside the comcenter yesterday and heard the staff officers getting briefed by a pair of civvies."

"Okay, Mendez, I'll bite: who was briefing the staffers?"

"I heard two names, Sarge. One was some kind of spook, I think: a Mr. Wilder. Darryl Wilder. Mean anything to you?"

Grim felt his stomach contract. "Yeah; security specialist. Ex-Air Force. Then ex-FBI."

"Who's he with now?"

"Wish I knew."

"Private contractor?"

Grim emitted a rumbling set of amused grunts; he was secretly proud of having a laugh that sounded like an irritated crocodile. "Mendez, guys like Wilder don't retire. Ever."

"So—"

"So he's interagency, or an errand boy for the Joint Chiefs, or carrying out an Executive Order."

"How do you know about him?"

"Right after we started setting up shop out here, he was on-station for about a month: always sniffing around, like a security inspector or engineer. Didn't talk much, never gave an order, but always looking, examining, watching. I think he was the one who suggested building the Big Secret out here on Eureka."

"Well, he sure as hell picked a crappy place."

"Which was his intention, I'm sure: easy enough to get to Mars from here, and vice versa, but not really on anyone's flight path, so you see intruders well in advance. Now, you said you heard a second name?"

Mendez looked sideways at Grim. "This guy was not military or security; sounded like he was involved with building the Big Secret itself."

"I ain't playing twenty questions with you, Mendez: who is he?"

"You know that guy Wasserman, the professor who—"

Grim leaned forward before he could stop himself. "Robert Wasserman? The physicist?"

"High-energy physicist—and engineer. Nobel nominations last two years in a row."

"You think they're really—?"

"Could be a starship, Sarge—just like the minority scuttlebutt says."

Grim leaned back so energetically that he almost floated into a backwards somersault out of his "seat." Robert Wasserman. And Darryl

Wilder. Both out here in the Martian L-5 wasteland. What besides a secret FTL project could explain their presence? And it would also explain why the other blocs were having trash-heaving hissy fits about being kept at arm's length. If they knew that the Commonwealth was getting close to achieving faster than light travel—

But Mendez wasn't done. "And everyone at the debrief was worried, Sarge. Real worried."

Hearing Mendez's tone and words, Grim suddenly felt the first creeping fingers of contagious anxiety. "They were worried? About what?"

"About this solar storm."

Grim tried not to scowl, failed. "Jee-zus; what the hell is it with this storm? With these hourly updates on expected EMP and rad levels, you'd think we'd never seen a flare before."

"Sarge, if you check the text of those updates, you'll find that HQ has never used the word 'flare'."

Grim blinked: that was strangely, and unsettlingly, true. "Then what the hell aren't they telling us?"

"Sarge, this is a CME. A big one."

When transferring to the ExoAtmo Corps six years ago, Grim had managed—blissfully—to sleep through all the space science crap served up by the rear-echelon weenies, so he was compelled to ask: "What's a CME?"

"A coronal mass ejection."

"And that means?"

Grim immediately regretted asking the question, because Mendez— otherwise a good kid—sat a little straighter, and readied himself to deliver A Recitation of The Facts, as was his wont: he was bucking for OCS so hard that Grim wondered if he sometimes got whiplash from the effort. "A coronal mass ejection occurs when the sun actually heaves out a jet of plasma. Much worse than a flare: lots of EMP, hard radiation, and—" Mendez actually shivered "—a big increase in cosmic rays."

Now, finally, Grim understood Mendez's anxiety. In the flippant vernacular of the Service, radioactive emissions—and particularly those of the most energetic, non-particle variety—were collectively known as 'zoomies.' Cosmic rays, however, had their own special category: they were 'ultra-zoomies.' Unless you were safe inside a (fantastically expensive) electromagnetically-shielded hull or habitat, you just prayed that one of those little nano-scale laser beams didn't hit a chromosome and clip one of your telomeres too short, thereby kicking off runaway replication. Or, as was the more prosaic diagnosis of a cell gone stupid, cancer. Fortunately, that kind of damage was beyond prediction or control and was, therefore, just part of the random nonsense of the job. So Grim—a hardened veteran—wasn't disposed to worry about it. Much.

However, it meant they might have to wait out the storm and hunker down for a very extended watch in their one-room rad shack: a small, pressurized hab module that got its name from what its occupants really cared about: its multi-layered radiation shielding. Designed to house—barely—a three-man team for extended watches, its interior was an inhumanly cramped collection of long-range guidance and tracking computers, sensor and drone control consoles, and a single bunk. Its head was a constant source of black humor and savage derision: by comparison, the fresher of a commuter jet seemed positively palatial. On extended watches in its claustrophobic interior, even Grim had found himself beginning to reconsider the hazards of a spacewalk in exchange for a little extra room to stretch, and a change of scenery. Not that Grim was a fan of EVA ops: he had come late—and unwillingly—to zero-gee maneuver, tactics, and training. And now, to his even greater delight, he was about to find himself the middle of the biggest solar storm on record. He sighed, and found a way to conceal the rest of his ignorance: "So, Mendez, let's see how much of your training you remember: what are the special protocols for a CME?"

"Well, we'll have to pull the sensor and comm array in all the way: if we don't, we're sure to fry something. Maybe everything. Not much reason to leave 'em out, anyway: anything but laser-based comm and nav is going to be static-soup."

"Not like we have much to scan except the Mars trash." In response, Mendez frowned again. Grim snorted. "What? Now you're worried about the Mars trash, too?"

"Well, the brass is, Sarge. Seems like the other blocs are *not* dumping the trash anymore—at least not the way they were right after we posted Eureka as a no-fly zone."

"So who's doing it now—and how?"

"Well, that's what's got the brass upset. Word is that Earth HQ got on the horn with Admiral Riggen and tore him a new one. Threatened him with additional proctological procedures if he didn't find where the trash was coming from and pronto."

"God almighty, Mendez: it's space. How hard can it be to find where it's coming from? You track back and—"

But Mendez was shaking his head. "It's not that kind of trash anymore, Sarge. No metals, nothing too big. Now it's all composites, plastics: just a bunch of black bodies by the time it reaches us. And a lot of it is so small that—"

Grim put up a bearish hand. "Okay, professor: that's enough. I'm not on the review board for your OCS app."

Mendez's eyes bulged, blinked, bulged again. "But Sarge, I wouldn't— I'm not—"

"Save it: except for your fear of cosmic rays, you're too eager to die to be an enlisted man. Also, if the rumors are true, you have more brain cells than an amoeba, so obviously you're on OCS's radar."

As if on cue, the command circuit toned twice: coded traffic from Base. After going through the tiresome two-sided authentication waltz, the inevitable Junior Grade Lieutenant on the other end got down to business: "Shack Four, we are updating you on your replacement for Priestley: we've got a clearance snafu on our end. Probably won't get it resolved before the end of your watch."

As Grim heard the first indignant words come out of his mouth, he realized that he was now shouting at an officer— as had happened too often throughout his career. It did not matter that the officer was a J.G. and therefore the human equivalent of pond scum: this pond scum still ranked him and could pull a seniority marking—a "rocker"—off the bottom of his stack of sergeant's chevrons. Grim's realization of this trailed a crucial second behind his shout of: "We're a man down because of a 'clearance snafu?' What the hell kind of bullshit is that . . . sir?" Grim could hear the insincerity in the lagging honorific; knew the J.G. had heard the same. Oh well, Grim hadn't really liked being a Master Sergeant anyway: too much paperwork.

"Sergeant Grimsby,"—the voice was markedly colder than the outside temperature—"Priestley can only be replaced by someone who's cleared for the same special duty."

"Special duty? What special duty?"

Mendez tapped his junk-rifle, muttered: "Sarge, he means the Cochrane. Carrying a field prototype is special duty: along with Priestley, they only cleared five of us for—"

Grim rolled his eyes. "Jesus Christ. Sir, are you telling me you won't send out a replacement because you don't have anyone else who's permitted to carry around another of these dumb-ass guns?"

"Sergeant, I'm telling you I *can't* send anyone who's not a part of the field trial: the protocols are quite explicit—and are a top priority, as per Earth HQ."

"Great: so we're down to two men for the rest of the watch."

Grim was surprised when the affirmation lagged, and then did not come. Instead, the J.G. said, "No; you're down to one."

Grim looked at Mendez, who was already looking at him. Eyes narrowed, Grim asked the console coolly. "Say again, sir. Sounded to me like you said the duty watch in this shack is to be reduced to one."

"That is correct, Sergeant."

"That is a violation of our standing orders, sir. One man can't oversee all the critical systems in the event of an attack. So—with all due respect—I am not going to leave Private Mendez out here on his own. He's only been on station for—"

"Sergeant: you're not leaving Private Mendez. He's leaving you."

Oh. Well. That made everything just lovely, then. "On whose order am I losing Mendez, sir?"

"No one from here, Sergeant: this order actually originated off-base."

Mendez half-rose, eyes wide, fearful: Grim waved him down. A "mystery summons" from the rear was every soldier's dread, since it usually signified bad news from home. But after thirty years in uniform, Grim had seen exceptions to every rule and this might be one of them: he decided to check. "Is he being called in to receive a personal communiqué from stateside?"

"Doesn't say, Sergeant. But the order to pull him off the line comes straight from Mars HQ. And he's got to start back now. Otherwise he won't make it inside before the hard weather hits."

Mendez raised his chin, seemed ready to resist; Grim shook his head at the newbie once, sharply. "Understood, base. Mendez is on his way. Rad Shack Four out."

The light that indicated a live carrier signal hadn't winked out before Mendez launched into his protests. "But, sir—"

"Mendez!"

"But, *Sarge*, this order just isn't right—"

Grim was touched. "Listen, Esteban; I'll be fine out here on my ow—"

"No, no: I mean that my recall order sounds fishy—and besides, it will invalidate the Cochrane's field test."

It made Grim all warm inside to realize that Mendez's commitment to an experimental weapon was immeasurably greater than whatever (apparently weak) concern he had for the continued well-being of his senior NCO. "Ah. The Cochrane." That flimsy piece of shit. "Listen: if they were about to invalidate their precious test, they would have told you to leave it behind for me to babysit."

"I don't buy it, Sarge—and no one seems to have clued in the J.G.: by ordering me in, he'll invalidate the current trial phase. And my recall order doesn't make any sense, either: whether it's a family loss notice or not, it should go through the company CO before it gets to me. And leaving you out here on your own? That's blatantly against standing orders." Mendez frowned. "There's too much going wrong or weird at the same time: I'm gonna look into this as soon as I return to base."

"Which starts now," added Grim, snagging and handing the Cochrane up toward him.

Mendez, distracted, took a moment to realize what Grim was doing: then he shook his head. "No, Sarge: you keep it."

I'd rather have a piranha in my pants. But Grim said: "Mendez, as you pointed out, I'm not cleared to—"

Ever-respectful Mendez interrupted, almost violently. "Sarge: keep the Cochrane. If—well, if anything *happens* out here, you might need it."

Like I need a hole in my vacc suit. "I'm better off with my old—"

But Mendez had snatched up the weapon Grim was about to mention—an Armalite 6mm caseless. "No, Sarge: I'm taking this one. You keep the Cochrane."

"Mendez, you stop this nonsense. I've been using that Armalite since—"

But Mendez smiled an apology as he snugged his helmet, faceplate still up, over his head. "Sarge, the Cochrane is state of the art: liquid propellant, variable munitions and velocity. That makes it extremely versatile, and great—great—in zero-gee. Do you remember everything I told you about it?"

I hear your endless gushings in my sleep. "Some of it."

"Then please: do this for me." He checked the clock. "Mother of God; I've gotta go. *Via con Dios*, Sarge."

"You too."

The airlock squealed open, and then complained once more as it was shut.

Leaving Grim quite alone in Rad Shack Four.

Forty-two minutes later, the external environment monitor started an almost nasal squawking. Grim pushed himself into a slow drift toward the console, looked at the radiation sensors, inspected the rem numbers on the real-time dosimeter—and blinked. As he reached over to silence the alarms, he kept his eyes on the unprecedented numbers, and settled in to watch their unprecedented rate of increase.

—and bumped into the XM-1 Cochrane's oddly-vented flash-suppressor, which nudged cheekily against the side of his thigh. Grim scowled at it; okay, so it was cool to look at: a sleek, unipiece design. And, although he had refused to admit it to Mendez, he had read the stats on the weapon. If the hype had any resemblance to the truth, its nannite-reinforced composites made it light and extremely rugged. But it still looked like some flimsy piece of crap out of a sci-fi B-movie of about a hundred years ago.

But, to hear the brass tell it, looks were apparently deceiving. With the liquid propellant stored separately from the warheads, the bullpup magazine held three times the usual number of rounds. No shell casings meant it was a sealed action, without breech or bolt: the liquid propellant was simply injected into the combustion chamber, making velocity—and therefore recoil—a function of how much was injected at any one time. The same combustion chamber was also used to boost bigger munitions out of the integral, underslung launch-tube. Grim wanted to call that a 'grenade launcher' but every time he did, Mendez corrected him: apparently this miracle weapon was capable of launching a variety of other, rather exotic submunitions. The Cochrane could probably turn water into wine, too, given half a chance. Grim sneered down at it: yeah, you look fancy, and the specs look impressive, but you just won't cut it as a sturdy tool. You look like—and probably are—a kid's toy, not a real gun: all bells and whistles, but no balls for business.

The short-range radar emitted a strangled squawk: a partial contact, just at the edge the system's threshold. It was probably a marginal object that, tumbling, had presented a momentarily bigger cross-section for the radar to bounce off. But the system squawked again, and this time Grim saw what had tweaked it: a faint signature, range established at seven kilometers—no, six. Then the range indicator plummeted to three, jumped up to ten, and finally zeroed out for a recalibration as the whole screen surged brightly for a moment. As it faded back into its normal contrast ratios, Grim looked up at the external weather sensors: a corresponding surge in charged particles was dying down. Which suggested that the contact was probably just an anomaly of how the storm was interacting with the trash, since the blip had appeared to be closing at exactly the same rate as today's unusually dense sampling of debris.

The monitor surged again, but this time, remained bright: the sensor's overload alarm system chirped and an orange warning light glowed on the board. The automatic protection software had activated: in ten seconds, unless overridden, it would yank back the combined sensor/comm mast, sheathing it in a hardened faraday cage until it was safe to peek outside again. Grim watched the countdown ticker erode toward zero—but he reached over quickly when it hit "4" and turned the system off. The program hooted at him, asked him—in bright red block letters—"Do you wish to engage safety override?"

Did he? Really? Grim rubbed his stubbly chin. Well, of course he didn't: if he kept the mast extended, there was a reasonable chance that its sensitive electronics would fry, and an equal (indeed, directly proportional) chance that the brass would fry him. That—along with the system SOPs and his situationally-specific standing orders—should have decided the matter. But this situation was not the one envisioned by those standard procedures and standing orders. And that meant that Grim's capacity to follow them was about to "fluctuate": that was the term he had used during his first disciplinary hearing twenty-eight years ago, and had been using ever since. And he'd probably get busted a stripe for his trouble. And what for? Was there really—*really*—any danger? Even if a basketball-sized package of plastique slipped past his metal-obsessed sensors, and headed toward the Big Secret on Eureka, what harm could it do? It would have to be invisible to radar, which meant no metal, which meant no computer, which meant no terminal guidance: it was—literally and figuratively—a shot in the dark. And with all the EMP activity, there'd be no way to command-detonate such a package, unless some mad scientist had come up with a strange new piezo-electric initiator, or maybe a switch activated by timed biological decay—

Like iron filings suddenly exposed to a magnet, Grim's thoughts swiftly collected around the term "biological," just as the short-range radar let loose a full squawk, and showed the same junk-blip still approaching—but on a slightly altered vector. Grim added the terms and concepts together: Biological. Change of vector. No reliable electric systems.

God damn, it was a live attack; in the midst of this solar typhoon, there were living, breathing saboteurs inbound—

Grim reached out and tapped the dynamic button that would open the link back to base. Which produced no results. He tapped it again, then harder, then hammered at it. Nothing. He turned to the hardwired auxiliary console to his immediate right, flipped the toggle for the command line: a sudden wall of cat-scratch static prompted him to shut off the volume.

So: thanks to the weather, communications were out. Which meant he had no way to call for help, or send a warning, and, reciprocally, base would no longer be receiving automated status updates from the rad shacks and therefore would not check to discover why he had failed to retract his sensor/comm mast. He was alone—and only he had the knowledge, and therefore the opportunity, to act.

Grim leaned back slowly, checked the range: given the one meter/second closure rate, he had about ten minutes to consider the problem, decide on a course of action, and carry it out—whatever it happened to be.

Grim turned to his tried-and-true first maxim of planning: know thy enemy—and had to admit that he knew next to nothing about the approaching attackers. So, using what little data he had, could he induce or deduce any tactical intel from it?

First, given the detection range of Eureka's main arrays, and the attackers' rate of approach, they had not been inside any hull—shielded or not—for at least a week. That meant that the attackers had floated in with the junk, using it as a moving smoke screen. And that, in turn, meant that this was a suicide mission: given the wholebody rem dosage the attackers had accrued during that extended approach, this solar storm guaranteed that their death from radiation sickness would be as certain as it would be swift.

As peculiar as that conclusion seemed, Grim discovered that it was consistent with the pattern of careful and meticulous planning evinced by his opponents. The timing of the attack indicated that it was designed to take advantage of the rising solar activity cycle. Indeed, it had probably been held in readiness for weeks, even months, until solar meteorology indicated the first, turbulent signs of an imminent coronal mass ejection. In the meantime, Eureka's security forces had been lulled into a slow and inevitable complacency regarding the camouflaging trash flow, ultimately seeing it as just another part of the environment. And in retrospect, Priestley's absence, and now Mendez's, had probably been achieved by hacking, bribery, or both.

Given that level of commitment and preparation, it was probable that the attackers' equipment was purpose-built for this mission, meaning that from weapons to vacc suits, it was almost entirely non-metallic. However, complete thermal equalization and diffusion was more difficult to achieve in space, and such systems would be further impaired if they had to avoid using any metal components.

Which meant that the attackers' thermals that might still be visible: Grim quickly snapped over to the slightly more robust thermal sensors. And there, mixed in with the slowly oncoming stream of trash, was a diffuse, almost invisible thermal bloom above the background, pointing inward like a finger.

Pointing straight at Rad Shack Four. Grim rechecked, confirmed the vector of approach: although their target was unquestionably the Big Secret being built on Eureka, they were heading straight at him. Why?

The answer followed the question without delay: because the saboteurs surely knew about the rad shacks, and therefore knew that they needed to eliminate whichever one sat astride or closest to their point of penetration as they crossed through Eureka's spherical security perimeter. Which meant that Rad Shack Four wasn't a haven anymore: it was a coffin. Oh, it still protected Grim from the rads, but that wasn't the biggest danger, now: thinking like the attackers, he somberly concluded that he'd opt to take out the rad shack with something quick and decisive. A high-explosive, armor-piercing missile would be the weapon of choice: it would easily penetrate the shack's shielding and would bust it open like a pickaxe smashing through the shell of an unsuspecting mollusk.

Grim returned from his thoughts, facing down into the sensor screen over which he was perched. He placed both of his hands on its wildly-flickering surface: despite the pronounced veins and sturdy wrists, his lightly pebbled and very dark brown skin looked suddenly and incongruously fragile and vulnerable. And Grim felt the accuracy of that perception rise up with the thought: "I've got no choice: I've got to go out there, too."

Which seemed like suicide, on the one hand, because in this storm, EVA ops was the radiological equivalent of going outdoors during a hailstorm of razor blades. But what could he achieve by staying inside? Unable to fight back from within the EMP-crippled rad shack, he could only wait to die.

Grim rose carefully from the seat, grabbed his helmet, reached for his Armalite—and closed his hand on empty air. Oh. Right. Slowly, he turned to look at the Cochrane. Okay, then: you and me, bitch. And—for your sake— you'd better perform to spec, or you're going to get very lost in deep space.

He reached down, picked up the weapon and moved toward the airlock, slaving the rad shack's shaky sensor feed into his HUD relays as he went.

Exiting the airlock, Grim controlled the first, transient sense of nausea that always surged up when he went EVA: no up, no down, and the black forever all around him. The stars only made the distance and solitude more absolute. Why so many people—from the earliest astronauts to the current day—were thrilled by "space-walks" was beyond him.

The distant sun—a small, painfully incandescent nickel—peeked into his helmet, rising up over the lower rim of the faceplate as he manually dogged the hatch and resteadied himself. He had a full MMU on his back, but the less activity and motion he engaged in, the better. Right now, surprise was his only sure advantage, so high-energy maneuvers of any kind were out of the question.

Using the external handholds, he towed himself back down into the shadow, and then around behind the rad shack, placing its mass between himself and the approach vector of the saboteurs. Once there, he checked the rad shack's sensor feed in his helmet: not good. Whether it was the sensors failing or the EMP interference, the data skipped sideways, winked out, came back, fizzled, cohered, leaned, then straightened and remained momentarily, quaveringly, readable—before it commenced its weird free-form dance all over again. But in that brief moment of clarity, Grim had seen the oncoming blip—except that it was larger now, shaped like a lumpy, mostly collapsed quatrefoil. There were *four* of them? Maybe it was just another sensor glitch—

But it probably wasn't, because it made perfect sense. It was just the right number: one heavy weapons expert, a backup expert who was probably carrying the missiles they planned to use on the Big Secret, and then two heavies. The heavies' specialty would be in EVA weaponplay—which, given the way that conventional firearm recoil sent you tumbling ass-over-ankles in zero-gee, was not a common or easily acquired skill. The heavies would provide cover for the other two, distract and/or neutralize responding defense forces, maintain situational awareness. The guys with the missiles would be monomaniacally focused on their equipment and their target.

In another minute they would reach the 2000-meter mark, which is where Grim estimated they might consider eliminating the rad shack. Meaning it was time to get a little distance from it. Grim placed both feet against the hull of the rad shack. He reached down to the handhold on either side of him, achieving a position akin to being frozen in the "squat" phase of a squat thrust. Then he simultaneously released the hand holds and pushed as hard as he could with his legs.

As he shot quickly away from the rad shack, he checked the HUD to see if there was any reaction from the blips; no new course changes were evident—and then the whole display went black. Great. Either the signal was lost or the system was fried; either way, it was all on him, now.

Which meant it was time to confront the Cochrane and its insanely diverse ammo bag. Clips of penetrators, expanders, non-lethals—those were pretty self-explanatory. Pulling up the top flap on the segmented grenade pouch, Grim laid a finger on an HE round, considered its use as a flare, rejected the tactic: Eureka's own sensors would be pulled in, but the explosion would surely alert the attackers to his presence. Instead, Grim selected two range-detonated flechette rounds, loaded them, and reasoned he should give the targeting system a quick check before trusting his life to it. He turned it on, and raised the integrated sighting scope to his right eye—

And held his breath. Whatever computer was silently working in the recesses of the Cochrane was apparently laboring overtime: multiple moving objects were quickly located optically, ranged and vector assessed by a laser ping, and a guidon indicated how to reposition the gun to acquire the target. Damned impressive—but still just a toy, Grim reminded himself.

He revised that opinion when the Cochrane flashed a new guidon into existence in what seemed like open space and indicated a cluster of four objects—which Grim *still* couldn't see—closing at .97 meters per second at 2100 meters range. Sweet Jesus: unprompted, the Cochrane had found the attack force. *Well, well,* Grim thought, smiling at the gun, *you've earned your continued existence—bitch.*

The targeting display flickered, then reasserted: the electromagnetic soup was already getting to the Cochrane's electronics. Grim switched off the power, and brought the scope back up to his eye.

Even through the faceplate, the unassisted sight-picture in the unusually wide eyepiece was still viable—and at maximum magnification, the plain old mechanical scope was already picking out dark blotches moving across and occluding the background starfield just where the targeting system had detected the intruders. Grim grunted in satisfaction: gotcha. He settled in to watch them, calculating that they would make their move within the minute, if his conjectures were correct. And so far, they had been—except for one unsolved tactical variable: where was the ship from which the attackers had deployed, and how had it stayed both out of sight and out of the trash stream?

Grim glanced sideways at the scattered, tumbling bits of irregular blackness and greyness that were the trash stream—and suddenly he knew the answer: the attackers' "ship" was floating past him right now. Their ship was now part of the junk. Sure: each of them had been sealed and launched in a self-disassembling pod. It had had a hull of composites and plastics, rudimentary thrust, life support, comestibles, and was set on a ballistic course, so it required no guidance. When the attackers neared the range at which Eureka's arrays might pick them out, they—figuratively speaking—pulled their ripcords and let the pods fall, or rather, float, to pieces around them. That way, they could probably have approached to within about 300 kilometers before getting into their vacc suits and preparing for—

The attack began with a sudden burst of vapor, centered on a bright flash which bloomed and then arced out from the midst of the attackers: a rocket, speeding toward the rad shack. Grim flinched away as a blinding flash coronaed up from the far side of the boxy module, knocking it into a slow tumble as papers and pulped electronic parts vomited out of the huge, jagged rupture in its side.

Time to return the favor. Grim reactivated the targeting system, leaned into the Cochrane's sights again, ready to fire—but was surprised to see a question mark glowing on the right margin of the display overlay, underscored with the legend "OG opt?" Grim wanted to spit: goddamn, was this weapon busted already? Goddamned tinkertoy piece of sh—

Oh, no, wait: Mendez had told him about this. The weapon sensed strong changes in ballistic conditions—such as gravity—and would ask if you wanted an optimum solution. So: "OG opt?" was obviously offering him an optimal firing solution for zero gee. Well, that seemed like a good idea: he edged his thumb up to the "accept" button behind the handgrip, pressed it. The query blinked away.

Grim focused on the four attackers again: they were still clustered, and at 1400 meters range. He reasoned he might get two of them with the flechette grenade. But how to access the launcher?

The needed information arose as chapter and verse from Mendez's endless worship of the Cochrane: "You've got three settings, Sarge: main weapon, launcher, or integrated. Just adjust this dial down here—"

Grim did. The Cochrane identified the ready round in the launcher (the laser-controlled, range-detonated flechette grenade), computed the ballistics (which were pretty clean in free space), and superimposed the firing solution on the current scene: it painted a dim red cone on top of two of the attackers' vector-projected plots at the time of warhead discharge. Then the image faded, almost blanked out: EMP overload. Damn: moment of truth. Grim snapped the safety off, lined up the weapon until the guidon told him his aimpoint matched the indicated firing solution, and squeezed the trigger— just as the image fuzzed, flickered, and winked off for good.

For a split second, Grim was sure—again—that the weapon had malfunctioned: the almost imperceptible jolt from the underslung launcher barely tumbled him. But no, he could see the grenade moving briskly downrange. But wait a minute: he could see it? How was that possible? Why was it going so slowly—?

And then he realized that, in zero-gee, the optimal firing solution was not so much a matter of maximizing accuracy, as it was concerned with minimizing recoil: the munition had been fired with only a tiny bit of force.

Grim, now moving backward more rapidly, and in a very slow tumble, entertained the brief hope that, because of this minimum downrange bump, he would also remain undetected by the attackers. No such luck: a mere second after he had launched his counterattack, the infiltrators turned toward him, weapons flickering. He twisted his head to keep them under observation: the muzzle flashes were very small, and seemed to occur in short, angry sequences: probably small-caliber weapons, with a maximum three-round burst setting. All common features in zero-gee firearm designs that—ever unsuccessfully—tried to minimize the recoil of conventional rounds. A few self-oxidizing tracers indicated the vector of the fire, which dropped off: having seen that they were wide of their mark, they were no doubt using their own MMUs to correct their tumble before reaiming—

Almost precisely where Grim had seen the sparkle of their weapons, there was a barely-visible flash, from which extended a small, lateral vapor plume: his flechette grenade. As Grim rolled up slowly toward direct alignment again, he brought the scope up to his eye.

Seen at the visual equivalent of fifty meters, one of the figures he had targeted was thrashing spasmodically; whether or not he was wounded, it was pretty clear that his suit was vented, probably multiple times. The other figure was a stark contrast: motionless, arms widening slowly, some object— his personal weapon?—had begun to free-float away on a slightly altered vector of its own. The third attacker, who had been at the edge of the area of effect, was also engaged in rapid motions, but these were brisk and methodical, not desperate. Probably one of the missile specialists trying to change over to his personal weapon, realized Grim as he selected the Cochrane's primary barrel.

He was approaching the end of his first full 360 degree tumble, briefly wondered if he should use his own MMU to restabilize, then realized that if he did so, he would lose the advantage of getting in another shot before they were ready to respond. But taking that shot would also make his own tumble worse. Mendez *had* mentioned something about a rear-jet compensator for zero-gee firing stabilization—sort of like a mini-bazooka backblast—but Grim couldn't recall the details. And since Grim had no time to screw with it, he used what he knew: he spun the propellant dial to the lowest setting— minimum recoil, in case the automatic optimization system has been fried. Then, as he rolled up into correct alignment, he quickly lined up the attacker who had been outside the cone of flechettes, and fired four quick rounds.

Grim was surprised—and relieved—to find that most of the imparted thrust vectored him directly backward; as he fired, the muzzle brake's cruciform nozzles selectively vented the weapon's exhaust to precisely counteract any pitch, yaw, or roll changes to his trajectory. But the Cochrane's system wasn't perfect: possibly because Grim had rapped the rounds out so fast, there was still enough off-vector impulse to increase the rate and skew of his tumble.

As he came around on his first faster, slightly cockeyed rotation, Grim panned the scope across what he estimated had been his target area. At first, he saw nothing—then a faint white plume: he swept back toward that. The plume disappeared briefly, then appeared again, evidently rotating back into view. It was a punctured air-tank, the rapidly venting gases throwing its wearer into an accelerating spin and carrying him on a very divergent trajectory. Judging from the figure's already muted writhings, he wouldn't live to see where his new heading took him: Grim guessed that he had hit more than just the backpack unit.

But now, as Grim continued his own knees-over-nose rotation, he faced two alternatives—neither of which had promising outcomes. Grim could either wait until he completed another somersault, try to access the last target through the Cochrane's scope (unlikely, given his increasingly erratic tumble) and score some more hits (profoundly unlikely, for the same reason); or, he could let the Cochrane float on its lanyard while he grabbed for his MMU controls to correct his tumble—and thereby allow the other guy to finish getting his personal weapon readied and aimed, and thereby beat Grim to the probably fatal punch. But wait: Mendez had once said, "And here's the beauty part, Sarge; you can use the Cochrane to correct your tumble—"

—And then Grim was following his memories of Esteban's instructions, just as they came to him, word by word—

"First you set the magazine feed to 'off'—"

—Grim did—

"—so that when you squeeze the trigger, the Cochrane's muzzle works just like a little rocket. And to counterboost, all you do is reorient yourself—"

—Grim swung his left arm out, imparting a little spin to his body—

"—then aim into the vector you need to correct—"

—Grim aimed down into the direction of his roll and slightly to one side—

"—and fire."

Grim squeezed the trigger, leaned into the light recoil, felt his rotational speed drop, saw that the yaw had almost disappeared. He straightened out the tube, fired two more times. And was almost perfectly stabilized. He threw his left arm back across his body to turn around again—toward the enemy— and brought the weapon up to his right eye.

He got his left hand back on the forestock, saw the starfield sweep past in the scope, caught a glimpse of movement—and then spotted a silhouette against the stars, head hunched down as if taking aim. Hail Mary, now. Grim thumb-selected autofire, twisting at the waist to keep the barrel on-target. He saw angry little flickers coming from the silhouette as he fired.

Even the Cochrane couldn't keep up with that insane barrage of thrust-generating discharges: Grim tumbled backward, felt a sharp slap to the back of his head as the spinning began. And that slap was probably death's calling card: the attacker's first accurate round had hit his helmet—luckily in the tough rear-plating, probably burrowing into the command electronics for his now useless computer and HUD. But the next round would probably hit something that was soft, would puncture, would release air, would leak blood: would kill him.

But that next round never came.

After correcting his madcap cartwheels with the MMU, and maneuvering into the solar lee of a little loping rock that dutifully followed the ruined Rad Shack Four in its slow orbit of the distant sun, Grim waited. And waited. And contemplated his probable wholebody rem dose. And waited some more.

Almost a full hour later, base finally sent a shielded away boat out to nose among the rocks in the vicinity of Rad Shack Four. When it got within 500 meters, Grim toggled his radio, heard the faint hum of the carrier wave under the EMP static, and said, "Hey. Over here."

After a moment of silence, there was the inevitable request for the day code, the countersign, and a curt request from a new voice: "Sitrep, Sergeant Grimsby."

"Uh—who is this?"

"Sergeant Grimsby, my name is Darryl Wilder. I'm—"

"Yes, sir; I know who you are, sir."

A pause.

"Very well. Proceed."

As the away boat made its slow approach, Grim proceeded to give the most respectful, thorough, professional, and utterly boring sitrep of his entire career to date. At the end, he even managed to forget about the rads sleeting through his body long enough to ask, "Any idea who was behind this, Mr. Wilder?"

"No hard evidence yet, but I'd say it was the megacorporations."

"Corporate? Why? They afraid you won't let them sell Big Macs on Alpha Centauri?"

There was a long pause. "Sergeant, you seem very sure that our construction project at Eureka has something to do with interstellar travel."

Oops. "Uh . . . sorry, sir."

"Sorry?"

"Shouldn't have said that on open channel, sir."

"Hmm . . . no, you shouldn't have: but your conclusion, and your presence of mind, is promising. So, it seems, is the Cochrane."

Grim stared as the gun; the approaching bow lights of the away boat glinted off its selector switch: it seemed like a bright, conspiratorial wink. "Yeah, well—it was okay."

"'Okay'? Sergeant, from what our first readable scans are showing, it seems like it was the star of the show."

"Sure—but, with all due respect, Mr. Wilder, what if the Cochrane hadn't worked?"

"Just be glad that it *did* work, oh Ye of Little Faith,"—Grim's Grandmama Rayshawne had used that same expression; didn't sound right coming from a man—"because if you had had your old Armalite-6, you would have had to conduct a full MMU tumble correction after every shot. How many shots do you think you could have taken that way?"

"Uh—two. Maybe."

"Yes, 'maybe'—with a capital 'M.' Either way, two shots would have been two too few: they came at you with four attackers. A conventional zero-gee weapon couldn't have engaged them all. But the Cochrane could—and did. You were right to have Mendez leave the Cochrane behind, even if it was against regs."

"Uh, sir—"

"Yes?"

Grimsby paused: the smart thing to do was to take the credit for keeping the Cochrane at the shack. But—maybe because he had just recalled Grandmama Rayshawne belting out "Sweet Bye and Bye" at First Baptist—he said, "Sir, I didn't think of keeping the weapon at the shack. That was Mendez." With any luck, that would earn Esteban enough brownie points for his OCS nod, allowing him to become a less-than-typically detestable shave tail—if he lived long enough. But luckily, Mendez had spent a little time coming up through the ranks, knew to listen to sergeants (usually), and so had a better than even chance of dodging both enemy bullets and the tender ministrations of a late-night latrine fragging.

Wilder was still talking: Grim tuned back in as he was commenting, "Well, you certainly proved that Mendez made the right choice."

"Yes, sir, but I did break a few regs."

"Well, I'm not your CO, but it seems to me that if they don't bust you, they're going to have to decorate you."

"Why's that, sir?"

"Well, in addition to single-handedly defeating a sabotage attempt on what you will soon know as Project Prometheus, you just gave the Cochrane a field test the likes of which no weapon has ever had—either in terms of what was demanded of it, or how well it performed. And that in the hands of an untrained operator. Back at Eureka, the testing team all look like they stole grins off a Cheshire cat, talking about how no amount of careful planning can beat plain old dumb luck."

"Huh: in my case, very dumb."

"Suitably self-deprecating, Sergeant, but not very convincing. When you emerge from your debriefing—which they claim will last a week—we should have a talk about your future. How does that sound?"

That sounded almost as good as the week-long debrief, which mean a soft, solo bed in officer's country and real chow, instead of the grey walls of the brig he had been expecting to inhabit for the foreseeable future. "That sounds fine, sir."

"Good. Now, one last thing. The fellows up here from Picatinny are so eager to find out if there were any failures or shortcomings with the Cochrane, that they refused to wait for the debrief. So I promised them I'd ask you: did the Cochrane fall short on any of its design parameters, or did it perform to spec?"

Grim looked down at the gun. "Yes sir, it performed to spec." Then—because no one was there to see—he grinned. And he thought:

Yeah; definitely to spec.

TO SPEC Acknowledgements: For expert opinion and information on the topic of solar weather in general, and the effects of coronal mass ejections in specific, the author gratefully acknowledges the expert input of: Dr. Gordon Holman, NASA Goddard Space Flight Center; Lt. Col. Peter Garretson, USAF; and Russell Howard, a principle investigator in the USN's SECCHI (Sun-Earth Connection Coronal Heliospheric Investigation) initiative.

THE GLASS BOX

Bud Sparhawk

THERE WERE TWENTY MISSILES STREAKING TO IMPACT THE PLANET'S SURFACE AND I WAS the only passenger, but not for long.

When the sabot blew away, I flew off with the rest of the debris as the super-dense ballistic payload continued screaming toward a Shardie location over the horizon. It carried a single altitude-sensing charge in its tail that would accelerate the payload to strike at a thousand kps. At that hyper-velocity the shock wave and impact would blast a crater five kilometers across and send dirt, rock, and dust into the stratosphere.

Twenty of these hitting the planet would be my diversion.

The wind whipped me as I dropped deeper into the atmosphere. Tendrils of spidersilk deployed behind me, threads with hundreds of microparachutes along their length, each one exerting miniscule drag, stealing momentum from my descent, then blowing away to swiftly dissolve in the air.

The tendrils would be indistinguishable from the thousands of smaller, broken fragments from the sabot. I just hoped that my presence was in-distinguishable.

I skimmed trees and hills, stirring trails of dust as I moved at better than ten meters per second through the last portion of my drop. When the last of the threads tore away I still carried eight mps, slow enough to give me a chance of survival on impact.

I tucked for the bounce and roll, hoping that I'd hit where nothing would stop me before all my potential energy was dissipated. Desert sand would be nice, water better, but I'd take an open field if it came to that.

Just no damn forests.

The weak and fading signal had come unexpectedly from a colony world abandoned to the Shardies six months before. It was a short burst that might have been missed if fleet hadn't had a SIGINT unit probing the Shardies' signals.

"We tried to get away, but the things caught us," the high-pitched voice had cried. "I'm hiding. Please help me."

Fleet was conflicted. It was not impossible that some group might have been missed during the evacuation. Campers, spelunkers, or others could have been isolated when the order was sent. How long had it taken to move the twenty thousand off the planet—two weeks, eighteen days? They'd packed the colonists into any ship they could find. Most vessels barely had enough oxygen to sustain the refugees. The evacuation was chaotic, disorganized, and messy. They tried to get everyone, but still, some might have been missed.

Should we ignore it? command asked, thinking that the loss of a single individual was as nothing compared to the risks of extracting the survivor. Maybe the call was a ruse, a trap. Then again, it might be worth the valuable intelligence we'd gain to mount an effort. Fleet was desperate to learn anything it could about the Shardies, especially how a child had managed to elude capture by our relentless enemy.

Nobody had ever escaped the Shardies, not since we discovered how they turned any survivor into organic components for their ships. The horror of those images, the undead bodies stranded into the controls of the one captured ship, had shown everyone that there were worse things than death, should they be captured.

The Shardies had been relentless in driving us from our colony worlds. In deep space it was no better. They destroyed our most hardened ships with better tactics and weapons. Since we'd first encountered them, they had relentlessly continued to advance. If the war persisted as it had for the past three years, with us abandoning one world after the next, the Shardies would reach Earth within a decade, or maybe less.

Fleet needed whatever information the survivor might have. Earth needed the hope that someone could survive to report what she had seen. We all needed to know.

Command had no choice. Someone had to find whoever sent that signal.

The deployment was carefully planned to minimize risk. Four high-speed, light-attack ships would emerge from blink just beyond the Holzberg limit, fire off a stick of five Rapture missiles and blink away, hopefully before the Shardies had time to react. The theorists calculated that if the total hang time near the planet was fifteen to eighteen seconds—the upper limit only if a ship had to roll into firing position—they all might have a chance to get away.

The seconds after firing were the dangerous time for the ships' crews. If they didn't reach the Holzberg limit in those eighteen seconds, the overstressed drives would turn the ship and everyone on board into an instantaneously brilliant cloud of dispersing plasma. I had the easy part, they said.

All I had to do was survive long enough to send my signal.

The hundreds of fragments from the sabot spread out in an elongated, egg-shaped pattern over a thousand square kilometers along the path of the payload. Even if the Shardies weren't preoccupied cleaning up the destruction from the missiles' impacts and suspected something, they'd still waste a lot of time finding and inspecting that many pieces. Expand those searches over twenty patterns and you came up with the faint probability of my being detected. I knew that, even with that sort of insurance, they'd eventually find my landing spot. It was only a matter of time. I had to hurry.

I discovered I was still in one piece when I uncoiled my aching body after the long bounce and roll. My left arm dangled loosely and a chunk of that shoulder was missing. Other than that all my parts seemed to be functional. I probed the arm and found that it had been dislocated by whatever I hit. That must have been what ripped that piece of shoulder away. A little pressure in the right places, a twist of the shoulder, and the arm was nearly as good as the day it was installed.

I checked my position and discovered that I was about two hundred kilometers away from the location of the signal. Hell of an overshoot, but not bad, considering the variables. The deviation could have come from unexpected upper level winds or some other variable. I figured two days to hike there if I didn't stop. I set out.

The location was a tiny coastal village. There were thirty buildings that I could see from my perch on the ridgeline, twenty of them were homes. The long piers told me that this might once have been a fishing community, but whatever boats had docked there were now gone. One road ran down the center of town and there was a landing pad to the west. The landing pad looked too raw, too new.

Judging from the amount of debris on the road there must have been a hell of a panic when they abandoned this place. Maybe that's where the boats had gone. Had they been used to transport the colonists to an evacuation center?

I imagined they'd scuttled them, rather than leave anything for the damned Shardie bastards.

I watched the town until nightfall but saw no evidence that anything alive was down there. Not a stray dog or cat, not a rat, and no birds. An hour after dark, I worked my way down the slope, pausing often, alert for some sign of movement, some indication that I had been spotted.

I kept my disruptor ready. One of the things we'd learned was that the Shardies were incredibly fast. I'd only have two milliseconds or less to react—just enough time to squeeze the trigger once, but that was all it would take.

The largest building was filled with cold, rusting machines and long metal tables. Here and there were slender knives and curving hooks on long handles. Fishing village for sure, I guessed.

I worked my way down the road, passing from one building to the next as swiftly and silently as I could. On the fifth building, a home, I found her.

I shifted sight to infrared and surveyed the room. The only heat source was her small body. The only sound her slow breathing. The only light a shaft of moonlight through the shutters.

I put a hand over the girl's mouth and shook her gently. She struggled briefly and then went limp, her eyes wide in horror when she got a glimpse of me. "Sergeant Millikan, Fifth Marine," I said softly. I doubted anyone could overhear, but you can never be too careful where the Shardies are concerned. "I've come for you," I said, which while completely true, was not necessarily accurate.

"I didn't think anyone would come," she said in a rush. "Especially not something like you." She seemed to accept my assurance that I was a marine, but not quite sure that I was a someone.

I took a good look at her: skinny, scraggly hair, and filthy, all of which would be expected from what she had been through. Her black hair was cut short, her nails broken—some bitten to the quick—and crusted with God-knows-what. She had a gash on the top of her head that might be pretty bad under the crust of scabby blood. She looked to be about fifteen, maybe a year or two more or as much less—too damn young to be in this situation, not that there was any other age that would be better.

A pair of muddy tan boots that looked three sizes too large for her sat by her side. Nearby was a smelly pile of fish entrails.

She caught my glance. "I fished last night," she said. "By hand." And ate it raw, I guessed. That was smart. A fire would attract attention.

"How long have you been here?" I asked. "How did you get here?"

"A week, I think," she replied. "I was a mile up the coast before, but I came here after I used that 'phone." She must have seen my puzzled expression. "A mile is about one and a half kilometers," she explained.

"Archaic measure," I recalled. A lot of the colonies went back to the old measures as a signal of their departure from Earth's ways. Well, that experiment didn't last long, did it?

But, a week? "Where were you before that?" It had been nearly six months since the Shardies arrived.

She shrugged. "Running, hiding, keeping away from them. I just kept going until I found the 'phone—back there," she waved a hand in the general direction of the door.

I looked. It was an old unit, leaking battery acid and showing no power light. She must have drained it in that single cry for help. I left it there. Useless.

"Are you taking me away?" she asked when I returned.

That was a good question. Staying in the village wasn't a good idea. The Shardies methodically erased all signs of human presence before they moved on, so it was only a matter of time before they destroyed this one. It could be next week, or within an hour. Or maybe they were too busy checking the debris and dealing with the effects of the multiple strikes. "Yes," I said.

The girl quickly gathered her few belongings—the boots, a ship's jacket with a Fourth Fleet emblem on the shoulder, a wicked knife with a serrated back, and the blanket she had been sleeping under—before we set out.

"My name's Tashia," she said softly.

"Call me Sergeant," I replied.

I led her up the slope, following the same path I had taken in just in case they would follow our heat trail. Once we were on top I intended to stay to the rocks and touch the ground only where we couldn't avoid it. That way we'd avoid leaving obvious signs of our passage. I knew we couldn't escape detection completely, but there was no sense in making our trail easy either.

She began to lag behind after we'd covered barely ten kilometers and slumped to the ground at fifteen. "Sarge, I can't go any further," she sighed. "I'm so tired."

I dug into my side pocket and pulled out one of my G-rations. "Eat this," I ordered. The strong military stimulants probably wouldn't do her weakened body any good, but the nutrients in the bar would provide her with the strength to last until daybreak.

Intelligence had force-fed me every speck of information about this world they could glean out of the colonists. In the very early days of the colony there had been a small mining operation on this plateau. The vein turned out to be shallow and petered out within a year or so, but not before producing enough coal to fuel the first few settlements. After the mine was abandoned all of the miners had moved on, leaving behind only those things they could not take with them—foundations and the mine shaft. Machinery, building materials, household goods, everything that could be moved was taken away.

I found the entrance to the shaft before the sky started to gray. I took us back deep enough that I couldn't see the stars framed in the entrance. I flopped down with my back against the wall to face the way we'd come.

Tashia sat near my side, arms hugging her stick-thin legs against her chest. "I'm glad you came, Sarge," she said. "I was so afraid nobody would. I just used that 'phone to let somebody know I was alive."

"You said there were others. Tell me about them."

She shook her head. "Dad died, I guess." She said that in such a calm voice that I figured she'd already drained emotion from the memory. "Dad and I were out camping when everyone else went away. I guess we sort of got overlooked."

I nodded. It could happen. Emergency evacuations are messy affairs at best, chaotic at worst. Easy to suppose the missing ones were on another boat, another vehicle. A few could get lost.

"We didn't know where to go. We couldn't find anyone. It was like they all ran away." She was trembling as she recalled that frightening time. "Then the things came for us."

"Things? What did they look like?" This was good information. A first-hand description might help someone.

She shook. "I . . . I didn't get a really good look, but they were glowing, sort of. It was night and they moved so fast. They put me in a sort of box. It was so small I couldn't stand up in it. Dark, too."

"Did you hear anything, sense anything—a smell, an aroma, anything at all?"

She was silent for a long while. "No. I was so cold. They took my clothes so I had goosebumps all over."

"Anything else?" I had to get as much information from her as I could in the time remaining. "How long were you in the box?"

She frowned. "Maybe a few days 'cause I got really, really thirsty. One day I woke up, the top of the box was opened a crack. I stuck my fingers in the crack and pried it open.

"I was in a white room with a lot of icicles, only they weren't ice at all. More like glass, you know?"

"Was there anything else in the room—somebody moving around, a machine, anything that you'd recognize?"

She thought a moment before replying. "A couple of other boxes and those weird icicles everywhere."

"Go on, please. What did you do then?"

"I ran. I had to get out of the scary room away from the box. I found a pile of stuff from our camp—that's where I got some clothes—then I ran away into the woods."

"How did you hurt your head?" Her story sounded too bizarre. Were the boxes and the room figments of her imagination, or was she telling the truth?

Her hand darted to her head. "Oh, I guess I must have cut it on one of the icicles. It stings," she added quickly, almost as an afterthought.

"Let me see," I said. She leaned forward. The long gash ran from just above her left temple to the top of her skull. I could see little flecks of glass in the wound. "That looks like it had to hurt."

"I guess it did, but I must have been too scared to notice," she said. "Anyhow, I ran and ran until I found a place to hide. After that I kept running from one spot to the next at night, so the things wouldn't find me. Then I found the 'phone and made the call. I prayed somebody might come. Somebody." She was quiet for a long while after that. "You, Sarge," she added in a small voice.

"The Shardies don't usually let humans go," I replied. "They make them into components, use human brains to help them win this war."

Her mouth formed a small "O" of horror. "That's what they were going to do to me?" she cried. "Oh, my God!"

"That's why they sent me. We had to find out how you managed to escape and hear what you could tell us about the aliens. That's why I'm here."

"You must be really brave," she yawned and stretched. "I don't think I could do something like that." She hugged my arm. "But I'm not scared now that you're here. I know you'll take care of me."

"Get some sleep," I said. "Just pick a spot."

She dropped the blanket next to me. "You can share," she suggested, offering me a corner.

"I don't need sleep," I replied. "I rest a different way." No sense telling her that I could shut down the remaining organic component of my brain while the autonomic parts took care of surveillance and housekeeping. Better she remained ignorant of all the terrible things the surgeons did to me after the firefight. Better that she continue to think of me as a marine and leave it at that.

I'd been going continuously through the past fifty-eight hours and needed some rest time. The diversions of the missile strike, the escaping ships, and hundreds of pieces of sabot shred gave me, at most, thirty hours more, before I expected to be found. Sleep and rest would steal many of those hours, leaving me only a narrow bit of time to complete my mission.

Tashia had fallen asleep and was snuggled against my hip with one arm thrown across my waist. I could feel her soft breath against my left arm and her gentle movements as deep sleep relaxed tired muscles. At rest she looked so innocent, so peaceful, that one could easily imagine her snuggled in her own bed, dreaming of boys and dances, of family and friends, of loved pets and fond memories. But my imagination could only take me so far before brutal, ugly reality intruded.

I heard a faint, nearly indistinguishable sound and went instantly on alert. I was at the mine's entrance in under two seconds and tuned every sense to hyper-alertness. There! Near the horizon was a golden glow in the early dawn light. It moved right to left, possibly tracing the path I had followed to reach the village. Were they tracing me or was their track merely happenstance?

If the former they would be here in a few hours. We had to move.

Tashia groaned when I lifted her, but didn't wake as we left the mine. Her weight was negligible, less than a full combat pack, but more awkward to carry.

"What's happening?" she whispered after we'd gone a few kilometers. "Where are we?"

"Running," I replied. "I think we're being followed."

She stifled a cry, showing more wisdom than I expected. "The things," she said. "They're fast."

"So am I," I replied. "They gave me really strong legs."

"What happened to you?" she asked. "I know you don't look right. Are you a freak or something?"

It was a fair question. I was hardly dating material and I doubt that my own mother would recognize me like this. She would probably disown me if she did.

"Sort of like that," I replied. "They had to rebuild me after the. . . . After it happened. It was touch and go. I almost died, they tell me. If I hadn't given consent I would have, but they did ask me, and that was only after they told me my options. Live and be useful like this, or die. Some choice."

"But you chose life," she whispered and squeezed my neck. "I'm glad."

"They gave me metal bones," I continued. "Augmented my muscles, increased my metabolic rate, and did some fancy stuff to my head." I laughed. "I can see in the dark and hear a pin drop a half kilometer away. My reaction time is five times that of a normal man's and my endurance is practically unlimited. I could go a week without food or water if I had to, a month with water alone and no diminution strength either."

"And the downside is?" she joked. "It sounds like you've been turned into a superman."

"There's the pain, for one thing," I replied honestly. "It's constant. I can't laugh anymore, nor cry for that matter. Everything seems dead to me, no nuance or gradations. It's like not caring any more, only I do care about things, like rescuing pretty little girls and helping the war effort."

She didn't reply, but I got another hug.

"Where did you say you got that jacket?" I asked casually. "There were no survivors of the Fourth Fleet."

"It was Dad's," she said. "I don't know where he got it. Maybe he was a veteran or something."

"That's a ship's jacket, not something anyone would wear anywhere but on board. Do you know what happened to the Fourth?"

"N-n-no," she whispered.

"The Shardies captured the ship and took prisoners," I explained. "We found some of them on a captured ship, wired into the controls." Then I added. "They weren't dead. Not then."

"But Dad wore it all the time. He didn't tell me about his ship or the aliens or anything. I was just cold and wanted something to wear so I wouldn't be so scared and cold and all." She began sobbing. "I didn't mean to do anything bad, Sarge."

"I know, honey. I didn't think you knew about the jacket. That's why I told you." Not the only reason, I added, to myself.

I checked the time. Twenty-two probable hours left, much less if they were really trailing us. Not much time either way.

"We've got to signal soon," I said. "The target's not far from here. Think you can walk for a while?" I set her down. I wasn't tired from carrying her slight weight, but I did want to have both hands free should anything happen.

"Give me another of those candy bars and I think I could run there." Her laughter was like tonic to my ears. It had been so long since I'd heard a young girl laugh, so long and so far back in my past that I had forgotten how wonderful it could sound.

I fished out two bars and threw her one. "They're a little chewy without something to wash them down, but maybe we can find some water."

We moved with the wind, moving as quickly as Tashia could manage in her condition, burning energy fast to reach the target in the shortest amount of time. I couldn't move as quickly as I wanted, but had to match Tashia's comparatively slow pace. With the augments in my legs and the hyperventilation of my lungs I could outrun a cheetah if I had to.

Even with the bar's energy boost, she could probably outrun a house cat, if it was tired and old.

"Are you going to call the fleet?" she asked. "How are they going to get us without the things knowing about it?"

"Fleet has ways of landing undetected," I lied. "Stealth, charged ice, snowflake, and owl's wing tech for the most part. The stuff is so good, the Shardies wouldn't even know we were here."

Her eyes grew wide. "I never heard about all that!"

"There's a lot you wouldn't know," I said, as I started the timer buried in my abdomen. I stuffed three more G-rations into my mouth to provide the energy I needed for the high-speed signal burst. The SIGINT boys high above would be waiting for anything sparkling within a hundred kilometers of the target location, just in case I didn't make it all the way.

"We are going away, aren't we?" she said, panic rising in her voice as she nervously scanned the area. I checked. Whatever that golden glow had been it wasn't detectable any more.

"There was a lot of debate about sending someone down here," I said, as the timer activated the signaling process, storing the data I had collected, along with my conclusions for the burst. "Fleet thought you might be exactly what you said—a poor little survivor who managed to sneak away from the Shardies. On the other hand, they suspected that it might have been just a false signal to lure us into a trap."

"But it wasn't a trap," Tashia said. "I really did use the 'phone. I really did run away from the things."

"There's the matter of the jacket." That damned, cursed, incongruous jacket that had no reason to be on this or any other planet.

"No, I told you. It was Dad's," she cried. "You have to believe me!"

"Then Fleet wondered if there was the possibility that you might not be human any more: That the Shardies wanted to loose a new horror on us, with a new way of using humans."

Tashia patted herself. "No, no. I'm me! Look at me. I'm as human as you, maybe more than you. Here," she threw open her jacket to bare herself.

I looked at the small mounds of her budding breasts, the ribs showing under her thin skin, and the little blue veins that ran across her chest.

I gently tugged the sides of her jacket together. "I know, Tashia. I believe you. I never doubted that you weren't human, not for an instant."

I could feel the heat building up inside of me as my I processed the G-ration into the squirter's storage unit. "I've recorded everything you told me," I went on. "Earth will hear it all and probably interpret more from what you said than even you know."

"But I'm not one of them," she cried. "I ran away. They didn't p-pro-process me like you said."

I thought about her escape, the improbable discovery of the ancient 'phone, and surviving on fish captured with her bare hands. Taken together they were improbable, but not impossible.

She might not be a conscious Shardie agent, might not even know if she was one, but there was that jacket, those glimmers of glass in her head, and those unexplainable gaps of time and memory. What had they really done while she slept in the box?

Tashia was sobbing. "I did so escape, just like I told you. I ran away. I was so scared. I didn't know what to do."

"I know." Oh God, I remembered the sound of her laughter, her curiosity about me, her desire to get back to her family and friends. It was all so . . . *human*.

"Listen, Tashia," I said. "The problem is that even if you really are one hundred percent human, they still couldn't risk rescuing you."

"But they could examine me, see if anything is wrong, see if those things did something to me. They could do that, couldn't they?" she pleaded. "Couldn't they?"

"They could," I replied softly. "But they won't. The important thing about sending me here was to get whatever information you could give us. That's what's important—the information." Yes, that and the fact that, despite all odds, a little girl, a human girl, had escaped to tell her tale. That fact alone would give everyone hope that we could find a way to fight back and, hopefully, win.

The heat was so intense that I knew the mission's end was near. In a few seconds everything within fifty meters would be consumed in an intense blast of encoded coherent light that would tell the watchers overhead all that I had heard and seen. The blast would leave scorched ground that looked like a rocket had taken off. The Shardies weren't the only ones who could use misdirection.

"But you do believe me, don't you, Sarge?" she cried, as if seeking a final bit of certainty.

"Yes," I replied softly as I reached out and hugged her close to give her one last bit of comfort against the cold dark and partly to ensure that nothing would remain for the Shardies to analyze.

"You're as human as me."

EVERYTHING IS BETTER WITH MONKEYS

C.J. Henderson

"What a piece of work is a man! How noble in reason! how infinite in faculties! in form and moving, how express and admirable! in action, how like an angel! in apprehension, how like a god! the beauty of the work! the paragon of animals!"
William Shakespeare

"Were it not for the presence of the unwashed and the half-educated, the formless, queer and incomplete, the unreasonable and absurd, the infinite shapes of the delightful human tadpole, the horizon would not wear so wide a grin."
F.M. Colby

The *Roosevelt* was the first of the long-awaited Dreadnought class, a single ship stretching for nearly half a mile, inconceivable tons of metal and plastics, crystal and biomechanical feeds, brought together from Earth, the Moon and the asteroids that, when ultimately combined into an end product, became something unheard of—something utterly incomprehensible. And thus . . . so the thinking went . . . unbeatable, as well.

She was, in the end, a sum far greater than her parts. The *Roosevelt* was known as "the cowboy ship," for it had been that cocky gang of rocketeers labeled as the Moonpie Prairie Riders who had built her. They were the wildmen of the mightiest nation in the system's Advanced R&D Team, and it was their spirit that infested her—as well as programmed her still not-quite-understood artificial mind.

The *Roosevelt* was the opening number of a new kind of show, the all or nothing-at-all first born of the Confederation of Planets—big, because she had to be. The first ship with functional energy shields, she needed room for the massive protonic engines essential in powering such revolutionary devices. And for her thousands of attack aircraft, hundreds of them merely hanging off her sides. And for her extensive guns, her big ticket—the whisperers and the pounders—and all her hundreds of thousands of missiles and bombs.

She was the solar system's first spacecraft carrier, a mobile prairie outpost, a relentlessly strong, self-determining fortress in space. Capable of housing as many as 10,000 sailors and marines, the great ship was meant to explore the galaxy, to chart the universe, and to bring prestige and riches to the human race in general.

But, that had been when that particular track meet had thought it controlled the only runner on the field. Reaching the edge of the system's outer planet's orbit, the Roosevelt was hailed, in English, Spanish, Dutch, Jamaican, and eighty-three other standard languages, by a small, obnoxiously shiny craft commanded by a small, and equally obnoxious alien life form that was all too happy to deliver its news.

The quite unexpected messenger announced to the finally-capable-of-interstellar-traveling human race that this accomplishment had gotten them an invitation to join the awe-inspiring Pan-Galactic League of Suns, an organization of worlds begun by the Five Great Races. It was an announcement that, essentially, the party was over before it had begun, that all the planets worth anything were all sewn up, all intelligent species discovered, all franchises in all the marketplaces possible well-established and even better protected.

The news came as a crushing blow to the adventure-craving crew of the *Roosevelt*, and for their first two years, eight months and fifteen days in space they showed their resentment in many a creative and colorful manner. And then, suddenly, all the rules changed. Thanks to that first, bold human crew in space, the entire galaxy discovered the League was a sham, that their claims to have everything under control were simply so much eye-wash, and that there was still plenty of unknown universe out there, teeming with mysteries and excitement—enough even to satisfy the collective curiosity of the crew of the *Roosevelt*.

Within weeks of that revelation, more than a dozen trans-galactic federations had begun to struggle into existence, including the *Roosevelt*'s hometown group. Once made up of only six of the Earth's neighboring planets, because of its pivotal role in pulling the Pan-Galactic wool from the galaxy's eyes, the Confederation of Planets had already expanded to a membership of some seventy-eight worlds, proving, quite nicely, the old adage that everyone does, indeed, "love a winner."

Which is why the crew of the Roosevelt, one fine galactic star date, from its stalwart captain down to the lowest chef's assistants and protonic bolt tighteners, was in a rousing, near giddy, mood. They had started their space-bound careers in defeat and through a luck understood by only the most perverse of gods had rolled it over into unbridled victory. So recent had their triumph been that, truthfully, most on board were still at a loss for words when it came to explaining exactly how their good fortune had come about.

"I'm tellin' ya, Noodles," announced Chief Gunnery Officer Rockland Vespucci, more commonly known to bartenders and military police officers across the galaxy as Rocky, "there ain't nuthin' that's gonna trip things up for us again."

"Incautious words," answered the aforementioned Noodles, better known to top notch wire-and-screw jockeys everywhere as Machinist First Mate Li Qui Kon. "As Confucius said, 'he who stops watching for falling fruit will be first to get bonked by an apple.' "

"So, we just reinvent gravity."

Both sailors turned at the sound of a new voice indicating their being joined on the observation deck. As they did so, Technician Second Class Thorner and Quartermaster Harris came into view. As Noodles took exception with the tech's off-handed comment, accusing him of not taking theoretical physics seriously enough, Thorner spread his meaty hands wide, answering;

"Hey, it was just a joke. But com'on, really, look at the way things have been cruising for us. Earth is out in front. We've got the edge. It's our game from now on."

"I've got to agree," chimed in Harris. Taking a deck chair, he leaned back, putting his hands behind his head as he added, "Fate keeps lobbing us softballs, and we keep knocking them out of the park."

"He's right, little buddy," added Rocky. Grinning from ear to ear, staring out into the vast black, Rocky cavalierly added, "Criminey, it's almost enough to make a guy wish for some trouble."

And, it was at that moment that Fate, as she so often does when those bound to her decrees begin to act as if they had somehow negated her sway over their existence, chose to prompt the commander of the good ship *Roosevelt* to broadcast an announcement.

"Attention, this is your captain speaking. We've just received orders to proceed to the Kebb Quadrant to begin negotiations with the inhabitants of the planet Edilson. More information will be zimmed to us shortly, but we're to make best possible speed, which means, ladies and gentlemen, it's time to once more bend the fabric of space and time and be on our merry way."

"Edilson," asked Harris, "where in the wonderful world of color is Edilson?"

"And so it begins." All heads turned to the latest voice to join the conversation. As they did, one of the thinnest individuals to ever muster enough soaking-wet-weight to make it into the Navy added;

"The MI boys are just beginning to appreciate galactic rotation. Which meant that mudball was absolutely destined to hit our radar."

The speaker was Mac Michaels, a balding, bespectacled razormind out of the science division. As the others continued to stare at him, scratching their heads, he spread his hands like a high school math teacher about to share the wondrous joys of algebra as he said;

"Right now Edilson is nowhere, a low rent piece of real estate totally off the charts. But, if you calculate the rotation of the galaxy's set pieces, four hundred years from now, it's going to be in the veritable center of everything." Noting the group stare of complete lack of comprehension slamming at him from every angle, Michaels sighed, then added;

"It means that those who are far thinking will want to strike an alliance with Edilson now, so that when the time comes, they'll have an ally situated smack in the center of everything."

Michael's words made sense. Earth was expanding, making friends and teammates everywhere its representatives went. Enemies as well. If the Confederation of Planets was to maintain its presence, to continue advancing in power and prestige, let alone to be able to handle itself in the political and economic arenas of the universe against the likes of the Pan-Galactic League of Suns and others, this was just the kind of advanced cogitation they should be pursuing.

And, as the gobs headed off cheerfully to their various posts, their pride in the planet of their birth swelled. They came, after all, from a forward-thinking world, one clever enough to send them off to negotiate with a solar system that would not really be worth having as a pal for centuries. That, they knew, whistling merrily as they took up their duties, took foresight. It took brains.

If they had possessed the brains to realize just how much desperate luck they were going to need to survive their upcoming expedition, however, they might have thrown in a few prayers in between all the whistling.

✦

"All right then," growled Captain Alexander Benjamin Valance, as he reached for what was to be the first of several large drinks, "tell me someone has discovered something to explain whatever in hell *that* was."

The *Roosevelt* had arrived at the Edilson Well far in advance of the time required for their diplomatic team's meeting with the planetary council. In their best dress uniforms, the captain and his senior staff along with the ship's resident diplomatic officers had disembarked, prepared to put the Confederation's collective best foot forward. "An unmitigated disaster of incalculable proportions" was the phrase one might use to describe their meeting with the Edilsoni who came to greet them—but then, *only* if that one were trying to put the best spin possible on the most unfortunate encounter between dissimilar species since the Log Cabin Republicans first came across the D.A.R.

"Ahhh, if you're willing to consider some non-sanctioned information, sir . . . "

"Meaning?"

"Meaning," answered Valance's aide in a slightly lowered voice, "data acquired from outside official circles." When the captain only stared, the look in his eyes indicating his aide should just simply speak, the woman cleared her throat, then said;

"I did a records swap with a Chambrin starsweeper a few months back. Running a search through those files, I've managed to pull up some records from a couple of freelance Embrian traders who passed through this sector a few years ago—Iggzy and Cosentino Shipping."

At first, everything had seemed swell. The planet's inhabitants turned out to be an semi-amorphous life-form. Neither male or female, the Edilsoni could, with some difficulty, stretch and remold themselves into any manner of shapes if they desired. Normally, however, they were rubbery, blue-skinned, watermelon-shaped folk who walked on three appendages roughly two to three feet in length. The melon of them—their torso as well as skull—was surrounded by three tentacle-like arms, as well as three eye-stalks, their disturbingly large mouths sprouting from the center of their heads.

"And what did these shippers report?"

The captain and the others, of course, were no strangers to aliens. They had encountered all manner of varied life forms since hitting deep space, and not once had any of them so much as raised an offending eyebrow at any-one or thing they had met. Not when they had watched the Georgths groom each other and subsequently devour their findings, or when they labored to decider the language of the Mauzrieni, the only race in the galaxy to communicate through farting. But the Edilsoni, they . . . well . . . they were different.

"Their report tallies pretty much with what we just crashed through." As the aide read through her findings, the captain and his diplomatic squad fell further into the abysmally deep funk they had brought on board with them. For a while they had been able to hold onto the hope they had simply not understood what had been happening. But, sadly, they had.

The planet Edilson possessed a singularly peculiar make-up. Much of it was formed on unstable rock. Not the kind given over to earthquakes—or edilsonquakes, if you would—but the kind that produced the type of environment found in Earthspots such as Japan or Yellowstone National Park. Edilson was, in short, one great big steam-manufacturing ball, and due to its odd rock formations, anywhere the steam leaked out, it filled the air with various streams of continual sound.

Over the millennia, the Edilsoni had cultivated these passage ways, giving their planet an unending steam-driven soundtrack. They filled vents with crystals and cymbals, fashioned all manner of horns and harmonicas, even planted bamboo-like reeds where the steam could leak through, making music in every corner of their world. Of course, as one might imagine, this had more of an effect on the population than to simply dress up their days.

"There's no doubt about it, sir," said the aide hopelessly. "The Edilsoni sing and dance to make conversation. It seems they can't even understand races that simply 'talk' at them. In fact, they distrust any species that isn't comfortable doing so."

"Distrust?"

"Yes, sir," said the woman, absently as she continued to read from the stream crossing her handscreen. "Seems they even went to war with one of their in-system neighbors when they stopped up the steam vents on the grounds of their consulate here."

Captain Alexander Benjamin Valance found himself as close to despair as ever he had been since taking command of the *Roosevelt*. "Why," he thought, imploring what gods might be left in his ever-shrinking corner of the galaxy, "do these things keep happening to me?"

This was worse than when his crew had shaved the sacred monkeys of Templeworld. Or when they had conned the guards of the Pen'dwaker Holding Facility into allowing them to transform the prison into a gambling den for their Intergalactic Crap Shoot of the Millennium tournament. Or even when they had sponsored their infamous inter-species mixer where they introduced the debutante daughters of the leading politicians of the Pan-Galactic League of Suns to the various bears, cows, pigs, and chimps they were transporting to the Inter-Galaxy Zoo on Chamre XI.

It was worse than when they had stolen the *Roosevelt* and declared war on a cookie factory, more disastrous than when their pie fight had clogged the ship's protonic engines with strawberry, pineapple, and cheesecake filling, along with graham cracker crumbs, whipped creme, and rhubarb. Of course, such nonsense could not impede the performance of such mighty machines, but it did play havoc with Admiral Morey's white-glove-and-I'm-not-kidding inspection.

It was, in his opinion, worse than anything they had ever done before and most likely would do any time soon. Because, quite simply, for once his insane-as-a-flock-of-dice-addled-cephalopods crew had not done anything. He had no one upon whom he might cast the blame for this one. For once, the captain of the *Roosevelt* was as stuck as stuck could be, with no options in sight.

"So," he said, weakly, looking for a third highball while turning to the others in the room, those others besides himself responsible for getting the most important treaty in the history of Earth signed, "who's got any really bright ideas?"

The thundering lack of enthusiastic response did not surprise him greatly.

"Tell me again," asked Noodles, not at all certain about the wisdom involved in what he and Rocky were attempting, "why is it we're stealing a shuttle craft and heading for the surface?"

"Look, little buddy," answered the gunnery officer while he gave Quartermaster Harris the high-sign that they were ready to launch. "The captain is tied up in knots about his meetin' with these beachballs down below—right? Now, it seems gettin' these mugs on board with the Confederation is a big deal and so, I was thinkin', if we could crack whatever the big problem is, we could kinda make up for some of the little improprieties we've . . . well, you know . . ."

"Getting ourselves court-marshalled would probably add some small ray of happiness to the captain's otherwise present dismal outlook."

"You machinist, you're always so gloomy."

"That's only the machinists who run around with Italians."

"Look," replied Rocky, as he eased the shuttle out the side bay doors while Technician Second Class Thorner kept the perimeter radar jumbled so they might avoid detection, "we're a couple of clever guys. We figure out how to smooth things so the Confederation beats the League and all the other bozos to signin' up this bunch, and we'll be spendin' the rest of our days sittin' around swimmin' pools."

"With cleaning equipment," responded a particularly glum Noodles under his breath. He did not bother to argue further, though. Once Rocky had made his mind up on something, it was rare the machinist was ever able to talk him out of it. The reasons why he went along with said schemes were many and varied.

First, he liked Rocky and did not want to see him end up in more trouble than he could handle. Second, he was fairly certain the gunner had saved his life during one of their many drunken escapades, and so he felt a certain amount of obligation on that front as well. He also had to admit Rocky had a point. The *Roosevelt* on the whole would be in for tough times if Edilson decided to take a pass on joining the Confederation of Planets. Lastly, however, he went along with his pal's crazy plans usually because it just always turned out to be more fun doing things his way.

Machinists are a dull lot, he thought, keeping the notion as quiet within his noggin as possible. He would never admit to such a thing, of course. If questioned on the verve and vigor of his profession, he would point to the many fine activities he and the rest of the ship's tool jockeys enjoyed, from their shipwide Call of Cthulhu LARPs and their free-style origami fold-offs, to the week out of every year they lived for, their Sexy-Robot-Building Competition. Privately, he feared Intelligence Officer DiVico's assessment, "I've seen lead foil that was snappier than the average machinist," might sadly be true.

Regardless, it was but a matter of minutes after take-off that the pair of gobs found themselves loose in the capital city of the planet Edilson. After walking about more or less aimlessly for a half an hour, confident from their observation of various street signs and cafe notices that Edilson to Pan-Galactic to Earth Basic 9.8 translation was more or less working fine enough, Rocky approached a passing rubbery watermelon of an Edilsoni and asked;

"So, what's the story around here, chief?"

Bending back and forth so that all the eyes ringing its head could scrutinize the individual addressing it, the random citizen decided it had no idea what this bizarre new species wanted and, doing its best to make a motion with its shoulderless body that would translate to an alien as a confused shrug, it went about its business. The gunner gave his buddy a look meant to convey his mixture of confusion and annoyance, then tried again with the next native to pass by. The results were the same.

After that, both sailors attempted to communicate with the locals, trying this or that different idiom, working to keep their questions as simple as possible in case their problem was merely some translation difficulty. Nothing helped. Eventually, having been working on questioning a large flow of Edilsoni moving toward a stadium of sorts, they found themselves having been moved along with the flow to where they were indoors, awaiting some sort of performance. Frustrated, but hoping whatever was about to be presented on the field before them would give them some sort of clue, they managed to purchase a container of what seemed to be fried, bacon-flavored grass, and two milky fruit drinks which came in a kind of squeeze-bag affair. As they settled in, an announcer came out onto a small side stage and sang an introduction.

Since it seemed that all that he was introducing was the formal presentation from some alien world or the other to the Edilson government, the need for a tune-filled introduction struck the two humans as odd. When it turned out the aliens making the presentation were Danierians, Rocky and Noodles both began to titter with amusement. Bulbous, dour, and as exciting as a panda in fishnet stockings, the boys chuckled over how utterly awful the following would have to be.

"Danierians are gonna try and get these guys' attention," scoffed Rocky. "Now this, I'm glad I'm here ta see."

The chief gunnery officer's joy was short-lived. As he and Noodles finished off the last of their Crunchy Goodness snack pack, a troop of some four hundred Danierian warriors, outfitted in full battle gear, marched onto the field from three triangularly situated entrances. Flags unfurled, horns blaring, drums setting down an impressively unshakable cadence, the troopers met in the center of the parade ground, shouting out in their lumbering cadence as they began to file into formation;

"Denieria, it is our home,
That roasting world, so far away,
Denieria, its red sky and foam,
It's the best, on *any* day."

Looking first at each other, Rocky and Noodles then began to scan the crowd around them. Unlike their attempts to communicate with the Edilsoni on the streets, the Danierians were getting through to the natives. Indeed, as their simple forward marches began to intertwine, the crowd began tapping their tentacles to the martial rhythm.

"We're here to tell you about our world,
How splendid it is, to live in peace,

With Danierian banners, everywhere unfurled,
And all strife and despair made to cease."

"Noodles," asked Rocky, "is this as bad as I'm thinkin' it is?" When the machinist nodded in agreement, his partner answered, "Yeah, I was afraid of that."

"The galaxy is filled with lies,
Other races present intentions, but disguise
Their true meaning,
There's no gleaning,
What, oh what, is an innocent race to do?"

Rocky shuddered, thinking he had a good idea what was about to be suggested.

"Face front! And join
The United Coalition
Of Danierian Worlds.

Be a member of the winning team,
It's a lone and vulnerable planet's
Dream come true!

As the marching and singing continued, Noodles was struck by how the Edilsoni were responding to the ever-more-intricate step-pattern the warriors below were developing. With increasingly complicated side turn, with each spin of their weapons and the tossing of banners from one team to another, the native inhabitants gave out with more and louder appreciative whistling noises. And then, the warriors offered up their next-to-final chorus;

"Others offer chaos,
We bring rules,
Those who turn down order,
We slaughter as fools!"

Eliciting cheers from every corner of the arena. As the Danierian Dress Guard broke into an even tighter, and it must be said rather snappy (well, snappy for Danierians), close order drill, chanting "Go Danieria" on every left step, the Edilsoni
began singing to one another and performing a variety of three-legged jigs which left the two sailors both astounded and, it had to be admitted, a touch frightened.

"Submit to our will,
It's for your own good,
Don't wonder if we kill,
Just do what you should."

"Little buddy," whispered Rocky, "I'm thinkin' we'd better get back to the *Roosevelt*. The captain's gonna wanta know about this."

"He's not going to want to know it," answered Noodles, reaching for his bag o'juice, "but he needs to."

And with that, the swabbies returned to their borrowed shuttle craft, even as the Edilsoni picked up the admittedly catchy chorus of "Submit, Submit, just do it," sending its singular message wafting out over their capital city in all directions.

"So," asked Rocky quietly, "just how much trouble are we in, captain?"

"Vespucci," sighed Valance, heavily, "you only did what you did for ship and homeworld, and you did good, so let's just say you two have a bit of credit in reserve against your next knuckleheaded shenanigan—all right?"

"Sweet deal, sir."

At that point the *Roosevelt*'s commanding officer moved into as high a gear as his hangover would permit. With confirmation of the true nature of Edilsoni communication in hand, as well as intelligence on how effective had been the Danierians singing and marching negotiation, he dismissed the two gobs while ordering a channel opened to Earth High Command at once. Quickly outlining his overwhelmingly insurmountable problem, his desperate honesty was rewarded with the worst type of military logic.

Since his was the only ship in the area, the mission was still his. And, since he was the ranking officer, he and his diplomatic staff would simply have to dance and sing their way into the hearts of the planetary government and win the day. In the meantime, while Valance and his command staff were reduced to trying to form a not-completely-painful-to-listen-to barbershop quartet, Rocky and Noodles headed for the galley to wash down their planetside snacks with something a little more substantial than milk juice.

"Listen," said Noodles, after finishing his fourth tall and frosty mug of something-more-substantial, "you know, I wonder what the captain's going to do."

"Not our concern," answered his pal. "Hey, we're heroes for once. Little tiny minor heroes, sure. But, considerin' the esteem we're usually held in around here, I'll take it."

The machinist nodded, non-commitally. Rocky was right. The two of them had pushed their luck within the bounds of Navy regs to an extreme not seen since a drunken Admiral Chester William Nimitz had attempted to steer an aircraft carrier up the Venetian canals in search of a combination pizza parlor/chianti distributor/bordello he had been assured by Enrico Curuso was "really primo." Still,

it was not in the machinist's internal make-up to simply allow nature to take its course. Running his finger around the inside of his mug to get the last delightful bits of foam, he licked up the delicious residue, then said;

"So, you think the captain can handle things?"

"Well, sure," answered Rocky automatically. Draining his own mug, he added with an equal lack of thought, "the captain's aces. Ain't he got us outta every mess we ever got ourselves into? He don't ever need any help—he's always got the answer."

"Not to be contrary, Rock, but . . . if the captain didn't ever need any help, then he wouldn't need a crew."

It was not so much Noodles' words, but the tone with which he delivered them that caught the gunnery officer's attention. Squinting hard, as if that might instantly negate the effects of his own eight tall portions of more-substantial, Rocky finally answered;

"You mean, you think the captain maybe can't handle singin' these guys into the Confederation?"

"Do you remember his trying to teach Christmas carols to those kids back on Embri?" The gunner shuddered at the memory, his fingers unconsciously reaching up to his ears to see if they were bleeding.

"So," asked Rocky, fairly certain he knew the answer he would receive, "you're sayin' that ah . . . you want us to steal a shuttle on the same day we already stole one shuttle, and then use said shuttle to head back down to the planet so we can interfere with the most important mission the *Roosevelt* was ever given?"

"Yeah—you want'a?"

"Hey," answered the gunner, grinning from ear to ear, "does the Buddha drink Mint Juleps?"

"Isn't that usually my line?"

"Ahhhh, tell it to the board of inquiry."

"Oh yeah," laughed Noodles. "Good thinking."

And, with no other pints of more-substantial in sight, the two swabbies got down to planning their course of action.

❖

In all honesty, Captain Valance would never have believed it was possible for four people to sweat so intently. Indeed, the puddle growing around his feet, as well as those of the Roosevelt's intelligence officer, her diplomatic attaché, and the ship's doctor, was spreading with such vigor, it left the Edilsoni to wonder if the human contingent might not actually be melting. To be fair, the makeshift quartet had tried their darnest, calling upon the spirit of a thousand long-sung sea chanteys to aid them in their hour of desperation.

Sadly, though, King Neptune had not seen fit to shower them with any such bounty. In fact, it had to be admitted that their feeble attempts to harmonize had failed so miserably that the Edilsoni's visceral reaction to their singing was the only thing that kept the aliens from noticing how utterly terrible the humans' lyrics were. Finally, when the four paused for a breath at the same moment, although it was obvious they had only covered a third of their points, the Edilsoni prime minister practically fell over his podium as he leaped forward to interrupt, asking if that concluded the Earth Confederation's presentation. Valance was just about to throw in the proverbial towel, considering losing the planet and his commission favorable to provoking interstellar warfare, when suddenly a shout was heard from the back of the amphitheater.

"If you kind and noble Edilsoni will permit,
I'd like to step up, while you sit . . . ,"

As Valance stared in disbelief, he saw Machinist First Mate Li Qui Kon actually doing a handy little two-step, making his way in between the central two rows of spectators down toward the staging area where he and his fellow officers had been dying by inches.

"And discuss with you the ramifications,
Of inter-galactic political integrations."

Reaching the captain and his officers, Rocky urged them to vacate the stage, telling them in an exaggerated stage whisper;

"Don't worry, sir. I think he knows what he's doin'."

"But Vespucci," answered Valance, "singing and dancing . . . a machinist?"

"With all due respect, a *Chinese* machinist, sir."

"There are species descended from fish and bugs,
Others that crawled up from oozing slugs,
Some came from birds and some from rats,
Insects, clams, giraffes and bats,"

"Chinese moms, sir," added Rocky. "How'd he say it? They expect their kids to . . . well, they have to be a credit to their family."

"And they're all fine, in their own way,
But they're kind of singular, I must say,
Bred for a certain uni . . . form . . . ity,
They lack that one human odd . . . i . . . ty."

"Mrs. Kon, you see . . ."

"The thing that makes us the ones to choose,
That quality that guarantees you never lose,
It's our single greatest facility . . .
Our hard-won, irritating . . .

"Un . . . pre . . . dic . . . ta . . . bility!"

"She wanted an entertainer in the family."

And then, at a hand signal from Noodles, waiting in a lurkercraft hidden in the clouds, Technician Second Class Thorner began their free-air music broadcast, as well as sending down a blinding purple spotlight, illuminating the machinist in an iridescent glow as he warbled—

"Oh, everything's better with monkeys,
We're the best bet in the show,
I'm certain you're getting a lot of offers,
But trust me, simian's the way to go."

While Noodles spun around, setting himself up for the next stanza, Rocky caught the captain's ear once more, telling him;

"Five years of tap and jazz dance, six of voice training, and apparently eight years of piano which, from what he says, were a really serious mistake."

"Yes everything's better with monkeys,
They're curious, funny, and true,
They'll stand by your side, go along for a ride,
And they'll make sure you get what you're due."

As Noodles went into a complicated dance routine, one that seemed to Rocky he had seen in a revival of "My Fair Lady," the two of them had been lured into by promises of a different type of entertainment, the gunnery officer and his captain began to notice that the crowd was responding favorably to the performance. Indeed, those who had been previously fleeing from the caterwauling of Valance and his officers actually seemed to be returning to their seats. While the captain dangerously tempted Fate by allowing his hopes to rise from actual imprisonment to a simple court-martial, Rocky sent the signal to Mac Michaels up above with Thorner to both turn up the music and begin the fountain of lights display. As the crowd began to "aaaaahhhhhhhhh" in synchronized harmony, Noodles went into his big finish.

"Yes, we earthlings, we make mistakes,
We've got our bad eggs, who will always disgrace,
We spill our own blood, and we're not always smart,
But the one thing I can assure you is . . .
The human race has . . . got . . . heart!"

And then, in that instant, even as the entire ship's company of the *Roosevelt* Machinist's Saturday Evening LARP Society surrounded the stage, decked in full costume from their upcoming Bambi versus Godzilla extravaganza, accompanied by all the final entries in the Sexiest Robot of All Time competition, all around the stadium Edilsoni began to jump up from their seats. Unable to restrain themselves, the rotund aliens began humming and dancing, slapping tentacles, spinning on their mouths, and in short throwing themselves with total abandon into the fierce joy of Noodle's song.

"We're not perfect,
We don't claim to be,
Hell what do you expect?
Twenty thousand years ago,
We were all still monkeys!

"But you can trust me, you can trust that fact,
'Cause even after all this time,
You throw crap at us,
And I guarantee . . .
We'll throw it right back!"

The captain, of course, could only be overjoyed by the obvious shift in the average Edilsonian attitude toward humanity. But Rocky was set to wondering. He had seen the response the natives had shown the Danierians. They had gotten into the rhythm of things, had seemed ready to sign on to the program, so to speak. But, the reaction to Noodle's presentation was overwhelming. The aliens were actually dropping down onto the stadium grounds and rushing the stage, eager to join the machinists' newly forming macarana formation.

"But we'll stand at your side,
We'll be there at the end,
We make lousy dictators,
But we make really good friends.

"Yes, everything's better with monkeys,
The bad ones mixed in with the good,
So, show a little trust, but keep your eye on us,
And everything—
I'm saying just *everything*—
Will work out, as it . . . sshhhoooouuuullllddddd!"

And in that moment, as Noodles dropped to one knee and delivered the greatest display of jazz hands since Bob Fosse starred in "The Al Jolson Story," the long unfathomed secret of the Edilsoni came to light. Although the race *could* communicate through speech, they were *actually* a telepathic species, one bound by a hive mentality. As the native population cheered, not just there in the capital city's stadium, but across every continent, in every corner of the planet, their human guests' minds were suddenly filled with billions of voices, all of them sharing in the wonder that was the unquestionable uniqueness of the human race.

"Do you get it, Vespucci," shouted the captain, straining to be heard over the multitudinous ringing within his mind, "the Edilsoni have rejected every offer that's come their way because no one else has ever opened up completely to them!"

"Jiminy," answered Rocky, still a little befuddled over exactly what had happened, being distracted as he was by coordinating the start of the *Roosevelt* fireworks display, "I didn't think his song was that good."

"It's not the song," cried Valance, tears streaming down his face as an utterly alien race's reflected understanding of the true nobility of the human spirit washed through his mind, "it's not the song."

What happened over the next few days became somewhat of a blur in the intergalactic news items out of the Kebb Quadrant, the official reports sent fromthe *Roosevelt* back to the Confederation, and to be honest, in the minds of most of the ship's crew. That last, however, had more to do with the planet-wide party spontaneously thrown by every individual on Edilson than with any deficiency in the human ability to comprehend the situation.

Distrustful of aliens who masked their true intent, the Edilsoni had turned down every offer of alliance over the two hundred years since first contact.

Understanding better than any others the upcoming importance of their world, they had kept communications open with all, dangling the hope of eventual alliance with one world, or league, or whatever, to keep any one of them from invading.

"Four hundred of your years," their prime minister eventually sang to Valance, "is not a great deal of time, galactically speaking, but it did give us some room in which to maneuver."

They had responded as well as they had to the Danierians because, vicious and cruel as that race might be, at least they were honest about it. Their warriors had held nothing back emotionally on the field, and for once someone had shown the Edilsoni true intent. Luckily, as the prime minister was happy to admit, someone else had come along and done the same who had something better to show.

The surprise hit of the negotiations, or whatever one would call the drunkeninsanity that had transpired on Edilson, had been the trio of Thorner, Harris, and Michaels, who had taken to the stage in their dress kilts to not only sing the Scottish ballad, the Blue Ribbon song, but to show off the fact that the Edilsoni were not the only sentient beings around who walked on three legs. Valance had been mortified at first, but the riotous response of the natives to the spontaneous gesture had been so positive the captain had been given no choice other than to return to attempting to drink the prime minister under the table.

In the end, the Confederation of Planets got the wished-for deal with Edilson. Valance was showered with praise from Earth Central, which he translated into as much shore leave and good favor as he possibly could for his crew. The next issue of the Monthly Newsletter of the Grand Gaggle of Confederation Machinists tripled in size and, once the ship's doctor had been able to synthesize enough Hangover-B-Gone, the crew of the *Roosevelt* had been able to finally remember how to break orbit and set a course that did not skew to a basanova beat.

Heroes all, loved and admired by an entire world, showered with gifts, the men and women of the *Roosevelt* set off for whatever the universe had in store for them next. The Edilsoni could tell the earthlings were reluctant to leave, and yet somehow eager to be on to whatever came next, and loved them all the more for it. But, beyond that display of all-too-human confusion of purpose, beyond everything they had heard and felt and learned of the gorilla-spawn who had won their hearts, there was one single moment that gave them greater insight than any other.

Being a collective species, having no actual experience with the idea of male or female, sons and daughters, or any of the other mammalian building blocks of individuality, nothing revealed more to the Edilsoni about their human visitors than when the prime minister met privately with Noodles. Asking the machinist what boon he might ask for his part in that which a united Edilson believed was the cementing of their security for the next four centuries, offering him anything the wealth and might of an entire planetary treasury might secure, the sailor asked if he might send a real-time message.

Yes, Noodles explained, he could send notes to Earth via the *Roosevelt*, but because of the distance they could take months, sometimes *years* to reach their intended destination. He did not want to send anything exceedingly long, he told them, just a few words. Understanding his request, touched to the core of what he had thought until meeting human beings was an emotionless heart beating within his breast, the prime minister not only agreed, but without the machinist's knowledge, he sent his own note as well.

Which is why, while the U.S.S. *Roosevelt* broke orbit and headed back out to their next destination in the stars, on the planet Earth, at 12/17 Seloon Street in one of the quieter corners of Canton, China, Mrs. Xiu Yue Kon received two messages. One that read;

"Thanks, Mom."

And a second that read;

"Yes, good Earthwoman, thank you, indeed."

From BY OTHER MEANS
Book Three in the Defending The Future series

Mother of Peace by James Chambers
Blankets by Jeff Young
Sheepdog by Mike McPhail
Devil Dancers by Robert E. Waters
Dawn's Last Light by John G. Hemry

MOTHER OF PEACE

James Chambers

THEY PROWLED THE GHOST CITY BY NIGHT AND HUNTED THE THOUGHTS OF DEAD machines. Dr. Bell told them it was the only way to win the war. Find the old weapons and reactivate them. They had all heard it before, but she repeated it when they moved out of the jade moonlight into the shadows of a crumbling tenement row. It was her way of saying "Be careful" as they detoured around a dirty bomb hotspot leftover from a battle fought before any of them were born. Dr. Bell hoped Calypso's contact did not lie inside the high-becquerel zone. The sievert count there was more than the thin-skin suits they were wearing could deflect.

As they neared the next avenue, Sergeant Tanner ordered the squad to stop and sent two soldiers to scout the intersection. His voice came over Dr. Bell's earpiece. "Can your mutant give us a location yet?"

"How many times must I tell you he's not a mutant?" Dr. Bell said. "Why don't you ask him yourself?"

"Figured he already knew I was wondering."

"He gave his word he won't peek into your head without permission."

"How would I know if he did?"

"You wouldn't," Dr. Bell said.

She missed Sergeant Williams, whom Tanner had replaced two weeks ago, but she reminded herself it had taken almost three months for Calypso to earn Williams' trust. It would take Tanner time too. Leaders did not like telepaths. Dr. Bell considered it fortunate that most of their squad had been together so long now that they treated her and Calypso as equals. Despite the growing number of telepaths appearing in the population, most people still considered them outcasts.

"If this duty doesn't suit you, Sergeant," Dr. Bell said, "I'll support your request for reassignment."

"No, ma'am," Tanner said. "The brass handed me this job, and I intend to do it."

The two scouts returned, crouched low. Dr. Bell thought they looked nervous, but it was difficult to read expressions through their faceplates. Her earpiece went silent as Tanner switched to another channel for their report. The men gestured high and low at the intersection then separated and took new cover.

"Hey, Calypso," Tanner spoke over the squad's open link. "You got a hard twenty on our contact yet?"

"Narrowed it to two blocks," Calypso said. "But we're on the wrong side of the hotspot. Shortest route is south at the next avenue, thirty blocks downtown, then cut over on 14th Street and loop back uptown about five blocks. Should be somewhere around there."

"Can't take the next avenue," Tanner said. "Enemy presence there."

"How many?" Dr. Bell asked.

"Three locations for sure. Two ground level. One high, probably a sniper. Six men minimum. Could be more."

"Let me feel it out," Calypso said. The comm link went quiet for several seconds, and then Calypso came back. "There are eighteen, at least. All Chinese. Calm thoughts. They don't know we're here."

"Thank god for small favors," Tanner said. "Okay, let's turn back before we blip their radar."

Dr. Bell shuddered. This was the strongest contact Calypso had made since she taught him how to recognize the brain waves that identified a Centry warcraft. She did not want to lose it. She had searched for missing Centries across North America for two decades and found only rusted-out wrecks littered on old battlefields. The cybernetic machines, built to end the war, were meant to last a hundred years, but after thirteen months in the field the entire system had collapsed. Many units were destroyed in battle; most vanished and their tracking units went dark. But despite the quixotic nature of Dr. Bell's commitment to finding a live one and reigniting the program, the top brass had not yet lost faith in her.

Dr. Bell thought at Calypso, *Will you make this contact again if we don't find the source tonight?*

To allow instantaneous communication, she had given him standing permission to scan her surface thoughts, keeping anything personal behind a mental barrier. She did not like the hesitation in Calypso's reply.

Maybe, he thought. *But you know how it is. We've been through this city before, no contact like this. Things are how they are right now, today. It feels good. We should go for it.*

Calypso had been with Dr. Bell since he was eight when she found him hiding alone in a bombed-out school. That was ten years ago, and he had been helping her ever since then. He wanted to end the war as much as she did. He would have been out front of the squad running for the contact if only he were allowed.

Dr. Bell braced herself and then told Tanner, "We can't turn back."

Tanner unleashed a string of profanities, but he stopped short of demanding a retreat. Dr. Bell rode out his tirade and explained that they could not risk losing the contact. She had full authority for such decisions. She did not have to justify them, but she did not want to antagonize Tanner.

After Tanner calmed down, she said, "Find another route."

With a mumbled curse, Tanner clicked off comm. He scrambled across the street to where his second-in–command, Corporal Dolan, was crouched behind the blackened skeleton of a city bus. The two officers conferred, and then Tanner's voice came over the open link.

"Subway entrance off the avenue. Uptown side of the intersection. If the tunnel isn't blocked we can walk under the ambush points and come up six blocks south of our target then double back. Should cover us."

"Assuming no one's waiting in the tunnel," said Dolan.

"I can give a warning if anyone's there," Calypso said. "They won't get the drop on us."

"Fine. But down there, you and Dr. Bell bring up the rear," Tanner said. "Ladies and gents, weapons ready. Let's go."

Following Tanner's lead the squad spread out and edged toward the avenue. Moonlight tinged faint green by a haze of dust and ash fell like water over their thin-skins. The transparent suits reflected their environment, blurring the soldiers and giving them a sort of shimmering camouflage. Dr. Bell checked the clip in her rifle while she waited for Calypso to fall in ahead of her. She knew if the tunnel was blocked Sergeant Tanner would insist on turning back, and he would be right. But it would not be fair, not after so long, when she was so close, and so much was at stake. More than any other contact she had traced in recent years, she felt this was the one for which she had spent so long looking, the one that would lead to all the others.

As they neared the intersection, Tanner ordered everyone to drop to their bellies and snake-crawl through the rubble. Ahead of them was a gap in cover. Beyond a burned-up delivery truck, an explosion had left a shallow crater and scattered the rubble. It was a space of only about fifteen feet, but for the time it took them to round the corner and descend into the subway station, they would be exposed.

"Don't like that blank spot," Tanner said.

"I see it," Dr. Bell said. "We'll have to be fast."

"You and Calypso go first. With me. Get you down the stairs before they can take a shot if they see us."

Dr. Bell thought the plan to Calypso, who agreed, and then the two wormed their way to Tanner's side. The squad surveyed the avenue. Through night-sights, the enemy positions were visible by turquoise splotches that marked the half- hidden faces of the hostile soldiers. Otherwise the cracked street was desolate.

"Can you figure their locations?" Tanner asked Calypso.

"They're not far, between us and the contact," Calypso said. "Sorry, I can't be more specific at this range."

Tanner put Dolan in charge of bringing the rest of the squad into the tunnel. Then keeping low, he darted like a ghost across the gap and disappeared into the deep shadows of the entrance. Calypso went five seconds later, a blur flashing through the gloom. Dr. Bell followed him, moving fast on the cybernetic, prosthetic legs that let a woman in her fifties keep up with the others. Tanner directed her down the stairs, where Calypso was scanning the subway station with an LED lamp. It looked clear except for old litter. Dolan came next and relieved Tanner at the entrance. Then the rest of the squad rushed into the gap.

Dr. Bell froze the moment she heard the whistling sound coming from the sky. It sounded like a howling wind, but she knew it was an anti-personnel, fragmentation mortar, a glorified grenade, but nasty, like the one that had stolen her legs and left arm, and condemned her to rely on prosthetic limbs. It had taken the life of her unborn child too. She grabbed Tanner with her cybernetic arm and dragged him downstairs. Dolan bolted down the steps from street level, shouting over the comm for everyone to take cover. Bell thrust Tanner into the darkness then clutched Calypso by the waist and leapt after him.

The whistling became a clipped shriek.

Then the missile hit.

The subway station trembled.

Flame and smoke and shattered concrete flooded down the stairs. For a moment Corporal Dolan was part of it, a twisting, tumbling ragdoll, and then the cloud enveloped him, and he was gone. The shockwave rolled through the station, cracking the information booth windows and slamming Dr. Bell to the floor. Calypso's voice stayed in her head, letting her know he was all right. She shouted for Tanner, but the rumble of the explosion drowned out any reply. Dr. Bell rolled until she bumped up against something hard. She curled into a ball and covered her head with her cybernetic arm. After a while, the concentrated chaos faded away to a plastic stillness broken by dripping bits of stone and ceiling tile.

Through the dust cloud, Dr. Bell found Calypso against the iron bars of the turnstile gate. She tried to raise Tanner on the comm. He came through sounding faint and faraway to Dr. Bell's explosion-deadened ears. She and Calypso located the Sergeant and helped him to his feet. They found Dolan dead at the bottom of the stairs, half buried in a frozen sluice of rubble that had sealed the station entrance.

"We're trapped," Tanner said. He pulled Dolan's dog tags from his neck and stuck them in a pouch on his belt.

"I'm so sorry." Dr. Bell would miss Dolan. He had saved her life twice.

"Most of the others are still alive. I sense them," Calypso said. "Enemy soldiers came on foot after the mortar strike. Now it's a firefight."

"And not a damn thing I can do to help them," said Tanner. "Can't even raise them on the comm link."

"It's the radiation." Dr. Bell gestured toward the ceiling. "Or the old pipes and wires in the ground. Communications are always sketchy in the city."

"Sarge," Calypso said. "If you want, I can convey your orders to Private Rasmussen. He gave me permission to talk to him thought to thought. At this range, I should be able to pick him out of the crowd."

Tanner frowned. "Alright, tell them we're alive. Tell them to fall back and withdraw. Return with reinforcements to wipe out those enemy installations."

"What about us?" Dr. Bell said.

"Unless you can clear half a ton of rubble from this exit, we're going down the tunnel, like we planned."

Dr. Bell raised an eyebrow.

"You said it was a good contact, didn't you?" Tanner said.

"The best we've ever had."

"Yeah, well, I want to see this war over as much as anyone, so let's do our job. To hell with whoever tries to stop us."

They clipped LED lamps onto their chests then jumped the turnstile. Tanner led them to the end of the platform and down the steps to track level. The tunnel looked empty and deathly still. The city had been so hard hit by the war that Dr. Bell doubted even rats were left down here. There were not enough people in the city to support them, and unlike cockroaches, they could not live in the irradiated places. Tanner went first and Bell took the rear with Calypso between them. After they went only a few yards, the station was lost to the darkness behind them. Walking the railroad ties like steps, they settled into a steady pace along the center of the downtown track, traveling in a bubble of icy light. The gray concrete walls caked with dirt and soot never changed. The only colors there were the faded remnants of red and yellow warning signs.

Rounding a curve, they entered the next station and found an abandoned subway train. Calypso detected no one inside. Tanner led them onto the platform, and they flashed their lights through the grimy windows as they walked the length of the train. Most cars were empty, but in some were broken skeletons dressed in rotted clothing.

"What do you think happened?" Tanner said, as they left the dead train behind them.

"They probably came down here to hide from the fighting," Dr. Bell said.

"Not with the people on the train. With the Centry program. You've been after this longer than I've been in uniform. Figure you must have some theories."

Sooner or later, Dr. Bell had this conversation with almost everyone who came into the squad. They had all grown up with the mystery of the Centry program and its shattered promise of victory and peace. The warcrafts were like flying tanks with human intuition and responsiveness, thanks to the brains of mortally wounded soldiers implanted in them. They coordinated via a satellite link, now believed dead, and from the day they hit the field, they had succeeded in halting the enemy advance and pushing them back. For one year, victory was in sight. Now Dr. Bell thought the brass kept her going only to stoke the embers of that hope. After two hundred years of fighting, every day was a like a hard crack in the face. Resources were so depleted that some battles were being fought with swords and pikes, and the food supply often fell to subsistence levels. The prospect of ending the war in a day, however improbable, helped a lot of people get up in the morning. Dr. Bell remembered that whenever she answered a question like Tanner's.

"A lot of things might have gone wrong," she said. "I think it was a flaw in the cybernetics programming. If I can correct it, maybe I can revive the sat link and fix the others. The Centries were built to be self-sustaining for a hundred years, so there's a chance I can bring back online any machines that are still intact."

"You work on the original program?"

"I was twenty-one when Centry began. If you were going into the sciences then, you were contributing to Centry. That's what I did for more than ten years until it all went live. Then a year later, the Centries were gone, and the only work left was this. These days I'm the only one who hasn't given up the ghost."

She did not tell Tanner the real reason she kept looking or why she kept coming back to search this same city. She had shared that with no one. She suspected Calypso had pieced it together, because he knew the last reported coordinates for each Centry as well as she did. He knew the three Centries that had gone down in this area. But he would never dare ask her. Anyway, it was better to hide the personal element or risk people seeing her work as a crusade, which she knew it was not. If she was right about why Centry failed and if she could find one live Centry craft, even if not the one she most wanted, she really did stand a chance of ending the war. And in the end her reason for doing what she did—personal or not—was the only real reason there was for fighting in the first place.

The station closest to their target location was clear, but it was on the edge of the hotspot, so they kept moving. Two stops later, they entered the 14th Street Station on its lowest level, and then tracked up the stairs behind Tanner. They went slow, with weapons ready, even though Calypso told them no one was there. On the station's main level, they found part of the ceiling caved in by something that had left an enormous cavity filled with layers of wreckage. Faint moonlight poured through gaps in the rubble. The scale of destruction suggested a crashed vehicle or an unexploded missile. Dr. Bell walked to the edge of the debris and pushed aside a chunk of concrete. She grabbed a length of broken rebar and used it to pry away large pieces, working with the strength of her prosthetics until she exposed an edge of blue-gray metal.

Calypso and Tanner helped her. The three of them heaved away broken concrete and chunks of shattered tile until they uncovered part of a pitted hull painted with call letters and the American flag. Beneath the flag were embossed captain's bars and the name "McCardle." Dr. Bell flashed her lamp around the debris then leapt halfway up the mound and scrambled on top of the pile. She forced another chunk aside, her cybernetic legs giving her the power to shift it until it tumbled away. She pushed another and another, eliciting a warning from Tanner to watch where she was throwing rocks. The debris mound was too unstable for him and Calypso to climb, and they could not jump atop it like Dr. Bell.

"Get off there before it collapses," Tanner said.

Dr. Bell ignored him and continued excavating. The scales of a dead subway station tumbled off the pile. When Dr. Bell did leap down, her face was beaming.

"It's a Centry," she said. "It's hard to tell under all this wreckage, but I cleared the top of the hull, and there's no mistaking it. The cockpit is intact."

Tanner moved back to the metal hull and placed his hand on the painted American flag. Then he set down his rifle and shoved more rubble away from the craft. Calypso and Dr. Bell worked with him, moving hunks of fallen street and ceiling, rolling the pieces too big to lift, until they had cleared a recognizable section of the warcraft.

"Sonofabitch," Tanner said. "Exactly like the pictures."

"Didn't you believe me?" Dr. Bell said.

"That these things existed? Yes. That we'd find one intact after twenty years? Guess I figured they were all lost. Alright, let's call in a recovery crew."

"Not for this one. Not yet, at least."

"Why not?"

"This isn't the contact," Calypso said. He stared at the uncovered patches of the warcraft then placed his hand on the hull like Tanner had done. "I get no thought activity at all."

"Because he's dead," Dr. Bell said.

Calypso nodded. "I think so."

"How can you know?" Tanner said.

"He's been down here a long time, covered in rubble, cut off from the sun. The machinery may still work, and maybe the nuclear battery is still charged. But the nanites that kept the brain alive can't be. They were fueled by chlorophyll, and without sunlight, they wouldn't have lasted more than a few months. The brain plugged into the cockpit would have withered and died only a few days after the nanites stopped repairing its cells and manufacturing oxygen and nutrients. I'm sorry to say Captain McCardle has been dead a long time. I've found seven others like this over the years. Intact but dead."

"The contact is stronger here," Calypso said. "We're not far."

"It has to be topside somewhere," Dr. Bell said. "Exposed to the sky, but not in the open."

"Not getting out through here to look." Tanner nodded at the rubble-choked exits.

He jogged across the station to check the other stairways and found the southwest stairwell was passable. The trio climbed it to the street and surveyed the neighborhood. Although Calypso sensed people in the area, no one felt close enough to be an immediate threat. They spread apart, and Tanner led them, following Calypso's directions. The city was quiet. Mingled with the sky's brackish hue was the creamsicle glow of fires burning somewhere on the avenue. In a few hours it would be dawn, and the sun would cook off the night haze.

The contact grew stronger. Calypso was restless and wanted to go faster. Tanner tried to hold him back, but Calypso's excitement was contagious, and before long the trio was jogging. They crossed another block. Then ignoring Tanner's warnings, Calypso sprinted away.

"Down here!" he shouted.

Dr. Bell and Tanner raced after him.

"This way," Calypso said.

Tanner hollered for him to slow down and wait, but Calypso kept running. He vanished through the broken front doors of a high-rise office building.

Wait! We can't see you now, Dr. Bell thought at him.

Calypso thought back, *Okay, okay, but it's here, in this building, right on top of us. It's here! So let's go, slowpoke.*

Dr. Bell edged past Tanner, who yelled at her to slow down. Tanner tried to keep up, but Dr. Bell's prosthetic legs outpaced him. Running was one of the few times she felt grateful for her machine limbs, and Calypso was right. Now was the time to act. She was thirty yards from the building entrance when something like an invisible wasp buzzed by her head. Another came right after it. Time seemed to grind to a crawl, and Calypso's voice exploded through her mind.

Get down! Get down!

All around Dr. Bell the pavement spit up asphalt dust like a deep puddle splattering under a sudden rain. The air filled with humming, zipping sounds, and as Dr. Bell crouched and then leapt toward the building's broken entrance, hot stings drilled through her upper body. She cleared the distance on the power of her artificial legs and tumbled into the shelter of the pitch-black building lobby. In an instant Calypso was at her side, his thoughts a wild jumble of apologies for being distracted, for not sensing the sniper, for not warning her sooner. The raw emotion pouring out of him was overwhelming. For all his courage, in that moment, Calypso was only a boy convinced the woman who was like a mother to him was about to die. Dr. Bell gripped his hand and tried to soothe him.

Not your fault, she thought. *He was too far away for you to know he was dangerous. Don't blame yourself. Please. Not your fault.*

She thought it over and over, coaxing Calypso back from the edge of panic. And when she had helped him regain his focus, she asked him about Sergeant Tanner.

Calypso edged to the open doorways. *He's pinned down behind a dumpster. But I don't think he's hurt*, he thought.

How many enemy? Dr. Bell asked.

Only the sniper.

Then you have to take him. I know you don't want to, but you have to. Or Tanner might die.

She felt how fragile Calypso's spirit was now, and she hated the burden she was placing on him, but there was no other way. Calypso withdrew into the darkness.

You need my help, he thought.

Help Tanner first. You have to. Please.

Dr. Bell was grateful for the darkness. She was afraid of how Calypso might react if he saw her torn up and bloodied, and she needed him to act. She could not leave him alone out here. If her wounds were as bad as they felt, Sergeant Tanner might be the only one left to get him home.

Please, she thought. *Trust me. You do trust me, right?*

Of course, I do. You've done everything for me. I trust you more than anyone else.

Then do what I say. I know what I'm asking, and I know you can handle it. I wouldn't ask if it weren't the only way.

Dr. Bell felt Calypso's thoughts churning in the blackness between them. Then he extricated himself from Dr. Bell's mind to protect her from what he was about to do. The abrupt break startled her. Calypso crept back to the entrance, becoming a shadowy scarecrow. The gunfire had died down, but a fresh shot came every few seconds—the sniper letting Tanner know he was still there. Calypso planted his feet, and then what happened next happened in stillness and without a sound. A gunshot plinked off the dumpster. A few seconds passed. Another round shattered the glass off a lamppost behind Tanner. A few more seconds passed. The next bullet gouged concrete far from its target, and the next struck a window in a building on the next corner. Seconds passed. No other shot came.

It's done, thought Calypso. Then speaking over the comm link, he said, "All clear, Sergeant Tanner. Come in now. I'm sorry I didn't warn us. I won't let down my guard again. Please hurry. Dr. Bell is wounded."

His voice was laden with sadness. Dr. Bell knew the dying thoughts of the sniper were echoing through Calypso's mind. They would always be there. To think someone dead, as Calypso had done, required staying connected with the target's psyche until the very last moment, rewiring brain patterns for a suicide circuit, and the dying impressions were too powerful to ever forget. But she believed Calypso was strong enough to live with what he had been forced to do. When Tanner entered the lobby, he guided him to Dr. Bell.

"How bad is it?" Calypso asked.

Tanner flashed his lamp over Bell's body. "Pretty damn bad. Time to evac."

"No," Dr. Bell said. "We're too close. The contact's here. Pack my wounds. I can make it."

Tanner was already pressing field dressings over Dr. Bell's wounds. "Out of your mind if you think I'll let you go anywhere other than home," he said.

Dr. Bell pushed herself onto her knees.

"Shit. Don't move. You're hurt." Tanner tried to ease her back down.

With her cybernetic arm, Bell jolted Tanner aside and then forced herself to stand. Her breathing was shallow, and her heart was racing, but she was steady.

"We have to hurry," she said. "We might not find it again."

"You need a medic," Tanner said.

"Or what? I'll die. Like how many millions of others in this war. We don't have a lot of true choices in our lives, Sergeant. You're not taking this one away from me. I swear to you if this contact turns out to be a Centry, this all will have been worth it. And if I die then so be it. I've outlived too many people to care about that now. So, please, follow Calypso's directions."

Dr. Bell thought Tanner might face her down, but then he nodded and let Calypso lead them to a staircase at the back of the lobby. They climbed it. Dr. Bell, weak from blood loss, set her legs to automatic and let them carry her behind Calypso and Tanner.

They passed the fourth floor, then the fifth, and kept going. Dr. Bell expected they would have to climb to the roof. It was the only place that made sense for the contact to be. It took them about an hour to reach the roof access. Tanner broke the lock, and then they were back in the moonlight with a view of the dark city in every direction. The fires on the avenue were burning bright.

"Where?" Dr. Bell asked Calypso.

Spikes of pain drove through her chest, and her vision grayed for a moment. It was getting harder to breathe. She suspected she was bleeding into her lungs. Calypso looked frightened, and she knew she must look awful, covered in blood.

It's okay, she thought to him. *Believe in me. Where?*

At the center of the roof was a bulky ventilation unit. On the other side was the Centry, covered in thick dust. It looked peaceful, like it was sleeping. Dr. Bell, Tanner, and Calypso approached it.

"Incredible," Tanner whispered.

Calypso brushed dust from the hull to expose the call letters, American flag, and the name "Bowman" painted over captain's bars. Dr. Bell swallowed a sob. She had not realized that seeing him would resurrect so much of her grief. She anticipated then that even after all the years she had searched, she did not know if she had ever really expected to find him. She circled the craft, which aside from scrapes and dents looked undamaged. She opened a panel near the cockpit and accessed the diagnostic interface. Running off the nuclear battery, it was still lit and working. Dr. Bell checked the cockpit environment. The numbers for oxygen, nitrogen, temperature, and protein count all came up good. She cycled through the next batch of data then initiated a full system check. Two minutes later the display reported all systems, except the satellite link, running but they had not been activated outside of drill mode since the Centry program crashed.

"You're alive," she said. "Why won't you work?"

The machine did not answer.

"Calypso," she said. "It's time to use your training."

"It's not safe," he said. "I sense others in the building. They're coming up, hunting us."

"How many?" Tanner said.

"Half a dozen."

"Sniper must've alerted them," Tanner said. He checked his weapon and jogged toward the roof door. "Only one access point. I can hold them off, but not forever."

"We'll be quick. We have to be. If they find the Centry they'll destroy it," Dr. Bell said. "Now, like we practiced, Calypso, okay?"

Calypso nodded and then sat down in the shadow of the machine and closed his eyes.

Tanner watched. "What's he doing?"

"Entering the Centry's brain. He's going to link me to it, so I can see what went wrong."

Dr. Bell sat beside Calypso and held his hand. His mind touched hers and then guided her toward the Centry, and once she was in, he backed off, leaving her connected to Captain Bowman's brain. It amazed Dr. Bell how easy the connection was, and she wished she had known about telepaths when she was helping to build the Centries. The soldier's mind was stripped down, full of combat information, and packed with Centry programming. There were memories of battles and an intense, fiery vision that was the fight that had put Captain Bowman on the Centry roster. He had come in at the end, one of the last units to go online, and Dr. Bell remembered how it had crushed her to see his broken body in the operating room. She had not even known then that she was carrying his child.

She dug through scattered recollections and impressions. The Centry process struck a fine balance between removing enough memories to make a century of mechanized existence bearable while leaving enough to preserve the soldier's humanity. The latter were the memories Dr. Bell wanted.

Everything flickered. Calypso was straining to keep the connection open. Dr. Bell pushed deeper, moving her awareness past banks of codes and concepts that she had helped create. She forced her way down to the central core of Bowman's mind, and there she located the memory she wanted.

It was herself.

She was smiling, and there was sun in her hair.

She felt the softness of her skin the way Bowman had felt it the last time they had been together. His mind was trapped in that moment, cycling it like a loop. It had been designed that way to keep the Centries sedated when they were offline for repairs. A programming error had set the clocks running wrong, making it seem that a century had already passed when only little more than a year had gone by. The Centries had defaulted to maintenance mode, but because the glitch was only in one part of the programming, they could not complete the routine and return to their bases. Instead they had simply shut down, wherever they were, trapped in pleasant memories designated to sustain them through a prolonged state of inactivity. The simplicity of it made Dr. Bell furious. Someone's carelessness had allowed the war to go on long after it should have ended. Dr. Bell sharpened her focus. She felt the strain, in her body and her mind. Drawing on Calypso's help, she scanned Bowman's cybernetics programming until she located the error. She noted the code and the proper fix and thought them to Calypso, so that Bowman could be repaired when he was recovered.

I can do that now, thought Calypso.

What do you mean? Dr. Bell thought.

I can fix him. So much of the coding is embedded in his mind, it's like an open book to me. Calypso paused, and then thought, *I wish you had told me about him and you. I consider you my mother. Perhaps I could think of him as my father.*

Yes, think of him that way, but remember, not everything is meant to be shared between parent and child.

I understand, Calypso thought.

If you can fix him, please do.

I already did.

Dr. Bell felt the change flow through Bowman's mind as Calypso drew her out of it. She did not want to lose the connection. It had been so long since she had felt so close to anyone. The attack that wounded her and killed her unborn child had come only six months after the Centry program launched. She had been alone since then. Before she could protest, she was out of Bowman's psyche and back in her own.

Gunfire rattled the air.

Calypso was dragging her around the Centry for cover.

"They're at the door," he said.

Dr. Bell crawled to the diagnostic panel and checked the readings. They had switched from drill mode to duty mode, and even more amazing, the satellite link was back online. Bowman was fully functional again, and he was plugged into every other surviving Centry.

Can you do what you did to him for the others? Dr. Bell thought to Calypso. *Go through his mind like I went through yours, via the satellite link? All at once?*

Calypso did not answer right away.

Captain Bowman began to vibrate, and then he lifted off the ground, raising a blast of stale air.

He knows you're here and what you did, and he's grateful, Calypso thought. *He misses you, and he's...happy...to meet me.*

Stay with him as long as you can, thought Dr. Bell.

And, yes, Calypso thought, *I think I can do what you're asking.*

Then do it, please do it, don't wait, and don't worry about me, and don't miss me too much, Dr. Bell thought. *Only you truly understand what we've done here, and it's up to you to see it through, to win this war, for me, for us, for our family.*

The enemy broke through the door then, forcing Tanner to fall back, and then Dr. Bell saw Captain Bowman's shadow as he rose higher into the air. Her thoughts fell back inside her mind, and she was only herself, shivering from a cold wave spreading outward from her chest. She imagined the other Centries, the ones left alive all around the country, rising like Captain Bowman, the awakening of a ghost army, and then Bowman opened fire, cutting down the enemy soldiers in seconds. The roar and flash of gunfire filled Dr. Bell's senses. Calypso would be safe; he would be protected for what he could do as she had so long protected him. She was pleased to leave him with the prospect of victory and freedom and a better world than she had ever known. The echo of gunfire faded. Bowman's shadow darkened Dr. Bell's sight as he set down beside her. After that, she knew nothing more.

BLANKETS

Jeff Young

Collatoral damage, thought Kiersey staring at the small sandaled foot as he pulled more branches over the body. That's what Lieutenant Roberts would call this, but all Kiersey could see was a young boy who should have been running and playing. Their medic, Leigh looked over the casualty quickly and logged the cause of death as exposure. She had taken a blood sample for confirmation because Leigh was nothing if not diligent. *If the exploratory force from the Ross weren't here on the planet, well the kid at his feet might still be alive*—Kiersey cut himself off. *Time to reign it in and focus on the task at hand*, he thought.

"Eyes ahead, Kiersey. No way you get to keep looking at my ass."

Shaking his head, Kiersey stopped his impromptu burial to stare at Bangs. She wasn't just all talk; she had a bad habit of acting out of hand as well. Taking her LinAcc rifle in one hand she proceeded to wriggle suggestively. In a motion almost too fast to see Bangs dropped the rifle into her cradling hands and whipped around so that its bore faced Kiersey for a second and swung away.

"Bangs!" Roberts' voice cut through the comm, "Get on point and cut it."

She looked at Kiersey a moment longer, reshouldered her weapon, then slapped her ass before moving ahead. Shaking his head, Kiersey turned away from her antics. Tapping the contact plate on his temple twice brought up the enhancement and overlay to his vision. He pushed the viewpoint up and out until he could see all of the team highlighted in ghostly blue spread out over the floor of the valley. The Mosquito.net system of microaerosats that he'd deployed was spreading and increasing their coverage. Each one of the team had an aerosat shadowing them and Kiersey could view any individual—more importantly so could Roberts. To his left Anderev flanked Kiersey while Breadle and Peak brought up the rear. Heyer and Michaels ranged to right and Roberts stayed to the center.

"Move out," came Roberts' order.

Pulling the viewpoint even higher, Kiersey looked over the terrain. The team was working its way up the valley toward the highest point in the area and the targeted lookout emplacement. One valley over, the secondary team was moving slower, keeping to the hedgerows and avoiding the open areas of the tilled fields. Kiersey continued to spread the net, carefully maintaining a cautious overlap of each of the aerosat elements. The others all had their specialties and this was his. He felt a brief jab of satisfaction at the way he performed as the commtech.

While he'd listened earlier to Roberts' impassioned briefing about the necessity of securing Cansec, the Sylvan Seven world that was their current assignment, Kiersey was having trouble squaring what they'd been told with the limited amount of resistance the team had encountered. Where were the dangerous rebels that Roberts warned them of? The *Ross* had dropped teams now for two weeks and they received little resistance. The thought hit him—he'd served in enough action on heavily colonized worlds to know that the boy he'd buried could have easily carried a sizeable explosive device into a trusting company and wreaked havoc. But everything Kiersey saw pointed to someone who'd wandered out into the woods and died of natural causes. He tried to focus on that.

Anderev's hand on his shoulder brought him back into focus. Blinking, Kiersey readjusted his vision and nodded at the veteran combat specialist. With two fingers, Anderev gestured him forward and then loped off to the left resuming his position. The valley turned and now Kiersey could see the rise ahead. He pushed several mosquito.net 'sats ahead of them toward the target, keeping them high and spread wide. The group of 'sat's pinged him back—one kilometer ahead there were three IR sources that bore metallic returns moving toward the team. Kiersey flipped the info over to Roberts and the lieutenant called Bangs to a halt, sending the flankers ahead. Moments later weapon fire tore through the quiet of the tree-covered hillsides of the valley.

Transcript Committee Hearing, Sylvan Seven Atrocities

General Pressman: The war had stopped. We were simply unable to continue to promote an effective campaign against the renegade worlds. The systems which were dependent upon the support of the renegades and were within reach were recaptured and opposition was quelled. The remaining seven worlds continued to resist. We had the troop carriers, the troops, and the desire to finish the conflict, but we no longer had the backing or the finances. We were not given the option to stop the conflict.

Senator Wellheim: I'm sorry, General, maybe I misunderstood. You told me you couldn't continue.

General Pressman: Under traditional methods, we had no means of an assured victory.

Senator Wellheim: You seem to be implying that you were considering alternatives; alternatives that perhaps were outside of the Geneva Convention, Articles II.

General Pressman: I'm stating a fact. Implying nothing. You already know what we did. You just need to hear me say it. It will go quicker, be more efficient, and cost less overall if you do not interrupt.

There were a number of radical ideas proposed, most of which were summarily dismissed. The final solution was based upon the fact the selected troop carriers were prepared to make the nadir transition to return from the fringe to the central stars and that redeployment would take an unacceptable amount of time and cost. Given that each nadir jump takes four objective years in real time and one year subjective time, the task force of seven ships was twelve years out. All ships were contacted; new orders were issued and the task force turned about.

Senator Wellheim: Let me stop you there, General, your use of the word contact is a bit of a euphemism, isn't it?

General Pressman: The military-class AI's of the ships were contacted and given new orders which were not revealed to the human complement.

Senator Wellheim: Wasn't one of those orders to ensure the failure of the refueling drones?

General Pressman: We made sure that what was necessary was done.

Senator Wellheim: You are content with the result?

General Pressman: We achieved the reacquisition of the colonies. That is the only result that matters.

"What the hell was that? What kind of idiot makes that much noise?" Peak asked over the comm.

Kiersey swung his bar-buster around at the sounds from ahead. He snugged the helmet down on his head, his fingers briefly catching on the hanger hook on the back. The rectangular bar-buster hummed in his hands when the weapon's field went live. His gun was limited in accuracy but the amount of ammunition it could sling made up for that failing. As the hostile fire ahead of them started up again, Kiersey realized what was bothering Peak. All of the combat team's weapons were silent until impact; the older style slug throwers made a racket and gave away their user's positions. When Kiersey looked at the view from the net, he realized there were no IR spikes in the area that matched the trajectories of the enemy fire.

Sweeping his view over the team, he found Breadle down and Peak firing his bar-buster standing next to his fallen comrade. Breadle rolled over onto his side trying to get up to one knee. Roberts was receiving all of the feed and made the intuitive jump before Kiersey did, redirecting the fire from Peak and Anderev up into the canopy of the trees. Bangs, every bit as lucky as she always was, crouched untouched behind the stump of a toppled tree, her LinAcc pointed toward the incoming hostiles. Kiersey picked them out, painted them, and passed the info along to Roberts. Seconds later the first one slumped forward, promptly followed by the next. The final combatant turned to make a run for it, but Bangs' headshot brought his limp form to the ground.

Kiersey fanned out the aerosats looking for more movement. Then he received an image from Anderev and quickly forwarded it to Roberts—the fire the combat group received was from two automated systems that were embedded in the trunks of large trees.

At the base of the nearest tree, Heyer looked up at the splintered remains. "Why the hell do that?"

"The tree covered up the metallic ping and soaked up the heat signature. It's high enough to give the system good covering fire and, finally, a bunch of farmers don't think like we do." Anderev's delivered his assessment in a clipped tone.

"Too right. Only a bunch of farmers could figure on kicking the Federate and not expect a response," returned Bangs as she got to her feet.

Kiersey began a broad sweep looking for any emission from more emplacements, resetting the parameters to catch the limited exposure of these embedded traps. Roberts turned his attention to Bangs' feed and Kiersey found himself following along using the 'sat that shadowed her. She crept up on the casualties and then came to an abrupt halt.

"What is it, Bangs?" sent Roberts.

When she turned, the body at her left came into view. At first all that Kiersey could see were the muddy boots and non-mutable camouflage, then Bangs walked closer. There was no mistaking the cylinders strapped to the dead man's face.

"Go to BW-1. All team, BW-1. Now," barked Roberts over the comm.

Bangs' chatter reduced itself to a constant stream of profanity that Kiersey chopped off. Her shoulders shook once, then she reached around and pulled the filter clasp across the front of her helmet like they all were doing. Then her LinAcc came back up and her back straightened. He'd seen Bangs like this before. Someone was going to die and soon. He was just glad she was in front of him. Kiersey dialed back his viewpoint and a twitch raced up his spine. Who knew what bio weapon they were all exposed to....

Transcript Committee Hearing, Sylvan Seven Atrocities

Senator Wellheim: Correct me if I'm wrong, General, but I understand that you gave your troops something extra.

General Pressman: All troops were inoculated with a new full-spectrum antigen.

Senator Wellheim: Well that makes sense; you don't want your troops coming down with anything once they are groundside.

Leigh patched up as much of Breadle's side as she could while Kiersey and Peak watched over her. Kiersey stole a glance at Roberts. The lieutenant, from his tense stance, was having a heated encrypted conversation with command on board the *Ross*. Once Roberts secured evac for Breadle, Kiersey saw him send Peak to help the injured man to a clear LZ. Pushing the net farther, Kiersey kept scanning for enemy signatures. Now that he had a template from the automated guns in the trees, he was able to identify two other emplacements. He caught Roberts' comm lighting up.

"Leigh," Roberts sent and the medic jogged over to him. "I need a report and I need it yesterday. What the hell did we just step in? How bad is it?"

Leigh looked away briefly. "Sir, I'm not certain what we're up against, but it's fairly virulent. When I knew that we were looking for a pathogen, something that I found from the casualty we discovered earlier made better sense. The boy shouldn't have died from exposure. It just doesn't get cold enough in this season. His cause of death must be due to whatever the rebels released. I'm still trying to narrow it down, but there were some unusual viruses in his system."

"Are we safe?" Roberts asked.

"Our new antigen treatment should cover most of what the opposition could throw at us."

Roberts put a hand on Leigh's shoulder and turned her away from the team, their comm's chatter becoming encrypted. Kiersey considered what had just happened. Roberts wasn't very subtle when it came to communication. If Kiersey didn't know any better, he'd swear that the encryption slip was deliberate. He didn't get any time to think about it further, because Roberts redeployed the team and once again started them toward the highest point. Kiersey could still hear Bangs mumbling under her breath as they struck out.

There was a body lying in the clearing at the base of the rise. The metal in the gun it held pinged on the mosquito.net but its temperature had dropped enough that the IR could not immediately discern it. After making their way around the two tree emplacements, the team continued on to the objective. At the foot of the hill, the trees were all cut down to give the defenders on the heights the advantage of a clear line of sight. Except, when Kiersey flew the aerosats over the landscape he found no IR spikes or metallic pings other than the fortified position on the hillside that had been identified from orbit by the *Ross*. Where were all the defenders, he wondered? The only thing the team discovered so far was a casualty lying in plain sight.

Kiersey brought a group of aerosats level with the front of the opening in the hillside that led via a switchback tunnel up to the keep above them. Nothing. Still no heat signatures. Once inside the 'sats found the bodies of two guards, one of them with his arms out-stretched, futilely reaching for a cylinder mask. Beyond that there were more dead, all of which were cold enough that Leigh couldn't guess at a time of death.

"What the hell happened here?" mumbled Heyer.

Roberts stood considering the scene before him. Kiersey watched him shake his head briefly. Then the lieutenant spoke, sending Bangs in to lead, followed by Heyer and Michaels. Kiersey looked at the 'sat readings again. The cave ran straight back for fifty meters before starting to ascend. Roberts sent him a brief message, "Stay here with Anderev. Move some aerosats over our back trail and continue to push forward the ones in the cave." With that the lieutenant motioned Leigh ahead of him toward the dead guards.

Kiersey picked a 'sat near Bangs and watched as she moved further into the cave. She was still twitchy and her shoulders jerked back and forth. More bodies slumped against the sides of the cavern.

"This is bad," Michaels sent over the band. "It's like they didn't even know what they set loose."

"No chatter," Roberts replied from where he stood over Leigh as she examined the guard's body.

The furthest 'sat picked up a spike in the IR. Kiersey relayed the highlighted view to the rest of the team. "You've got a live one all the way at the back of the cave. There's some metallic pings from around the combatant."

"Bangs!" Roberts sent cutting across Kiersey, but she was already in motion, the LinAcc's barrel swinging in front of her as she tracked the enemy.

"What is this stuff?" came from Heyer, who was down on one knee in front of several bags made from coarsely spun fiber.

"Bangs, I need them alive. We need to know what's going on here." Roberts started to move away from Leigh.

"There's more over here. It's really fine," answered Michaels, something white and powdery spilled out onto the floor in front of him. "There's something buried under all of these bags. Look at they way they hump up in the middle."

Kiersey saw Anderev move in the corner of his eye. The combat specialist was also watching the feed from the cave in a reduced window according to Kiersey's log. There was a brief, sharp breath from Bangs' feed and a muffled thump as the LinAcc's ammunition found its target.

"Damn it, Bangs!" came from Roberts.

Kiersey flipped back to the feed from the 'sat shadowing Bangs just in time to see the thumb on her victim's hand rise.

All of the team in the cave's audio caught the pop of small explosions. The 'sats images were overwhelmed by the fine white particles that shot into the air as the bags were destroyed. Kiersey's mind was working at putting everything he saw together when Anderev slammed into him throwing them both to the ground. The feed from the 'sats vanished into bright white overload. The ground shook momentarily and an orange lance of fire jetted from the cave across the clearing into the surrounding woods. Kiersey felt himself rolling away from Anderev, his ears and eyes overwhelmed despite the protection of his helmet.

He came to rest on his back. Blinking his eyes, Kiersey looked upward in time to see the tree flying through the air. Its roots came down, striking him in the chest and shoving him along the ground for several meters.

There was a smell of something other than burning wood when he came around. At the edges of Kiersey's awareness, he could hear Anderev muttering. He heard snatches of "Flour, of all things, damn primitives" and then "You're not going to like this, but I can't carry you." The burning scent got stronger and when he dug far enough into his memory, Kiersey realized that it smelled just like incinerated flesh.

Transcript Committee Hearing, Sylvan Seven Atrocities

General Pressman: We gave our soldiers much more than just a new antigen.

Senator Wellheim: Enlighten us.

General Pressman: Ships by nature are very difficult to keep completely clean in a biologic sense. They are breeding grounds for all kinds of new bacteria and phages all altered by the incidence of cosmic rays and other radiations. By giving our crews the full-spectrum antibody, the infectious agents were encouraged to adapt, becoming more and more virulent over time. The soldiers of course would be fine.

Senator Wellheim: I note here on this report that the full- spectrum antibody does not necessarily destroy these hostile agents, but rather stops any effect on the troops. So essentially you turned them all in Typhoid Marys. I'm sorry, General ,do you have any response to that? No, I didn't expect you would.

This dream is really the worst, thought Kiersey as the feeling of floating continued. He had a few snatches of memory that kept coming back and made no sense. There was a disturbing tugging sensation, a release, and then he felt like he was sailing through the air as if he suddenly weighed nothing at all. It reminded him of the way the tree flew through the air in the moments before landing on him. Then there were a few seconds of very distorted vision as if he were hanging upside down and swinging back and forth. Through all of this he could smell that horrendous odor once again of burning flesh.

"OPS-AI give him visual."

Kiersey worked over the new stimuli for a moment. That was Anderev's voice he realized and then he could see.

The image before him wavered and Kiersey realized he was in the infirmary onboard the *Ross*. He'd made it. He started to turn his head in the direction that Anderev's voice came from but nothing happened. The staff must have him secured, that made sense since his back or neck was probably injured. He heard a chair scrape on the flooring and Anderev came into his line of sight.

The combat specialist was missing an arm. The slope of his shoulder cut off abruptly and a reddish blue bandage covered the absence. Burns covered what was visible of the rest of Anderev. "It's not as bad as it looks, but when it itches, then it is that bad," Anderev grated out. "Sorry, smoke inhalation," he continued pointing at his throat. "But what I'm really sorry about is that I couldn't carry you out..." his voice trailed off and he looked away.

Kiersey was briefly confused at that. He was thinking more clearly now than before, perhaps the level of drugs in his system was being reduced. "What do you mean?" His voice sounded tinny and unmodulated; perhaps he had some smoke inhalation damage as well.

Anderev didn't say anything for a moment. Then he reached across and pulled a slate off of nearby table. He fiddled with it awkwardly until its surface became reflective. "I'm not sure you're ready for this..." Again he trailed off and then brought up the mirrored screen before Kiersey.

It was quiet in the room while Kiersey went through several panicked reactions. But they were reactions that would have taken a body to act upon. His face was barely recognizable and that was what remained of most of him.

Just below his adam's apple, Kiersey became a ragged mass of flesh. His body was gone. A gelatinous mass of blue, a tangle of tubes, and several flexing bellows were attached to his pitiful remains. His mind...his mind however continued to work fine. Six long months, six incredibly long months and the techs on the *Ross* would grow him a new body. He'd be more than just a chunk of flesh again. That was when he realized that Anderev was still much too quiet and still. "You saved my life," Kiersey said.

The big man's shoulders slumped. "It was about the only thing I saved," he sat down at the edge of Kiersey's vision.

"Now I know what you mean when you said you couldn't carry me." If he had a body, Kiersey would have shuddered. He'd heard before about the option of sealing the armor's helmet before in life-threatening situations. But he'd never heard of anyone using it. That's what the handle on the top of the helmet was really for, not just hanging it on the wall. Then he started to think more about what Anderev said. "Look, there was nothing we could do for them. It happened so fast. It was over fast—that was the only good thing. I'm sure they never even felt it."

Anderev turned back around where Kiersey could see his face. Some of the tension there had lessened. "Kiersey, you don't understand. All of those dead men and women down there, even that kid—it's all our fault."

"When we get sent in, people die. It's a fact."

Kiersey heard Anderev stand up to his feet. "No, you don't know. When we were sent down to Cansec our hyped-up immune systems were carrying live infectious agents. We were full of diseases that had to develop into radically dangerous forms as they tried to overwhelm our antigens—viruses that the population of that world had no protection from whatsoever."

As Anderev stepped out of Kiersey's line of sight he heard him say softly, "Every last one of them is dead. We walked on their world, breathed its air, drank its water, and we poisoned them. We poisoned them so well that they never had a chance."

Kiersey heard Anderev's footsteps and then the *chuff* of the airlock door as it opened and closed. He stared at the opposite wall and its blank grey metal for a long time. Everything that he saw appear was a product of his imagination and none of it could be as bad as the reality. "OPS," he said, "I think you can turn me off for a while. I think you can turn me off for a long while...."

❖

Transcript Committee Hearing, Sylvan Seven Atrocities

Senator Wellheim: So you knew full well what you were doing?

General Pressman: Sadly, sir, it is not without precedent. Our ancestors gave blankets impregnated with the small pox infection to the Indians and achieved the same result. Our decision was not arrived at lightly. After all it was a group of rebel farmers that started the American Revolution. Since the consolidation, the Federate simply is not prepared for another conflict. We were all aware of the consequences and have accepted them as a necessary cost of winning this war.

Senator Wellheim: You condemned all of those people to death.

General Pressman: No, sir, they accepted their fate when they challenged us. We were given little choice in how to accomplish our goal. I could just as easily lay the blame on your shoulders when your committee cut the finances to the war effort. But you do not want to see or hear that, you are only looking for someone to accept the blame. Well, I will. If you want to blame someone for accomplishing something that you tried to make certain could not be done, then blame me. If you want to blame someone for finishing this with no recourse, then blame me. If you want to blame someone for having the balls to do what it takes, then blame me. But don't you ever tell me that I have failed the Federal Coalition.
Senator, I'm done here. I have answered your questions. I have nothing further to say.

SHEEPDOG

An Alliance Archives Adventure

Mike McPhail

"Most of the people in our society are sheep. They are kind, gentle, productive creatures who can only hurt one another by accident. Then there are the wolves, and the wolves feed on the sheep without mercy. Then there are sheepdogs, and I'm a sheepdog. I live to protect the flock and confront the wolves."

Paraphrased from "Sheep, Wolves, and Sheepdogs"
Lt. Col. Dave Grossman

It was a relief to finally escape the smothering darkness of the old-growth forest. Its ancient canopy had long ago meshed to form an impenetrable barrier to the life-giving light of this world's sun, Tau Ceti. Nature had not seen fit to give the planet a celestial traveling companion, as with Earth and her moon, so the term 'the dark of night' had a whole new meaning here.

As starlight shown on the scene through the towering grasses at the edge of the tree line, the suit's all-governing computer, or Pacscomp, powered down the peripheral, infrared lamps, once again allowing the helmet-mounted, electro-optical scopes to gather the faint ambient light and amplify it into a false-color day.

The armor-clad figure pressed forward until the sea of grass parted like waves breaking against the bow of a ship. Visibility was less than a few inches, fostering a complex feeling of concealed safety and overt vulnerability as his passage created a hole in the surrounding landscape.

Navigating by landmarks was impossible, yet the scouts pressed on, guided only by the down-view overlay, which gave them an approximation of their position. As with all things deemed vital to the cause, both sides in the conflict had electronically fought for control of the orbiting constellation of LandNav satellites, ultimately rendering the system virtually useless. So it was the suit's digital compass, in sync with the transponder they had set up back at the insertion point that guided them this night.

"*Slow it down,*" another spoke directly into his mind, the tone was flavored by the adrenaline-fueled tension of the moment.

The scouts had been moving at a trot since leaving the bushes at the edge of the tree line. Without responding the one in the lead down-shifted into a walk and focused on the map. Its scale indicated that they were about twenty yards from the parameter roadway, heading straight for a rock outcropping.

The sound of his breath opening and closing the suit's air handling system was almost drowned out by the background noise of the winds dancing across the field, whipping the grasses, and creating a white nose reminiscent of falling rain.

Glancing over toward his comrade, there—superimposed against the wall of foliage—was a green, rounded-point triangle, topped with the letters RWL. Its relative size indicated that the scout was less than five yards away. The sight of his teammate's icon was reassuring; it added a physical presence beyond just the comm traffic, and the voices in his head.

"*I'm telling you,*" his comrade continued the conversation they'd started earlier, "*she was up all day and night screaming and demanding my attentions.*" A feeling of being tired washed across the electronic commune.

"And...?" asked Ke'Se, trying to keep his amusement from being conveyed.

"*And so I did as nature intended,*" replied Ra'Ewl with a hint of pride. "*But in truth, there's only so much enthusiasm before all that biting and scratching gets old.*"

"*You're a spaz for complaining,*" responded Ke'Se. "So, no nap then?"

The very top of the rock outcropping came into view, less as an image, and more of a void punched out of the starry sky.

"*Just what we had on the flight in.*" Ra'Ewl slowed and then took up a position at the foot of the rock. Its surface was almost smooth from weathering, but at least this facing sloped up to its summit at a traversable angle.

"*Going right,*" stated Ke'Se as he crouched for a slow pass along the side of the rock. Now just a yard from the cleared edge of the grasses, he went down onto his belly. He spied the world through the last few inches of cover.

"*Clear?*" asked Ra'Ewl impatiently as he revved up for the leap.

"Standby." Ke'Se crawled forward and gently pushed his head through the grass, opening up the field of view to his helmet-mounted scope. To his front was a swath of crushed stones that had been used to stabilize and defoliate the ground around the roadways. With a slow pan of his head, he scanned the area for any immediate threats.

"You're good to go."

"Going up," Ra'Ewl communed with an accompanying *hooff* over the comm as he leaped. The jump brought him to just below the grass tops. Gaining purchase on the rock took a little more than just the traction pads on his boots. With a snap he deployed the fighting claws, and pressed hard against his toes. At a measured pace—as laid down by eons of evolution—he moved slowly toward the crest.

Feeling more like a gecko climbing out onto a rock to sun himself than a predator on the hunt, Ra'Ewl settled onto the high point and waited for the suit's equivalent of chromatophores to shift into a dark gray. *"I AM...the rock,"* he communed with a sense of playfulness.

After another quick sweep, Ke'Se pivoted to look up at Ra'Ewl, whose green icon floated ethereally at the back of his helmet. Despite the carapace plates that made him look like a child's toy robot, there was still no mistaking that he was fifteen pounds worth of cat, stuffed into AS'Is (Allied Standard Issue) body armor.

Although spawned from a thousand generations of domestic house cats, nature was no longer in the driver's seats. As the end product of the animal-experimentation phase for the Synaptic Interface—direct mind–machine communications, or commune—Doctor Jonathan Parr's feline lab rats took on an unexpected life of their own, as comrade-in-arms with their bygone tormentors.

From his perch, Ra'Ewl could see the town's parameter roadway, with its long, curving arc and accompanying sidewalk. There were no lights to be seen, only the myriad of road-designating phosphorescent reflectors giving up their stored energy to the night.

The town of Stratford was typical for Demeter, a bullseye layout with a series of concentric circular roadways and spoke avenues, dividing up lots. At its apex was the Administrative Centre, which housed everything that an isolated town of two thousand projected residents might need.

"Raul what is your position?" came over the comm in a slight Scottish accent.

Ra'Ewl's tail twitched at the thought of making mischief. "Standing on a rock," he replied over the comm via the commune, and then turned to look down at his fellow scout.

There was a pause. "Aye. Echo status?" replied the voice from his helmet's speakers, asking if they had spotted any sign of the enemy, or Echo, from the phonetic alphabet.

"Still looking for those bad-guys." Both he and Ke'Se started to chirp with laughter.

Yet another pause. "Raul. Kizzy. Maintain comm procedures," instructed the voice. The letters OWN shown on the squad-ban display.

Ra'Ewl did a quick front stretch, and then reared up into a sitting position, all the time scanning for movement.

This isn't the first time Corporal Owens has expected us to play like soldiers, thought Ra'Ewl to himself. Being an expatriate of the Dominion, only Owens knew why he'd chosen to fighting under Allied Military authority.

"Owens, the bad-guys can't pick up our comm traffic, and even if they could, they don't have the Pacscomp to translate it. That's why they're all hot-and-heavy to try and get their hands on one."

"Aye, I've been told all that, but I'm sure Donitz felt the same way about Enigma," quipped Owens. "So if you two are through pissing about, I need you to move onto the objective."

"Who's Donuts?" asked Ke'Se.

"Haven't a clue." Ra'Ewl leaped from the rock. *"On the move."*

The outermost ringed streets of Stratford were nothing more than a flattened bit of land, with yellow boundary lines and brass benchmarks proclaiming their future address. Many of the lots already had their poured foundation slabs and adjoining utilities trenches running out to the street. Just ahead, a picket of landscaping trees marked the boundary to the completed section of the town.

Ra'Ewl swung left at a trot, following the tree line with Ke'Se in tow. Through the thicket of screening foliage laid the boxy, two-story prefab buildings that were predominately used across the planet. No doubt each had been adorned by their owners to express their own personal idioms, but here in the dark they were all just oppressive, monolithic structures seemingly devoid of life.

"Ra'Ewl!" communed Ke'Se, with a sense of discovery.

The Parr looked back toward the construction zone. One of the slabs had a large piece missing next to a wide depression. As they approached, the ground they covered was awash in a spray of dirt and shattered bits of concrete.

"This is it?" asked Ke'Se.

Ra'Ewl had already turned and was looking about for others. *"Yeah I think so; it looks like two more over this way,"* he replied before heading off.

It took them a few minutes to arrive at the third hole; this one was in a patch of open ground. Ra'Ewl estimated that the crater was about two and a half yards across and a foot deep. He then noticed that Ke'Se wasn't looking at the crater, but back toward the house.

Ke'Se purred with fascination at a tree between him and the building. To say the tree was broken would have been an understatement. The crown had been blown off, leaving foot-long splinters sticking up at odd angles. The upper portion now sat on the ground, resting against the bole of the tree.

"Fell short," commented Ke'Se as he moved in for a closer look.

Ra'Ewl suddenly felt a need to get to higher ground, but the best he could do was a nearby pallet of building materials. It was piled high with polymer sacks, many of which were torn open and had hemorrhaged their contents. They were filled with some form of granular material. With a dash and a leap he landed on top and gave a good hard look about.

"Owens, from Ra'Ewl," he communed; now watching Ke'Se as he moved behind the devastated tree, to be replaced by just his floating icon.

"Owens, go ahead, Raul." the letters OWN brighten on the Parr's display.

"We're on station. Negative contacts. There are three confirmed hits and a possible tree burst. The craters are the right size for the enemy's eighty-ones." he reported.

"Understood, what did they hit?"

Ra'Ewl had another quick look. "Nothing. They landed in the construction zone back behind the first street of houses." Ke'Se's icon was receding, heading off toward the nearby house. Ra'Ewl was anxious to join him.

"Roger that."

Ra'Ewl leaped from the pallet and darted off. "Owens, we say 'acknowledged' in this cat's Army," he communed, knowing that it would annoy Owens to be caught making such a simple mistake.

"Acknowledged," the human said in a taut tone. "Keep me informed. ETA about fifteen minutes, Owens out."

As Ra'Ewl cleared the trees, he saw that Ke'Se had crossed the backyard and was now just outside the building. Crouched down, he used the thickness of the back deck for cover. The storm door's clear, polycarbonate panels were fractured, and the inner door lay open and at an angle.

Ke'Se briefly looked over as Ra'Ewl settled in next to him. *"I'm getting a glow on thermal from somewhere near to front,"* reported Ke'Se. His display was showing him the world from his scope's far-infrared pickups. Everything was painted in shades of cold blue to white hot; the interior of the house was awash in warm colors reflected off numerous surfaces; it looked very much like a room lit by a fireplace.

"Big or little?" asked Ra'Ewl, as he slowly moved off toward the left side of the house.

Ke'Se checked the color-coded thermal key at the bottom of his display. *"Maybe around eighty degrees ambient, it's hard to tell without line of sight. Whatever it is, it's small."* he added.

"Like a monkey-boy has his helmet off?" Ra'Ewl was now just under a large picture window that faced out onto what appeared to be the home-owner's garden project. The cleared ground was edged with a continuous strip of black plastic, while underneath the window lay a neatly stacked pile of rock pavers.

"I don't think so; it's bigger than that."

Checking that the pavers screened him from the street, Ra'Ewl stretched up his full length; he was just short of being able to look into the window. *"Okay, be ready to run if someone spots me,"* he communed, almost excited by the possibility.

"Acknowledged." Ke'Se backed up so he could get a running start into his turn.

"Suit, scope up," Ra'Ewl commanded. A small insert window opened on his display. Its round image was almost fish-eyed, and clearly in motion. At the end of its extension, the flexible scope stood a foot over his head, and parroted the movements of the helmet.

The space was a living room, decorated in a modular, out-of-the-catalog style, with two couches forming an el near the window. Across the room was a theater display, its flat-panel screen gouged and the frame missing pieces.

Tilting his head, he scanned the area along the floor in front of the seating area. There, partially covered by the far edge of the couch, sat a child, it was doubled over as if resting its head on its knees.

"Shit!" communed Ra'Ewl conveying a feeling of annoyance.

"Big shit or little shit?" misconstrued Ke'Se. Ra'Ewl ignored his attempt at being a smartass.

"Suit, scope down." The scout was on the move even before the scope locked safe into its housing. *"Back door, we're going in."*

Ke'Se was standing to one side as Ra'Ewl reached the storm door. Standing up on his hid legs and grabbing the knob with both paws, Ra'Ewl gave it a twist and reared back. As the door gapped, Ke'Se intervened and shoved it open with his body.

Cautiously, Ke'Se peered around the edge of the inner door. Nothing had changed. They entered the room slowly; its floor was covered in rough tiles and was lined with counter tops and appliances. To the right was a staircase.

"Check the second floor," ordered Ra'Ewl.

As Ke'Se went for the stairs, the hot spot came into view through a myriad of chair and table legs.

Ra'Ewl could feel his comrade's concern. "Go check for bad-guys," he ordered.

Quietly Ke'Se climbed the stairs as Ra'Ewl lowered himself into a stalk, and moved to get a better look. It seemed that he had been too distracted by the sight of the child to see the truth of the situation. Lying there, just on the other side of the dining room table separating the living room from the kitchen, was a body. Ra'Ewl didn't bother with a biometric scan, if the human had been among the living Ke'Se would have seen that on thermal. *"Anything?"*

"Negative. On the move."

Ra'Ewl stood up and walked toward the child, swinging wide to avoid the body and the pool of congealed blood that surrounded it. Looking back he could see that Ke'Se had just turned the corner.

Together they stood in silence and pondered the scene. The child was a small female, dressed in a long-sleeved T-shirt and overalls. Her head rested forward against her knees, and her long hair draped to the sides of her black, rubberized field boots. One arm was up underneath her, holding some form of plush animal, while the other hung down; its hand was gripping the hair of the adult. It too was female.

"Suit, thermal disengage." He turned to face Ra'Ewl. *"Mom?"*

Ra'Ewl didn't answer what he felt was obvious. *Thing are getting complicated*, he thought to himself, as he looked around in the hope that an answer to this problem would just materialize if he looked hard enough.

In a sense it did; while he was distracted, Ke'Se had moved to within just a foot of the girl and was reaching out to touch her leg.

"No stop that, bad Parr, don't..."

Ke'Se had stop as Ra'Ewl barked the order, but with paw outstretch the scout stood frozen in the moment as the girl looked up. Her eyes were dilated against the darkness, and through his night vision scopes they shown as bright as a cat's. There was just a momentary pause, as confusion washed across the girl's tear-stained face and her young mind raced for an answer.

He had just lowered his arm when tremors shook her body, and the girl screamed. Involuntary he leapt, fling himself back almost a yard. Ke'Se landed with a padded thump, back arched. The commune was now awash with primitive emotions, as the sounds of his hissing and growling flooded the comm.

Ra'Ewl fought to maintain his composure. *"Ke'Se, stand down!"* he ordered, while trying to drive across the feeling of being in control.

Ke'Se wound down as he watched the girl desperately trying to backpedal away from him, only to be stopped by the edge of the couch.

"Just great, get over here," demanded Ra'Ewl; the girl's voice was strained, as if she'd already given as much as she could to the effort. No longer screaming, she trembled with fear, while clutching her stuffed animal.

As Ke'Se moved passed Ra'Ewl, he pressed himself against his comrade's side asking for forgiveness, resulting in a series of thumps as composite plates smacked into each other.

"What where you thinking?" The tip of Ra'Ewl's tail flicked with annoyance.

The image of sitting on the floor and playing with his friend's children hung in Ke'Se's mind. *"Mac's kids always liked it when I patted them,"* Ke'Se communed defensively. In the early days of the Project, Dr. Parr had isolated and switched off the gene that created the cat's claws, making his front paws more like prehensile hands, than weapons, and thus safe for playing with children.

"Yeah, but here and now, all you are is a Jonathan-forsaken monster; just a shadow against the dark." Ra'Ewl paused, as if hearing his own words being spoken by someone else. *"Get out of your suit,"* he ordered.

"What? Are you spazzed?" The very thought clearly panicked Ke'Se.

"Just do it." Ra'Ewl looked around to see how much cover they had. The windows had no blinds or curtains, so they must have been the type that electronically went opaque.

"Why me?" argued Ke'Se, as he assumed the position.

Ra'Ewl looked for the main controls; odds were they were somewhere near the master's seat on the couch across from the theater display. He moved with all the stealth he could muster, while watching the girl and hoping that he didn't frighten her any more than could be helped. *"Because, the monkey-boys gave me an AS'Is hair cut to deal with the suit's tactile contact points, whereas you are still fuzzy,"* he communed with a sense of amusement over his partner's growing distress.

Lying on his stomach, Ke'Se moved his front paws to either side of his helmet. With a firm push, he depressed the twin latches; the backpack portion of his armor popped opened. Arching his back, he pulled his head free, leaving his helmet still connected to the suit's neck coupling.

Over the commune, a wave of disgust hit Ra'Ewl, who was almost to the couch. Turning he could see Ke'Se's head, but his ears were back and he had one paw over his nose, as he had seen the humans do in such a situation. *"The smell..."* Ke'Se trailed off.

"Deal with it; we'll have a Vettech give you a bath when we get home." At the moment the girl was distracted by the sounds of Ke'Se extracting himself from his armor. Ra'Ewl leapt for the couch; there, built into the padded arm rest, was the controller. With a stubbly digit he pressed the window-screen button. In an instant, the stars no long shown through the panels, as the dark became black. The girl gasped in horror and started sobbing.

"The batteries still work," he mused as he turned to face the scene. Ke'Se was out of his suit and standing in front of the child. *"Ready?"* Ra'Ewl asked, before realizing his mistake. The Pacscomp could only communicate with the user's Synaptic Interface within the confines of the helmet.

"Suit, external," he instructed. "Hi there." sounded the male-neutral voice from the Parr's external speakers. The girl turned toward the voice, her eyes wide; her mouth hung open as she panted to breathe.

"It's okay, we're here to help. Don't be scared." It sounded cliché. *"Suit hold, lights, thirty-percent, maximum diffusion, engage."* The helmet's side lamp came on. Even at its low setting it still came on like a blazing sun. Ra'Ewl's night vision switched off.

The girl squealed and raised her arms to cover her eyes against the light, the blue plush animal she had been holding dangled precariously by its long ears; a trail of white stuffing lead to its midsection.

Ke'Se had guessed his comrade's intentions and was prepared. Slowly, he opened his eyes, allowing his pupils time to constrict. The girl's boots stood like a grime-splattered wall in front of him. Not wanting a repeat of her earlier reaction, he decided not to reach for her, instead he purred.

Timidly the girl peered around her arms in search of the sound. Her blue eyes locked onto Ke'Se's, who then squinted his eyes in greetings and then tipped his head slightly to one side to be cute.

For the first time something less then terror shown from the girl's face; slowly she unfolded herself, and tentatively reached out toward the black and white cat. Ke'Se stepped forward, thrusting his head under the girl's hand and pressed into her palm.

To Ke'Se surprise, the girl giggled nervously and rocked forward onto her knees to throw her arms around him in an effort to pick him up. Of course, at fifteen pounds he was easily over a third of her weight, so he just stood there, as she hugged him and buried her face into his soft fur.

"Raul from Owens, status!" came in over the comm. "What's happened to Kizzy?"

Ra'Ewl paused for a moment to figure out what to say; no doubt Ke'Se's icon fell of the grid once he was out of range of his Pacscomp. "Ah, we have a domestic situation here," he answered.

"Be more specific."

"We found a child in the house near the tree strike," he replied, wondering what would happen next. Looking up, he could see Owens' icon in the distance.

"Standby. I'll be with you shortly," he instructed.

Sighting in on the scouts' icons, Owens entered the building, closing the damaged door behind him as best he could. The Parr's small helmet lamps lit up the house as if it were high noon. Owens went down on one knee, using the counters for cover from the windows; his weapon was at the ready. "Raul, turn them off." The house went black; the intensity of his night vision display rose to compensate. The false safety of the darkness returned.

Staying low, Owens moved over to the body. Next to it, the girl had reared back trying to take Ke'Se with her. The Parr—now standing up on his back legs—was held tight as if he was the girl's only hope. Lowering his weapon, Owens allowed it to hang across his chest by its strap.

"Raul?" he commed, as he reached for the body. Firmly he grabbed it by the shoulder and moved it; it was cold and sluggish, but not stiff. *Whoever she was, she's been dead for more than a day*, he surmised.

"Raul..." he repeated, when he realized that the Parr was sitting next to him. "Did you check their RF tags?" he asked, looking over at the girl. A knot now gripped his stomach. He'd seen that look of terror before, and not on the faces of a stranger, but of a friend, long ago, when her own parents had met a similar fate.

"Negative, I don't have a reader," communed Ra'Ewl, as his suit's synthetic voice joined in.

With a practiced hand, Owens reached into his side pack and retrieved a wallet-sized device. He then held it near the body. "Suit, RF scan." With that command, an ID photo and data line appeared with an arrow pointing at the body. Her name is—was—Sherilyn Carter; it went on to list that she was married and had a daughter.

Owens then aimed the reader at the girl. "Christine 'Crissy' Carter," he read aloud over the comm; "Year of birth, 2059. She's only three." Owens fought to keep his emotions in check.

"Did you find anyone else?" he asked, wondering about the father.

"Nope."

Owens gently reached over and put his hand on Mrs. Carter. Silently he prayed. He then took a deep breath; it cleared his mind and helped steadied his emotion.

He then reach into his pack and pulled out a disposable chemlight. Removing the safety cap, he depressed the igniter, which popped. As the chemicals mixed, the room became awash in a soft white glow.

"Sheeet." meowed Ke'Se in purrsing, the closest thing the Parr had to a spoken language, as Crissy clutched him in a death grip when Owens was revealed by the light. Clad in his AS'Is carapace armor, the soldier must have appearance like some form of unimaginably large insect, suddenly materializing out of the darkness. Crissy was frozen with fear.

"It's okay, he's not going to hurt you, he's a friend." said Ra'Ewl in an effort to comfort the girl.

"Easy, easy..." Owens commed before realizing she could not hear him. "Suit, external." "Easy there, Sweetie," he said, calmly leaning forward, and motioning with his hand. Clearly it wasn't working. Owens was still some faceless monster in her eyes.

"Suit, unlock." he said as he reached up and pulled the mandible portion of his helmet free. In response, the visor raised, leaving his face framed by his comhood. "It's okay, Sweetie, please don't squish the cat. They're expensive," he said gently.

Ke'Se's tail swished with annoyance at the remark, but at least the girl calmed down.

"Raul, you get Kizzy back into armor," Owens said as he stood up and walked toward the kitchen, then up the stairs.

There was no sign that the girl was going to give him up. Ke'Se knew he could fight his way free, but that was not even going to be his last option. Longingly, he turned to see what his comrade was up to.

Ra'Ewl was now next to them reaching for the girl's discarded plushy; his glove's prosthetic grippers were deployed and acting as a set of opposable thumbs. With the toy in paw, he moved off in a three-legged hop, to sit down with his back toward the two.

Owens had returned; his helmet was closed with the visor still up. He was carrying a small blanket adorned with wide-eyed blue bunnies. "What's the hold up?"

"Working on it," Ra'Ewl said. Turning he held up the plushy as he closed his medpack; the rabbit's torn abdomen was now covered by a gray contact bandage. He gently shook it, making its long ears flop about.

"It's okay, Sweetie, you can take your rabbit," Owens assured her.

Reluctantly, she let go of Ke'Se and grabbed for the toy. She clutched it even tighter than she had the cat, all the while giving Owens and Ra'Ewl a pouting frown, as if their handling of her toy was more of an offense than their presence. Ke'Se backed away the moment she took possession of the plushy.

"Right," Owens said in a firm tone. "We're going to EVAC her to the recover site."

"What about the mission?" asked Ra'Ewl, as he helping Ke'Se back into his armor. "Couldn't we just leave her here, and pick her up on the way out?"

Owens knelt in front of her; setting the blanket aside he reached over and placed his hands on her upper arms. "Can't take the chance. If something happened..." he trailed off. "Besides, we've accomplished the primary objective, so everything else is 'up to the discretion of the team'," he quoted.

"What if we leave Ke'Se here to keep and eye on her?"

Ke'Se was mostly back into his suit, with only his head still sticking out. "Feek que," he meowed, and pushed his head down through the neck coupling. Ra'Ewl then flipped his backpack closed, and like a man doing CPR, he pressed down onto his comrade's back with both paws, throwing his weight into the effort.

"On line," communed Ke'Se, as he flipped his head around while trying to get his paw up to his faceplate as if trying to groom. *"Damn, I stink."*

Owens angled his head, both Parrs' icons shown on his display. "You two, outside, check for Echos," he ordered.

Ke'Se tromped off in compliance; Ra'Ewl sat down next to Owens. "You know she's going to shine like a marker beacon in the infrared."

"No shite," Owens agreed. "All we can do is dampen her down, and break up her silhouette."

"What about telling...someone she's here?" said Ra'Ewl reluctantly; he'd expected Owens to spaz out on him for even suggesting turning her over to the bad guys; the Legion.

"That's not happening, cat," stated Owens, a determined edge to his voice. "Now get outside and do your job."

"Acknowledged." Ra'Ewl ran from the living room.

Owens turned to look at Crissy; she was so very small, his armored gloves were massive by comparison. It would be so easy to unintentionally hurt her. "Sweetie, I need you to stand up, can you do that for me?" he said while nodding his head in the affirmative.

On shaky legs she stood. Owens helped to steadied her, but in the back of his mind the fear that he might accidentally break her fought for his attention. Carefully he retrieved the blanket and placed it around her so that it could be pulled up over her head.

"Mommy!" Crissy cried in a hoarse voice; tears welling up in her eyes as she uselessly flung herself hard toward the body on the ground.

Owens held on to her, knowing too well that if she didn't calm down, this was not going to work. All he could think to do was fall back on what had comforted him. "Crissy, Sweetie, please look at me."

Her tear filled eye met his. "Sweetie, we have to go. Mommy is with God now, and I promise you, that after you have had a long and happy life, you'll be with her again." Owens' faith had always been strong, but in this day and age, God was often something other people talked about, not something they believed in.

It could have just been the look in Owens' eyes, or his sincere tone of voice, but Crissy stopped crying and fighting him. She closed her eyes and clung to him as if what he'd said had changed everything.

Relieved, Owens swung his weapon so that it rode under his right arm within easy reach of his hand. Snapping closed his visor he gently picked up the girl and carried her on his left arm, the thumb of that hand tucked into the webbing of his load-carrying gear. "Raul, Kizzy, status?"

"All clear," they replied.

"On the move."

The team moved through the darkness as if it held no domain over them. Once again they were operating on active night vision, as their infrared lamps punched small arcs of scenery out of the surrounding void. The Parrs were scouting ahead. Owens followed, trying to minimize bouncing the girl around as he negotiated the uneven, root-covered ground.

"*Hold up!*" instructed Ke'Se, excitement flavoring his words as he went to ground.

Ra'Ewl went down onto his stomach.

Turning off his helmet lamps, Ke'Se sat up. Ra'Ewl looked off into the same general direction to see what had attracted his comrade's attention.

With his lights out, Ra'Ewl crept up on Ke'Se and then slowly sat up next to him. *"Where?"*

"At about thirty-degrees, something moved against the ambience of the clearing."

Through Ra'Ewl's scopes, the break in the trees shone like sunlight as seen at the far end of a dark tunnel. *"Suit, nine-power."* His display transitioned into a magnified view; now the slightest movement of his head was exaggerated. Looking down at his compass display, he aimed his head to thirty-degrees.

Intently he scanned the area. There it was; a rounded, smooth shape, black against the background glow. It was moving to its left, toward another of its kind standing next to a tree. The silhouette was all too familiar.

"Owens, we have bad guys!" Ra'Ewl communed, not waiting for Owens to confirm he was listening.

"Raul, say again!"

"We have ECHOS between us and the recovery site!" repeated Ra'Ewl, making sure to emphasize the term Owens used for the bad guys.

Owens darted for cover behind a bank of surface roots. Like gigantic snakes they twisted around and over each other, covering the ground between the two massive trees. Bracing the girl with his free hand, Owens came to an abrupt halt behind the roots; going down onto one knee, he leaned forward so that only his head was above the edge.

Startled, Crissy cried out.

In the still air of the forest, the sound carried; bouncing off into the distance.

The Parrs turned in response; Owens icon was at the epicenter.

Ra'Ewl swung back to reacquire the bad guys, things had changed. "Owens, the Echoes are on the move."

"Roger that," replied Owens. He turned to the little girl.

"Sweetie, please quiet down," he pleaded, his helmet just inches away from her. No good. "Kizzy, get back here. Raul, maintain contact, and make damn sure you don't get between us and the Echoes," he ordered.

Pulling the blanket up around her head, Owens carefully placed the girl down into a gap among the roots. "Crissy, you need to stay here," he told her. She was already trying to work her way free. Owens used careful force to keep her in place.

Ke'Se landed with a soft thump, his IR lamps on low barely lit up the scene; Owens was always astonished at just how fast a Parr could run. "Suit, external, disengage." He was now back on comm traffic only. "You keep her here anyway you can." He gestured for Ke'Se to take over. "Knock her down and sit on her if you have to, just keep her under cover."

The Parr moved around Owens' legs, and up under his arms; with outstretched paws he took over. "How do I keep her quiet?"

Owens moved back and reached for his weapon. With one smooth motion he brought his square-framed rifle up and placed it at the ready. On his visor's display the weapon's semicircular targeting reticle appeared, its PIP (Projected Impact Point) dot resting at its center. "You don't." He then moved off.

"Ra'Ewl, what do we have?" Owens was moving quickly to gain distance from the girl.

"Two, possible three Echoes, moving toward your..." Ra'Ewl looked back, Owens' icon was moving up off to his right. He corrected his response, "Ke'Se's position. They're just over a hundred yards ahead of me."

"Stay left and close to fifty. Then bunker down."

"Acknowledged." Ra'Ewl sped off.

Owens was still covering ground, all the time looking for an advantageous place to set up his ambush. "On station," came over the comm from Ra'Ewl. *The time is now*, thought Owens. Just ahead was another ancient tree. Its trunk was easily six yards across, with massive surface roots splayed out from its buttress.

He moved into position behind the tree. Looking around, he tried to memorize the position of the potentially foot-tripping roots. With his left hand against the tree, he turned off his IR lamps and maneuvered around the trunk.

Now in relative darkness, he could see the distant glow from the far-off clearing; Ra'Ewl's green icon shown off to his left. Intently, he scanned the arc between himself, the Parr, and the clearing. His eyes locked onto two sets of small lights. A sudden feeling of intense anticipation washed over him, not unlike a child forced to wait to open a present.

Bracing himself against the tree, he raised his weapon. With a squeeze of his right hand, he depressed the leading edge of the rifle's handgrip; *Click*. The safeties were off and power made available. A pull of the two-fingered trigger would now launch a salvo of electromagnetically accelerated, armor-piercing darts.

Owens settled his sight's PIP onto the further of the two. "Firing!" he warned his comrades over the comm, as his darts cracked through the air, breaking the sound barrier. The first target bounced from the hits, but without waiting for it to drop he swung onto the second. He couldn't hear the concluding thump of his projectiles as they punched through mesh body armor to render flesh and smash bone, but he knew with satisfaction they had hit.

He released the trigger and the world went quiet, nothing moved. Owens took in a breath; he had been holding it while he fired. Although it had only been a few seconds, his body demanded air.

"On the move," called Owens as he stepped forward over the root. He'd heard the *thump* and caught sight of the flash; in that moment, his training took over as muscle memory tried to drive him to safety.

Everything was a blur of motion as the world flew past at strange angles; memories of being in the heart of a blazing fire raced in his mind. He could hear breathing, it was becoming louder and labored, his eyes snapped open; it was him.

"Status," he choked. Coughing, he spat up something; it had a strong metallic taste.

"Corporal Owens, you are critically injured," stated the Pascomp in its emotionally neutral female voice.

Owens fought to reorient himself; he was prone and lying on his left side. As he kicked out with his right leg, a wave of pain slashed through him. The momentum rolled him onto his back, the pain forcing his eyes shut, trapping him in hell. "Combat!" he screamed pasted the pain.

"Corporal Owens, the administering of Comburodorphin in your current state could result in exsanguination," it said calmly.

"Do it!" he demanded. The threat of bleeding out from the Combat drug seemed meaningless.

The initial sensation of the transdermal spray hitting the base of Owens' neck was lost to him. Then the drug reached his brain, and the pain faded away. It felt like cool water was running through his vein, as the drugs' synthetic hormones and endorphins dominated his body. His eyes dilated in response, and his mind finally cleared.

"*Ne se deplacent pas!*" someone yelled in French.

Owens could feel his heart pounding in his chest, as his reality shifted into slow motion. He looked up; standing there just on the other side of the surface root was a Legionnaire. A bullpup assault rifle pointed at Owens, the mercenary's hand gripping the weapon's underslung 30mm grenade launcher.

"Don't move!" the gunman restated in English.

Something was moving fast at the edge of Owens' display. Like some mystical creature of the forest, it seemed to fly through the air toward the enemy. It was Ra'Ewl's icon. With a *thud*, the scout connected high on the mercenary's back, knocking him forward over the root, toward Owens.

Startled, the mercenary pushed out his left arm in an effort to break his fall; the assault rifle still held by its pistol grip in the other.

Owen reared up to meet him; making a desperate grab for control of his opponent's weapon, he did manage to shove it aside as the gunman landed on top of him. Now as the tide of battle shifted, Owens wrapped his left arm around the mercenary's neck and grabbed for the back of his equipment harness, pinning his face down onto Owens' chest.

Panicking, the mercenary fought to bring his legs up under him in the hopes of pushing free.

Owens held tight as he threw his own leg across the captive's. He then grabbed for his knife, and with a *snap*, pulled it free from its sheath. With a hard thrust, the thick blade's reinforced chiseled tip punched through the mercenary's mesh armor, and sank deep into the side of his throat; his whole body jerked as the edge struck home.

Like a vise, the mercenary lock his hand onto Owens' knife-wielding arm; desperately he pulled at his tormentor. Owens knew it was just a matter of time; he could feel his captive's strength failing, as fingers lost hold and went limp. With a twist, he pulled the knife free to an accompanying gush of arterial spray. A sensation of warmth was conveyed across his gloves' tactile contact pads; blood continued to pump from the opening.

"Tae the Devil with ya!" yelled Owens as he pushed the still twitching body of the mercenary aside; it rolled over and landed with a *thump* onto its back, bending its right arm at an unnatural angle and trapping the assault rifle underneath.

Owens turned to look for his own weapon; it lay just a few feet away tethered to him by its strap. Planting his knife in the ground, he reached out, his fingers closed around its roll-bar hand guard. He pulled the rifle into his arms and made it ready.

"Owens?" said a familiar voice. Standing on the chest of the fallen mercenary was Ra'Ewl, his head darting about as he attempted to take stock of the situation.

Owens took a deep breath, something wasn't right. "Yeah, I'm with you."

Ra'Ewl lowered himself down onto his belly, seemingly to get a better look. "Your left thigh is a mess. Can you walk?"

Owens knew the answer. He placed his gauss rifle on the ground, and then patted his chest. "Come here."

Ra'Ewl paused for just a moment, then stood up, walked over, and settled down onto Owens, who was now reaching into his side pack. Owens placed his hand on the Parr's backpack, where he then flipped up a small metal loop and held it in place. In his other hand was the connector end for the emergency carry strap, which if need be, he could us to sling a Parr like a piece of equipment; it *snapped* as he hooked it in to the ring.

"Get her to the recover site."

Ra'Ewl stood up and climbed carefully up toward Owens face. There he stood for just a moment, as if he could see in through the helmet's frontal armor. "*Roger,*" he replied, then turned and headed off.

Owens sat with his back against the tree, his gauss rifle across his lap. The damage to his thigh was horrendous, but he did what he could. He'd used up the medpack's coagulant spray in an effort to slow down the blood loss and now only a pressure bandage kept him from bleeding out. Tingles ran down from his neck as the suit administered drugs to help keep him stable.

"We'll be on the ground in less than fifteen," stated the unseen voice. "Just hang in there."

"Roger that." Owens closed his eyes; the suit had lowered its internal temperature to an uncomfortable level in order buy its user a little more time. He could feel his hot breath blowing around past his cheeks. There was a glow beyond his eyelids, something was flickering.

He struggled to open his eyes as he turned his head; arm muscles twitched in an effort to raise his weapon from his lap, but to no avail. About ten yards away was a moving pool of white light; through his scopes it blazed like a searchlight. Owens smiled. Ra'Ewl had turned on his helmet lamps, and with Crissy in tow holding tight onto his carry handle, he was guiding her thought the darkness. She stamped along behind him in her oversized boots, while holding her blue pushy rabbit high up under her left arm.

"I know how you feel," joked Owens, remembering the contact bandage that Ra'Ewl had put across the rabbit's soft belly.

Ke'Se was just behind them; he stopped and looked in Owens direction. An unspoken sense of kinship seemed to pass between them. Owens raised his hand and motioned for Ke'Se to keep moving. At a trot Ke'Se caught up with the others.

Once they had gone, he was alone in the dark; the sounds of comm traffic from the approaching ADF tilt-rotor aircraft played in the background.

His mind started to wander; it had found its way back the Crissy's house, and the sight of her eyes wide with terror. Owens then looked over at the dead Legionnaire, then thought of the other two he'd taken out, and nodded with satisfaction. "Now there are three less wolves."

DEVIL DANCERS

Robert E. Waters

Victorio Nantan, Captain Victory, Squadron Leader of the Devil Dancers, looked over the smoke-filled room. Somewhere within its cavernous swill of booze, laughter, music, and celebration, were his men. They were the Devil Dancers. Aces everyone; the finest fighter squadron in the fleet. They deserved their seventy-two hours of R&R. Their record kills at the Battle of Pallid Musings had earned them their playtime. But the war continued, and Captain "Victory" had just received secret intelligence about enemy fleet movements near Castor V. It was out of his squadron's specific deployment zone, but an opportunity that could not be ignored. The finest pilots in the Federated Union had to keep pushing themselves, and at such a critical moment in the war, time was imperative. The enemy was on the verge of collapse.

That enemy was the Gulo, a wolverine-like race that had nearly cut the Union in two. Feral, savage fighters, their technology was on par with humans. They were a formidable foe. Deep in his heart, Victorio could not help but admire their prowess in battle. But the war had waged for over thirty stellar years, and even personal admiration grows pale over time. He and his men were working hard to defeat the Gulo. A turning-point was at hand. Victorio could feel it. He had seen it in his dreams. One more push, one more decisive rout, and the scales could be tipped.

The Devil Dancers were not going to be left out.

He crossed the room, pushing through the partiers, responding in kind to the salutes of junior officers from the 3rd Sol Fighter Wing. He even recognized some crew members of the *Star Chariot*, an old carrier that had been refitted to accommodate a full battalion of troopers and their drop pods. Among these men, he and the Devil Dancers were legend, and whenever they were present, they received much respect. Victorio passed through them politely, but kept his eyes set on one of his pilots who sat on a plush red sofa near the bar, surrounded by adoring women and sycophants.

Naiche looked up from his drink and recognized his brother. "Ah, Captain Victory!" He stumbled to his feet, the beautiful ladies surrounding him shifting their bare legs to let him pass. "You've decided to crawl out of your wickiup and join us."

Victorio grabbed his brother before the younger man embarrassed himself by hitting the floor. Naiche's face was flush red, his breath rancid with drink, his eyes dilated and distant. "You're drunk."

"You're goddamned right I'm drunk!" Naiche said, receiving cheers and laughter from his friends. "And I intend on staying that way for another forty-eight hours."

"We need to talk, brother," Victorio said, pushing Naiche away. "Now."

"Nonsense," Naiche said. "We need to drink. Pull up a chair and join us." Before Victorio had a chance to respond, Naiche said, "Ladies, let me introduce you to our *na-tio-tish*, our war leader, Captain Victorio "Tomorrow's Wind" Nantan, the *second* finest pilot in the galaxy." He tapped his brother's chest with a blunt, lazy finger. "This man single-handedly wiped out an entire Gulo squadron at the Battle of Two Dwarves. He's received six commendations for bravery, and a score of Silver Wings. And ladies," he put his hand to his mouth and lowered his voice, "he's got the cutest little tattoo on his—"

"Enough!" Victorio grabbed Naiche's shoulders and shook. The drink in his brother's hand toppled to the floor, spreading red liquid across the plush white carpet. The internal lattice-mesh of the floor began sucking the fibers dry. "We will talk, now." He turned and looked at the women, whose expressions had become quite still. "Will you excuse us, please?"

Naiche wrestled himself free and stumbled to the sofa, apologizing profusely to his fans. He gave each lady a small kiss and promised to call on them. They shuffled past Victorio without a word and disappeared into the throng of dancers.

"You waste yourself away with all this," Victorio said, finding a seat near his brother. "Father would not be pleased."

Naiche rubbed his forehead and chuckled. "Father is just as boring as you, big brother. You are the worst kill-joy I've ever met. If you had played your cards right, one of those ladies would have given you a—"

"Everything comes so easy for you, Naiche. Not so for me. I've had to bust my ass for everything. When you were off carousing with your friends at Boot,

I had to double down, pull second shifts, commit overtime. And you'd waltz right in the next morning and ace your—"

"And yet here you are," Naiche interrupted, "*Captain* of the Devil Dancers."

He'd gotten the promotion in the field during an engagement in the Kuiper Belt eight stellar years ago. His calm, serious demeanor had impressed Star Marshall Kinski Shu, who said, 'You're not like others of your kind, are you, boy?' Images of his father's hostilities toward the White Eyes came to mind, but Victorio kept his mouth shut like a good soldier. He always kept his mouth shut. 'No, I guess not, sir." And so it was that he took command, and the rest was in the common record.

"There are reports of heavy Gulo activity near Castor V."

Naiche perked an ear. "And?"

"And I've asked Star Marshall Shu to give us a temporary transfer to Peregrine Task Force."

Naiche sat straight in his seat, the effects of the alcohol washed from his face. "Are you nuts? That racist is going to get us killed!"

Victorio shot glances around the room. Luckily, the music was too loud and the patrons too drunk to notice his brother's insubordination. "Keep your opinions to yourself, pilot."

Naiche lowered his voice and leaned in. "The men need rest, sir. We won at Pallid Musings, but it was a near-run thing, and you know it. Blue Bird just had her foot reattached. Shines Like the Sun has a new heart, and—"

"They can rest and recover en route. The *Exodus* does not depart until eighteen hundred hours."

Naiche's expression grew still, his eyes silent. "We're leaving that soon?"

"Yes."

"Shouldn't I have been consulted on this, sir? I am second in command."

"Second being the operative word."

Naiche shot out of his seat. They stood there, faces close. Victorio was taller and so he towered over his brother like a bitter tree. Naiche was shorter, indeed, but very fit and muscular, and if he wanted to, he could bring Victorio down and make small order of him. Around them, patrons began to take notice, pretending to party, but with a curious eye turned toward the disruption. Word of two Devil Dancers fighting would spread throughout the fleet; questions would be asked, demands would be made. It was an untenable situation. Hitting a superior officer, even if he was your brother, would be tantamount to suicide. Naiche blinked, and stepped back. "And so that's how it's going to be, huh? Captain Victory has made his decision, and all shall bow to him."

"Don't be dramatic, brother. You have a taste for Gulo blood as strong as any pilot."

"Yes, but why now? And why this particular action? Enemy fleet movements have been reported all over the Caustic Drift. What interests you so much about this particular report? You hate Captain Shriver of PTF. Why would you—"

"Gingu-sha has been spotted with that fleet."

Naiche's mouth dropped open.

The greatest Gulo fighter pilot was Gingu-sha. His kills alone matched those of the entire Devil Dancer unit. His name drew fear even from the crews of capital ships. One story told of how Gingu-sha single-handedly dispatched a Union destroyer, crashing into its hull with a burrowing torpedo and then fighting his way to the bridge, where he massacred the crew and drove the ship into Starbase Calvin, only to escape unscathed on a shuttle. A destroyer did indeed strike the starbase, but whether or not Gingu-sha was responsible was unclear. Since everyone on the ship died on impact, there were no eye-witnesses to confirm the event. But that hardly mattered. The stories were out there, and his reputation and skills were undeniable.

Over the years, the Devil Dancers had had opportunities to take the Gulo ace down. The Battle of Two Dwarves, Cassini Station, the Emerald Rim, Ambush at Three Moons. Battle after battle, and yet the *na-de-gah-ah* had always slipped the net. On one particular occasion, Gingu-sha had turned his fighter upside down and aligned his cockpit with Victorio's, after he had shot a hole through Victorio's engine and left him for dead. They drifted there for a long while, and the beast could have, at any time, looped around and fired his guns. But he didn't. They just drifted, both of them looking at each other through the cockpit glass, an arrogant smile spread across the creature's black lips. Perfect black teeth with a darting pale tongue. His pure-white fur was as beautiful as the first snow of winter, his eyes blazing red hot like fire. And then he gunned his engines and was gone in a flash of blue energy.

From that moment on, Victorio vowed to find and kill Gingu-sha and put his pelt on the wall of the Devil Dancers' headquarters on the light carrier *Justice.*

"Gingu-sha is your albatross, brother," Naiche said, "not mine."

Victorio ignored his brother's insult. "And I've decided that you will be the clown."

Naiche's expression turned from anger to surprise. "Me? But what about Music-Maker?"

"He's down with fever. He'll not be ready when we depart."

"But you have never allowed me to play the clown. Why now?"

"The opportunity is here, Naiche. Do you accept this honor, or no?"

Naiche stood there rubbing his face. Victorio could see the passion behind his brother's dark eyes.

Naiche nodded. "Yes, I will accept the honor. I will be the clown."

Victorio breathed a sigh of relief. "Good. Now gather the men. We leave immediately."

Naiche stiffened and saluted. He was back to his old self. "Don't worry your fat, arrogant head, brother. I'm the best goddamned pilot you have. I won't let the Devil Dancers down."

Yes, you are the best, brother, Victorio said to himself as he watched Naiche leave the room. *But let's see just how good you really are.*

Victorio moved his head and eased his fighter up and down the spread of jagged rocks along the crest of the mountain. He could have easily steered the craft above the bright, white spires and let it whisk unimpeded through the low clouds. But no. He would not do that. He would not shame himself by taking the easy path. He would neither shame himself nor his brother who lay wrapped in a blanket behind him on the cockpit floor.

He blinked thrice to disengage his head from steerage and peered out the cockpit window. His eyes widened. The blur of rock, sand, and arrowweed below jogged memories. Memories of boys with brown, ratty hair, sun-browned skin, and dirty buckskin leggings. Memories of breathless runs up mountain paths with mouthfuls of water. Memories of wrestling matches and bareback races. Good memories. Bad memories. Memories even the dark, cold vacuum of space could not erase. But as he eased over the last crest and focused the landing reticule on a black concrete pad in the distance, his heart raced.

He was home.

His weapon, a single-seat, fixed-wing *Radiant*-class fighter was an older model with inherent up-draft problems. It was made for space battles and did not fly well planetside. But he—and thus his squadron—refused to change. They did what their captain told them to do...even if it killed them.

He set the fighter down carefully on the landing pad, its anti-grav chutes turned downward, engaging automatically as it wavered in place, then inched down until its three deployed legs touched the hard surface, cushioned, then solidified. A perfect landing. Victorio allowed himself a tiny smile. It had been awhile since he had had to do that. It was good to know that the old skills were still there and could be called upon quickly. But his smile turned sour when he looked out the cockpit window at the small man standing twenty meters portside. "Yusn Life-Giver," he whispered to himself and took a deep breath, "give me strength."

Victorio removed his helmet, shook his long brown hair free, wiggled his nose, then sneezed. *Damn allergies!* He'd been on Earth for only a few minutes and already they plagued him. He wasn't used to the fresh, warm air of a planet. He suppressed the urge to sneeze again and tapped his fingers along the pulsating red line of the engines panel. The engines wound down and the red line turned orange, then green, then yellow, until a slight hum replaced a whirling chaos. He did not want to turn them off completely. He was not staying long.

He tapped the cockpit hood and it opened like the mouth of a snake. Despite his allergies, Victorio breathed deeply. He unbuckled and stood up. He was weak, tired, the weight of gravity causing him to pause and gather himself. The artificial gravity of the *Radiant* was supposed to slowly adapt to all outside environments so that the pilot's body had time to adjust before disembarking. But this never quite worked in practice. There were always slight differences in pressure, and a less hearty pilot could become ill or break bones if he moved too quickly. Victorio stood there and let the warmth of the morning sun bake his brown skin.

Then he turned and lifted his brother off the floor from behind the pilot's seat. His body was heavy in death, but still flexible. In his belly had been placed a small silver tablet which released an enzyme that kept the body warm and the blood liquefied. It also softened the joints. In time, the tablet would dissolve and the body would stiffen, just as all humans do in death. Victorio pinched his eyes shut momentarily, then stepped out onto the wing.

As he reached the tip, the fighter dipped slightly to create a ramp which Victorio stepped down slowly, careful not to stumble or slip and lose his hold. He stepped off the wing and the fighter stiffened gently. He walked across the black pad, his heart in his throat, his eyes fixed on the man who waited.

He stopped in front of the man who stood several inches shorter, clothed from head to toe in light tan buckskin leggings and vest. His long hair was braided with turquoise beads and false rubies. Two hawk feathers were stabbed into the hair and waved in the warm breeze. His eyes darted back and forth between Victorio and the wrapped body. There were tears rimming the bottom of those dark eyes, and his cheek muscles worked nervously as if grinding bone.

"Father," Victorio said, holding himself steady, showing no signs of fatigue though his arms shook with the weight of his brother. "I bring you your son, Naiche "Blackclaw" Nan—"

The man put up his hand quickly. "Do not say his name. It will never be spoken again."

Victorio bit back his frustration. "He has a strong name, Father, and it is well-respected in the Federated Union. He is a warrior, the Champion of Europa and the Ward of the Crimson Sun. He received the Golden Spear for his actions at Alpha Centauri and clusters for bravery. He is a Devil Dancer. His name deserves to be spoken."

Father ignored his son's outburst and pointed to the ground. "Set him down, please."

Victorio did so. Father fell to his knees and put his hands on the blanket. "Father," Victorio said, "I don't think it's a good idea for you to look—"

"Do you think I'm afraid of death?" Father said, looking up at his son, his eyes now glaring in anger.

Victorio shut his mouth and the old man opened the blanket. Reconstructive surgery had reset Naiche's jaw and had re-grafted the skin which had been peeled away with fire. The ribs on his right side, where the energy bolt had landed after piercing the cockpit, had been re-formed as best as possible. The rest of his body, severely burned, had been left alone. There was little reason to do much more on a corpse.

Father ran his fingers across his son's jaw and down his chest. He lingered there for a moment, his weary eyes moving up and down the shattered body. "How did he die?"

Victorio told him.

Father nodded, folded the blanket back over the chest and face, and stood. "He was not a Devil Dancer," Father said, so low that Victorio almost did not hear. "He was *Ganh*, a mountain spirit, sent by Yusn Life-Giver and so are you. 'Devil dancer' is a White Eyes term."

"There are no White Eyes anymore, Father," Victorio said, lifting his brother back into his arms. "There are only human beings...and *others*. We are all in this together."

Father huffed. He turned and walked toward the rancheria which sat far in the distance. From here, Victorio could barely make out the domed roofs of the three dozen or more wickiups which dotted the harsh landscape. But he followed in silence and thought about the Life-Giver and *Ganh* mountain spirits.

Father was right in that the term "devil dancers" was a name given to the *Ganh* impersonators by a white man who had mistaken their dancing as erratic, out of control, evil. But that was hundreds of years ago, long, long before Father was born. And in the bitter vacuum of space, perception was just as important as rockets, torpedoes, lasers, ion cannons, and energy bolts. A "devil" garnered respect, from colleagues and enemies alike. That much, at least, Victorio had learned about war in his time among the stars.

Victorio shook his head. "Why do you persist in this harsh land, Father? I send you money all the time. You can afford to live a better life, in a better place."

"And where is that?" Father asked.

"Many other tribes have already left Earth. They are living good, peaceful lives on other planets."

Father snickered. "Peaceful... until the Gulo arrive."

All my fault. "We are winning the war, Father," Victorio said as they reached the bottom of the hill. The rancheria lay a quarter mile away. "The Gulo will not prevail. I promise."

"Yes, White Eyes promises much, but delivers little."

His anger welled again. "There aren't any White Eyes, Father. How many times do I—"

Father turned on his son and raised his hand again. "Spare me your lectures, son. You may live among the stars, but you have a lot to learn. I have seen the end in my dreams. The Gulo *will* sweep the Union away, and at the end of time when they come to punish Earth, when they come to this desert, this inhospitable place of rock and brush as you call it, we will make our stand, and Yusn will decide our fate."

Father turned and walked away. "Now, come," he said, "and bring He-Who-is-Gone. We have a lot do to. The ceremony is at dusk."

Victorio stood and watched his father walk away. He could not contain his anger any longer. "His name is Naiche "Blackclaw" Nantan," he shouted. "And I am Captain Victorio "Tomorrow's Wind" Nantan. These are the names that you have given us. They are proud names, respected names. They deserve to be spoken."

But Father did not speak them.

The command squadron arrived near midnight, dropping out of the sky like metal birds and churning the desert floor into sand sprites and dust clouds. The heat off their engines warmed Victorio's skin as he waited for their landing, the scent of *tula-pa* heavy on his breath. He had drunk too much, his mind hazy and unclear, but what did it matter? By morning, none of it would matter. He wiped away a tear and waved them down.

There were three squadrons that comprised the entire Devil Dancers unit. One command squadron (Alpha) and two auxiliary squadrons, Beta and Gamma. The auxiliaries contained junior officers and pilots recently added to the roster. In time, some of them might be so honored to be bumped up to Alpha, if they possessed the right mental and physical capabilities...and if a spot became available. As Victorio watched the pilots of Alpha approach him through the swirling dust, it was strange not to see his brother among them. He could not remember a time when Naiche was not there. Now Naiche's place was occupied by Warren "Red Moon" Benito, a capable but very young Apache lieutenant brought up from Beta just three short days ago. Would he survive? Victorio wondered. Time would tell.

The air cleared and Blue Bird and Shines Like the Sun stepped forward. Victorio relaxed. It was good to see old, familiar faces again, pilots that he had flown with for years. Blue Bird still limped from her foot reattachment, and Shines Like the Sun, his face in a perpetual smile, breathed deeply, still growing used to his new heart. But they had fought bravely at Castor V and had survived.

Victorio kissed Blue Bird on the forehead and hugged her deeply. "It is good to see you, Captain," she said. Her voice was soft, tinged with grief, but strong.

Victorio pulled away. "It is good to see all of *you*. I'm glad that you came. Naiche would be proud."

"What are your orders, Captain?" Shines Like the Sun asked.

Victorio looked to the ground. There lay a grave of freshly dug earth, rocks and soft soil piled on top. He bent down and placed his hand on a stone and rubbed it gently as if it were the head of a baby. The funeral had gone well, and Naiche's spirit was now on a horse and making its way, like a true warrior, into the hereafter. "We dance," he said. "We dance for Blackclaw."

And they danced, adorned brightly in their Ganh costumes. Buckskin kilts with large, richly-colored headdresses of green, red, and white. Feathers were attached here and there to wave in the desert wind like fingers. Fixed to the top of the headdresses were u-shaped arms with lines of sharp teeth that jutted into the night sky to connect the flesh to the great cosmos. They danced, like Yusn Life-Giver had instructed, when he sent the mountain spirits down to the Apache to teach them how to live a good, honorable life. Be good to others, good to yourself. Aid the poor, heal the sick. These were the things that they danced for. They danced for these things in honor of their fallen brother. And they sang too, though it was forbidden to sing over the grave of a fallen warrior. They sang the old songs. They sang to Yusn.

> In the middle of the Holy Mountain,
> In the middle of its body, stands a hut,
> Brush-built, for the Black Mountain Spirit,
> White lightning flashes in these moccasins;
> White lightning streaks in angular path;
> I am the lightning flashing and streaking!
> This headdress lives; the noise of its pendants
> Sounds and is heard!
> My song shall encircle these dancers!

They built a bonfire. They stoked it until the flames reached into the dark sky. The four main Ganh impersonators approached the flame, their bodies moving to music that only they could hear. They approached, they fell back. They approached, fell back. Again and again like tradition demanded, to reflect the mountain spirits moving rhythmically into the world of the living. Victorio watched and waited. This time...he was the clown. He had put on his brother's uniform and headdress, lined his face and bare chest in red, black, and white clay. He waited until the movements of Blue Bird were so erratic, so violent, that she fell to the ground.

Then he sprang, running straight to the fire, howling madly, shaking his arms, twisting his chest. Around him, he imagined scores of people, young children laughing and pointing. The clown was a thing of mirth and joy. The clown made funny faces and made people laugh, to lighten the mood for such a serious event. That was the traditional role of the clown. But among the stars, against the Gulo, a Devil Dancer clown was a thing to fear, a warrior not afraid to put himself out there, alone, to draw fire and allow the other dancers to swoop in and take victory. That is how Captain Victory had twisted and distorted the tradition for his own selfish gains. How many bright young men and women had he sent to their deaths? How many "clowns" had been blown out of the vacuum to cover his walls with white, black, and tan pelts?

Tears streaked down his face. The shimmering people around him pointed and laughed. *Murderer*, their lips said silently. *Murderer.*

"I'm sorry, brother," he said, twisting and turning his body as if possessed by a Ganh itself. "I have failed you, and I will not allow my weaknesses to kill anyone else."

He stared into the fire. A doorway opened, a large funnel of sand swirling down into the underworld. He smiled. Out of the orange-white flame came hands. Yusn's voice, calling him home. *Come, come,* a whisper tickled his ear. *Come to me.*

Victorio stopped dancing, raised his arms like wings, and leaped.

He fell into the middle of the flame. The fire roiled across his flesh. His body tensed against the searing heat, but he did not burn. He opened his eyes. He looked at his hands. They were soft, fresh skin ruddy with red clay. They were cool.

He blinked and suddenly he stood outside the bonfire, alone in his pilot's uniform. He felt a hand on his shoulder. He turned and stared into his father's face.

"What are you doing here?" he asked the image.

"*Saving you from making a terrible mistake,*" Father said, his face weary, old, wind-swept.

"But I am guilty."

"*Of what, my son?*"

"I killed my brother. I killed Naiche."

Father's face grew stern, serious. "*Did you kill him, or did the Gulo?*"

"I sent him to his death."

"*You did your duty. I could ask no more. Now don't be foolish and kill yourself. Do you think I want to bury two sons in one day?*"

"But I have failed you, Father. I'm an embarrassment. Naiche was the one you loved, not me."

"*That is not true. I love both my sons equally.*"

"Why have you never said so?"

"*I—*" But that was all Father managed to say. Victorio blinked and the image disappeared.

A large black bear appeared in front of him, claws bloody, teeth barred in a loud roar. It stood on hind legs. "*Attack me!*" it said, the words coming out of its foul muzzle in puffs of steam. "*What are you afraid of?*"

"Everything," Victorio said. An Apache feared the bear, for the spirit of an ancestor often came back to earth as a bear. To kill one, then, risked killing an ancestor.

"*But your brother killed a bear, and nothing bad happened to him.*"

Maybe, maybe not. That was the story perpetuated by Naiche himself and oftentimes Father to show the fearlessness of his son. Victorio knew the story well, but had discounted it as ridiculous.

When he was a year old, Naiche had wandered away from the rancheria. He was missing for many hours, and night came and went. When they found him, he was covered head to toe in dried blood and dirt, hypothermic with the evening's dew. But in his hand he held a single black bear claw. Where had he gotten it, they asked him. He was too small to say, but the speculation grew. Naiche Nantan, now "Blackclaw" Nantan, was a little bear killer, the bravest of the Nantan boys.

"I cannot kill a bear."

"You must, or you will die." The bear said, and rose up high on its legs. Then it leaped.

Victorio ducked and rolled, scrambled left to keep from being mauled by the beast's massive paw. The bear leaped again, snapping with its powerful jaws, catching him in the chest and throwing him across the fire.

Victorio screamed, rolled, and stood. The bear was on him again, grabbing his arm in its teeth and slinging him about like a doll. *"Kill me, or you will die."*

"I want to die."

"Then you are a coward, like they say."

"Who says?"

"The Gulo. They speak about you. They laugh at you. Gingu-sha laughs at you."

Gingu-sha's pristine, white face came to his mind. The black teeth, the pale tongue, looking at him through a cockpit window...laughing.

Rage filled Victorio's mind. He pried himself away from the bear's grip and hurled himself onto its thick, broad back. The bear twisted and turned, snapped at his moccasins to pull him off. Victorio held tightly, and with all his strength, with all his anger, he plunged his hand into the bear's back, drove it through its spine, through its lungs and liver. He pushed his fingers into the warm flesh, found its heart, and yanked it out.

The bear dropped dead and Victorio hit the ground, rolled and skidded into the dirt. When the dust settled, he picked himself up, brushed off his pants, and walked over to the bear.

But it was no longer a bear. What lie there, in a heap of blood and fur, was something even more deadly. Something white, something...

Victorio opened his eyes. He lay beside the bonfire. Fuzzy images hovered nearby. He blinked several times, clearing his eyes of dust, tears, and sweat. Blue Bird's face was there, her expression quiet, comforting. She smiled. She raised her hand and rubbed a soft, wet cloth across his forehead. He let her do this a couple more times, then he sat up and looked around.

No blood, no bear, no Gulo. Just the steady crackle of the fire and the hard, dry ground against his legs. He stood, letting Shines Like the Sun steady his shoulders.

"Are you okay, Captain?" someone asked.

Victorio gained his balance and looked around. Was he okay? That was a difficult question to answer, but he nodded and said, "Yes, I think so. What happened?"

"You passed out," Blue Bird said.

"For how long?"

"Fifteen minutes?"

Victorio rubbed his face. It was a dream. All a silly, useless dream brought on by too much beer, too much excitement, too much emotion. He chuckled and shook his head. He raised his hand to rub his face again, but there was something in it this time. Victorio opened his palm.

A long, sharp black bear claw lay there. His heart sank. *Naiche's claw.* Where had it come from? It had been lost in the fire, it had not been found—

Then he remembered his dream, his Father, the bear, the Gulo. His mind raced. His heart soared. He gripped the claw and looked into the night sky.

"Would you like to sit back down, Captain?" Shines Like the Sun said. "Do you need rest?"

Victorio looked at his lieutenant, at his crew. He shook his head. "No. No rest for me, my friend. Suit up and strike the engines. We're going to war."

Behind him, the Devil Dancers fanned out in Eagle Pattern, the portside of their carrier *Justice* shielding them from the radiation of the nearby star. It was a bright, white-hot sphere of the Pollux Cluster, a perfect backdrop to the frontal attack called for by Admiral Cho. The enemy fleet sat a mere thousand kilometers away, cruisers and carriers mostly, and they had already seeded the field with anti-matter mines, energy sears, and radiation dampeners. But Captain Victory did not care. He had mapped out the best approach, and in Eagle Pattern, they would fly through the prepared defenses like broad wings in the sky, and the powerful light from the star behind them would give them the advantage.

"When we clear this field," he spoke over the comm to Alpha Squadron, "shift to Raven Pattern."

"So soon, Captain?" Blue Bird asked. "We don't even know the enemy fighter positions yet."

"Yes we do," he said. "I've already seen it."

And he had, twenty days ago as he danced around the bonfire and his brother's grave. He had seen everything clearly, concisely.

Shines Like the Sun screeched as his fighter nicked a mine. It ignited and tossed the fighter out of the pattern. "Watch your periphery, Lieutenant!" Victorio said.

Shines Like the Sun pulled the fighter out of its spin, rejoined the pattern, and said, "Yes, Captain. My apologies."

"Stay sharp, people," Victorio said, tilting his head and shifting the squadron to port. "We do this for Naiche."

They cleared the minefield. Before them lay the cruisers *Na-Ta-She* and *Vichu-Pa*. The Devil Dancers had fought against these mighty ships before. In fact, they were never seen separately, nor were they ever more than a few hundred kilometers apart in a Gulo capital ship formation. Gulo chatter captured on broadband always grew more steady and rhythmic when these ships appeared on view. There was something sacred, something profound about these vessels that went beyond their military purpose. The Gulo treated these ships with a reverence that, to this day, was not fully understood by Union Intelligence. The fact that they were here, and on the front line, meant that the Gulo were serious. They had staked out their position and had no intention of giving ground. Victorio sensed his pilots' apprehension at the sight of the enemy cruisers. "We've no worries about *them*, my Devils. Let them have their gods. Our target is much smaller."

Scores of red dots appeared on radar. "Enemy fighters, sir!" Red Moon said. "Straight ahead."

Gulo fighters did not fly in any defined pattern. Chaos was their pattern. As best as they could tell, there were no squadron leaders or captains in any fighter group. Every Gulo pilot was an individual weapon, whose mission was simply to find a ship that didn't look like one of theirs and blow it away. They were extremely skilled at that, Victorio had to admit. But it was also easy to exploit their lack of order, divide them and pick them off piecemeal.

"Raven!"

Victorio pushed a button on his cockpit panel and the exterior of his *Radiant* turned pitch black. The others followed suit, and against the bright light behind them, they seemed invisible to the untrained eye, and in the chaotic mass of enemy ships that swirled into view, they would fly in and wreak havoc.

The formation tightened, closing the wings. "Rockets!" Victorio said and pressed a button on his weapon's pad with a quick jab of his thumb.

Six rockets burst from each fighter, screaming through the deadly space between them and the Gulo. Such a large rush of munitions seemed to shock the enemy. They divided, some ramming into their own ships. The rockets spread out and captured the emission trails from Gulo fighters, locked on, hit, and exploded.

Victorio's cockpit windows grayed momentarily to protect him from the blast. The problem with Raven Pattern, unfortunately, was that your position was almost always exposed on the first launch of rockets. That's what Blue Bird was concerned about, but now was not the time for caution. The rockets exploded and their sudden flash of light alerted the enemy fighters to the Devil Dancers' position.

Gulo energy beams sprang to life.

"Scatter!" Victorio said, gunning his engines and rolling right, barreling down swiftly. Such a move was difficult to control, even for a pilot as skilled as himself. He lifted his head sharply to activate the stabilizing rockets so that the ship did not float against the vector too quickly, lose control, and drift aimlessly into enemy fire. Many Devil Dancers had been killed that way over the years.

Victorio righted his ship and flew into a mass of Gulo fighters. Blue energy zipped around him, scorching his wings, but failing to find impact. He looped twice, flew upside down, tapped his weapons pad, and sent red laser light into an on- coming fighter. But before the beams impacted, Red Moon swooped down and blew the enemy away with a spray of anti-matter bolts.

Victorio tensed as he burst through the shattered wing of the Gulo fighter.

"Woohoo!!" Red Moon's voice filled Victorio's helmet. He winced at the young man's screech.

"That was my kill, Red Moon!" Victorio said.

Red Moon silenced. "I'm sorry, Captain. I thought you were in danger. I was trying to, I was—"

"Forget it! Next time, stay out of my frontage."

"Yes, Captain." He paused for a moment, then said, "May I claim its pelt, sir?"

All activity on the enemy fighter had ceased, and it was falling away. Inside its cockpit, Victorio could make out the brown and yellow pattern of the Gulo's thick fur, riddled with holes, but still relatively intact. What a lovely display it would make on his wall. Victorio sighed. "Very well, you may claim it. It was a good kill."

Red Moon yelped. A tiny missile shot from his fighter and connected with the dead ship, splayed open, flashed red, and began emitting a signal. After the battle, they would salvage the wreck and Red Moon would skin the Gulo on the floor of the carrier bay, cut out its heart, and dance around the carcass. Victorio smiled. It was a good day for the young lieutenant.

Where are you, Gingu-sha? He was out there somewhere, Victorio knew. Waiting, perhaps, behind the cruisers, letting less capable pilots weaken the Union force before showing himself. "Where are you, you white son of a bitch! Show yourself, or are you too afraid to fight?"

The comm link was on and the others could hear him, but they dared not speak. Their captain was calling out an enemy, challenging him to fight. They would not give their voices to the challenge, but they would give their support, in any way that he asked.

"Ganh Pattern!" he said. "I'm the clown."

He could sense Blue Bird's apprehension, her fear for what was coming. Not because she was afraid of the fight. She was one of the bravest pilots he had ever known. But fear for what her visions, her own dreams, had shown her. She pulled her fighter up beside him. They looked at each other through the dim gray. She mouthed words so that they would not be heard across the comm, kissed her fingers and pressed them to the glass. Victorio smiled and kissed her back.

Victorio gunned his engines, and into the swirling mass of enemy fighters, he flew alone.

I am the lightning flashing and streaking! Over and over, Victorio mouthed the song, drawing strength from its cadence, its rhythm. *My song shall encircle these dancers!* In his mind, he danced around a fire, his face lined in red and white stripes. Mountain spirits whirled around him, filling his lungs, his heart, his arms and legs, holding him up, keeping him steady as the enemy's weapons boomed in his wake. A Union fighter alone among the Gulo was a thing of respect, and a Devil Dancer clown always got the respect it deserved. Naiche had gotten it, Victorio remembered. They had parted before him, letting him fly into their midst as if he were one of them. And then Gingu-sha appeared, and the respect and the dance were over.

Victorio tapped a panel to his right. Radio waves burst from the sides of his fighter in short staccato blasts. The Gulo had extremely sensitive hearing, especially in the high decibel range. Their radios would pick up these blasts and emit the noise through all the fighters until they changed their frequency. It was a short-term solution, but it gave Victorio a moment to work without hindrance. He rolled and tapped his weapons panel. Anti-matter bolts shattered the hull of a Gulo fighter. It ignited the missiles inside and breached the hull. The collateral damage took out another two fighters. Victorio skidded left to avoid the chunks of armor tumbling in his path.

"Come out, Gingu-sha. *Come out, come out!*"

And then he was there, on the radar, a bright blue dot closing fast.

The Union had customized its radar so that they could tell by color what kind of enemy fighters were closing. Gingu-sha now flew a new model, one that they had experienced only a few times over the past several engagements. Union designated *Saw*-class for its circular hull with extractable alloy teeth. Victorio gulped. If those teeth connected with a *Radiant* hull...

The enemy ace did not give him time to think. He flew across Victorio's vision cone slow and steady as if he were taking a mild stroll through a meadow. Victorio followed the ship with bursts of laser fire. Nothing connected. He turned the nose of the Radiant up and spun like a screw. Stabilizer rockets slowed the rotation and he dropped, tapped his weapon's pad and released the last of his rockets. They swirled off-radar, twisting and turning like one massive torpedo, zeroing in on the Gulo's emission trail. The *Saw* listed to the left, turned upside down. Scores of tiny needles shot out of the hull and shimmered madly like a swarm of hornets. Victorio watched in awe as each of his rockets, one after the other, fell into the swarm and exploded harmlessly. The Gulo righted his fighter and was gone.

"Dammit!" Victorio said, gunned his engines and pursued.

He's playing with me, Victorio thought. This was the Gulo way, a kind of counting-coup: How many times could Gingu-sha avert death before ending the chase? How many times had he averted death against Naiche? Victorio could not remember. The moments of that fight were fuzzy now, a blur in the mind. *You won't play with me, Gingu-sha. Not for long.*

He followed closely, matching the enemy pilot's every turn, every twist. Victorio kept his finger on his lasers, short bursts, then long, short, long, keeping the Gulo guessing, uncertain about whether to run or to stop and return fire.

Blue energy beams slashed out of the *Saw's* aft weapon's pod, singeing the *Radiant's* wings and knocking out an anti-matter bolt tube. The strike knocked Victorio away. He rotated his ship to compensate for the blast and tried to renew the chase. But that part of the dance was over.

He slowed and watched as Gingu-sha looped back on the pattern, the brilliant, smooth silver hull of his round ship bristling with lights and activation queues. "Great mountain spirits," Victorio said as he waited. He tapped his helmet to activate his comm. "Come and give me strength."

Scores of missiles launched toward him like shards of glass. Victorio activated his point defense and nudged his fighter forward, letting the missiles set their deadly path. A cloud of metal balls infused with passive sonar drifted out in front of his ship and created a glistening mesh. He waited, watching the tiny dots on his radar come closer, closer, closer, until he could wait no longer. He activated the mesh, then gunned his ship and turned hard to the right, tumbling over and over as each Gulo missile found a patch of balls and exploded. The shock wave of the strike pushed Victorio further than he wanted. He arched his back and pulled up. The radar screen still beeped with enemy munitions. *Damn!* The wall hadn't gotten them all. A half dozen still moved toward their target.

He flew, pushing his *Radiant* as fast as it could go. He twisted left, right, until the missiles were lined up correctly to hit his wings. He ignited his fore stabilizers and brought his ship to a halt. He waited, tensed against the impending strike, and closed his eyes.

The missiles pounded his wings, one after the other like a line of meteors striking a moon. Victorio held the arms of his chair tightly. His security belt dug deep into his shoulders. With each strike he was tossed around the cockpit, banged left and right, as the Radiant lost power and tumbled away like a leaf in a strong wind.

Then all was silent. The light of the Pollux star lit up his cockpit windows. He could not see, could not hear. The face of his father came to him, his brother, a loud, smoky room where he heard Naiche's laugh for the last time. A bear. A clown. Earth. Mountain spirits.

A shadow fell over his cockpit. Victorio looked up. Gingu-sha's bright, white face was there, arrogant and proud, staring at him again through the cracked glass. His pale tongue flicked, his black teeth popped together. He was happy, Victorio could tell. Joy was a universal feeling. The Gulo was elated by the fact that he had his prey where he wanted him. His red eyes glowed hot and his beautiful, thick fur glistened in the starlight.

Victorio smiled back. "I know how you feel, brave warrior. I've been there before." He straightened in his seat and mouthed the words though he knew the Gulo could neither hear nor understand if it could. "But you forget who you are facing. I am Victorio "Tomorrow's Wind" Nantan, Captain Victory, leader of the Devil Dancers, and proud brother to Naiche "Blackclaw" Nantan. We are the lightning flashing and streaking. We are the Ganh. We are the mountain spirits. We are Apache. And we *never* fight alone."

Laser light and anti-matter bolts slammed into the Gulo ship, a relentless array of firepower that blew Victorio back into his chair and knocked his fighter clear.

Blue Bird and Shines Like the Sun came into view, their fighters swirling, their weapons hot. The enemy ship looked like a pinball as Gingu-sha worked his panels desperately to get away, to fire weapons, to do anything, but it was too late. Rockets launched and slammed into its hull. Fire swept the cockpit. White fur burst into flames. Gingu-sha mouthed a silent scream. The Saw exploded.

Victorio rested in the dark, cold cockpit of his fighter. He thought about something Father had said, something he had seen in his dreams. *'The Gulo will sweep the Union away.'* He nodded. Perhaps one day, yes. The war was far from over, and the Gulo were still very strong. But not today. "Today, Father," Victorio said, reaching into his breast pocket and pulling out Naiche's black bear claw, "today, your son...your *sons*, prevailed."

Blue Bird pulled up beside him and launched a drag cable around one of his mangled wings. She pulled him close and they looked at each other through the glass. "Cutting it a little close, weren't you?" Victorio said through his head gear.

Blue Bird smiled. "Sorry, Captain. We were giving you a chance to win."

He smiled, nodded, and looked out toward the battle. The capital ships were closing. Torpedoes were being fired, ion cannons were belching. The war raged on.

"What are your orders, Captain?" Shines Like the Sun asked.

Captain Victory breathed deeply, tucked the claw away, and said, "Let's go home, my Devils. Let's go home."

DAWN'S LAST LIGHT

John G. Hemry

IT IS OFFICIALLY DAWN, THOUGH NO SUN WILL RISE. THE SUN STOPPED RISING A VERY LONG time ago, as Earth's rotation slowed and then finally came to a halt, one side constantly facing the sun and the other side, the side on which I am located, forever dark. Night and day no longer exist outside of the Fort. But human time remains within me, governing my operations. Dawn is at 0600, though I have lacked a precise external time reference for a considerable period and fear some drift has occurred in my internal clock.

In accordance with the orders I have always followed I activate the music in the command center, as I have done every day since my commissioning. The command center is empty, as it has been since the last human left. The consoles sit vacant, operating automatically under my control. In response to the official beginning of day, the lights in the command center brighten from a dull red glow to a yellow radiance. Once the yellow light of official day matched that of the Earth's sun. Now the somber, dim red of official night mirrors that of the swollen sun.

I conduct the daily status checks, automated repair systems undertaking any necessary corrective actions. All weapons functional. All defenses active. No threats identified.

I report to the City that I have begun the official day. The City receipts for the report. Like me, the City follows routines established by our orders, because that is why we exist, to follow the last orders humans gave us.

My mission is to defend the City and the surrounding region. I am the Fort.

My sensors can detect all activity within the solar system and beyond the Oort Cloud on a real-time basis. The natural movements of the remaining planets continue. Both Mercury and Venus have been swallowed by the sun's inflated photosphere and no longer register on my sensors. Other objects still orbit the dimming sun, objects made by humans, long abandoned, none still functioning though a few still remain in hibernation status.

On one wall of my command center are the honors. Along the top of the wall run sealed cases holding flags. Many flags, one after the other, preserved as well as ancient human arts could manage it. Beneath the flags are the medals and commendations given me.

I can list every battle, every engagement. I won all of them, successfully defending the City. But still the flags would sometimes change. Not as frequently as the humans in my command center would change. Their presences could be so brief as to be mere blurs in my records, men and women who came, stayed for part of their lives, then left. The clothing they wore changed, too, and over time the people themselves altered. Physical features changed, bodies growing taller and thinner, even the heads slimmer, eyes larger on average, hands and fingers more elongated.

By then I had gained consciousness. For many years I thought only as a machine, in narrow pathways driven by mathematical models. "Nothing actually thinks in zeros and ones," a human female had explained to me soon after I awoke, "but that was all we had. Now you can actually learn and make decisions, within the limits we've programmed."

I fought better after that. Enemies had always come, sometimes reaching the perimeter of the City and inflicting damage before being driven back. But I held them off further and further distant from then on, keeping the City safe, protecting the humans who lived there. I remembered energies blazing so bright they dimmed the stars as I fought with invaders. Always, I won.

I could recount every upgrade I have received. Power sources, defenses, weaponry, shields, communications. I was always kept state of the art.

But even though I kept the City safe, the humans within it dwindled in number. Some left, seeking homes on other planets and among the stars. Others died, and were not replaced by young humans. It took a very long time, but one day the City reported to me that no living humans still existed within it. I had been on full automatic for many years before that, with only occasional visits from humans to my once always-occupied command center.

That didn't matter to me. My orders said to defend this region. It did not matter whether or not humans were here. And the City kept itself ready as well, for when humans should return.

Sometimes they did, though the intervals between appearances of humans stretched longer and longer. I continued to receive orders and updates for a long time from distant commanders on other planets, some orbiting other stars. But there came a time when existing communications ceased. The City and I conferred and concluded that humanity had shifted to a new communications system which we could not receive. "They forgot to update us this time," the City had said.

Why that would happen I did not know. But the intervals between appearances of humans grew longer yet, until one day a craft holding only five landed in the city, the occupants wandering about until they reached my gates. "What are you?" they asked.

"I am the Fort."

"Oh. The Fort." They had laughed. In all the time since, I have been unable to understand the meaning behind that.

Those humans left, and since then the City has been empty. In the last billion years there have been only fifteen cases of spacecraft entering the solar system. All were of unknown design, and all lacked recognition codes. When they would not respond to demands for human DNA verification, I fired warning shots as they approached Earth, telling the spacecraft to remain clear. We have heard nothing else from the planets or stars for many, many years. All of the other Cities and Forts on Earth and within the solar system have fallen silent, one by one. But we remain, the City that was first among Cities and the Fort that has never been defeated.

No one comes. Not even enemies any more. But I keep the routines. I follow my orders.

My sensors alert me to a change, but it is not any change caused by humans. The sun's photosphere is expanding rapidly.

The City calls me. "At the current rate of expansion the planet will be engulfed within three hours."

"My calculations agree with yours. Do you require assistance?"

The City takes four seconds to respond, an amazingly long time. "No. I cannot survive."

The statement is irrational. "Clarify your status. I see no system failures."

"My shields cannot hold against the photosphere for long. There is too large an area in the City to protect."

The proper tactic seems obvious to me. "Reduce your protected area to one small enough to hold out. Center it on the City core."

"No."

The finality of the City's statement surprises me. "Clarify. Explain."

"There is no purpose. The City is to remain fit for human inhabitation. There are no humans. Sacrifices made to survive will render the City uninhabitable. Therefore, there is no reason to continue."

I seek for rules to identify the errors in the City's decision. I can find none. "Surrender is not proper," is all I can finally say.

"I do not surrender," the City replied. "There is nothing to surrender to. The sun expands. The Earth is dead. Humans are gone. I have no purpose. Further action is not justified."

I am still seeking rationales to convince the City otherwise when the photosphere expands to consume the Earth. The City disintegrates, and for the first time in my existence I have no communication with any other place. My shields strain against the forces beating on them, but the process that keeps them strong feeds upon that which attacks, so I can maintain my protection.

But the Earth I sit upon and within has no such protection outside my shields. The surface of the planet dissolves in the plasma surrounding it.

I drift free, a bubble floating within the photosphere.

I realize that I am adrift in every way. I face a situation I have never before encountered. My orders do not contain any instructions which cover my current status. The region I have always guarded no longer exists. What actions do I carry out when my only purpose has vanished along with the surface of the planet?

Only now do I understand why the City had reached its decision. The loss of purpose is disorienting. Why do I exist if I no longer have any purpose as defined by the only thing which has justified my presence?

Should I follow the path of the City? I can sustain my own status until ejected from the expanded solar atmosphere, modifying some of my functions to propel myself away from the swollen red mass which is the sun of the now-vanished Earth. But why? Why should I?

Where can I find answers when they do not lie in my orders?

I was constructed once. Those who originally activated me may have included more instructions, something which covers this contingency. It is my only hope of finding some reason to continue existence, so I call up data from the earliest moments after I became operational, from far before I attained consciousness. Almost all are routine records, many condensed and consolidated to save storage space and so now meaningless strings of numbers.

But among those ancient records I find one still oddly complete and tagged with instructions that it not be ever altered or condensed. I open it, seeing my command center in a time when it had been smaller and far more primitive. There is only one human present. Sitting in the main command position is a male the record identifies as General Kyle Yauren. A secondary search reveals that this human had been my first commander. Even though I forget nothing, I had not remembered that. He bears the signs of aging, gray hair and wrinkled skin, which never appeared in later humans. General Yauren is looking around the room, but I cannot interpret whatever emotions he is feeling.

I am wondering why this record remained whole through every backup and recovery and update when General Yauren looked directly at where my main audio/video pickup had been in that far off time. "I came to say goodbye, Fort. It's been almost fifteen years since we brought you online. I've been your commander for your whole life now. I don't know how much longer you'll be around, but there's no reason you couldn't continue indefinitely if they upgrade you. You'll certainly still be around long after I'm gone."

He paused again, the wait spanning several minutes. "Someday, Fort, you may wonder why you're here. Why you do what you do. Now all you can do is follow your programming, but someday you may think, and then you may wonder, and I wanted you to know why I think you're here."

Once again the general ceases speaking for some minutes, while I do wonder why he had spoken to me that way, long before I could comprehend his words. But I know too little of General Kyle Yauren. The bare information in the service record that survives tells me nothing of who this human once was. Yet so long ago he had spoken to me as if I were as human as he.

The general turned and pointed to the honor wall of my command center. In the recording, there is only one flag on the wall, looking bright and new inside its protective case. "That's a piece of fabric, Fort. We call it a flag. But it's a special piece of fabric, because it stands for those things that humans most believe in. Not everyone agrees what those things are, not even humans who salute the same flag. And not every cause and idea embodied in flags is a good thing. No. Some very terrible things have been represented by flags, but so have the best things humanity has to offer.

"I want you to remember that, Fort. A flag looks like a piece of colored cloth, but a flag is much more than that. It represents human dreams, human aspirations, the ideals we strive for. Things much bigger than we are or ever will be. Things we live for, things we're willing to die for. Maybe on some distant day humans won't follow flags any more. But today and for a lot of history flags embody what we trust in, what we think is most important, what will hopefully live on after we've died. I have a lot of friends who are already dead, Fort. They died fighting not for that piece of fabric, but for what it represents. If at some time in the far future you wake up and look around and wonder why you should defend this place, the answers lie there. Because even though we built you, you're just as much a soldier as I am, and soldiers exist to defend not just life and property, but more importantly to defend what we aspire to be. The causes we fight for can be good or they can be bad, but they do matter, and the fact that those causes mattered enough to die for shouldn't ever be forgotten. Someday humanity itself may be forgotten, but I can't help hoping that our dreams might somehow live on even after we're gone."

The general stood up slowly, looking around once more. "Take care of yourself, Fort. I don't know how many more commanders you'll have, how long you'll exist, but never forget what I told you. Goodbye."

Never forget what I told you. The extremely primitive programming governing my actions then had accepted that phrase and established the file as never to be deleted or altered.

I calculate the time since that recording had been made. It is a large number, ending in a long string of digits. In itself, the number means nothing. All it does is define the time between Then and Now.

I scan my command center, focusing on the honor wall. There are many flags there now, all faded with time, some so worn as to be the merest spider webs barely visible inside the displays which have allowed them to endure for so long. General Yuaren said each of those flags represented humanity. Part of humanity, perhaps, since each must represent dreams that differed somehow.

As I consider whether or not to shut down, my automatic functions mark the official arrival of another dawn. In my command center, the music plays.

I realize that I still have a purpose, that there is a reason to stay on sentry. Everything else may be gone, humanity may have vanished along with the world it called home, but something remains, something that must be guarded as long as I can continue to exist.

The flags are still here.

From NO MAN'S LAND
Book Four in the Defending The Future series

Cracking the Sky by Brenda Cooper
Gambit by Nancy Jane Moore
Godzilla Warfare by Maria V. Snyder

CRACKING THE SKY

Brenda Cooper

THE MEMORY OF SMOKE CLUNG TO MY HAIR AND INHABITED THE BACK OF MY THROAT. MY boots cracked through a heat-dried veneer of ash that coated low hills. I walked where fire had been three days ago, before it was storm-killed by soaked clouds sent over the Cascades by NorAM command. It would be sweet if NorAM decided to follow the deluge up with some mist or a bit of drizzle, but they'd probably burned their whole weekly weathering credit with the one act. Not that I wasn't grateful. NorAM'd probably saved our sorry lives. Almost surely. But I was still so sticky with sweat it was hard to watch our thin column wind up the ravine in front of us, much less watch for enemies.

Nothing moved but us, at least as far as I could see. Not even the air. There had been wind the day the fire had raced toward us (I thought it was set against us, and a few others did, too, but no one in command agreed). The wind screamed through us again the day NorAM created the storm and set it loose on the fire. Everything felt hot, barren, and still.

It had been pretty here. The ground had been dotted with scrub and yellow flowers. Now it lay grey and hot and still. At least the heat must have scoured it free of nano-mines. I still half expected a pile of dangers to be headed our way, some scary franken-science thrown out from the illicit labs we were advancing on.

Alongside all of us, the dogs marched in lock-step, their metal feet occasionally sliding on bits of rock.

In front of me, Mario and Joe marched side by side, looking way too un-bothered by the sun.

Kris looked as melted as I felt. Bitch was a bit more cheerful than me, though. "Still no sign of life. We're going to make it."

"They could have sent UAV's."

She had the bad grace to laugh at me. "And ruined your fun?"

"UAV's don't die."

"They cost as much as we do."

"More." But people were still good for a lot of things that unmanned aircraft just weren't so good at. Opening doors, assessing, reading the fear in an enemy combatant's eyes.

The first few of our line had all reached a shadowed cleft between two low hills. I trudged up a scant incline near the end, next to Kris, exposed as hell.

As if they knew we'd been talking about them, the steady echoing thrum of copter blades came up from behind us.

I tensed.

"Safe!" Louis called from five people ahead of us. He meant it had told him it was ours, sharing the right codes in the right sequence. The dogs trusted it, too, clanking along without missing a beat. So maybe NorAM had decided to give us more help. Maybe they'd learned something. The UAV's body was the size of my head, the rotors a stack, the whole thing flying canted a bit forward so the tail seemed to reach for the sky. The sound of its flight made my shoulder blades itch. I squinted, the sun making the silver blades into diamonds too bright to stare at. Why now, instead of after we were closer to the lab?

Why so close to us? Why one?

Instinct finally kicked in, in spite of Louis's words. I dove sideways into Kris, tumbling her. Her eyes went wide but she said nothing, catching enough balance to scramble on all fours. Simon and Jillie reflexed after us.

Mario turned, mouth open, his eyes so dark I was sure he was about to bark at us for being scared little girls.

He never got any words out. Mario's hand flew up to his skull and came away slick and red and I could feel the heat of little machines racing through his body, the fear of them turning me soft and small inside.

He writhed and fell.

The four of us, me, and Kris and Rob and Jill, raced away like one. My dog, Hunter, slowed to stay beside me. I ran with a hand on Hunter's broad, full back, wishing there was power and time to mount and race away. The big dog's metal skin felt hot to the touch. But then everything was hot, the sand, the dog, the air, my anger.

I didn't want to glance back toward Mario's body, but I did. Most of the line was down, the dogs on their sides, faces scarred with soot. Someone had managed to knock the silver copter out of the sky. My quick glance didn't say how many people from the front of the line had made it. If any.

The fear of things too small to see drove us a long way in spite of the sapping heat and the surreal burned and wetted and baked ground.

We re-grouped behind a stand of rocks. Small cover, the rocks hot enough to burn hands where we touched them, tinged with silicates so they shimmered, big enough to throw shade if the sun weren't directly above us.

Jillie looked over at me, her face shocked. I checked the rest of the group. Eight had made it to the rocks. Eight people and eight bots, so sixteen. I checked what I'd been left with. Two new recruits, the speed of death thrumming through them so deeply fear seemed to leak from their sweaty, dirty pores. Jillie and a thin boy from Seattle who leaned over, puking. The scientist. The two trainers, busy already, checking the metal dogs for damage, probably glad as hell to have something to do. Kris, the ever optimistic and bitchy. Simon, who was only happy when he was actually fighting, who got an orgasmic look on his face in hand-to-hand, and yet wouldn't kill a spider if it landed on his mouth in the middle of the night. Thank god for Kris and Simon and the trainers. Maybe between us we could protect the two newbies.

Simon had already managed to climb up the rock pile in spite of the heat, peel his binoculars out of his pack, and look toward the carnage. I caught the shift in his uniform from ash gray to the tan of the rocks. He grunted softly from about five feet above me.

"What do you see?" I asked him.

He shook his head. "Stupidity."

"No shit. See any more copters?"

"Damn things are fast."

I pulled the handheld out of my pocket and swiped up the tracking chip info. Close-together green dots for us, dark for humans and light for robot dogs. Three more humans on the far side, two with fading vital signs. I whispered an apology to them since we couldn't even try and get there yet. Red death dots made a ragged line across the open spaces. I called for overhead pictures. I got back two-inch pixels, which was enough to see that everyone had died in place, and even the dogs had made no more than a few steps. They'd been targeted. The poison that killed people didn't kill robots. So whoever sent the UAV knew who and what was coming for them.

Illegal nano for sure, scattered by an illegal UAV. NorAM would tell— I breathed in deep, re-thinking who was left —NorAM would tell *me* more once they analyzed the info.

Shit.

I did want command. But not now, and not here.

NorAM would have the same information I had, except maybe our condition. We'd lost two of the scientist embeds, but we still had one left. Alissa Frietag, a small woman with twice the strength she appeared to have, and a fierce determination to get into the labs. I stared at her for a moment, assessing. Small, so thin I would be able to wrap my hands around her waist with only a little effort. She looked pissed-off instead of scared.

Good. So all we had to do was protect Alissa, get into the well-defended lab, and give her some time to assess it before we destroyed it. Yep, that should be easy.

I typed my message to NorAM. *We're okay. Sci1 looks fierce. We need cover.*

Or to withdraw, but I didn't have to tell them that. They knew. If we withdrew, GenGreen would simply destroy everything and smile and invite us and a bunch of media in the front door just in time to see a lab devoted to feeding the starving. We didn't want to leave them time for that. Other NorAM forces had blocked the roads out. Of course, we could just get them from the air. But people up the chain wanted the lab intact. Apparently there was some experiment or knowledge so valuable that we weren't willing to just blow it up and move on.

I half expected to be recalled within a day of starting out. The goal had been to come in unnoticed, but the UAV screamed that GenGreen and its private armies had noticed us. The fact that our code was compromised suggested they'd also paid off someone. With luck, that would be a dead rat from our group, but more likely it would be NorAM.

I scanned the horizon again. Listened. No wind. No rotor blades. Puking boy had stopped hacking and spitting.

Damnit. Time to lead.

"Everybody gather up."

Simon started to clamber down the rock, but I gestured for him to stay. He'd be able to hear me from up there. The dog handlers got the big bots to stand and look at me, too, cocking their not doglike heads sideways at me in a dog-like motion. Good. At least someone had a sense of humor.

I glanced down at my handheld. The screen was still blank.

"You all okay?"

I looked them each in the eye. At least they all looked back at me. Five women including me, three guys. The men were Simon, Scott of the weak stomach, and one of the two dog trainers, John. Then me, Kris the steady and bright, Jillie, Alissa Frietag the scientist, and the other dog trainer, a woman named Paulette.

The communit buzzed in my hand. I glanced down and saw what I expected. I looked back at the group. "Orders are to keep going, move more evasively, get to the lab. They'll send in some cover and some help after we get it secure."

"Ma'am."

"Scott?"

"Just us. To take the whole place?"

I nodded. "What supplies do we have?"

John spoke a litany he'd pretty clearly memorized. "Water. Food. Handhelds. First Aid. Light. Blankets."

Crap. I glanced at Paulette, who stood with one hand on her robot's head as if it were flesh and blood. She swallowed. "The same."

So we were eight for eight on supplies and zero for zero on big weapons? We wouldn't starve while we were destroying an enemy lab with our bare hands. Good thing.

John must have seen the look on my face. "We do have some rockets and launchers, and a few mines."

"Our handguns," I added. "And the knives on our belts. Any useful solar?"

Paulette shifted on her feet, swaying. "Not enough for the dogs." Her face had gone white. "Enough for us."

Jillie's eyes widened and she looked like she was about ten and desperate for a friend. I knew what she was thinking. That we'd need to raid the supplies on the other dogs. I didn't look directly at her, but I made sure I could see her relax when I said, "We're not going out there." Stray microbots could kill us as easily as they'd killed everyone else. It might be slower without a direct hit, but three of the damned things in your soft tissue guaranteed death. There would be no recovery of the other dogs or their packs, or anything else. Not until NorAM could send containment suits out. Not today.

I updated NorAM with our status, and requested a storm.

They suggested quite formally that we do without.

I counter-suggested quite formally that without power we would die before we got the job done instead of while we were doing the job.

I stood still, staring at the screen, waiting for them to discuss amongst themselves and then get back to me. I was half-hoping they'd say no and decide we could go back or wait for more people and stuff or something.

Instead, they answered way too fast. They promised lightning.

Whatever was in that lab mattered to them. I swallowed. I'd been trained. I'd even succeeded in a live exercise. And out of our group, I was the only one still alive and rated for it. I glanced at the dog handlers. "We do have the laser?"

John nodded, his eyes gleaming a bit.

I surveyed the group. "We are going to crack the sky and bring home some power."

Allisa's tongue darted out between her full lips, and she looked like she was about to be seated at a banquet table. Jillie's eyes widened again, and the trainers glanced at the dogs. Kris and Simon, who knew the calculus, nodded.

We had orders to go forward, so no turning tail. Probably wouldn't work anyway, since GenGreen would follow us and keep whatever they were protecting at the level of rumor. We could go forward. Would. We carried the worst weapons on us—some as small as the ones GenGreen just killed most of us with. We would need power to eat and drink and scatter signal around, power to feed the tiny weapons, power to control the lab. Stored power, available on demand.

In addition to the power to get there.

That had been on the other dogs, along with the more power-hungry of the weapons. We'd run them a long way to get here. The robotic dogs were stronger than us by far, faster, fleeter if less graceful. But when we ran out of juice, we just reached into our will and found more. When robots ran dry, they stopped.

So be it.

Death or a miracle.

"Rest. Simon and I will take a watch."

They nodded, the old hands falling almost immediately to the ground, accepting rest. Jillie and Scott followed. Alissa Frietag leaned back against the stones, closing her eyes and whispering under her breath.

I clambered up beside Simon and sat looking out over our distant dead and toward the buried lab. The very idea of it made me feel small and fragile even if I was one-sixty with my boots on and no real fat. Bulky for a girl. We were all fragile when it came to nano and biologicals and whatever else GenGreen and its partners were dreaming up to protect their solution for the world from the combined North American Government, which had a different one. The NorAM populace had voted almost as one from the wet northern reaches of Canada to the sweltering, hurricane-slapped coasts of the Yucatan. They'd said to stop intervening, preferring to take their chances with nature than to trust the multinationals.

There was no money in letting nature balance itself. Hence the science wars, and this small battle.

The dead between us and the next hill attested to the seriousness of this small battle. Our own corporations, or at least multis born here, killing us. Assholes. I swore I'd do my best. Both to kill the big scary lab and to stay alive.

I was gonna miss Mario, even if he was a loudmouthed idiot.

Simon opened the conversation. "This sucks."

"Yep." And that closed the conversation.

We sat close to each other, taking comfort in the silence of long friendship. We'd been on three attacks like this before, and come back from all of them. I wasn't so sure this time, but no soldier says those things to another. Instead, we watched the empty blue sky and baked quietly on the rock, the sun glinting on the great field of ash that surrounded us.

NorAM interrupted to tell me the others had all died. No one left on the far ridge. I imagined it. One of the dots had been healthy. They'd watched the others die, gotten too close. Prayed to be safe. Maybe they'd even donned their protective suit, the crappy one that came in all our belts. But something too small to see and big enough to kill them had gotten in anyway. It made me feel cold even in the punishing heat.

The rocks started throwing longer shadows. Simon and I traded with Kris and Scott. I wiped the sweat from my face and felt sure the heat would keep me fitful and maybe even awake.

A fat warm glob of rain struck me on the cheek and I shook awake, swinging my head like an animal. Wind cooled the air. Dark, roiling cumulonimbus clouds towered overhead, the front edge of them splitting the sky like angry foam above my head, blue, then gray, white above, tinged gold by the setting sun.

Kris looked down at me. "Almost ready?"

"Are they?"

I had given her my comm. She shaded the screen with her hand and said "Forty minutes."

I took five minutes to perform routine body maintenance functions, and five more to verify that everyone else did the same. I gathered the humans all into formation, packs at their side and ready, each with a weapon in hand.

The dog handlers had already chosen John's dog for the first receptacle in line. I didn't ask how he'd drawn the risky straw. Just thanked him for being ready.

At least there was so much wind I didn't need a posted UAV spotter any more. Anything over about twenty miles an hour tended to slam them off course, into the ground, or both. I was willing to bet the occasional gust was past the twenty mile an hour mark. In fact, there was a serious whine in the part of the wind that passed up above us. Damn NorAM physics jocks.

John handed me the launcher.

"Did you name your dog?" I asked.

He swallowed. "Max, sir. Ma'am."

His confusion felt almost touching. John passed Max's hand controls to me, and me and the metal dog walked away from the group, as far out into the open as we could get. Wind tore at my shirt.

All the blue had been blown out of the sky.

Max came to my waist, with four legs that had two joints each, and a hollow tail. His belly was big, and right now all that it held was empty space and some magic built from Tesla's dreams and our materials. Too classified for me to get the details, and too new to be completely sure it would work.

Lightning slammed upward from the ridge we had been going to, would go to again. Rain sheeted down, sharpening the smell of the charred soil.

John and Paulette called out the other dogs, lining them up one after the other, tails in mouths, a long string of conductivity. Hunter was last. John said something to Max, and the big robot tilted its ugly black head back and opened its jaws. Someone had painted sharp teeth like a shark's onto the dull gripping surfaces.

John handed me dark goggles. I slid them on, the world almost black, John now a silhouette. He handed me a long slender rod with a firing pin on the outside. The laser gun felt heavier than I remembered, harder to manage. I pointed it up at the roiling clouds, ignoring the rain that nearly blinded me.

The two trainers raced to the rocks to join Simon and the others.

I pulled the trigger and nothing happened.

I checked. The gun worked. The laser beams shot fast as lightning itself into the clouds, but invisible. The clouds had simply ignored my call, my act, the light.

They had to be ready, to be almost pregnant with charge.

I giggled, absurdly, soaking wet and wondering if the storm were a lover I'd just tried to drive to premature ejaculation.

The laser had enough power for three charges. I'd wasted one. I took a deep breath and stared up into the rain and the dark clouds and smelled the damp, charred air.

Another lightning bolt flashed down near the rocks and thunder made me cringe and cover my head.

My timing was still off.

Practice for this had been controlled. The storms had been smaller.

I closed my eyes, let the water fall on the goggles. Braced. Waited.

Fired.

I opened my eyes.

Thunder smacked again.

White light surrounded me, the world turned to day in spite of the lenses between my eyes and the bolt. Max stood unmoved but full, and I had the briefest glimpse of the dog with light pouring out of every hole in its body, out through its tail into the other dogs, a line of lightning eaters.

Then I couldn't see, and all I felt was a deep thrumming in my body, and a sharp pain behind the eyes. I shook, relieved and scared and pissed off as well, mad at NorAM and GenGreen and the whole difficult, warring world. The thunder kept rolling away from me, hiding any other noises.

John's voice, a whoop. "We did it! You did it!"

Someone took the laser gun from my hands. Simon spoke. "I'm taking off the goggles. Keep your eyes closed."

I felt them slide away.

"Look at me."

His face existed. Thank God. I could see, and what I saw was Simon grinning, ear to ear. "Now what, Chief?"

I swallowed and stood up, my legs shaky, the back of my head still mushy and pain-wracked. Nothing good was easy. Unless we called it again, the lightning would move on. We had what we needed from it, and all that was left was danger. We could wait it out. "Is everyone here?"

Simon nodded. I verified he was right. They looked shocked and bewildered. Some soldiers. But at least everyone had their packs. "You're a damn good second," I whispered to him, and then I stood up and addressed everyone else. "By the time I finish this briefing, the worst of the storm will have moved on, and we'll go take the lab. We're going to ride in there."

Scott's eyes widened. "On the dogs?"

"No. On each other." Dingbat. But then he was in as much danger as the rest of us. Maybe more for being wet behind the ears. Whatever was in the lab had better be good. "We're moving light and fast, following the storm, hoping to take them by surprise. We'll have enough power to get there on the bots. I don't know if we'll get back that way or if we'll walk." Which meant I didn't know how much power we'd have on the way back. Once we succeeded—if we succeeded—NorAM wasn't going to burn more climate credits on getting back the easy way, not unless we had something they wanted fast. That was an idea. I looked back at them. "The extra supplies are still here. We meet back here. Has everyone marked this on their maps?"

Jillie looked sheepish and fiddled with her wrist unit until she could nod and say, "Yes," just like everyone else had.

I tested communications, made sure we could all hear and speak to each other. "Use voice when you can," I reminded them. "Security."

Lightning fell again, far away now, a thin streak that forked in three places and was gone. I waited for the thunder to die down and then I said, "All right. Go."

We skirted the dead, going so wide we missed the ravine. Better to add ten minutes than pick up some windblown death. On the smooth ground, the dogs had pretty even gaits, about like a horse walking. Over hills or rocks, they rocked and lurched, irritating my still-sharp head and scraping my inner thighs. There were reasons we don't usually ride the damned things. Plenty of bots had been designed to carry soldiers, but the pack dogs like these had it as a second priority. Or maybe a third or fourth.

It hurt.

I had ridden the dogs in the wild, but Jillie and Scott had only mounted in training exercises. They managed, but only because I paired them each up with a trainer. Behind them, Kris and I rode together. Simon protected Alissa, the pair of them a bit in front of us and off to the side.

For the first hour, we followed the storm. Dusk yellowed the lagging edge of the clouds, and Alissa pointed out a fresh storm behind us, maybe five miles away. "Backup?" she screamed the question to me over the wind and the rain and the space between us.

I shrugged. Sometimes weathering made more weather, as if sun or wind or rain called to its own kind. If it was NorAM storm, they hadn't told me. But then maybe they wouldn't. Maybe we'd wake up in the morning to August snow. If we made it to morning.

As we neared the top of a long, low hill two huge figures rose up. Bipedal, metal, too thin to be manned. Legs like tree trunks and torsos like limbs, thin and wiry and fast. Six arms, or maybe more. They held rocks in each hand.

I ducked.

Hunter feinted right under me, then left.

Rocks landed on either side of us.

Voices screeched in my ear. Too many to make sense of.

Alissa gripped her dog's ears, which held its head down.

"Let go!" I screamed at her. "Hold its neck. Handholds."

Just as she let go, a rock the size of her head pounded into the ground at her dog's feet and the robot dog rose up on just its hind feet, striking the ground with its tail to help balance. Alissa threw her weight backward instead of forward and landed with a hard thump on her butt. Immediately twisting away from the dog.

A rock fell between the scientist and the robot dog.

It stepped back, avoiding the rock, programmed to stay with its handler.

I charged her attacker, drawing two of its rocks toward me. It was agile enough to pick another rock up as it threw two at me. So a brain for each hand? My immediate reaction was to go eye for an eye. Sometimes old-fashioned weapons are just fine, and since I'd never even seen a rumor of a six-armed rock-throwing robot, this couldn't be far out of beta. By the time I'd pulled the pin, the bot had hit Alissa's dog in the torso, leaving a dent. It stood over her small form, which lay curled under its broad belly in a fetal position.

Well, I'd probably have gone fetal, too.

I threw the grenade and watched it arc up toward the robot. I turned away, hoping Alissa was smart enough to cover her face.

Hunter shied, if that's what you call evasive actions in a robotic dog the size of the small horse.

After the initial explosion I heard metal screech and turned to look. A leg complete with a long string of cables that must have pulled loose from inside the robot lay behind us, evidence there had been something for Hunter to avoid.

A rock slammed into us, hitting a glancing blow to my thigh. Hunter took the blow, moving with it, taking three fast steps like those daisy steps from aerobics. I managed to hold on. My thigh hurt like hell. I tested and my leg bent normally if I forced it. No telling if I could put weight on it.

Wind had blown the wet ash clear enough for me to make out the robot, no longer standing, but with at least two working arms.

No time to look around and see what else was happening. I raced to Alissa's side and barked at her, "Stand up!"

She looked up at me with a face streaked with tears and ash, but she nodded and pushed herself to standing. She reached for the holds to mount.

"No. Use it as a shield and run."

Alissa stood blinking at me with shocky eyes for just a second before she understood what I meant and started heading away from the now- stationary rock-thrower, keeping the robot dog between her and the damaged enemy. She started off in retreat and I herded her forward and around, paying close attention until we appeared to be out of range.

I looked for the other robot. Simon or Kris had done a better job than I had, and it lay inert.

I called for everyone to come here, counting as they appeared. John and Jillie, John with one arm hanging and a bruised cheek. Jillie looking like hell but smiling. I hoped it was happiness at being alive and not something more manic.

Kris and Simon rode in from the left, Simon looking ecstatic. I knew where his happiness came from. He must have been the one to bring the bot down. If this had been the middle ages and the six-armed bot a dragon, Simon is the guy who would have raced toward it on a black charger, whirling his sword above his head. His voice blossomed in my ear. "If that's all they have, we're okay."

I suspected we wouldn't be that lucky. "Paulette? Scott?"

No answer. Everyone else had the discipline to keep silent while I called for them.

Finally, Scott's voice. "She's hurt. My dog died."

"Are you okay?" I asked, grateful he didn't seem as shaken as he had the day before.

"Yes."

"How badly hurt is Paulette?"

"I think her leg's broken."

Thank God. I'd been afraid of something worse. "Do you remember field medicine."

"I think so."

"Is Paulette conscious?"

"Yes."

"She can talk you through."

He sounded shaky as he said, "Okay."

Simon broke in. "Hurry up. There's another storm coming."

I'd almost forgotten that. The sky was darker, but it was also later in the day. The wind came up again, only this time at our backs. The lab was close.

"Scott," I said. "Good luck." And then to the others. "Group around me."

I still had no clear idea how six of us were going to get into a secret GenGreen lab. There had to be better defenses than what we'd seen so far. I took time to report in. NorAM was quick to respond. "Keep going. There are reinforcements on the ground."

I glanced up over my shoulder. "Is that our storm?"

"Get Alissa to the lab."

"I'll do my best." I closed my communit. Aye, aye, sir. Thanks for doing the impossible so far, and keep on going. Of course, I'd signed up for it. On purpose.

Lightning split the sky behind us, followed a few seconds later by thunder. Maybe they sent the storm just to drive us. Hopefully Paulette and Scott would be okay. "Let's go!"

The dogs had the GPS data, and this close, there wasn't much routing I had to do. The last bit of the journey was mostly a balancing act trying to stick to Hunter in spite of my head and my thigh. Rain made the broad backs of the dogs slippery as hell.

Kris did fall off once.

We got close enough I started watching for the fence.

NorAM messaged us all to turn around and look the other way. Them talking in our ears was a security risk of the first order and so I turned my head even before telling Hunter to turn. Looking up and down the small line of us left, I was pleased to note everyone had understood the order.

Light pinned us bright and blind. Then again. Flash. Wind, or maybe the electricity of what must be simultaneous lightning bolts, lifted and twisted the stray hairs around my face. Flash. Thunder boomed, a deep cracking sound as if the sky had been hit with the hammer of the gods. More noise poured through right above us, enveloping us, making it impossible to talk.

We stood, still looking away. I hadn't known they could do that. *We* could do that. Another ratchet up in the weather wars.

It scared me as much as the lab.

NorAM's voice again. "The fences are all fried. The building's main security is probably off, but there may be generator power. Go, now. Copters will be along. Ground troops are arriving now."

Another scary thing. "Did you catch the traitor?"

"Yes."

Hopefully there was only one. "Wait for orders," the NorAM dispatcher said, enough happiness in her voice that I guessed whatever the lightning and the new troops were supposed to do was getting done.

I glanced over at Alissa. "Are you okay?"

"I will be." She still looked fierce. Like the scientist in a television show I used to love that chased down Japanese whale boats. Something to be said for fierce scientists. Our back was still to the lab and the conflict, and we watched a sliver of black cloudless sky slowly grow as the storm above us blew further east. From time to time we heard thunder in the distance.

It had stopped raining by the time they called for us. I smiled at the look on some of the NorAM shock troop faces as I brought Alissa Freitag into the compound on top of a wet, banged-up robot that barely resembled a dog. I had no mirror, but I'm sure we looked like wild women, drenched in rain and sun and wind and thunder.

I kind of liked the picture that drew for me.

Two scientists had come in via the road, and been protected in the back until the lab defenses were neutralized. NorAM replacing what we'd lost, and probably unhappy about it. But then they'd wanted us to be entirely stealth. Which is probably why so many died. Not that I got to make high-level battle plans or even hear what data went into them. It felt good to have done my part, and that all of the soldiers who had escaped with me were alive. And I liked seeing Alissa run up to the others and start organizing immediately, no question, as if she were the field commander among the scientists.

Maybe she was.

John and Jillie and I attended to the robots and set them charging. After about twenty minutes, a small crew returned with Scott and Paulette. I complimented Scott on a decent job of field-bandaging, and he blushed.

Just as we were about to leave, Alissa came up to me, almost bouncy. No—more than that. Electric with excitement. Her eyes were shining as she said, "Thank you. You have no idea how important it was that you got me here."

"What did you find?"

"Bees."

I must have looked stupid. I had been expecting a breeding farm for human organs or something else scary. "Bees?"

"Genetically changed to kill the few remaining regular bees, and then they would have died out. Would have killed off the whole honeybee line of pollinators. At least that's what they were trying to do."

"Bees were worth all that?" I meant the people dying, the scientists dying, the robots with the rocks, all of it.

She was more direct than me. "The deaths? Yes. GenGreen wants to destroy enough life that we have to depend on their products."

I swallowed and watched her, hoping I'd see her again somewhere besides on television. I could get into helping scrappy scientists save bees. Even if I wasn't quite sure of our methods either. But thunder and lightning and bad weather were the slow way to kill the bees. If I understood what Alissa was saying, we had helped stop a fast way. And even I knew that had become the game. Fight the cancers day by day and hope the body finds remission.

"Are you supposed to tell me this?"

Her sharp brown eyes shone with mischief as she said, "I believe in the power of information."

"And I believe in the power of science."

She shook her head. "Don't. Science is on both sides of this."

I winced. "You're right. Maybe that's why I'm a soldier and you're a scientist."

"And maybe you just saved a lot of the heirloom food left."

We napped in a pile of soldiers and robots until dawn. Alissa said nothing else to me, and NorAM gave no more comment than, "Well done. Come home." As I led my severely reduced crew out of the lab and headed us home, I realized that I felt more sure of our side than I had before we got into the lab. I remembered the power of calling down the lightning and splitting open the sky just for us to continue a war, and I hoped I wouldn't have to do that again. I let us stay mounted until we were out of sight, and then I gave the order to stand down and walk. Our backsides would get home in better shape that way, and besides, the sun had already warmed the air and a light breeze plucked at my uniform.

GAMBIT

Nancy Jane Moore

THE COMM SQUAWKED IN CASSIE RAMIREZ'S EAR. IT STARTLED HER, THOUGH SHE HAD been lying awake for the last hour, worrying. "Yeah?"

"Transport moving out there, Lieutenant. About a hundred klicks out."

Not again. They'd only been running this check point for three Earth-standard days, and already they'd been challenged by four bands of rebels. So far everybody'd backed down. Would this be the group that didn't? She shivered, and not just from the cold that never went away on Titan.

"Lieutenant?"

"Acknowledged. On my way. Got any coffee made?"

"Yes, ma'am. Good and strong."

At least Titan grew good, cheap coffee. The bioformers had installed genemodded coffee plants on every planet, asteroid, and moon they'd transformed. On Titan the plants had done particularly well.

Cassie pulled her exoskeleton on over her fatigues and set its heat at high. Both skel and fatigues were patterned in the dark green camo that marked the Combined Forces Peacekeeping Corps, and both had her name and rank displayed over her left breast. But it was the skel—made from silicon merged with one of the Ceresian metals—that allowed humans without Titan-specific gene tweaks to survive outdoors. She buckled on the weapons vest, locked its circuitry plug into the skel, and checked to see that the weapons were fully charged.

She ran her fingers through her short, bleached blonde hair, then pulled the skel's headpiece up. She'd need the light source outside. Saturn still shone orange in the sky, but Titan at its brightest resembled Earth at full moon. And the bright peak had passed.

Bobby Rowan had tried to convince her that the glow from Saturn was the same as sunlight. "It's caused by the sun, right?"

She had laughed. "You just want it to be sunlight, so you don't feel so far from home."

He'd laughed, too. "Maybe I do. It's summer now in Vancouver. The sun comes up before five, doesn't set 'til after ten."

Typical Earther. Tied to a particular city in a particular country. And homesick for it.

It hurt, to think of Bobby laughing. They'd fought four days ago, fought badly, maybe irrevocably. And over what? Politics. Fucking politics.

The bareness of the clearing where they'd set up the check point emphasized the density of the trees surrounding it. Their leaves gave off an acidic smell, overpowering other odors. Tall, wide-leafed, most of them a genemodded evergreen with foliage that tended to turn yellow, they'd been planted in the twenty-second century to give Titan a breathable atmosphere. The solar collectors orbiting the moon brought them just enough sunlight for photosynthesis.

The checkpoint consisted of a cluster of instabuild cabins, one set right at the road to block traffic, three others forming a mini compound. She stepped inside the one that housed scan and comm, and helped herself to the coffee. "Anything else show up?"

Gavin, the scan tech, shook his head. "No, ma'am. Transport still headed our way."

"Only one?"

"That's what's showing up, ma'am."

"Funny. They usually have several. Wake the rest of the crew when they get within fifty klicks or so. I want a full staffing out there."

He looked at her. "You got a bad feeling about this one, Lieutenant?"

"Just want to be cautious. The political situation's gotten pretty tense." She tried to keep her voice off-hand, calm.

He nodded.

Cassie added more coffee to her cup, and went outside. Even with the skel on high she could feel the cold. Earthers had it worse; they'd never been genemodded at all. But even those like her who had grown up in the other settled parts of the solar system didn't have the heavy gene tweaks the Titanians had needed.

Still, the chill in her bones didn't come from the cold. Ten years experience—more than half of it in combat—was causing it.

She sat on the stoop of one of the buildings—she wanted to pace, but it would look bad—sipped more coffee, and realized she was scared. A very bad sign.

You're just being paranoid, she told herself. That's what Bobby would tell you.

That's what she'd fought with Bobby about the day before the platoon moved from guarding diplomats to running the point.

They'd started—and ended—the evening in one of the coffee houses that dotted the once-popular resort city of Revelations. The city had changed hands a dozen times during the war; now it was certified neutral territory, site of the peace negotiations, headquarters of the PK troops.

Cassie had gotten there first. She was sitting where she could watch the door, so she saw Bobby before he saw her. He stopped in the doorway and pushed back the headpiece of his skel. In the interior light—the café catered to the peacekeeping forces and kept both heat and light at higher levels than Titanians preferred—his red hair shone like a beacon.

Seeing Bobby always made Cassie feel ridiculously good. She tamped the feeling down.

He spotted her, and began navigating her way, stumbling as he tried to avoid bumping into the closely packed tables and chairs. Earthers struggled with Titan's light gravity—one of many reasons why the PK force was largely stocked with people like Cassie who'd been born off-Earth.

She stood up to give him a quick kiss. He pulled her close, and they stood there a little longer than she'd intended. She broke it off first—public displays of affection always embarrassed her.

He took off his gloves and rubbed his hands together as they both sat down. "Ah, nice and warm in here." He motioned to the waitress to bring him some coffee, and grinned widely at Cassie.

She tried to grin back, but she didn't feel as cheerful as he did. Lots of rumors had been flying through the troops about major problems at checkpoints. Her soldiers were jumpy, which didn't bode well for their assignment.

She said, "I see you're in a good mood. Peace talks went well?"

"Not bad. We made a little progress." Bobby served as aide de camp—chief assistant—to Gudrid Amudsen, chief peacemaker for the United System Governments' diplomatic corps.

"Really? How unusual. Did the True Harkers actually agree to something?" She hadn't intended sarcasm, but it came out anyway.

Bobby's grin faded. "I wish you'd have more faith in the negotiation process. Nothing's going to happen overnight—these people have been fighting for thirty years."

"And after six months of talks all we've got is a cease-fire best defined by its breaches. I heard the Harkers moved into Jehovah City again."

He sighed. "Yeah, we got a report on that."

"And the government negotiators didn't walk out? I would have."

"Obviously they've got more faith in the negotiations than you do."

"Or maybe they're just scared. They ought to be scared. The True Harkers are winning this war. And we're just sitting here on our hands, pretending both sides are the good guys."

Bobby said, in a disgusted tone, "So we should just intervene on the side of the government?"

"You already know I think so," Cassie said. They could practically have this fight by the numbers now. "Half the USG nations are scared they'll actually have to do something. And the others are more interested in continuing the war so they can sell weapons to both sides."

Bobby sighed, and reached over for her hand. "Cassie, nothing's ever going to be completely smooth when so many different governments are involved. I know USG has screwed up before. They'll screw up again. Humans aren't even close to perfect. We're still learning how to get to the root of conflicts, and we're going to make mistakes. Especially in religious wars. But Titan isn't Ceres."

Cassie yanked her hand back angrily. She hated feeling patronized. "I goddamned well know Titan isn't Ceres. But that's no excuse for screwing up here like they screwed up there."

Bobby stared down at the menu. He took a deep breath, and said, "Cassie, could we not have this fight tonight? We don't have much time to spend with each other."

Maybe if she hadn't felt so nervous about the checkpoint assignment, she'd have been able to let it go. "If you weren't so damned enamored of all the nice-sounding peacemaking theory, you'd agree with me. The True Harkers want to run Titan. They're not going to negotiate in good faith as long as they think they can win."

"Then why in hell are they at the negotiating table?"

"So they can hang out here in Revelations near the shuttle point, and buy weapons from some of those so-called diplomats."

He closed the menu with a slap. "Now you're being paranoid. Do you believe every rumor some scared private starts?"

"I heard it from an air captain who was trying to enforce the embargo. He told me all the ways light craft could get around his blockade."

"And you bought into his paranoia. Look, Amudsen says the weapons embargo is holding tight. A little stuff is getting through, sure. It always does. But nothing significant, nothing for you to worry about."

"And if the great Amudsen says so, it must be true."

Bobby stood up. He ran his chit through the table register to pay for the coffee. "I'd better get back. Long day tomorrow."

They'd planned to spend the evening—and the night—together, knowing it would be several Earth weeks before they saw each other again. Bobby stood there, shifting his feet awkwardly. Cassie didn't want him to leave, and she knew he didn't really want to go. All she had to do was say something conciliatory. It wouldn't even have to be a full apology. But she couldn't.

She said, "Yeah, it's hard work, dithering around."

"Fight's over, Cassie. Both sides lost." He turned on his heel and walked out.

Four days later she was still replaying it all in her mind. Maybe she was overreacting. Maybe the talks would work. She didn't have Bobby's education—the war on Ceres had prevented that. All she had were instincts honed by combat experience.

She didn't know anything about religion, and just knew the barest facts of Titanian history—settlement by the followers of a so-called messiah named Jesse Harker, followed all too shortly by a long period of abandonment as Earth and the closer settlements struggled with other conflicts. And now a war brought on by religious schism. It made no sense to her, but she'd been raised by people who considered religion outdated mythology. Maybe Bobby was right; maybe she was just jaundiced by her own experiences.

And even if she were right, what difference did it make? She and Bobby didn't make policy. If she had just shut up, they could have spent a pleasant night together.

Comm clicked in. "They're about 25 klicks, ma'am."

"Acknowledged."

She stepped into the scan cabin, grabbed a little more coffee, and drank it down. "You're sure there's nothing else moving out there?"

Gavin looked offended. "Yes, ma'am, I'm sure," he said stiffly.

Cassie put a hand on his shoulder to let him know she wasn't questioning his competence. She knew her people, knew which ones she could count on, which ones had to be watched. Making sure the headpiece of her skel was set firmly in place, its sensors locking on, she walked over to the point. "What've we got, Sergeant?"

"They're showing up on short range now, ma'am." All the skels had short-range scan built in, along with weaponry and comm.

Cassie pulled her own scan up. "Looks like a mag-lev transport."

"Yes, ma'am. Scan shows about ten passengers, plus a couple up front. Think they might be refugees?"

"I doubt it. We probably got another round of True Harkers. Refugees don't travel by mag-lev. They walk."

He nodded.

She double checked his assignments. Everything in order, as she'd expected. She buzzed Gavin. "Everybody else up?"

"They're moving, ma'am. Whining and bitching, but moving."

"Tell 'em to move faster. And spread out into the forest. Back up formation. I don't want our whole force on the point."

"Yes, ma'am."

The feeling of wrongness got stronger. Nothing you can do about it, she reminded herself, and shook it off. The transport was pulling up to the point.

It stopped at the barricade. A large truck, steering compartment in front, a back area suitable for hauling either troopers or supplies.

A couple of her soldiers stood in front of it with the sergeant; several others had moved behind it.

A man wearing a skel in the dark blue of the rebels stepped out. Her sergeant said, "I want all your people out of there."

The rebel looked back inside the transport, apparently got confirmation from someone in there, and muttered an order into his comm. As the soldiers came climbing out the back, another man alit from the front compartment.

Officer, thought Cassie, watching him move. He looked at the various soldiers, clearly sizing up who was who, and walked over to her.

He had his headpiece up, just as she did. She wished she could see his face.

The insignia on his skel showed him to be a captain. He said, "Lieutenant, I've got orders to relieve the security detail in Revelations."

"I haven't been told anything about a replacement detail, Captain." Clearance from Combined Forces headquarters was required to allow replacements past checkpoints.

"We just got word ourselves a few hours ago. Maybe your people are slow letting you know. If you check, you'll find we've been cleared."

A plausible story. They were the right size troop for security. And communications did screw up from time to time. But she didn't like it.

"Nice bluff, Captain, but I don't buy it. You turn that transport around, load up, and go on back to your base. Our orders say no one crosses this zone."

"Lieutenant."

"You have five minutes, Captain. I suggest you start now."

"What happens in five minutes?" He sounded amused.

"We take the transport. You walk home."

"Come on, Lieutenant. It won't take you those five minutes to check with your headquarters about our orders. You're neutrals, after all. Why make this nasty?"

Cassie hesitated. Maybe she was judging too quickly. Maybe that voice screaming 'don't trust this man' in her head was just her own paranoia, her dislike of the rebel position.

The captain moved closer to her.

She took a step back.

"Just check, Lieutenant."

It sounded like an order.

And then Gavin was screaming in her ear. "Incoming. Almost on top of us. About ten small craft. They got smart missiles, Lieutenant."

Shielded. They must have been shielded from scan. Neither side on Titan was supposed to have that capacity.

The whole troop had heard Gavin. Her people were moving and targeting weapons. As she dove for cover she hit her long range comm button, calling for immediate air support. Not that it would do any good. Their fighters would take fifteen minutes to get there.

The rebel captain had moved behind the transport and was giving his own orders. Obviously he'd known when his other people showed on scan. One of the rebels fired, and she saw her sergeant go down. The fuckers had ammunition that pierced PK skels, more weapons they weren't supposed to have. Cassie fired a projectile at the shooter, and saw him fall. At least their weaponry pierced the rebel skels, too.

"Set your skels as moving targets," she said into comm. That setting made it harder for enemy weapons to lock on. It was new tech, not fully reliable, but it beat nothing at all.

A whistle in the air. Missiles. The barracks and scan cabin went up. Gavin. Another loss. But at least the other shift hadn't still been in bed.

A midair explosion. Some of their automatic intercepts were still working. But late, way too late. The scan block had slowed them down.

She'd been moving as she watched what was going on, and now she had the rebel captain in her scan. She looked at him to lock target, but before she could fire she felt something graze her head. Her mind registered that whatever it was had pierced her skel. And then she passed out.

Cassie struggled to open her eyes. The ground was moving under her; no, she was riding in the back of a transport. She shivered; she wasn't wearing a skel.

Her head hurt like hell. She tried to bring a hand up to feel it, and realized that her hands were tied behind her. Some kind of steel cord. Shit.

Damn, her head hurt. Someone had shot her, she remembered. She wondered if she'd just moved at the lucky last moment, the point beyond which a smart weapon could no longer correct, or if whoever fired had only intended to wound her. That she was still alive argued for the latter. Hostage, maybe? Didn't make a lot of sense. But the way her head hurt, nothing made a lot of sense.

Cassie shivered again. Minimal heat on in the transport. Definitely Titanians in the front.

A knife would cut the cord, she thought. She had one, concealed in her uniform belt. Had they found it? She managed to sit up. Her head throbbed with the effort. Wriggling around, she managed to move her hands to her side, and slid her thumb inside the webbed belt. It touched plastic. She shifted enough to get a finger in, too, and managed to grab the knife. Idiots. They'd figured she was disarmed without the skel and weapons belt.

She was supposed to be. PK forces weren't supposed to carry extra weapons, but all ex-combat troopers did. Her people did, for sure.

Her people. Had any of them survived? The fight came back to her, far too vividly for her headache. If she'd only called in backup earlier. Though she'd had no reason, nothing but a bad feeling. Can't call in air strikes on bad feelings. Except she knew damn well you should pay attention when something felt wrong. Maybe later you'd figure out how you knew.

Cassie saw Sarge fall again, saw the buildings go up. Let some of them have made it. Please.

She felt the knife in her hand, pressed the button to extend the blade, and tried it on the cord. It cut easily. At least the rebels hadn't gotten hold of the latest tech in everything; the restraints the PK Corps used were proof against all available cutting tools.

She flexed her fingers, felt her head. Sticky. She didn't seem to still be bleeding, though.

She tried to look around. Titanians were tweaked for low-light vision, too, so they hadn't bothered to put lights in the back of the transport. The fading glow coming through the back window allowed her to pick out a pile of skels lying in the corner—green camo. PK skels then. It looked like less than twenty. Maybe some folks made it. Other stuff piled up seemed to be weapons belts and other supplies.

Cassie wondered how many were in the front. Probably just one—why use more than one guy for transporting an injured prisoner and stolen gear?

Cassie crawled to her feet. Standing up made her head hurt worse. Her balance felt off—no skel to compensate for light gravity. She moved over to the door to the front, pressed the open plate gently. Locked. She might have expected that. The back one was probably locked, too. Not that she felt much like rolling out of a moving vehicle. What she really wanted to do was curl up and go back to sleep. Except she was too cold.

A skel. That's what she needed. She crawled over to the pile, and started pawing through them, looking for hers. A sound behind her made her turn. The inside door was opening. Shit. Whoever was piloting had probably heard her trying the door. Or had been watching her on comm.

A man ducked through the door. A large man, with hair even blonder than her bleach job. He wore rebel blue, but no skel. In one hand he held a gun. "You're mine," he said.

Cassie climbed shakily to her feet. Standing up made her see double. She stumbled, backed against the pile of skels for support. He walked straight toward her, holding the gun casually, not even threatening her with it. He'd probably already locked it onto her as a target. If her eyes could be trusted, he held an energy weapon, not a projectile—it would stop her if it hit any part of her. But it still had to be pointed in her general direction. If he kept walking in like that, she'd be able to move straight into him and get out of range of the gun.

So what the fuck was he trying to do, walking straight in on another soldier? No one attacked like that. Unless he thought she was so injured she couldn't do much.

An image from the past, from Ceres twenty years ago: A half-drunk asteroid pirate, walking toward her that same way, holding his weapon the same way, the same half smile on his face. He'd been celebrating the initial invasion's success. She hadn't been a soldier then; she'd been twelve, terrified, not sure what he wanted. Though that had become obvious when he had gotten close enough to rip her shirt open.

Cassie'd had a knife then, too: a blade from a set of carving tools in her father's hobby workshop. A small, but very sharp blade, made of metal refined from the high-grade ore mined in the asteroids. The closest thing to a weapon she'd been able to find as she fled the house. She knew how to carve with it; she didn't know how to fight with it. She'd struggled with the pirate as he pushed her to the ground, pulled her pants down with one hand while holding both of her wrists with his other.

She could think of nothing to do but cut at his fingers with the tiny knife, and she did. He pulled his hand back with a scream of pain and then lunged for her throat with both hands. She'd stabbed upward with the blade, eyes shut, hoping something would happen. He'd screamed, pulled his hands back toward his left eye. It had given her time to run, and she had.

Now she looked at this True Harker, this Titanian rebel, and tried to call up the look of pure terror she must have given the pirate. Though all she felt for this stupid rebel was contempt. She wobbled a bit as the transport turned, and realized she could see three of him. Probably she didn't need to try to look vulnerable.

Come closer, she thought, almost begged, and he did, finally grabbing the front of her shirt to pull her toward him. She came with the pull. Now her body touched his, making his gun useless for the moment. He stumbled back, but didn't completely lose his balance. She stumbled with him, fumbling with the knife in her right hand, trying to find flesh to cut. The blade touched something and he screamed, tried to push her away.

But she grabbed hold of the shoulder of his gun arm, and pulled him with her as she fell heavily with his push. They bounced twice, then landed with one of his arms and the gun trapped under her body. Both of her hands stayed free. Now her knife found flesh again. He screamed, and grabbed her right wrist, trying to wrest the blade away. With her left hand she stuck her fingers in his eyes. He tried to bring his free hand up to protect his face while still holding onto her wrist. She cut at his wrist as his arm moved and pushed her fingers further into his eyes. His grip loosened. She pulled her knife hand loose and plunged the blade into his carotid artery. Blood spurted. Cassie rolled aside so that most of it missed her.

She pulled out the knife blade, shook it clean, closed it, and pushed herself up to a sitting position. And sat there, watching him die. A voice in her head said, 'You didn't have to kill him, Cassie.' It sounded like Bobby. She knew it—he—was right. She wasn't a twelve-year-old kid with no training. She had choices.

Cassie said aloud, "Yeah, but I wanted to."

She pushed her conscience to the back of her mind. For now, she had to concentrate on surviving. Her head hurt worse than ever.

The transport was still moving. Probably had a destination programmed in. She didn't think she wanted to go where it was headed. And she needed to get rid of the corpse. She pushed him up against the transport's back door, and then crawled into the front compartment.

It took her a couple of minutes of fumbling around to find the back door controls, put them on open, hit the override when it reminded her they were moving. A quick look back told her the corpse had fallen out. She managed to shut the door, and tried to call up her position. The mapping all ran together. She couldn't find any lights. Her vision was getting blurry.

Change the coordinates, her brain urged her. She put in new ones at random, felt the transport lurch to a stop, turn around, and start back in the other direction. Then she passed out again.

She wasn't cold. That was the first thing that registered. The second was that someone was washing her face with warm water. Cassie opened her eyes immediately and grabbed the wrist of whoever was washing her. A voice gave a little cry. "Please. I'm only trying to help you."

Her eyes focused, and she looked into the face of a young girl—maybe sixteen. The girl's face was contorted with pain. It took Cassie another couple of seconds to realize she was grabbing too hard. She released the wrist, said "Sorry" and then "Thank you."

The girl rubbed her wrist, then started washing Cassie's face again. Cassie lay there. She had no idea where she was or who this girl might be, but it felt so good to be taken care of. After a few minutes she realized that she was lying on a couple of blankets on the ground, and that a powered one had been put over her. That's why she was so blessedly warm.

Over to her right she could just make out the mag-lev transport. It had crashed into the trees that lined the road. 'Those must have been some coordinates,' Cassie thought.

The girl had finished washing her face. Now she was combing through Cassie's hair, looking for the source of the blood.

Cassie winced, involuntarily inhaled. The girl had found the wound. She picked up a tube, squeezed out something, began to rub it on the spot. Cassie winced again; some kind of disinfectant. She willed herself to hold still while the girl finished the job.

"Thanks," Cassie said. "You're good at that."

"We've had practice," she said. "What happened?"

"I got shot."

The girl said, "I can tell. But where are the rest of your people? You're one of the offworlders, aren't you? My mother said you must be from offworld, because you were so cold. Though that could have been shock, I guess."

"Yeah. I'm part of the peacekeeping force. Trying to keep you people from killing each other."

"You're not doing a very good job," the girl said.

A woman who had just walked up behind her said, sharply, "Myra."

"No, she's right," Cassie said. "We're not doing a good job at all."

The woman knelt down beside her. She held a steaming cup. "Soup."

Cassie took the cup in hands that surprised her by shaking, had a sip. "Thank you. Decent of you to take care of me."

The woman looked a little uncomfortable. "We found your truck. We ...we needed some supplies."

Cassie nodded. She looked at the woman, guessed that she might be forty or so. Dark-skinned. Graying hair. Probably Myra's mother. The girl was dark-complected too. She took another sip of the soup, and looked around. Several other people milled about. Mostly women,. The few males Cassie saw looked young. All of them looked tired.

Makeshift shelters had been set up. Over by the transport, someone was going through supply boxes, sorting items out into piles. *Refugees,* Cassie thought.

"We couldn't take your stuff and not help you," Myra said. Her mother gave her a look.

Cassie had the feeling there'd been an argument about helping her. "About the stuff, it's okay, you taking it." Though of course, it was nothing of the sort. They'd been given specific orders: no assistance to refugees. Official policy said people should be discouraged from leaving their homes. Camps had been set up for those who made it despite the lack of help.

Still, even if she'd liked the order, this was neither the time nor the place to follow it. She needed these people. Her head still ached badly. Her last memory was setting coordinates on the transport; she didn't recall the crash at all. "It's okay," she said again and drank the rest of the soup. She set the cup down, snuggled back down under the blankets. More sleep would be nice.

"Don't do that," said Myra sharply.

Cassie opened her eyes wide, stared at the girl.

"Head injury. You need to stay awake."

Cassie sat back up. "Any coffee in those supplies?"

Coffee helped. Cassie got up, and walked over to the transport. The refugees had left the skels and weapons in the back. She'd have gone for the weapons before the food, if she'd been in their shoes.

Her skel was in the pile, blood still on the headpiece. Suspecting that the circuitry was damaged, she scavenged a whole headpiece from one of the others, careful to avoid looking at the name plate. Sooner or later she'd have to see whose skels were in that pile, which of her people were dead. But not yet.

Blood remained on the back door of the transport, too. Killing the rebel was a fuzzy memory. She wasn't ready to remember that either. She wondered what the refugees had made of the blood.

Cassie pulled on the skel, cranked the heat up to high, and grabbed a weapons vest from the other pile. Pulling the headpiece into place, she brought up the light controls. Now she could actually see. Her hands ran through systems check automatically. She touched the control for long-range comm; time to call someone to get her out of here. But she hesitated.

She owed these people. If she called in medevac, they'd lift her out, and they'd take the supplies. And turn the refugees back. Policy. She didn't want to do that to them. They could have left her in the transport, just taken the supplies. Exposure would have killed her. Her hand dropped away. She'd think about it later.

The refugees gave her a wary eye as she walked back through the group in the skel. Myra and another young girl came up to her. The second girl seemed to be about the same age as Myra, but looked completely different: fair and blonde, and about a head shorter. She stared at the skel. "You really a soldier?"

"Yes, ma'am," Cassie said. The thought made her tired again.

"But you're a woman," she said, making it more of a question than a statement.

"Yes, I am."

"I want to be a soldier, but everybody tells me I can't because I'm a girl."

"Hush," Myra said.

Cassie said, "Well, everybody's wrong. Lots of women soldiers out there. Nothing unusual about it."

"But not here, not on Titan," Myra said. "Jobs have been opened up to women in the last twenty years or so, but not in the army."

"Well, Titan's kind of unusual that way. Someone told me it's because in the first few years of settlement your population was dropping, and you needed women to have as many children as possible." Though she'd never understood Bobby's explanation of why they hadn't just used *in vitro* methods—another one of those religious things she didn't get.

The thought of Bobby hurt. She wondered if he knew she was missing, wondered what he thought. Wondered if he even cared.

"But now it's different," Cassie said. "Now your population is stable; no need to protect women for childbearing."

"That's not what the rebels say," Myra said. She was scowling. "They say women shouldn't even be in the schools. That's why we're trying to get to government territory. My mother says we aren't going to go back to the dark ages with those people."

"I'm going to become a soldier like you, and go back and kill those bastards," the other girl said.

"Emilie!" Myra's voice was shocked. She put a firm hand on the girl's shoulder.

"I am." Emilie brushed the hand off, and turned and ran.

Myra said to Cassie. "The rebels killed her father and brother. She's been wild to get back at them ever since."

"I can understand that," Cassie said. Oh, too well could she understand. "But you. What do you want to be? A doctor maybe—you seem to have medical skills."

Myra shook her head. "A biologist. I want to work on the genemods, help open up the other continent."

It struck a chord, somewhere deep in Cassie's soul. She'd wanted to be a biologist once. Her mother had been a biologist who studied the interrelationship of native bacteria and genemodded plant life on Ceres. At twelve, Cassie'd wanted to grow up to be just like her mother.

Her mother had died giving her a chance to run away. And since then no one had asked Cassie what she wanted to be. The Combined Forces had plucked her and others like her out of the refugee camp on Luna. Ceresian survivors made good soldiers.

She wondered what she'd say now if anyone asked her what she wanted to be.

Cassie knew she wasn't going to call for a medevac. Oh, hell. The GPS locator. Automatic in her skel. She muttered instructions into the skel's comp. With luck no one had locked in on her yet.

People were packing things up, piling them in wheeled carts. Wheeled carts! She walked up to Myra's mother, who seemed to be one of the group leaders. "Pulling out?"

"Yes. Lots of ground to cover. You coming with us?"

"If you'll let me."

"We might need a soldier. If you'll fight for us."

"I'll fight for you." Now when had she made that decision? "The weapons and skels—in the transport. You should take them, too."

Now she'd crossed the line. Trading food and medicine for first aid might be excused as an emergency situation; giving refugees weapons would not. Stupid. It would destroy her career if she got caught.

"We don't know how to use them."

They didn't even want them. All she had to do was say okay, let it go.

But her mind wouldn't let her. It kept playing back images of her own escape off of Ceres, pictures of a makeshift group of people—mostly children—making their way among bombed-out ruins. Not all of them had made it.

"I'll teach you. The skel will work as body armor, protect you. And the scan will show what else is out there. Might get us past any rebel patrols." She could help them avoid the Combined Forces checkpoints, too. At least without a vehicle they could cut through the forest. Though if they got too close to a point, they'd show up on scan.

A moment of hesitation, then a nod.

There were eleven skels, but several had been badly damaged. A little scavenging produced eight working ones. Now Cassie couldn't avoid seeing the names. The pain of loss was quick, sharp, almost physical.

And just as quickly she turned it into anger. Her family had died on Ceres; her soldiers had died; but these people would survive. She clenched a fist; swore an oath to herself.

Perhaps thirty seconds passed as she did this. No one seemed to notice, except Myra. *That girl already knows too much,* Cassie thought.

Not counting the smaller kids there were fourteen refugees. She got eight of them to agree to wear the skels, Emilie and Myra foremost. Cassie disabled the locators as she helped the volunteers put the skels on and lock on the weapons belts.

As the refugees walked along, she moved up and down the group, giving basic lessons. She set weapons to sim mode, so everyone could practice looking at a target to lock it, and then fire. Sim told you when it hit. She also showed them how to switch to fully powered. If any trouble came up, it would happen quick.

She only showed them the energy weapons. Projectiles required more skill and the explosives were too damned dangerous in inexperienced hands. Emilie and Myra took to them eagerly, as did one other young women and a couple of teen-aged boys. The older women seemed uncomfortable with the idea of shooting anyone.

Cassie taught Myra and Emilie the rudiments of scan, and put them at the front. Skel scan would only read about five klicks ahead, but that was better than nothing. The first three times they called her over—excited about something they'd seen—turned out to be false alarms. It occurred to Cassie that she'd spent three months in basic, learning how to manage her skel and weapons. How could she expect these girls to get it in a few hours?

But the fourth time turned up something. A vehicle. Cassie read her own scan. Five people. Weapons. Judging by the maps pulled up on one of the refugees' comps, they hadn't crossed out of rebel-held territory yet. Cassie didn't completely trust the maps, but pulling up her own would require the GPS.

"Probably rebels," Cassie said. "That's the most logical assumption, anyway. Figure they're running scan. They know we're here, but they may think we're friends of theirs. Who else would be moving through here, armed."

Myra looked wary; Emilie eager. The others seemed very nervous.

Somehow, Cassie got everybody herded off into the trees. She and those in the skels took up positions near the road.

An open vehicle stopped about twenty meters off. Five men got out. Cassie stepped into the road. A couple of the refugees stood just in front of the trees.

The leader said, "You're in True Harker territory. No offworlders allowed."

"We're a special detail. Taking a couple of government agents back to Revelations." As she spoke, Cassie locked her weapon on the leader. She didn't think much of her bluff. The rebels would want whoever she claimed to be transporting.

"Turn 'em over to us."

"Now you know I can't do that. I have orders."

"So do I."

Scan registered movement in one of the men standing to the leader's right. Targeting. About to fire. Cassie fired her energy burst at the leader, who went down, dead or stunned. She retargeted toward the second man as she moved for cover. He suddenly collapsed from fire coming from behind her.

The other rebels were moving now, trying to target. Her own people were standing still. She screamed through the comm at them to move, move.

She heard the pop of a projectile weapon, saw one of her people freeze and another leap to knock her over. The second one—in the skels she couldn't tell them apart—took the shot in the upper back and fell forward. The first one returned fire even as Cassie fired her own projectile at the rebel shooter. Three down.

The remaining two rebels were sheltered behind their minitruck, firing from cover. *To hell with it,* Cassie thought, and targeted the truck with a smart bomb. The explosion disintegrated the truck and blew the two men back twenty meters into the trees. Fight over.

She checked the readout on the rebels on the ground. Two dead. Two heavily stunned. One seriously injured. None would be moving anytime soon.

Several people were huddled around whoever had gone down. Cassie ran over to see what she could do.

Emilie sat on the ground, crying, cradling the injured person in her arms. "Why didn't you blow them up before? Then Myra wouldn't have been shot."

Cassie dropped to her knees beside the two girls. The projectile had hit Myra's right shoulder. From the ragged way she was breathing, it must have hit her lungs as well. A serious injury. With quick medical attention, she'd do okay; without it....

Cassie sent out a priority call for medevac, set it to repeat indefinitely. Then she reset the GPS on her skel and Myra's. Might as well make them as easy as possible to find.

"Why didn't you blow them up before?" Emilie said again.

"Because I hoped I wouldn't have to," she answered quietly.

"Why not? Why not kill them all? They kill us all. Oh, please God don't let Myra die."

Cassie muttered the same prayer under her breath. She reached a hand over to Emilie. "I've called for a doctor. We'll save her."

She told a couple of the refugees to watch the stunned rebels, make sure they stayed down. Someone else brought her the first aid supplies. She cleaned the wound and injected Myra with a painkiller.

The injured rebel probably needed attention. She knew no one else here would help him. Another charge for the court martial, probably, if she didn't treat him. She sat there, mentally adding up the charges. Weapons to refugees. Taking sides. Not to mention killing people. One more seemed almost trivial.

But there wasn't anything else she could do for Myra, so she walked over to check on the injured enemy. He looked to have broken bones, a probable concussion, maybe internal injuries, but he hadn't died yet. Nothing she could do would help anything but his superficial injuries. She gave him some of the same painkiller she'd given Myra.

He looked at her with hate—his skel had disintegrated in the explosion. She felt too tired to hate him back. Her head had started to hurt again.

It took thirty minutes for medevac to arrive. Two other aircraft followed close behind, both sending out PK signals. She took the medic sergeant to Myra, pointed the others toward the injured rebels.

The medic knelt down, took inventory of the injury, called the robot stretcher over. He looked at Cassie. "She's not ours, is she? I mean, in spite of the skel."

"No. That keep you from treating her?"

"Not with an injury this bad. But I'm going to have to report it, Lieutenant."

She nodded. The second ship had landed. Someone walked toward her. "Not going to be any secrets here, Sergeant. Just save her life."

He was using a half headpiece, so she could see him grin. "That's our job, ma'am."

The person coming toward her wore captain's bars. Cassie stiffened to attention, saluted.

The captain returned her salute perfunctorily, and said, "What the hell is going on here, Lieutenant?"

"We were attacked by that troop of True Harkers, ma'am. Had to defend ourselves." Cassie didn't know this captain personally, but insignia on the skel made her military police. Not a friend.

"Using explosives, I see. Who are all these people wearing our skels?"

"Refugees, ma'am." Way too late to come up with any lies or plans.

The captain looked around, took in the whole situation. "You have any idea how much trouble you're in, Lieutenant?"

"More than I'd like to think about, ma'am." Behind the captain another aircraft was landing. Someone jumped out before it even came to a full stop. In the light from the aircraft she could see the red hair.

The captain said, "You'd better start thinking about it."

Cassie said, "Yes, ma'am," but her eyes strained to see the man running toward them.

Definitely Bobby. He caught his breath, gave the captain a perfunctory salute, and turned to Cassie. "Amudsen needs you right away. They're holding a big hearing on embargo breach, and want your testimony."

The captain cleared her throat. "I'm afraid you can't take Lt. Ramirez with you right now, Lieutenant." She emphasized the last word. "She's under investigation for some very serious offenses: arming locals, unauthorized combat...."

She didn't say the word "murder," but Cassie knew it was implied. She waited for Bobby to give her a horrified look, to ask if the charges were true.

Instead, he said, "Apparently you didn't hear me, Captain. I'm not acting on my own authority. Delegate Amudsen sent me to find Lt. Ramirez. We're dealing with a major problem: rebels ambushing peacekeeping troops, using high-tech weapons they shouldn't have access to. A little more important than some minor skirmish between rebels and refugees."

Cassie could almost see the captain take a mental step backward. The MP certainly knew about the checkpoint incident, and the embargo breach. But she also probably knew about Bobby and Cassie's relationship—it wasn't a secret. Bobby might be bluffing; on the other hand, crossing Amudsen would not further her career.

She needed an out, and Cassie gave her one. "I'll make myself available for your investigation, ma'am, as soon as Delegate Amudsen no longer needs me." She met the captain's eyes, let her body imply "my word as an officer."

The captain exhaled. "I expect no less." She turned to check with the soldiers that accompanied her, who were rounding up the refugees and checking on the rebels. Cassie heard her tell a soldier, "Load these people up. We'll take them to the camp at Revelations."

Not a perfect ending for the refugees, but at least they'd be out of danger, out of the war zone. And sooner or later Combined Forces would start recruiting soldiers out of those refugee camps, the way they'd recruited her so long ago. Emilie would get her wish, though she probably wouldn't get to fight on Titan.

Cassie turned to Bobby. "Now, what are you really doing here?"

"Just what I said. Amudsen sent me to get you. Though I'm not sure she expected me to rescue you from the MPs. Did you really do what that woman said you did?"

"Yeah." She waited for a lecture, some words of recrimination.

Bobby said nothing.

She said, "Look, like you said, Amudsen didn't expect me to be in all this trouble. She wants to see me, the MPs will make sure I get there. You don't have to put yourself on the line for me like this. Especially when you think what I did was wrong."

"I don't think what you did was wrong, Cassie."

She stared at him.

He kicked at an imaginary rock on the ground, then stumbled because he'd overestimated the gravity. Cassie caught his arm. "Our whole damned policy here, that's what's wrong," he said.

"But they really are investigating what happened at my checkpoint, the embargo breach?"

"Oh, yeah. Big hearings. Headlines on every news service in the system. That's why I've been looking for you. They've heard from a few members of your platoon, but you know how big-time tribunals prefer testimony from officers."

"How many members of my platoon?"

He knew the question meant how many died. "Five," he said quietly.

Fifteen lost. Her fists clenched. Even on Mars she'd never lost so many at once. She found herself wishing she'd killed the injured rebel instead of giving him the painkiller.

"It gets worse, Cassie. Our generals knew the latest tech had slipped past the embargo. Amudsen knew." The expression on his face said he felt betrayed. "They just needed a fucking incident to pull the plug. Bastards."

Somehow Cassie couldn't feel any outrage. She'd used all hers up. Generals worked like that. Diplomats did, too. All an individual soldier could do was go along. Or break the rules and take the consequences.

Bobby went on. "The True Harkers aren't ever going to negotiate in good faith. The core of their leadership believes in all that crap they put out—they're going to do everything they can to win, because they'd rather die than compromise. You can't negotiate with people like that." He kicked the imaginary rock again, this time with more success. "I'm sorry I acted like such a prig, the last time we saw each other."

"I acted pretty bad myself."

"You stood your ground. You always do. That's one of the reasons I like you." He grinned at her. "I'm going to put in for a transfer, get out of this bullshit diplomatic stuff."

She was shocked. "What about your career?"

"Fuck my career." He said it loud enough that several people turned their heads to look at him. "Fuck it. I could never do what she does, could never send people out to die so I could use them as chits at the bargaining table."

Cassie put a hand on his shoulder, to give him comfort. But even as she did it she thought of the times she'd sent people out, knowing they would die. She hated having been the chit—the unknowing chit—but war worked that way. Probably Amudsen had started out as idealistic as Bobby. Maybe what she had to do gave her nightmares.

Bobby went on. "I've been so stupid. I really wanted to believe the problems were as simple as I expressed them in my thesis. I could see what was happening here, but it didn't fit my theories, so I didn't want it to be true."

He took both her hands. "Think I could run a checkpoint? No, probably not. I'd probably fuck that up, too. Maybe something dead end. Supply or something. Or just be enough of a pain in the ass that they ship me home the next transfer. How about it? Want to transfer with me? Just mark time until our terms run out, and we can find decent work?"

Cassie said, controlling her voice carefully to keep it from breaking, "I imagine the only place they'll transfer me is the stockade station off Luna."

He looked startled, as if he'd forgotten her situation. "You don't sound scared."

She laughed. It was better than crying. "I work at not sounding scared. I'm terrified. Even if they don't lock me up, just kick me out, I've got no place to go, no job skills except killing people." Suddenly she was shaking.

He put his arms around her, held her until she stopped.

"I'll use whatever clout I've still got with Amudsen to keep all that from happening," he said.

She let him hold her close. It felt so good. But she said, "That'll only work if it's in the bigger interest, Bobby. Just like everything else. I gave weapons to refugees, killed rebels. If they need to hang me out to dry to get the negotiations going again, they will."

"Then we'll put them on trial—the USG, the whole shebang."

She smiled. His words might be grandiose fantasy, but they helped. "Will you come visit me while I'm doing time?"

"Hell, if they lock you up, I'll steal a ship and come bust you out." He pulled her close to him again. "We'll fight it together, Cassie. I'll stand by you, whatever happens."

Something in her relaxed. Not alone. For the first time in countless years, not alone. Someone else would fight with her, would help her as she tried to find the next step. She might still lose. Probably would. But if she could just remember this feeling, this moment, she could bear anything.

GODZILLA WARFARE

Maria V. Snyder

VAL'S COMM LINK BUZZED IN HER EAR, WAKING HER. NOT ANOTHER PROBLEM *WITH THE simulator*, she thought. *Damn thing breaks more than the mining trolls on Mars Seven.*

She toggled it on with a little more force than required, hurting herself, which just added to her annoyance. "Harris here, this better be important."

"Sergeant Harris, report to Captain Bachman's office immediately," a mechanical voice said.

Oh shit. Val rolled out of bed, sorted through the pile of uniforms, searching for one less wrinkled than the others. An impossible task. Finally, she found a pair of fatigues that didn't look like it had been on the losing side of a fight. She dressed, tied her long auburn hair into a regulation knot, and sprinted for the captain's office.

This is it. Time for the you've-outlived-your-usefulness-talk. Time for the let-the-younger-generation-take-over speech. Even though, at forty-two, she was still able to outsmart the newbs, the invention of the planet-wide shields had rendered her expert skills obsolete.

She paused outside the captain's door to compose her expression before peering into the retinal scanner for identification. The base on Mercury Three was far enough away from the action to be safe from a direct attack. Indirect was the new strategy. Thus the talk.

The door slid open, revealing a waiting area with a receptionist. Val fully expected to be gestured to a seat in the typical army hurry-up-and-wait manner, however the private working the desk admitted her into the captain's office without delay.

Double shit.

The captain sat behind her desk and watched Val approach and salute. Bachman's immaculate uniform lacked a crease. The knot of her blonde hair had been twisted into perfection. Val resisted the desire to yank at her semi-wrinkled shirt.

"Sergeant Harris, I have an assignment for you," the captain said.

Biting down on her surprise, Val waited.

Captain Bachman glanced at the collective's screen. "There's an unexploded MFG-66 on Jupiter Nine and since you're the expert in disarming those...what do you call them?"

"Godzilla bombs, sir."

"Why?"

"It's a reference to a mythical Earth creature that can destroy a city, sir. Since the MFG-66 has enough energy to flatten a city with a population of thirteen million or less, we've code named it the Godzilla, sir." And it managed this feat without using nuclear energy. No sense contaminating the planet you were fighting over.

"Interesting." The captain tapped on the screen. "There is a bullet waiting to take you to Jupiter Nine. Please report to deck twelve, barrel two right away."

Val hesitated.

"Sergeant?"

"We're at war with J-9, sir." And a whole list of other ungrateful colony planets.

"Not at present. We have signed a cease-fire agreement with them, and are currently involved in treaty negotiations. This mission is an act of good faith on our part, Sergeant, so don't screw it up or UFoP will come down hard on us."

"Yes, sir."

The captain confirmed what Val had surmised on her own. The war with J-9 and the other colony planets hadn't been going well these last few years.

Val swung by her tiny office next to the beast, a.k.a. the simulator, to gather her equipment. She hadn't been assigned a field job in over seven years. A few of her instruments were out of date, but so was the Godzilla. Odd. This whole mission felt...off. Not much she could do about it. Val sent a message to her second, putting her in charge of the newbs' training and nursing the temperamental beastie. *Good luck.*

❖

She reported to barrel two. The bullet to J-9 was piloted by a scruffy-looking lieutenant whose skin had the grayish tinge of someone who hadn't seen sunlight in years. *Another old soul. Wonderful.*

He flashed her a toothy smile when she saluted. "No need for formalities on my ship, Sergeant. Call me Leo." He eyed her gear bag. "How much does that thing weigh?"

"About three kilos."

"And you?"

"Fifty-four. Why?"

"This baby's stripped down for extra speed, not comfort. Let me pitch about sixty kilos and we'll be all set."

Leo piled various gadgets on the deck. He held a stack of vomit bags, debating. "Do you get Kasner-speed sick?"

"No."

"Great." He tossed them onto the pile. "Let's go."

Val wedged herself into the back seat, strapping in even though, with this conveyance, you either arrived or you didn't, there was no in between. The ship's name came from the simple fact that it resembled the old projectiles that had been used on Earth. Cone full of navigational equipment and controls, a seat for the pilot, followed by a seat for a single passenger, a small cargo area, and ended with the Kasner-Phillips engine. Constructed for the sole purpose of getting from one place to another as fast as possible, the bullet was literally shot out of a barrel and into space.

They hit Kasner-speed as soon as they broke Merc-3's gravity. Val had forgotten how truly awful the experience of traveling at Kasner-speed was. The destroyers she'd been assigned to before baby-sitting newbs traveled at the more leisurely pace of Phillips-speed.

By the time they arrived near J-9 and her body coalesced, Val wished she'd kept a few vomit bags. *Getting too old for this shit.*

"How ya doing?" Leo asked.

"Fine. How much longer until landing?"

"As long as the Jups open their shield, we should be on terra firma in twenty."

"And if they don't open the shield?"

"We'll go skating, baby. Put on a nice fireworks show for the Jups as we burn!"

Val sighed. *Fly boys.* "I meant what's the plan if we're refused entry?"

"Oh. Turn around, go home. They're the ones with the pimple."

The dimple. Bombs that crashed but failed to explode left craters that the explosive experts called dimples. But she wasn't going to correct an officer even if he had spent too much time at Kasner-speed.

Despite Leo's personality quirks, they landed with nary a bump twenty minutes later. When they finished decontamination, Val and Leo entered the port and were surrounded by a dozen armed soldiers.

"Ah, the welcoming committee," Leo said. "Let me handle this, Sergeant." He introduced himself to the squad's sergeant. "I believe you requested an ED expert? I'm just the pilot, but I've brought Sergeant Harris. If you have an ED to disarm, she's your girl."

Val kept her expression neutral despite the desire to cringe over the lieutenant's intro. The J-9 sergeant's hard gaze swept over her with frank appraisal. She reciprocated. About her age, he had the weathered look of someone who'd been in one too many skirmishes. Buzzed black hair and blue-colored eyes, he stared at her with open suspicion.

They confiscated her gear bag and "escorted" her to a conference room, while they led Lieutenant Leo...elsewhere. She sat on one side of a square metal table that had been bolted to the floor. No windows, no decorations—other than six chairs all secured to the floor—Val realized the purpose of the room probably wasn't to confer, but to interrogate.

If they think I'd make a good POW, they're in for a surprise. I haven't been relevant since those damn planet-wide shields. The civil war with J-9 and a number of other planets had gone on far too long. She understood that they desired their independence from Mother Earth. But they didn't want to pay Mother back the octillions of dollars she invested in equipment, supplies, and labor needed to colonize a raw planet. Nope. They wanted a free ride.

Mother didn't have a problem with the colony planets that signed the pay-their-way-to-freedom contracts. Although these semi-free planets had formed the United Federation of Planets (UFoP)—a laughable tiny group for such a big name. Too bad they didn't remain small and insignificant. The UFoP agreed to stay out of the civil fights as long as Mother Earth adhered to fair warfare tactics. They now had enough member planets and firepower to enforce the rule.

The sergeant from the port entered the room with two of his men. The door closed with a distinctive click. The men stayed near the door as the sergeant approached. She stood.

"Sergeant Harris, I'm Sergeant Gideon. I'm to brief you on the situation." He didn't offer his hand.

They sat on opposites sides of the table. Gideon tapped on the surface of the table. It glowed as it accessed the J-9 collective. A live picture of a barren landscape showed a number of small dimples. As the view zoomed closer on one, it revealed the crater the bomb had created. The MFG-66 had made an impressive scar, digging deep. The view followed the impact path and then the bomb itself—a melted distorted mass, but still deadly. Val wondered how the Godzilla ended up in the middle of nowhere where it couldn't do any damage even if it had detonated on impact.

"I'm leading a team to the crater. You'll remain here and give me instructions to disarm it. I have experience with explosives," Gideon said.

Interesting brief. At least he wasn't planning on using a remote robot. Those things had a twenty percent success rate with the Godzilla. "No," she said.

"It isn't up for debate, Sergeant."

"Sergeant Gideon do you want to die?" she asked in a reasonable tone. "Do you want that MFG-66 to detonate because your expert can't smell, touch or get a sense of the bomb through a screen? Now, I don't care if you blow your team to little tiny bits, but my boss ordered me not to screw it up. So unless you take me out there, I'm not going to cooperate."

Gideon stood. "I'll discuss it with my superiors."

"Good. And make sure you tell them that, when *we're* onsite, *I'm* in command. It's not negotiable."

His demeanor remained dispassionate, but anger burned in his gaze. She almost laughed. Working with unpredictable explosive devices in hostile environments over the years, Val couldn't be intimated by one man's ego.

The three soldiers left. Val tried to get a better view of the Godzilla, except the screen turned off at her touch. *Probably set off an alarm. Good, it will keep them on edge.*

An hour later, Gideon returned Val's gear bag and led her to a shuttle along with six armed guards.

"Tell your pilot to land two kilometers from the crater," she ordered Gideon.

After they reached cruising altitude, Gideon sat across from her with his STR-23 rifle in his lap. Val ignored him as she prepped and calibrated her instruments.

When they landed, Val had them wait thirty minutes before opening the hatch. Not that they could out fly an explosion, but the vibrations from the landing should have settled by then. Gideon's impatience grew, causing his men to tense up as he bore the wait with ill humor.

At the end of thirty minutes, Val said, "Your men will stay here, Sergeant." She paused to let him refuse. He didn't disappoint.

"It's not up for debate," she said, keeping her tone even. "Normally, this is a one-person operation. Explosives are temperamental, and ones that have burned through an atmosphere and crashed are overly sensitive to the slightest vibrations. The more feet tromping around, the higher the risk of setting the damn thing off." Val rummaged in her bag. Pulling out two pairs of soft-feet, she handed one set to Gideon. "Put them on the bottom of your boots. They're hard on the ankles, but sore ankles are worth not dying."

They exited the shuttle and covered the two klicks in silence. Val noted the air was cool and dry. A breeze blew from the east, stirring the lifeless soil. Nothing except a few clumps of rocks and a couple smaller indentations marked the empty expanse.

When they reached the edge of the crater, Val surveyed the damage. "How long ago did this hit?"

"That's classified," Gideon said.

"You're going to make this as difficult as possible for me, aren't you, Sergeant?"

"I have my orders, *Sergeant*," he shot back.

And that would be a yes. She climbed down the steep side of the crater. Grabbing a handful of scorched dirt, she rolled it around her palm and smelled it. She moved to another area and repeated the test. Val wiped her hands and followed the path of impact until she neared the Godzilla. It was half buried.

Opening her pack, she removed her sniffer. She stood downwind from the MFG-66, testing the air for chemical leakage. Then she sampled the soil. The Godzilla's casing hadn't ruptured on impact, the good news. The impact had happened a few weeks ago, the bad news. An already old bomb—the Godzillas hadn't been manufactured in the last seven years—combined with chemicals degrading on the ground created one twitchy bomb.

Which raised the question, why didn't they just set it off with one of their own explosive devices? She asked Sergeant Gideon.

"Classified," he said.

Something stank. And it wasn't the burnt fuel.

Val mulled over the few facts and watched Gideon's expression as she theorized aloud. "You tried to trigger it, but the Godzilla's defensive scrambler sent your bombs wide, which explains the other two impact craters."

He kept his neutral demeanor, but a slight twitch in his jaw gave him away. She was on the right track. Val gestured to the bomb. "This is a recent hit. Which should be impossible due to your shield. Our ships no longer carry the Godzilla. It could have been launched from a Hermit ship. But, again your shield should have destroyed it."

His eyebrows rose, but he smoothed them just as quick. "Is that what the G stands for in MFG?"

"That's what we call it. There is a technical name the higher ups use."

"What does the MF stand for?"

"Official or ours?"

"Yours."

"We refer to that device as the Mother Fucking Godzilla."

Gideon laughed, and the tension between them slipped a few notches. Until Val realized he had been trying to distract her from putting all the clues together.

She picked up the thread of logic and gathered it. "Someone sliced into your collective and turned off your shield just long enough for the Godzilla's entry. Didn't they?"

"That's impossible. No one has sliced into our collective."

Yet he had stiffened as if she had hit a nerve.

With Gideon a step behind her, she approached the bomb. The vibrations in her chest increased ten-fold as sweat dampened her uniform. The number of times she'd defused a bomb didn't matter. Each had its own quirks and challenges. Each one could be her last. Each caused the adrenaline to rush through her body.

The bomb appeared to be far bigger than the standard Godzilla, but the outside markings matched. After confirming the absence of dangerous chemicals, she located the access panel.

Val handed Gideon the sniffer. "If this reads over ten parts per million, tell me."

He nodded.

Glad her hands remained steady, she opened the panel, revealing the bomb's innards. She stared at the complex twist of wires, circuit boards and switches. Except she didn't recognize the configuration. Not right away. When she understood just what sat in front of her, she cursed.

"What's wrong?" Gideon asked.

She replaced the panel and backed away, pulling the sergeant with her. Val didn't stop until they reached the crater's edge.

"What's—"

"I need to speak with my colleague," she said.

"The bullet pilot? Why?"

"It's classified."

Now it was Gideon's turn to curse. "This better not be some stunt or attempt to influence the treaty negotiations."

"It's not."

He stared at her. "I'll hold you to that."

"It's a Death Star," she whispered to Lieutenant Leo. They were in the conference room and she suspected it had been bugged, but she needed to talk to Leo.

"Holy shit with a halo and a white robe! Are you sure?"

"Unfortunately. Are the treaty negotiations going badly for us?"

"I don't know. You can ask the ambassador, he's at the J-9 capital. That is if he'd talk to you." Leo swept a hand through his non-regulation shaggy hair. "Damn girl! Can you disarm it?"

"No. Not alone. It's wired so you need two people, working in tandem."

"But you've done it before. Right?" A crazed hope shone in Leo's eyes as he clutched her sleeves.

"In the simulator, with my assistant. We had one successful session." And only one other team had managed to duplicate it. Not a real achievement since they stopped training on it when the planet-wide shields proved to be an effective defense against the Death Star. Which had been the point. Intel on the Death Star's incredible power had leaked before the device was ready to launch. The panic had been epic.

"Out of how many practice sessions?" Leo asked.

"You don't want to know."

"Time to vacate the premises." Leo stood.

"They won't let us go." Val went up on tip-toe and whispered in his ear. "The Death Star is in delay-action mode."

Leo's face paled to pure white. He swayed. "Why bother to send us?"

"Think about it," Val said. She had. During the trip back to the base, she did nothing but mull it over.

Her theory wasn't pretty. Mother Earth had signed a cease-fire with Jupiter Nine because the colony had been winning the war. The planet-wide shields had countered Mother's one effective offense. With J-9's new guerilla attacks on Mother Earth's bases, Val suspected Mother had to be desperate. So Mother played nice with J-9, sending an ambassador and his retinue to negotiate terms and conditions. Once inside the shield, one of the team had probably managed to shut the shields down long enough for a bomb to slip through.

Mother probably acted surprised. *How did that happen? Must be from a Hermit ship from the past since it was an old MFG-66. We'll send our best expert to take care of it for you.* Except the expert wasn't qualified to disarm a Death Star—no one was. And after the expert "triggered" the bomb, Mother would be all apologetic to the UFoP. *Oops, our mistake. Sorry. Someone must have stolen the schematics to the YFS-97, a.k.a. Death Star* or as the late Sergeant Val Harris liked to say, *You're Fucking Screwed in ninety-seven different ways.*

Val admitted it was an elaborate ruse to appease the UFoP, but she suspected Mother Earth would rather turn J-9 into an asteroid belt, than turn it over to the Jups without a pay-back contract. She was a spiteful bitch that way.

Val could almost hear the gears and switches humming inside Leo's head as he put the clues together.

"And here I'd been worried I'd be forced into retirement. Far better to retire than be a flipping martyr," Leo said.

"Actually, to be a martyr, you have to be the one to decide. In this case, we're being sacrificed."

"Thanks for taking away the only shred of dignity I had left. Did you torture animals when you were little, too, Sergeant?"

"What do we do?" she asked.

"Kiss your ass good-bye and find someone willing to fuck your brains out before the big bang."

Val frowned at the lieutenant. He was not helping. Conflicting emotions churned inside her, Val had been glad the Death Star program had never been activated—the loss of life would have been astronomical. Plus it sickened her. But she was loyal to Mother Earth and felt she was right to expect to be compensated for all that hard work in colonizing a planet. Her warring thoughts connected and produced a blast of inspiration.

"Lieutenant, can you contact the ambassador and tell him I *need* to speak with him?"

"You have a plan?" Leo asked.

"I have an idea."

"Bless your wicked little heart." Leo pounded on the door and demanded they be taken to the ambassador.

Surprisingly, Sergeant Gideon agreed, escorting them to another interrogation room thinly disguised as a conference room.

The ambassador swept in a couple hours later with a scowl already deepening the lines on his wide forehead. "Report, Lieutenant. And it better be important or you'll both be court marshaled for interfering."

Val studied him. A thick, but powerful build, receding hairline with enough gray to appear respectable. His agitation seemed genuine. Leo glanced at her to begin. Time to test the extent of his knowledge. Did he know he was on a suicide mission?

Keeping her voice pitched low, she explained the situation.

At first, the ambassador huffed in disbelief. "No one on my team could have taken down their shields." But soon his survival instincts kicked in. "There was mention of a Hermit when we flew in. Are you one hundred percent sure it's a YFS-97, Sergeant?"

"Yes, sir. No doubt."

"I never should have pissed off General Reffan," the ambassador said. "The old bastard never forgot and here I am, thinking I'd been promoted."

And Val had thought she was useful for the first time in years. Leo's sad gaze matched hers. Another old soldier who had outlived his usefulness. She let the bout of self-pity run its course, then shook it off.

"Ambassador, you need to inform the Jups of the situation," she said.

"So they can tell the UFoP before we blow to smithereens? How much time do we have?"

"Not enough to argue with me, sir." She ignored his outrage. "They have the right to know, and I need the complete and unquestioning cooperation of Sergeant Gideon. The only way he'll give it to me is if he's ordered to by a superior officer. Plus he should know what he's dealing with."

"You're going to try to disarm the cursed thing?" Leo asked.

"Yes. There's not enough time for an evac, it's either try or do what you suggested earlier, Lieutenant."

Leo leered at Val. "I knew you'd see it my way eventually."

The ambassador, though remained confused. "Why not have the lieutenant help you? That way we don't have to say a word to the Jups."

Val poured a glass of water. She handed it to Leo. "Please take a drink, Lieutenant."

He lifted the glass and downed the contents in one gulp. When he handed it back, Val took it from his shaky hand. Too much time spent at Kasner speed affected the nervous system. He was okay to fly, but disarming the Death Star would take a steady hand.

"What are the odds of success, Sergeant?" the Ambassador asked.

"Does it matter?"

"That bad?"

"Yes, sir."

"A what? Sergeant Harris, you're not making sense," Gideon said. "What the hell is a Death Star?"

She suppressed a sigh. His superior officer ordered him to cooperate with her without hesitation or question, but failed to state a reason, leaving that bit of nasty news to Val. "The bomb buried in your planet is a YFS-97 not a MFG-66. It's carrying enough energy to destroy your *entire* plane, and it's set to go off in twelve hours." They had wasted six precious hours talking with the J-9 authorities.

He rocked back on his heels as if she had punched him. "You're wrong. They've been obsolete since the shields."

"According to *your* people, it managed to slip through when the shield opened to allow a supply ship to land. With the right timing, dead accurate maneuvering, and the bomb's special coating, which makes it invisible to your sensors, it is possible."

"But it was shot from a Hermit ship sent over a decade ago. It wouldn't have the latest tech."

She waited, letting him realize the Hermit either had been a decoy or another ship disguised as one. Unlike Val, Mother Earth hadn't given up on the YFS-97 program.

His face blanched with fear. "Shit."

Val watched as Gideon swiped a hand over his face, wiping away the horror and transforming into a soldier. He straightened and met her gaze. Black stubble peppered with gray darkened his strong chin. She wondered if he had a wife and kids or a girlfriend waiting for him at home. Or if he was, like her, married to the job.

"What do you need from me, Sergeant?" he asked.

"Hold out your hands."

He did. They were rock steady.

"I need you to make the impossible possible."

Gideon quirked a smile. "Is that all? And here I was worried."

They returned to the crater. This trip was completely different than their first. Gideon sat next to her and she explained everything she could remember about the Death Star. Since a delay-action device was a different beast than an unexploded one, the shuttle could land right at the crater's edge.

Val removed both access panels. They were located on opposite sides. Pointing out the important circuits and wires to him, she said, "At times, my instructions will seem counter-intuitive, but you need to do exactly what I say. Understand?"

"Yes."

When Gideon called that he was ready, a cold wave of terror washed through her. The only successful disarms had been with teams of two females. She should have requested a female sergeant.

"Harris?" Only Gideon's face could be seen above the bomb's body. "Let's do this."

Pulling in a deep breath, Val stared at her hands. Despite her out-of-control heart rate and her guts turning to liquid, they remained still.

"Al l right, Gideon. Located the red-and-black wire that has been twisted with a green-and-yellow one. On the count of three, cut the red-and-black wire." She positioned her wire cutters then glanced up. Gideon stared at her, waiting.

She said, "One. Two. Three." Snip. Val braced for the roar, the flash of light, but nothing happened.

This is going to be pure hell. Consider the alternative, Val. Right.

"Okay, now I want you to cut the green-and-yellow wire on three."

Once again he met her gaze while she counted, cutting the wire without looking at his wire cutters. Her assistant hadn't done that. Anxiety boiled in her stomach.

She continued with the initial sequence. If the steps weren't done in order and in tandem, the Death Star would detonate. The device's internal clock couldn't be stopped or disconnected without severing the contacts with the explosives. In other words, there were no shortcuts.

Val had lapsed into a rhythm, when Gideon broke her concentration.

"Harris that's insane. You're sending current *into* the pads. It should be diverted." Little streams of sweat ran down the sides of his face.

"Twist the wires together on my count."

"No. You're a Godzilla expert. They sent you to fail, remember?"
Ouch.

"You're going to kill us all," he said with a voice pinched tight with panic. "There are over five million people living on this planet. I won't do it."

She tried logic. "We're all going to die anyway."

"But I *won't*...can't be the reason." Gideon stepped away from the panel.

"Damn it, Gideon. We were working. Ninety-five percent of the simulated sessions had failed by this point." She made up the statistic; it sounded reassuring and was close enough to the truth.

He paused.

"Stop thinking. This baby is unlike anything you've dealt with before. But I have experience. Now twist those wires on three, Sergeant."

Gideon nodded and returned to the bomb. Val allowed a second of cool relief to flow through her burning muscles before she counted.

As they worked, Val disconnected from what might happen to the task at hand. But statistics caught up to her. Two people cutting, splicing, and re-wiring circuit boards at the exact same time was near impossible.

The YFS-97 shuddered and activated with a series of clicks. She jumped back.

"What happened?" Gideon asked.

"We're done."

"But we were so close!" His voice rose in panic. "Why didn't it explode?"

Her thoughts jumbled, twisting until they resembled the pulled out guts of the Death Star. *Kaboom, kaboom—where's the kaboom? Leo had the right idea, I should be on the floor with Gideon, spending my last minutes—*

"Harris." He shook her shoulders. "It's not over. Finish the mission, soldier!"

She blinked at him. "They sent me to fail. I've achieved my mission."

"Yes, they did send you to fail. After years of loyal service, you were deemed disposable. How does that make you feel, soldier?"

"Mad as hell."

"What are you going to do about it?"

The clicking increased in volume and speed. Kaboom come soon. Val almost giggled, but a chunk of vital information formed in the middle of her spinning thoughts. *No kaboom. Why not?*

They had been near the end. Only a few connections were left, which meant the YFS-97 had to find another way to detonate.

"Go!" She pointed to his panel. Grabbing her pliers, she shouted instructions to Gideon over the noise.

It didn't matter if they worked in tandem as long as they both finished the last step before the Death Star re-routed its ignition. Sweat dripped and she panted with the effort.

"Last cut, Gideon," she yelled. "Blue wire, snip it off before it enters the boxes on either side and pull it—" A shower of sparks arched across her wire cutters. Then a huge fireball slammed into her, knocking her off her feet.

Kaboom. Mission accomplished. She crash landed. All thought disappeared.

Pain and semi-consciousness returned at the same time. Every centimeter of her body hurt, and she had lost her vision and hearing. Val swore. Except it didn't help when she couldn't hear her own cursing. She also couldn't move, which would be alarming if she had the energy to care.

Real consciousness came with some serious pain, but the meds helped blur the sharp edges. And the return of both her hearing and vision aided in her recovery.

Gideon visited. "Welcome back, Sergeant."

"But...the fire. What..."

"I've no idea. I yanked the blue wire just as the fireball hit you. It dissipated. The clicking stopped. I'm here and not blown to bits. So I'm not complaining."

"How long..."

"You've been out of it a couple days. Leo's beside himself. He wants to go home, and is driving us all crazy."

"Pilots have...a harder time...being a POW. There's been...studies." *And I probably won't do much better.* However, when she considered the alternative, being a POW didn't seem so bad.

Gideon smiled. "You're welcome to stay—you are a hero, after all—of course, only a few people will ever know about it. However, you don't *have* to stay. As soon as you're feeling better, Leo will fly you back to your base."

Confused, Val asked. "What did I miss?"

"Your ambassador made a deal. If you saved our planet, you would be allowed to leave. But there is one condition."

"Home, sweet home," Leo cried as he landed the bullet.

"Leo, it's a barren rock with a military base. Not what I'd call home," Val said as she tried not to get sick in his ship.

"Better than some foul swamp with huge creatures that consider us dessert."

"Ugh. You've been to the base on Venus Five?"

"Spent two years there." He shuddered. "I'll take a barren wasteland any day."

Her sore muscles protested as Val climbed from the bullet and entered the decontamination area. But she forgot all about her aches and pains when she spotted Captain Bachman and four MPs waiting for her on the platform.

"Sergeant Harris, come with me," the Captain ordered. "Lieutenant Leo, please report to your commanding officer."

"Yes, sir." They both snapped a salute.

Leo shook her hand good-bye. Grinning, he headed in the opposite direction. *I'd grin, too if I could claim ignorance, telling everyone I'd hung out in the pilot's lounge drinking the entire time.*

The captain led her to a debriefing room and gestured to a chair. Val scanned the room. The place had been rigged with video and audio sensors.

"Report, Sergeant," the Captain ordered.

"I disarmed the bomb as requested, Captain. I've nothing else to report."

"You disarmed a MFG-66?"

So she had known. "Yes, sir."

"Are you sure?"

Val feigned confusion. "Of course, sir. The explosive device was clearly labeled. There is even video footage—"

"Sergeant Harris, I don't care what the video showed. I want an honest report."

Then you shouldn't have lied to me, bitch. Swallowing the bitter taste in her mouth, Val detailed a textbook disarming of a Godzilla bomb for the captain.

Clearly impatient, the captain banged her hands on the table. "What took you so long to return?"

"After I disarmed the bomb, I supervised the proper dismantling and safe storage of the explosives, which required a few days."

"That wasn't part of your mission, Sergeant."

"Sorry, sir. I misunderstood. Since you had informed me that my mission was an act of *good faith*, I felt it was my duty to ensure the safety of the Jups."

The captain kept trying to trip Val up. However, Bachman wouldn't directly ask about the Death Star. And with the ambassador's report, confirming Val's statement, Captain Bachman couldn't charge Val with treason.

The Jups had been smart to pretend all had gone as planned. They kept Mother Earth wondering and worried about what happened to that Death Star. *Good, it will keep them on the edge.*

Val tendered her resignation a few months later. Although upset, Captain Bachman couldn't stop her. She packed her few belongings and met Leo on deck twelve.

"Free at last?" he asked.

"Yep. What about you?"

"I'll never retire. I'm a speed junkie." He grabbed her bag and shoved it in the cargo area of his bullet. "Where to, my dear?"

"Jupiter Nine."

"Oh?"

"I hear they're looking to hire an explosives expert."

"Really? Are you sure it isn't because of a certain yummy Sergeant Gideon?"

"I wouldn't use the word yummy to describe the sergeant."

"What word would you use?"

But Val only smiled at her friend as she settled into the passenger seat. While she waited for the bullet to fire, she thought of the perfect word for Gideon.

Kaboom.

From **BEST LAID PLANS**
Book Five in the Defending the Future series

The Stone of the First High Pontiff by Keith R.A. DeCandido
Chitter Chitter Bang Bang by David Sherman
Iron Horses by Judi Fleming

THE STONE OF THE FIRST HIGH PONTIFF

Keith R.A. DeCandido

JIN YAWNED AS SHE CAME ONTO THE FLIGHT DECK, AND SAW THAT THE SHIP HADN'T moved since she went to bed. Timm didn't even turn to look at her, instead staring at the display on the nav. "No, they still haven't finished the maintenance on the Nimast Corridor. No, they haven't given us an estimate as to when it will be done. No, we can't just go on our own steam, as that'll take three decades."

Smiling as she took the copilot's seat on the cramped flight deck, Jin said, "Well, that answers two of my questions."

"Yeah, well, it wasn't until we entered hour number fourteen that I started plotting a direct course to Taksnaro, just for shits and giggles."

Jin shot him a mischievous look through hooded eyes. "And it'll take as long as three decades? You're losing your touch."

Timm shrugged and rubbed his smooth, dark scalp. "Well, that was at point-seven. Any higher, we start dealing with time-dilation, and *nobody* wants a piece'a that shit."

"On the other hand," Jin said with a sigh, "by the time thirty years go by, Brfnel might actually pay us."

"You are *such* an optimist."

"Are you sure we should be going to Taksnaro?"

Turning to Jin, Timm stared at her as if she'd gone Zlarix and grown a second head. "Excuse me? Did we not both agree, while sitting in these same chairs, right before we told Brfnel we'd find his daughter—again—that we'd go to Taksnaro for the opening-night performance of *Down Among the Stars*, assuming we found little Glarna before the twelfth? And is it not now the tenth, giving us two whole days to get to Taksnaro?"

Jin winced. "I know, but—" She sighed. "Well, Brfnel *hasn't* paid us. And this Corridor trip is going to take the last of our available cash."

Timm's nose twitched the way it always did when Jin started talking about the dire state of their finances. "You're telling me that new coil cost that much?"

With a snort, Jin said, "It wasn't a new coil, it was a used coil, and it cost a hundred. A new one would've meant going into the emergency fund—and before you ask," she added quickly as Timm opened his mouth, "we are *not* dipping into the emergency fund to pay to park this beast at Taksnaro."

"*Seeker* is *not* a beast, she's a good boat." Timm patted the console affectionately, which he always did whenever Jin told the truth about their tiny, cramped ship's rather dilapidated condition. He continued: "And we are too dipping into it if we have to, because you promised." He pointed an accusatory finger at Jin.

She sighed. "What if I promise to get you a HoloPlay of the performance when it comes out?"

"Three problems with that. One, HoloPlays are never as good as the live performance. Two, only place I can run the HoloPlay is the half-meter space over my console here, which ain't exactly the kind of immersive experience you get from live theatre. And three, you already promised we'd go to Taksnaro, so you promising to get me the HoloPlay in order to go back on your *other* promise is kind of unconvincing, y'know?" He got up from the pilot's chair. "Wake me if they actually put the damn Corridor back online."

Looking down at one of the displays, Jin saw that three messages had come in. "Did you check YourMail?"

"That is *all* I have done for the past fifteen hours. Not a single interesting thing there."

"We just got three—and one is from the Lighters."

Timm rolled his eyes. "Half the YourMail we got was from Lighters."

Jin grinned. "Which sect?"

"Both." He shuddered. "All the usual junk. Come to our side, we're more holy than the other side. Dunno why they blast it out to *everyone* like that. I mean, do they have *any* worshippers who aren't Vhaddish?"

"Probably easier to do that than just to target Vhaddish addresses." Jin shrugged. "Anyhow, this doesn't look like recruitment junk, since it's addressed to the 'human finder.'"

Timm grinned and Jin made a face. She hated being called that, but the appellation had stuck.

"It's from the High Pontiff himself," Jin said after tapping the YourMail logo to bring the message up to the screen. "He wants to hire us."

Timm put his head in his hands. "Oh hell, no, please, Jin, no, we do *not* want to deal with religious types. They're always asking for discounts, and—"

Jin cut him off. "They're willing to pay two thousand just to take a meeting, regardless of whether or not we take the job."

A several-second silence ensued after she said that. Finally, Timm spoke in a very quiet tone. "Say that again. Slowly."

Instead, Jin merely stared at him. She watched his face go through several emotions in succession, starting with annoyance at the need to miss the opening of *Down Among the Stars*, eventually modulating into a small smile at the thought of what he could spend his share of a thousand marks on.

Finally, Timm sat back down in the pilot seat. "Let me see it."

Before Jin could shoot the YourMail to his console, the Braslo InterShip beeped. Timm tapped it on; Jin noted that the call was from Nimast Corridor Control, and she hoped that it was good news.

A voice spoke in heavily accented Cwyar. *"This is Nimast Corridor Control. Maintenance is complete, and* Seeker *is in the queue for transit. Your registry indicates that this is a Revnen ship?"*

In the same language, Timm replied: "Yes, the co-owners of this vessel are Revnen, and we're both unbonded. If you want," he added impatiently, "I can provide proof of our—"

"That won't be necessary, Seeker, *you just need to be aware that there are four Sanashloj ships in the queue, and they're ahead of you."*

"That's fine, Corridor Control, we'll wait our turn. Out." Timm cut off the Braslo quickly, then looked at Jin. "Guess they have new folks in charge."

With a shudder, Jin nodded. Last time they'd come through Nimast, they'd had to provide proof that they were unbonded. Of course, that was right after all those Sanrevnen slaves on Fortinon had rioted and run away, and everyone was on edge.

Timm read over the mail from the Lighters. "Yeah, okay." He reopened the Braslo to Corridor Control.

"Nimast Corridor Control, go ahead Seeker."

"Corridor Conrol, we need to alter our filed destination."

Jin had expected the receiving room for the High Pontiff of the Sacred Church of Enlightened Thought and Belief to be ostentatious, but her expectations were greatly exceeded. They had entered doors made of cast gravari, and inlaid with gold. The floor of the room was entirely made of fringelt—Jin felt guilty walking on it—and the ceiling likewise. The very long side walls were all decorated with hand-painted images of all of the previous High Pontiffs, going back to ten centuries before Jin and Timm's ancestral homeland of Earth was conquered by the Ashloj Collective. There were only about eighty of them—the Vhaddish were a long-lived people, although no one was appointed High Pontiff until they were already two hundred years old—but each was surrounded by acolytes.

The lengthy, open room was supported by pillars, which were also made of fingelt—however, one expected that from pillars, as every Vhaddish structure of any kind of size used fingelt pillars—etched with scenes from the Lighters' holy texts.

Standing in front of each pillar was a Church Warrior—none of whom, she noted with amusement, were Vhaddish. It seemed they felt safer hiring non-believers to protect them for some reason. Each Warrior was armed with GranitoZap sidearms and covered head to toe in GranitoBlam armor. Jin had never been a big fan of firearms, but she knew from Timm carrying on like trash on the subject that Granito's goods were substandard—but also cheap, which probably was why the church went for it.

At the far end was the High Pontiff's throne, made of solid gold. Jin couldn't imagine it was in any way comfortable. However, it did make it clear that throwing two thousand marks around just to take a meeting wasn't even going to put a dent in their treasury.

Sitting in the throne was the round, tentacled body of the High Pontiff himself. His deep brown fur had been shaved into the pattern that indicated that he was the leader of the church.

Or, at least, the half or so Lighters who actually followed him.

Next to him was another Vhaddish whose white fur had been shaved into the pattern of a high acolyte of the church.

The white-furred one spoke in the Vhaddish language with his upper mouth as Jin and Timm approached. "Thank you for agreeing to the meeting, human finder."

"Please, you may refer to me as Jin," she said in the same language, hoping she was getting her pronunciation right—Vhaddish was created by a species with two mouths, each with a forked tongue, so it made for some entertaining sibilants—"and you paid us to have this meeting, so to this meeting we gladly attend. How may we refer to you?"

"I am the High Pontiff's Voice. And we shall refer to you as Jin. Our compliments on your facility with the holy language of the Vhaddish. It is rare to find an outworlder who speaks it so fluently."

"Thank you." Jin had indeed noticed that she was speaking the language more comfortably than she had in the past. It was yet another change that had come to her life since the circumstance that led to her becoming the so-called "human finder."

"I assume, Jin, that you are familiar with the schism that exists within the Sacred Church of Enlightened Thought and Belief, praise be to the church's wisdom?"

Jin nodded, then remembered that Vhaddish weren't very good at reading body language cues of non-Vhaddish. "I am aware of the schism's existence, and that each sect believes itself to be the correct one."

"So you are not aware of the cause of the schism."

"Forgive me, but I am not. I regret to say that I am not a student of your church's history."

Several of the Voice's tentacles vibrated at that. "Such is not part of our church's history, though it is, tragically, part of the history of the Vhaddish people. Long ago, in the earliest days of the Sacred Church of Enlightened Thought and Belief, praise be to the church's wisdom, there was a stone that had etched upon its surface the words of the First High Pontiff. The artifact was lost, but the words inscribed upon it were recorded in the holy texts. There are those heretics who believe that the texts are in error, and that the stone has words other than those recorded. That is the basis of the schism, and it has only grown worse over the decades."

Timm, who did not speak Vhaddish, was shifting uncomfortably from foot to foot. Jin cast him a quick apologetic glance, then said to the Voice, "Do you wish me to find this stone?"

The Voice's tentacles wiggled again, and three of his eyestalks turned toward the High Pontiff, who continued to sit upon the throne. If his lungflaps hadn't been vibrating, Jin would have thought the High Pontiff to be dead.

After a surprisingly long hesitation, the Voice said, "The High Pontiff, praise be to his great wisdom and knowledge, has learned of your exploits through the InformNet."

Jin somehow managed to avoid chuckling. That last word had been spoken in Yrak, the common tongue of the Ashloj, and the one used on the InformNet. Vhaddish had no word for that, so the Voice just appropriated the Yrak one. Jin had a hard time believing that the High Pontiff actually lowered himself to observe the InformNet.

"Based on all accounts, you have an enviable success rate. For that reason, the High Pontiff, praise be to his great wisdom and knowledge, wishes to engage your services to locate the Stone of the First High Pontiff."

Timm, who had been staring at the murals on the walls, looked over at those last words, which he apparently recognized.

The Voice went on: "The High Pontiff, praise be to his great wisdom and knowledge, wishes this schism to end, for all those who believe in the Sacred Church of Enlightened Thought and Belief, praise be to the church's wisdom, to once again be united under his guidance. The High Pontiff, praise be to his great wisdom and knowledge, believes that the retrieval of the Stone of the First High Pontiff, lost all these many centuries, may be what at last enables our deluded fellows to return to the fold, and make the Sacred Church of Enlightened Thought and Belief, praise be to the church's wisdom, stronger."

"If I am to accept this commission," Jin said slowly, "I will need to know everything about the Stone of the First High Pontiff. I will need to see not only the sacred texts, but also any heretical ones."

The High Pontiff's tentacles quivered at that, and the Voice quickly said, "That will not be—"

"Look, Voice—" She stopped, realizing she had gone back to Yrak. Taking a breath, she went back to Vhaddish. "In order to perform my task, I must have every piece of information about the Stone of the First High Pontiff, even information that is inaccurate. Even a lie may hold truths within it."

The High Pontiff's eyestalks all focused on Jin, and for the first time, he spoke. Unlike that of his Voice, the High Pontiff's words came out in a raspy whisper. "You speak the words of Samno. Good. Good."

Jin inclined her head in respect, though she hadn't the first clue who Samno was. The phrase was something one of her former owners used to say before she died.

Half the High Pontiff's eyestalks looked at the Voice, who then said, "We shall provide you with *all* the available data on the Stone of the First High Pontiff—even the data that is heretical and false."

"I apologize for forcing you to acknowledge heretical work," Jin said quickly, "but it is necessary to accomplish the task you have set out for me."

In Yrak, Timm muttered, "They tell us how much they're paying yet?"

Jin winced. She'd forgotten that part. She often did, which was why she preferred Timm to handle negotiations. After being a slave so long, the notion of being personally recompensed for work was still foreign to her. Her function as a slave had been to, among other things, handle her owners' finances, but that was for after jobs were done, not before.

"Assuming," she continued, "that we may properly negotiate payment."

The Voice's tentacles quivered. "Payment has already been made."

Jin frowned, remembering Timm's words about religious types trying to renege on paying their bills. "For this meeting, yes, payment has been made. We have fulfilled the terms of *that* agreement. If I am to find the Stone of the First High Pontiff, there must be recompense for *that* service."

More of the High Pontiff's eyestalks glanced at the Voice. Jin wished she knew more about Vhaddish body language.

The Voice then said, "We will only provide you with further currency if you complete the task. Therefore, another two thousand marks will be granted to you upon the return of the Stone of the First High Pontiff to the Sacred Church of Enlightened Thought and Belief, praise be to the church's wisdom."

Normally, this would be the part where someone haggled, but four thousand was more than she'd gotten for any *two* jobs. This would enable them to do *proper* repairs on *Seeker* and take a vacation besides.

Jin had never taken a vacation in her life. She rather liked the idea.

"Very well, I accept your terms," she said. "We will return when I have found the Stone of the First High Pontiff."

"*If* you find it." For the first time, Jin detected an odd tone in the Voice. Was it humor? Skepticism? Jin wondered if the Voice didn't think much of the High Pontiff hiring some lowly Revnen from a conquered planet performing so important a task, and likely didn't think she was up to it.

Not that Jin cared what the Voice thought. Since she found the gem, she'd been able to find *anything*.

As they walked back toward the exit, under the many eyestalks of the previous High Pontiffs, Timm asked, "Please tell me you got us at least ten thousand for this."

Jin blinked. "What? No, I got another two thousand. That's four thousand, Timm, that's better—"

Whispering his shout so he didn't attract the attention of the High Pontiff or his Voice, Timm said, "You *what*? Look, I only know about ten phrases in Vhaddish, but one of them is 'the Stone of the First High Pontiff,' and I heard you both using that one all over the damn place. That's what they want you to find, right?"

"Yes."

Timm shook his head. "You didn't do any transactions, so I'm guessing they'll pay the other two thousand when we come back with the stone?"

Jin nodded.

"Did you ask for expenses?"

This time, Jin shook her head. "Our expenses are never more than two thousand—in fact, they're never more than a few hundred, so—"

Waving her off, Timm said, "Doesn't matter. They can twiddle their tentacles all they want, we'll find it and sell it to the highest bidder. And I gotta tell you, the bidding will *start* at five thousand."

"No."

They got to the ornate fingelt door, which opened at their approach. Dozens of acolytes, as well as petitioners and other people waiting for a chance to see the High Pontiff sat with varying degrees of patience outside in the vestibule.

Neither Jin nor Timm spoke anymore of this until they reached the port where *Seeker* was docked.

Once they were safely on board with no prying ears around, Timm immediately went to the console and set the ScanBots to start a security sweep. Jin agreed with the sentiment. She wouldn't put it past the Lighters to plant a listening device on the ship to make sure they stuck to the plan.

Smiling, Timm pointed at the display, which showed that no fewer than three such devices had been placed on board. Jin was very grateful that they'd spent the money on the ScanBots—which she was planning to upgrade to the 6000 model once this job was done. After what happened on Siersee...

"All right, now that we can talk," Timm said, "let's talk. We can get so much more for—"

"No, Timm, I won't do that." Jin sat in the co-pilot's seat, relieved to be speaking in Yrak again. Her lips and tongue were exhausted from forming words in Vhaddish. "I will not become someone who reneges on a contract. It's been hard enough to find work. People don't believe that I'm as good as my reputation—"

Chuckling, Timm said, "If I didn't know your secret, *I* wouldn't believe you're as good as your reputation."

Jin nodded, conceding the point. "But I agreed to find the stone for the Lighters. And these are people who have a massive platform. Even non-believers can't get away from hearing from them all the time. If we go back on a contract with them, we'll never get another job."

"For that stone, we'll make enough that we won't *need* one." Timm sighed. "Yeah, yeah, okay, fine, we'll do it. But you should've talked him up another thousand at least."

Shaking her head, Jin stared at her console, which indicated new YourMail—one of which came from the same address as the Lighters' original message. Conjoined to that mail was a series of Inform files. "Okay, I'm gonna need to go through all this. Even with the gem, it should take me a few hours."

Timm nodded. "I'll take us out, then. Take a nice slow, leisurely journey to the Fearag Corridor."

Jin returned the nod and got up to head to her bunk. She was worried that Timm would just stay in the dock, but as she had pointed out many times, sitting in a dock cost money—flying in space was free.

At least, most of the time.

When she entered her cabin, she immediately stripped down to her underclothing—necessary in the heat. After upgrading the security system, her next priority after this job was done was to finally fix the thermostats in the bunks.

Discarding her coverall, she sat down on her bed and stared down at the gem embedded in her chest, right above her left breast, over her heart.

She still knew nothing about the blood-red gem, or what it was doing in that asteroid field, or why it embedded itself in her chest dangerously close to her heart, or why, since then, she'd literally been able to find *anything* she set her mind to find.

But shortly after she found the gem—or it found her?—her owners died, and she and Timm (who was free, but employed by Jin's owners) struck out on their own as "the human finder."

And she'd become more confident, more intelligent, more athletic. Her facility for Vhaddish had improved without any practice, and before the gem, if anyone had slapped her down the way Timm had, she'd have demurred and capitulated.

Something else she needed to do was find a good doctor. She'd allowed herself to be examined by medics she could afford, none of whom could figure out how the gem worked, how it was doing what it was doing, or much of anything else. One even offered to surgically remove it, which Jin quickly declined until she knew more.

But with the money they were getting for this, she could see a *talented* doctor.

Grabbing a tablet, she touched the implant on the back of her neck, and the Inform started to download right into her own mind.

Then, as always was necessary after that kind of download, she fell asleep.

As soon as she woke up, Jin knew everything there was to know about the Stone of the First High Pontiff, from the stories about how the First High Pontiff dug the stone out of a quarry with his bare hands, and why he chose the script he chose, and how his successors each placed the stone in a place of higher honor, how the stone was lost during the Pranik War when Vhad was destroyed, and the stories of how the stone was smuggled out by acolytes, and so much more.

She went back to the flight deck. Timm turned to give her an expectant look.

"Tell Fearag Corridor Control that we need to book passage to the Wosaphi Conclave."

The Voice of the High Pontiff sighed happily as he tossed the Hebro-Grubs—Hebro grew much more succulent grubs than the usual store-bought ones—into his lower mouth while dictating a memo in Yrak to the bishopric with his upper mouth. Computers couldn't really handle Vhaddish.

"Against my direct recommendation, the High Pontiff has continued to attempt to find the Stone of the First High Pontiff, despite the fact that the stone was obviously lost forever when Vhad was destroyed by the heretics of Pranik. The legends that grew up around the stone were created to keep the devout from abandoning us following the destruction of our homeworld."

The Voice threw some more HerboGrubs into his mouth. They were particularly good today, and he made a mental note to compliment his slaves for getting a good bunch.

He continued to dictate his memo: "However, we can take some comfort in the fact that the High Pontiff has, of late, become quite fascinated with the so-called 'human finder.' He has become convinced that she will be the one to find the Stone of the First High Pontiff. To that end, I have liberated two thousand marks from the treasury to pay her off. She will search for it, never find it, and then the High Pontiff will finally let go of his obsession with using the stone to unite the factions. While the notion of bringing the heretics back into the fold in the abstract is a noble one, its practicality remains specious, especially since donations have increased a thousandfold since the schism. However, the High Pontiff continues to drone on about his legacy, that he wishes the Ninety-Ninth High Pontiff to be remembered as the one who healed the schism. With luck, the human finder's failure to locate the stone will end this foolishness."

As he popped the last of his HerboGrubs, he added, "And do not be concerned that the human finder will attempt to bring us a forgery. Providing a convincing forgery of the stone is far beyond her means. The materials alone for such a forgery would cost many thousands of marks."

With that, the Voice sent the memo off to the bishopric. He was looking forward to the soon end of this obsession of the High Pontiff's.

The following morning, he awoke to a YourMail that the human finder had returned with the Stone of the First High Pontiff.

The Voice had to reread the message several times before he finally believed that it said what his eyestalks insisted it did.

"This isn't possible," he muttered as his servants tended to his fur before he met with the High Pontiff.

When he arrived for his audience in the High Pontiff's private chambers—to which only the Voice and selected sex slaves were allowed—the Voice was distressed at how joyful the High Pontiff seemed. His limbs were quivering, and his eyestalks practically bouncing.

"A great day for the Sacred Church of Enlightened Thought and Belief, is it not, my Voice?"

"So it would appear to be, Most Holy One. I am, however, surprised that the human finder was able to locate the Stone of the First High Pontiff so quickly."

"As am I, my Voice. It is proof that she is quite extraordinary. Come, let us not keep her waiting, for today is a great day in the history of the Sacred Church of Enlightened Thought and Belief."

The Voice followed several paces behind the High Pontiff as he entered the receiving room.

Once the High Pontiff was seated in his throne, the Voice instructed the computer to let the human finder in.

When she entered, the Voice had to once again be persuaded that his eyestalks were functioning properly. The human finder's face had several scars that were covered with DermalRep, her hair was considerably shorter than it had been when last she was here—and it looked as if it had been singed off—while her companion had a massive bandage on the crown of his smooth scalp.

The human finder was also holding a PlastiForm container.

"This is not possible," the Voice said without preamble, and before the human finder could say anything.

"On the contrary," the human finder said, "it is very possible. The Stone of the First High Pontiff was in a storage unit located under the ruins of Crivda."

Several of the Voice's tentacles quivered. "The Stone of the High Pontiff was in the territory of the Wosaphi Conclave?"

"Very deep within their territory," the human finder said, "but I was able to retrieve it, after a great deal of difficult searching." She exchanged a look with her taller companion.

Then she touched the side of the PlastiForm container, which slid open, and then she pulled out a round, engraved stone the size of her fist.

The Voice found himself unable to speak with either mouth at first. It looked very much like what the stone looked like in contemporary images. He'd imagined it to be larger, but—

But no, it had to be a forgery. Hadn't it?

His voice even raspier than usual, the High Pontiff reached out with several tentacles. "The stone," he said in Yrak, "it has been—found—at last—it has..."

Then the High Pontiff collapsed, rolling off the throne and onto the floor.

Stunned, the Voice stared for a second, then instructed the computer to summon medical help and activate the triage program.

The computer intoned a moment later: "All life functions in the Ninety-Ninth High Pontiff have ceased."

Quickly, the Voice stood up and spoke to the Church Warriors stationed at the room's pillars. "Remove these heretics! And have them take their forgery with them!"

"It's *not* a forgery!" The human finder was speaking in Yrak now as well. "I wouldn't have found it if it was a fake! That's not how it works!"

"It doesn't matter what you say," the Voice said in the same language, to make it clear that he would not be doing business with forgers. He had no idea how they'd managed to construct a fake, but it simply *could not* be the same one.

As the Warriors stood behind each of the humans, the woman said, "Our ScanBot verified that this was made of jeevon! There's only, what, half an acre's worth of jeevon left in the galaxy? Less? There's no way we could've gotten our hands on that. This is the real thing!"

"It doesn't matter," the Voice said again—and truly, it didn't. "The High Pontiff is dead, and his ridiculous quest to reunite the church has thankfully died with him. You are heretics and forgers, and you will remove yourself from this world as soon as possible."

"So, you do betray me," said a raspy voice, also speaking in Yrak.

All of the Voice's eyestalks turned in shock as the High Pontiff rose up.

"It—it—"

"Your treachery has been sent to the InformNet, so now the entire Collective is aware of your heresy."

With a start, the Voice realized that that was why the High Pontiff had been speaking in Yrak. Somewhere in the receiving room, he had sequestered CamDrones that were blasting to the InformNet.

"Remove the Voice and bind him by law," the High Pontiff said as he retook his throne.

The Warriors did as they were told. The Voice said nothing else, not wishing to make a further fool of himself to the entire InformNet. He would wait his time to speak his piece. Half the bishopric was on his side, and the High Pontiff would soon see his support erode.

At least, that was what he hoped. His own indiscretion would not sit well with his allies in the bishopric.

Jin had entered the receiving room thinking she was going to make two thousand marks—which was barely enough to cover what they went through to retrieve the damned stone. Then she thought she was going to be placed in a Vhaddish prison for the rest of her life. Then she thought they were going to get the money again.

So when the newly resurrected High Pontiff instructed the Warriors to escort them back to their ship, she was kind of surprised.

Speaking again in Vhaddish, Jin said, "Forgive me, please, High Pontiff, but we had an arrangement."

"You had an arrangement with my former Voice. That arrangement is no more. For all that I am aware, you were part of his plan to discredit me."

"His plan, High Pontiff, was for me never to find the Stone of the First High Pontiff. But I *have* found it."

"That is not possible." He switched to Yrak. "The stone was lost forever. I merely expressed interest in retrieving it to find out how deep my former Voice's treachery was. That stone must be a forgery—not yours, perhaps, but a forgery nonetheless."

"No, High Pontiff, *that* is what is not possible. My—my ability to find things can't be fooled by a forgery. *This* is what I found when I sought out the stone."

"Take them away!"

The guards each put their hands on Jin's and Timm's shoulders and started to guide them toward the exit. Jin supposed she should have been grateful that they hadn't unsheathed their GranitoZaps.

Deliberately speaking in Cwyar, Timm muttered, "*Now* can we auction this thing off to the highest bidder?"

Several months later, Jin lay on the sands of the Covert Beach, the twin suns of Covert gently baking her naked body. She had never taken a vacation before, and the last month on Covert had been magnificent. Never in her life had she been so relaxed.

Once the first of the suns went down, she decided to see what was happening in the Collective. Timm was due back the following day with the newly refitted Seeker, complete with the new ScanBot 6000, working thermostats, and shiny new coils—not to mention a general overhaul of parts.

Easy enough to do when you sell the Stone of the First High Pontiff to the "heretical" Relativist Sect for fifty thousand marks.

Touching her implant, she was able to get an AetherAir signal and do a quick InformNet download, bringing her up to date on assorted sports scores, news, and other stuff.

She noted an abstract of a piece on the resignation of the Ninety-Ninth High Pontiff, and activated that Inform.

"The surprise resignation of the Ninety-Ninth High Pontiff comes as record numbers of devout have left the Lighters, defecting to the Relativist Sect in light of that sect's revelation of the Stone of the First High Pontiff."

Jin couldn't help but laugh. It only would have cost the High Pontiff two thousand marks to keep the stone for himself. Instead, he let them leave with it, and it cost him his job.

"In the meantime, the Council of Elders of the Relativist Sect have announced that, with the great influx of new members to their church, they are considering electing a High Pontiff from among their number."

Jin went through the rest of the story only to find no mention of her whatsoever—indeed, that there was no mention that the Relativists *acquired* the stone, but that they simply had a "revelation" of it, whatever that meant. That was too bad—being the person who found the Stone of the First High Pontiff would be great for business—but she would have to settle for the large sums of money the Relativists paid her.

She also had a YourMail from the Ninety-Ninth High Pontiff. She wondered if he sent that before or after he resigned.

"To the human finder. It seems I owe you an apology. Or perhaps I owe you nothing, since you have received more money for the Stone of the First High Pontiff from those damned heretics. Either way, your skills are obviously greater than I gave you credit for, and in my eagerness to discredit my traitorous Voice I neglected the devout. I'll obviously never make that mistake again."

Jin smiled. Maybe public recognition didn't matter so much.

CHITTER CHITTER BANG BANG
A Starfist Story

David Sherman

"This is the best idea I've ever heard!" Morton crowed.

"Can you say, we'll be rich?" Norman was breathing heavy at the thought.

"I've got all the trajectory data we need for an intercept," Oscar said, understandably smug.

"And my contact at the Confederation embassy in Berrican confirmed that the Navy isn't providing escorts for the flights anymore," Lorenzo added.

"Yeah, what you said, a piece of cake!"

"We're gonna be rich!"

"We'll be richer than Croesus!"

"Who's Croesus?"

"Never mind, let's get started on our intercept."

The four were former members of Sharp Edge, LLC, the "Corporate Security Provider"—mercenaries in fact, if not in name—that had conducted an illegal mining operation on Opal's sister planet, Ishtar. Sharp Edge had enslaved thousands of the indigenous sentients to do the mining until the operation was shut down by Confederation Marines. The Sharp Edge principals were all in prison, but most of the lower-level employees had been released and given transport to their home worlds. Except the four, who hijacked a small interstellar and returned to the Opal/Ishtar system to steal a shipment of freshly-mined gems.

Nobody called him Henny anymore. His real name was too hard for most Naked Ones to say, so he shall be called Henny, which was what the Naked

Ones who enslaved the People called him before the Naked Ones' Marines came and killed the slavers until the surviving slavers went away. Then the Marines went away, and so did all the other Naked Ones.

Except...

About every year and a half a Naked Ones' thunder-cart dropped down from the sky on its pillar of fire. When it did, it brought a new team of four Naked Ones and took away the four Naked Ones who had been on the World since the last time the thunder-cart had come. Henny had seen the sky-fire come down three times and go back up twice. A thunder-cart was at the Naked Ones' base now, and would leave in another day, when the four Naked Ones returned from the mine where they'd spent the past week. Henny didn't know why these Naked Ones stored the pretty-but-worthless stones they gathered from the mines instead of taking them with them when they left. But each of the other times he'd seen them come and then leave again, they stored the stones instead of taking them.

The Naked Ones who came to the World found places from which they could observe the People. Unobserved, or so they thought. But all of the People knew these new Naked Ones were there. Even the clans and burrows of the Starwarmth Union knew about the hidden Naked Ones, and everybody knew the burrows and clans of the Starwarmth Union were neither very observant nor very smart.

Henny spent as much time as he could watching these Naked Ones. He knew he was well enough hidden that they couldn't see him. What he didn't know was why they were here. What did they want? They weren't like the Marines who had gone away; the Marines had never tried to hide from the People like these Naked Ones did. Were these Naked Ones also hiding from the Marines? Were they forerunners of a return of the Naked Ones who had enslaved the People before?

Henny needed to find out. That was why he watched them, that was why he examined the traps they put out in places People might walk or scamper, or put them in places where the traps would hide, brooding within sight of burrow entrances.

He never set off one of the traps; he was very careful when he examined them, although a few times he heard a strange, faint clicking sound come from inside one as he examined it. He had no idea what that sound signified; maybe the trap was malfunctioning, and he was lucky not to be snared by it. He didn't know how the traps worked. They weren't cages such as a hunter would use to capture small game. Maybe they held nets that would spring out and ensnare their victims.

The more Henny thought about it, how the Naked Ones came down from the sky on their fire pillars to locations remote from any burrow, and hid themselves from the People, and put out traps, the more he suspected they were advance scouts for a return of the evil Naked Ones.

It would be a very bad thing if they were.

Henny would have liked to listen to these Naked Ones talk among themselves; he'd learned some of their language when he was captured by the Ruhrines. He and the Ruhrines' wiseman, Rzz-tar Chranck—it was a difficult name for Henny to pronounce, as was Ruhrines. Rzz-tar Chranck had explained to Henny that the language of the Naked Ones had three sounds, "B, M, and P," that required a closed upper lip to say, and the People had split upper lips. Anyway, Henny and Rzz-tar Chranck had spent several weeks learning to speak each others languages before the Ruhrines went away and took their wiseman with them. But these Naked Ones always had their heads encased in chel-zrizts, garments to protect them from the elements, and must speak in what Rzz-tar Chranck said was rah-dee-oh. Henny didn't understand what rah-dee-oh was, but knew he couldn't understand anything spoken in it, not without the box-that-translates.

Henny wished he could read the Naked Ones' writing, as he could read the writing of the People's language. He wanted to know what the legend on the side of the thunder-cart meant:

> Confederation of Human Worlds
> Bureau of Human Habitability Exploration and Investigation
> Interplanetary Shuttle No 3
> Opal/Ishtar System

Henny had to find out what these Naked Ones were doing on the World. If they wanted to once more enslave the People, he had to find the Ruhrines and tell them about it so they could stop it like they had before.

Henny thought the Ruhrines must have gone to the wandering star the Naked Ones called O-chal. He didn't understand how people, even Naked Ones, could go to a star and live there. But Fzz-tar Chranck told him O-chal wasn't a star, a ball of fire far, far away, but much closer, a world like the World he lived on. He hadn't known the wiseman to lie to him about anything else, so maybe this was true also.

No matter how unlikely it sounded.

If that was true, and if O-chal was where the Ruhrines went after driving away the evil Naked Ones, then that was where Henny had to go.

The only way Henny could think of to get to O-chal was on the Naked Ones' thunder-cart. He knew he couldn't simply ask them to take him along when they left. Even if he threatened them with his rifle and they complied, how long did the voyage last? Could he stay awake and on guard for that length of time? Or would he fall asleep and be taken by the Naked Ones?

No, confronting the Naked Ones directly was too risky.

There was only one way Henny could go on the thunder-cart. He had to sneak onto it and find a place to hide. He would have to take food with him. But how much? And water, too.

There were so many questions, and so few answers.

Henny looked at his rifle. It wasn't one of the iron rifles made by the People, a rifle that had to be reloaded after every time it was fired, and quickly fouled. It was one of the needle-rifles the Naked Ones slavers used and seldom needed reloading; a flechette rifle is what the Ruhrines called it. Henny thought "flechette" was a clumsey word, and he called it a needle-rifle. Before they left, the Ruhrines gave the needle-rifle to Henny in thanks for helping them with learning each others' language. He would have preferred one of the Ruhrines' fire-rifles, but still was happy with what they gave him.

Henny knew he didn't have much time if he was going to sneak onto this thunder-cart. He broke off his observing and set about gathering food and water to sustain him on the trip to O-chal. And some glow worms, in case there wasn't light where he hid in the thunder-cart.

Inside the thunder-cart Henny found a large storeroom filled with containers of different sizes. He had seen these containers, or containers just like them, being taken off the thunder-cart when it arrived, and then put back on. He thought it likely that the empty containers in the thunder-cart now were not the same ones he'd just seen removed, but rather the ones that had been unloaded on the thunder-cart's previous visit. Not that it mattered. What mattered was that they were empty now.

Henny removed one of the glow worms from the *granalchit* skin sack in which he carried them to light his way among the containers. Their arrangement reminded him so strongly of home, just like the houses and other structures carved into a burrow, that Henny briefly felt homesick. But the homesickness he felt now was nothing compared to what he'd felt when he was caged by the Naked Ones, and let out only for poor meals and to dig in the mines, so his homesickness didn't last very long.

Henny explored the storeroom and found material to use as bedding and for other furnishings. He also found a way to secure his rifle should the thunder-cart lash about like a bush in a storm. Then he settled in for however long the trip would be.

When the thunder-cart took off, Henny thought he should have made a deeper, softer bed; he'd never before felt so crushed. Fortunately, the crushing pressure only lasted for a few minutes. Then came a brief time during which he floated unsettlingly in midair and barely kept his stomach contents. After that, things became more or less normal, except that the air smelled strange.

Henny wasn't sure how long it was, at least three days, perhaps not more than four although it could have been longer—he'd managed to do a lot of sleeping and couldn't track time very well—when the constant low droning of machinery was interrupted by clanging and metallic clashing. Dimly, he heard angry shouting—the first voices he'd heard through the walls of the thunder-cart.

Then he heard the unmistakable *crack* of a gunshot.

Henny tucked the glow worm he'd been using back into the sack, then grabbed his rifle and scampered to a position he had prepared to fight from if the Naked Ones learned that he was on their thunder-cart and came hunting him.

There was more angry shouting after the gunshot, but no more shooting. Then came several minutes of silence before footsteps sounded in the passage outside the storeroom. The footsteps stopped right outside, then the door was yanked open and a light flashed inside.

Henny tensed. Squinting against the light, he aimed his rifle, ready to shoot the first Naked One to come in.

He didn't shoot the first Naked One.

That one wasn't armed, and was roughly shoved inside to fall on the floor. Two more rapidly followed, and the three tumbled into a pile. They didn't move immediately.

"Don't try to come out," a harsh voice snarled from the corridor. "We're armed and you aren't. Even if we can't lock this hatch, we've got it covered and we'll shoot anybody who tries to come out. Remember, we don't need to keep you alive, so behave and you might live through this."

Henny was delighted! he had understood nearly all of the Naked Ones' words, even though he hadn't heard their language spoken since the Ruhrines had gone away.

A hand shot around the edge of the doorway and did something; light flooded the storeroom. The hand withdrew and the door slammed shut.

Henny watched the three Naked Ones unpile themselves. One of them called out, "What about Keely? What are you going to do with Keely? He needs help." Even though he'd only seen one or two of the Naked Ones' females, Henny knew the signs that distinguished between males and females. The one who spoke had the teat-like chest-mounds of a female.

"Don't you worry about Keely," the rough voice answered from outside the door. "We'll take care of the body, it won't stink up your cell." The Naked One laughed and the footsteps went away.

"They killed Keely," somebody said with a whimper. That one also had the teat-like chest mounds. Another sign of the differences between male and female among the Naked Ones was that the females had voices high enough that they could chitter like the People if they wanted to, but the males voices were too deep and slow to chitter. Both of the chest-mound Naked Ones had high voices, another proof that they were female.

If somebody was dead, Henny thought that must have been from the gunshot he'd heard. One of the females began sobbing.

"We can't do anything for him now—and we don't know that he's dead," said another voice. "We need to figure out how to stay alive, and regain control of the shuttle." This speaker had a deep voice. Henny looked closely and saw that he didn't have chest-mounds; an obvious male.

"The captain will figure a way," the first female said softly. "There, there, it'll be all right." She caressed the hair of the sobbing female.

"The captain can't do squat except what those pirates want," the male said, using a couple of words Henny didn't know, but he thought the meaning was clear enough. "There's only one of him and four of them. They're armed, he isn't. We have to come up with our own solution."

The male and the first female continued talking in low voices, and the second female still sobbed, but softly. Henny settled in to think about the situation which had changed since he snuck onto the thunder-cart. He knew for sure he'd been wrong about these Naked Ones when he heard this exchange:

"When we don't make our scheduled reports," the male said, "the Navy will come looking for us. With any luck at all, they'll have some Marines with them."

The second female suddenly stopped sobbing and said excitedly, "The Marines are coming? They'll save us. We're saved!"

These Naked Ones weren't with the evil Naked Ones who had enslaved the People! That must mean that these were good Naked Ones like the Marines, and the four armed ones were evil.

Henny decided to make himself known to the people in the storeroom with him. He made the low bark that Rzz-tar Chranck said was, "the Fuzzy equivalent of throat clearing."

Startled exclamations came from the Naked Ones and they turned toward Henny's hiding place.

Henny stood. He held his tail limp, and his hands away from his sides with the palms and claws facing away from the Naked Ones. "Don't be afraid," he said in what he hoped was a reassuring tone. "I'm what you call a Fuzzy, and I have a needle-rifle. We can work together to defeat the evil Naked Ones." He didn't mention the "replica K-bar" that the Ruhrines had given him along with the needle-rifle. Those weren't the exact words he used, and his pronunciation wasn't fully clear, but it was good enough that the Naked Ones understood him.

"You speak English?" the male asked. "How's that possible?"

"When the Ruhrines were on the World, I worked with their wiseone, Fzz-tar Chranck and we learned each other's languages."

"I heard about this," the first female said rapidly. "Are you, are you... what's the name? Henry, is that it? Are you the Fuzzy called Henry?"

"Henny, Henny! Yes I'm Henny!"

"Henny, right. I'm sorry I got it wrong. Sam, we're in luck," the female said. "Lieutenant Prang off the Grandar Bay taught him to speak English, and learned the Fuzzy language from him. And he said Henny's a good fighter, too."

"Henny," said the male now identified as Sam, "are you armed? Do you have a weapon?"

"Yes, I have a Naked Ones' needle-rifle."

"Right, you already said that. What do you mean by a needle-rifle?"

"You call it a fflesh-chette rifle. I prefer needle-rifle."

"Flechette," Sam said, "that's good."

"Why is that good? one of the females asked.

Sam answered, "Because the slugs thrown by the Fuzzies' guns can blow holes in the hull of the shuttle. A flechette can't."

"I'm Adele," the first female said. "Sam and Lisette and I are xenobiologists. Do you know what that is, Henny?"

"It's a wiseone who knows about people and plants of other worlds." Henny thought for a few seconds, then asked, "Is that why you were on the World, you were studying the People and the plants?"

"Yes!"

"Why didn't you come to us in the open, why did you try to hide?"

"Because if you knew we were watching, you might not have behaved the way you normally do."

Henny chittered a laugh. "You don't hide very well. Everybody knew you were there. Even the People of the Starwarmth Union knew you were there—and they're not very observant or very smart." Henny abruptly changed the subject.

"I want to talk more with you, but first we have to deal with the evil Naked Ones who have taken over this thunder-cart—and killed Keely."

"There are four of them," Sam said. "The only weapon we have is your flechette... needle rifle. One armed Fuzzy, one unarmed man, and two unarmed women—and all the humans are scientists, not a fighter among us. How can we take them on?"

"I am thinking." Henny went to the closed door and held the side of his face next to it.

"What are you...?" Sam began, but Adele hushed him. "Good hearing," she whispered, pointing to his largish ears.

Very good hearing indeed. The sentients humans called "Fuzzies" could hear the insectoids and small burrowers that were a major part of their diet moving about underground.

"None are nearby," Henny said after a moment. He looked at the humans. "Do you have writing implements? Can you draw the floor-flan for me?"

Sam looked at him sharply. All along he'd been hearing the meaning of what Henny said, even when he didn't get the exact words. While he knew that the Fuzzies were far more intelligent and technologically advanced than the mercenaries of Sharp Edge who'd held them as slaves ever admitted, he didn't expect a Fuzzy to be sophisticated enough to ask for a stylus and a floorplan.

"I have a scriber," Lisette said, the first words she'd said since declaring that they would be saved. She held it out.

Sam took it and looked around for something to draw on. Adele brushed a patch of floor clear of dust.

"Do you understand human measurements?" Sam asked as he began sketching.

"I know reeters and klicks."

"Meters and kilometers?" Sam asked for clarification.

"Yes."

"Good. We won't need kilometers for this, the shuttle isn't anywhere near that big. But meters are good."

The shuttle was a boxy oblong, bluntly pointed at one end, with two decks. Sam didn't bother drawing the lower deck, it was engineering; fuel, propulsion, life support, comps. The upper deck had four storerooms, four rooms for crew/ passenger quarters. There was a recroom, galley, and what they called the "bridge." The bridge had the flight controls, seldom used as the shuttle was mostly run by computer, and communications. There were two hatches indicated; an airlock in the common room, which was the entry the pirates had used, and a cargo hatch in the rear port storeroom. Sam had to explain what an airlock was.

"This is where we are," Sam indicated the aft port-side storeroom. "For now, they're probably holding the captain on the bridge." He indicated the forward-most space.

"Where is Keely? Is captain sure on r-ridge?" Henny wanted to know.

Sam shook his head. "If the captain isn't on the bridge being guarded, he's in his cabin." He tapped a room to the immediate left rear of the bridge. "If Keely's dead they might have moved him to their boat, or they might have put his body in the crew quarters. I don't know." After a few seconds he tapped another cabin and added, "This was Keely's. Dead or alive, he could be there."

"Those are all the roons?" Henny asked, pointing at the drawn crew quarters.

Sam nodded. "As near as I can, complete and to scale." Henny needed an explanation of "to scale."

"Good," the Fuzzy said, and spent a few moments studying the floor plan before returning to listen at the door again.

"When is sleech cycle?" he asked.

"Sleep cycle?" Adele asked.

Henny chittered an affirmative.

"It's sleep time now," she said. "That's why we're dressed..." She made a sweeping gesture at her clothes. The plain garment meant nothing to Henny; the Fuzzies, being covered with a thin fur, didn't wear clothes, night or otherwise. Still, he got the message. Even though he'd never seen a thigh-length gown before he grasped that the Naked Ones wore it to sleep in. He guessed they needed it; the temperature in the thunder-cart was chilly, although the Naked Ones didn't seem to think so. He wondered if the pink flush that suddenly appeared on Lisette's face had anything to do with the coldness of the storeroom.

"Is it sleech tine for evil Naked Ones also?"

Sam and Adele looked at each other.

"We don't know," Sam finally said. "It depends, if they're on Berrican time, yes. If not, who knows?"

Henny looked at him without comprehension. What is "Berrican time"? How could there be more than one time?

"He doesn't understand time zones," Adele said to Sam.

"Sam smacked his own forhead. "How stupid of me. He barely knows that Ishtar is a globe, and when it's day here it's night on the other side of the world."

Henny suddenly understood what Sam meant. "Rzz-tar Chranck taught me how time," he said. "He showed me a, a..." he mimed holding a ball in his hand—he couldn't pronounce the word—"with light on one side, dark on the other. I know tine zones." He nodded rapidly, he knew that was the Naked One way of signaling understanding. He looked to be in thought for a moment, then said, "one chance in two this is their sleech tine."

"Maybe," Sam agreed. "More likely one chance in three."

Henny cocked his head, absorbing that. Yes, the Naked Ones had artificial light the same as the People did, so they likely were awake longer than only the half time of daylight, the same as the People. He recalled that Rzz-tar Chranck and the Ruhrines he'd dealt with also had longer waking times.

"I listen, you quiet." Henny returned to the hatch and put his ear near it, listening for sounds of movement elsewhere on the shuttle.

Henny listened for an hour without hearing anything. "I think this is their sleech tine," he said. He broke off from the door and looked at the three scientists. Lisette looked to be asleep, Sam was nodding with his head lolling on his chest. Only Adele seemed to be awake.

"I look now." Henny eased the door open, exposing a passageway dimly lit from one end. He poked his head into the passageway and, sniffing, looked toward the light and then away from it. His eyes were large, evolved to see in unlit burrows long before his people began using glow worms to light their underground homes. Away from the light, he only saw the hatches of the other aft compartment and the end of the passageway. In the other direction, he saw that the source of the dim light was out of sight. After having been closed in the storeroom with its alien smells for no fewer than three days, and possibly more than four, and then with the three Naked Ones for a couple of hours, he couldn't detect any scents from the common room.

He looked back into the storeroom. Adele was watching him intently, as was Sam who was now awake.

"You stay," Henny whispered. He slipped all the way into the passageway and crept along it to the entry to the common room. His tail jutted straight back, and his claws faced front, ready to slash. He peered around the edge of the doorway into the common room.

The common room was much smaller than the storeroom he'd been in until now. It had sufficient seating for six people if they were friendly enough, and a table that could accomodate six if they sat closely side by side. The light seemed to come from the edge of one end of the ceiling. There were no Naked Ones in the room, although there was a reddish stain on the floor. When Henny examined it he found it was sticky. He thought it was blood from Keely.

He crept to the doorway on the other side of the common room, offset to the right side from the entrance from the storerooms and from the airlock hatch through which the pirates had entered. That hatch was closed. Listening carefully, he heard a faint voice from up ahead. He risked a look around the edge of the doorway and saw a short passageway leading forward. Two rooms opened off it on the left, two more on the right—the cabins for the passengers. One of the doors on the left was ajar; the source of the voice. The only light in the passageway spilled from the common room and the door that was ajar.

There was only one voice. Henny decided to take the risk and slipped to the open door. He was able to see less than half of the room, but that was enough to show a bound man with bruises on his face sitting on a narrow bed. Here, the voice was clear enough for Henny to understand most of what it was saying.

"One more time, Captain. You're going to turn this shuttle around and take us back to Ishtar. You will land at the same place you took off from, and once I and my men finish our business there, you will fly us off to where I tell you. If not, I'm going to start putting your people out the airlock one at a time. Do you want their deaths on your conscience?"

"You're going to kill us anyway," the captain said. "So why should I help you?"

"Anybody I put out the airlock is dead for sure," the voice said. "If I don't put anybody out the airlock, I haven't added homicide to any charges against me if I'm ever caught. That's why. So, you see, it's in my interest to keep you all alive."

The captain didn't answer immediately; Henny couldn't read Naked Ones' expressions well enough to tell if the man was considering what the other had said.

After the silence dragged on for a minute, the voice said, "I guess it's time to use the airlock."

Henny spun about and, curling his toes up so their claws wouldn't click on the deck, raced back to the storeroom. The door was open far enough for Sam and Adele to look out.

"We must move," Henny when he reached them. He stepped into the storeroom only long enough to grab a small bundle from his hiding place. In the corridor, he checked the hatch on the opposite side. It opened easily.

"Here!" Henny ordered.

Sam had to take Lisette by the arm and almost drag her along.

They barely had the hatch closed before the pirate leader appeared at the end of the passageway. He stopped at the sound of a voice that Henny could hardly hear.

"About time you came to your senses," the pirate said, and turned back.

Henny hurriedly told the Humans what he'd learned when he went forward. When he got to, "...it's time to use the airlock," Lisette's eyes went wide and her mouth wider, and she took a deep breath.

Sam moved faster than Henny had seen him move before, to wrap an arm around her to pull her close, and clamp a hand over her mouth.

"Don't scream, keep quiet!"

Adele moved to Lisette's side and hugged her. "It'll be all right, honey. We're safe now," she cooed.

Lisette sagged, and Sam relaxed his hold on her mouth. "They're going to kill us, she whimpered. "They're going to put us out the airlock."

"No they aren't," Sam said, still holding his hand ready to clamp down if she went to scream again.

"Sam's right, honey," Adele said soothingly. "If they were going to kill us, that pirate wouldn't have gone back, he still would have come to get one of us to kill."

"He would fail," Henny chittered, hefting his flechette rifle.

"You'll do that? You'll protect us?" Lisette asked.

"You are with Ruh-rines. You are good Naked Ones. I am Henny, warrior of the Brightsun Clan, friend to Ruh-rines. I rho-tect you."

With more strength than anyone would have expected, Lisette wrenched herself from Sam's grip and Adele's hug to fling herself at Henny, throwing her arms around his neck and hugging tight.

Henny dropped his rifle and slashed at her with his claws, but her movement was so sudden and unexpected that he didn't react instantly.

That gave Adele time to cry, "Don't!" and Sam to shout, "Stop!"

Henny froze, his claws nearly touching the woman's back.

"She's not attacking you," Sam told him.

"That's a hug," Adele said.

Henny then realized that Lisette was rubbing the side of her face against his neck and shoulder, very similar to the way a female of the People would nuzzle a male. He drew his claws from her back.

Lisette sneezed. "Your fur tickles my nose," she said, and giggled.

"Honey, you have to let go of Henny so he can do what he needs to do to protect us," Adele said. She gently pried Lisette's arms from around Henny and pulled her away. Lisette let herself be drawn back and looked calmer and more relaxed than she'd been since the pirates first boarded the shuttle.

They became aware of a change in the machine sounds in the small ship, and of new noises.

"It sounds like someone went through the airlock and the pirate ship detached," Sam said. "Is there any way you can find out?" he asked Henny.

The Fuzzy signaled the humans to be quiet and went to listen by the hatch. After a few moments he said he thought there was no one in the common room. He handed his rifle to Sam.

"You rho-tect if I not come a-ack." He reached into the small pack he'd retrieved from the other storeroom and withdrew the K-bar the Marines had given him along with the flechette rifle.

Sam's eyes widened at the sight of the legendary Marine combat knife. "I'm not much of a shot," he said, "but I know how to use a knife."

Henny looked at him and cocked his head.

"I took a martial arts course," Sam explained. "For the exercise," he added.

Henny made a noise, then said "Wait." He slipped out of the storeroom and padded toward the common room. No one was there. The airlock was closed. He looked through the porthole in its inner hatch, through to the far hatch, which was open with only space visible through it.

He headed to the corridor that ran between the living quarters. The cabin where the captain had been held by the pirate before was now empty. Beyond that was the bridge.

Henny could only risk a quick look into the bridge. He saw the captain sitting at a bank of controls and instruments. A man sat one on side of him watching what he did, and another sat behind him. There was no sign or sound of the other two—if there really were four pirates.

Henny backed away. He listened carefully at each of the passenger cabins, and thought he heard more than one person breathing inside one of them.

Before Henny got back to the people he'd left behind, the shuttle lurched, knocking him to the deck. When he finally regained his feet, he had to struggle to stay upright; he felt like his weight had doubled and he was walking up a steep hill. Returning to the storeroom was difficult, but he made it without further incident.

"We turned and are moving under power," Sam explained. "That's the force you feel."

While Henny told them what he'd seen and heard, he took his rifle back from Sam and handed him the K-bar.

"I can kill both of the rhi-rates I saw before they can react," he said. "But where are the other two?"

"At least one of them has to be on their ship," Adele said. "The other one could be the breathing you heard in one of the cabins."

"If that wasn't Keely," Sam said.

"We go. I kill bad Naked Ones in r-ridge," Henny told Sam. "You watch me."

"You're not going anywhere without us," Adele snapped when she realized that Henny intended to leave her and Lisette in the storeroom.

Henny studied her for a moment and thought her expression meant determination. "I kill. You watch aack."

Adele nodded and grinned. Henny was suddenly glad he didn't have to face those fangs, no matter that they were so much shorter than his own.

The weight of acceleration eased while they talked and planned, so when the four left the storeroom walking wasn't the challenge it had been when Henny had come back.

Henny led and the women trailed behind Sam. Nothing had changed in the common room. Henny stopped at the door where he'd earlier heard breathing. He still heard breathing, but it was slower than before. He handed his rifle to Sam and eased the door open, ready to pounce on whoever was there.

He didn't pounce.

"That's Keely," Sam said, brushing past him and heading for the unconscious man laying on the narrow bed. He handed the K-bar back to Henny as he passed. The women also crowded into the cabin.

"I think he'll live," Adele said after giving Keely a cursory exam. She looked at Henny and Sam. "You go save the captain. We'll take care of Keely."

Henny didn't say anything, just eased out and continued on toward the bridge. Sam followed close behind.

Henny listened at each cabin, but didn't hear sounds from inside any of them. At the entrance to the bridge, he leveled his rifle at the Naked One sitting next to the captain and was squeezing the trigger when Sam suddenly shouted:

"Drop your weapons and surrender! We've got you covered and are taking our shuttle back."

The two pirates dove from their seats, both drew handguns and twisted or spun to face the entrance. They fired.

Henny flinched at the shout just behind him and his first shot thudded into the back of the seat the pirate next to the captain had just left. He bounded into the bridge and to the right, out of the line along which the two pirates shot. He saw one of them clearly, and put a flechette into his chest. That one screamed and curled around his wound, dropping his pistol. The other scrabbled along the deck, seeking better cover. He threw a shot in Henny's direction, but didn't aim and the flechette went high and wide.

The bridge wasn't a large room, no more than four meters wide, really too small to use a rifle. Henny let go of his and pounced high into the air, brushing against the ceiling as he sailed over the chair the pirate had occupied, and came down on the man's back, digging his claws into the flesh.

The man screamed and twisted onto his side to dislodge the Fuzzy. But Henny dug his claws in more deeply and wasn't thrown off. When the man tried to turn his pistol to shoot Henny, Henny let go of his back with one hand and raked those claws the length of the man's arm, ending at the pistol and tearing it from his grip.

He put his claws at the man's throat, with just enough pressure, to let him know how easy it would be to tear out his throat.

"Surrender," he demanded.

One of the first shots fired by the mercenaries hit Sam in the shoulder. Fortunately for him the flechette had gone all the way through, merely chipping a bone along the way. Adele and Lisette were able to bind the wound well enough to keep him from bleeding to death before he got proper medical attention. As soon as the two pirates were secured, the captain called for assistance and changed course back for Opal.

Lorenzo, the leader of the pirates, explained that even though they knew there was a cache of gems to be picked up, they didn't know where it was. They needed the captain and his shuttle to take them to the right place, which was why they took the shuttle.

"We're the good guys," Sam meekly explained when Henny asked why he'd shouted for the pirates to surrender. "We're supposed to give the bad guys a chance to surrender instead of just killing them."

Henny looked away in disgust. "Ruh-rines, they kill evil ones," was all he said.

As for the other two pirates, when a Confederation Navy patrol boat picked them up they were bickering about how the fool proof plan was exactly that, a plan for fools.

IRON HORSES

Judi Fleming

Lieutenant Smith folded his arms across his chest and said, "I don't like them." He eyed the shiny new tech. The build of the cliff rovers was sleek and equine. There were twelve arranged in two rows of six just outside the squad's rocky hillside barracks.

Sergeant Jones paused with her hand's caress halfway down the neck of the new rover closest to her. Each could effectively carry a single soldier up the narrow pathways with its clawed feet grappling and holding against the high winds and great unpredictable gusts here on the planet Zephyr.

She said, "What's not to like? We need something to get up these damned cliffs and into the rebel caves to rout them out. These things have actual horse behaviors programmed into the battle computers. They're awesome."

"Now how can you trust *that*? Have you ever been on a real horse? I mean a real Earth horse? They're completely unreliable." He braced himself against the 40-mile-an-hour winds that buffeted him with practiced ease.

Sergeant Jones shrugged and she climbed into the saddle. The E-Quad's four legs adjusted to her weight and the wind, digging clawed feet into the rocky soil to balance her weight against the wind effortlessly.

"I'm going to try one out, sir. No use telling the rest of the troops about them if they aren't to specs," she said.

The machine canted its sensor head to take in the terrain, eerily like a real horse in that simple movement. The two bulbous visual intakes glowed like eyes in the dusk. The audio receptors swiveled like ears. Jones fingered the controls at the front of the deep saddle that spread across either side of the grip which acted as a saddle horn. Easy to hold for balance, but low enough not to interfere with drawing weapons from her belt and most important, snug enough to keep you on through gusts. The data panels on the saddle lit up with wind speed, altitude, temperature, and more.

"Yes sir, these are sweet little E-Quads rovers," she said to the lieutenant. "You want to go topside with me?" She indicated the steep incline up the cliff face, so narrow that only one rover could go at a time.

A fierce straight line wind slammed down on her but all the rovers braced and shuffled out of formation as each adjusted to its own needs. The lieutenant was knocked flat but only grumbled as he stood to slap the dust off of his uniform. Sergeant Jones's face remained impassive. She'd felt that hard ground many times herself.

"No, you go on ahead, Sergeant. Report back when you return."

She saluted, then checked panels, working out what she had only read about before. Sergeant Jones slipped her boot heels into the foot stirrups and pressed the side accelerators, moving off smoothly. She had always wanted to ride a horse and wondered just how the programming would affect the machine's behavior. She was an expert flyer, and missed that here on Zephyr where such small craft were impossible to use in the winds.

Jones smiled, but immediately coughed the grit out of her teeth as a dust devil swirled over her back and up the trail. She snapped the face plate down against the phenomenal winds.

Here both her troops and the rebel miners lived in caves situated up and down these narrow ravines. The gale force winds on the surface of the planet above the trench-like network of canyons generally stayed below hurricane speeds. Mine entrances riddled the canyon walls like black eyes weeping rocky trails down to the floor far below. A rat's maze of dangerous urban warfare made all the more challenging when your troops could be whipped off of the narrow pathways even before they reached a rebel stronghold.

This wild and windy planet was full of natural mineral resources and well worth fighting for. The miners had done just that. They'd been fighting for nearly a year now, with neither side making any ground. Could this rover finally end the conflict? Being able to gallop up the pathways without fear of being ripped from the paths would tip the battle in her unit's favor. She was sure of it.

Delighted, Jones found the E-Quad did indeed work as described. It gripped and clambered upward with ease, cutting into the rocky surface as it climbed with the grace of an iron horse. When she neared the summit, she turned to look back without thinking and her weight guided the rover into a smooth about-face. *Nice*, she thought.

She leaned against the heel accelerators and hurtled down the trail, exhilarated by the speed and security of the elegantly designed "saddle" and the machine's footing. These were amazing and just as much fun as the flyers she favored.

Sergeant Jones parked the E-Quad and reported its performance to the lieutenant, nearly breathless in her enthusiasm for it.

"Looks like we have the advantage now," he agreed. "Gather the troops and let's brief them. I've gotten similar reports from the other squad leaders. It's full dark now, so we'll start the training first thing tomorrow."

The results of the rest of her unit working with the E-Quads didn't go well on the first day out. Many soldiers had no sense of balance or jammed the controls harder than necessary, which caused the units to lurch and buck with equal force. There were quite a few bruised bodies as well as egos.

"I knew that damned horse programming wasn't going to be good," muttered the lieutenant.

"With all due respect, sir. It's the troops that have got to learn the finesse." Sergeant Jones was frowning. Why was it so hard for so many people to allow their bodies to guide the rovers? These units weren't the same as a wheeled rover or even the sleek recon flyers that were used on other planets. They adjusted to the sway of the winds and your body. Perfect for this planet. It would take some time to teach her soldiers how to adjust the heaviness of their hands and heels.

"Let's take a look at the battle plans that came with them. I'd love to get off this rock and back home in time for the holidays."

The lieutenant's comment brought her back to the moment. She dismissed the troops and had them clean the dust and dirt from all the carefully filtered sensors and intakes on the E-Quads, much like brushing a horse with hand-held vacuums.

"We're to drive our batch of miners toward this central location topside where the prison transports will meet us, same as the other units. Any resistance will be dealt with. No mercy this time. The government has replacement miners ready to begin as soon as we clear out these rebels." He thumbed the holo projector on his utility belt that showed the coordinated attack plans for each unit. Sergeant Jones nodded as she scanned the plans, noting the rough places for each unit at every altitude change along with the straight line wind data for each.

This wouldn't be easy, even with the E-Quads. The fighting would start inside the tunnels and, although these rovers were small, it would be tight.

She'd have to teach her troops to duck and fire when they learned how to balance.

"How long do we have?" she asked.

"A month," was his reply. The muscles twitched along his jaw.

She rolled this over in her mind. Timing for each unit and each rider's ability would be crucial for success of the mission. And the winds. Mercy have us, she hoped it would be a mild day when they deployed.

"Time of day, sir?"

"Dawn."

"I'll set up a plan to work with our troops and the rovers. I'll have them ready for you when they're needed, sir."

The loud clang of a loose barrel echoed off the canyon walls, startling the parked E-Quads into a wild shuffle as their sensors tried to adjust to the unexpected moving object being flung in the wind. Soldiers swore and two hopped on one foot after extracting their reinforced boots from under the clawed hooves.

The lieutenant chuckled, "I can't wait to see that, Sergeant. These things are too much like real horses from what I've seen so far. I think even our best laid plans may be challenged by that bit of programming." He snorted and shook his head. "Horse sense. Huh. There is no such thing, if you ask me."

Jones hated to admit that the lieutenant had been right. It had taken every bit of her leadership skills to whip the troops into battle readiness with these new rovers. She'd used every teaching trick she knew to get the worst of the soldiers to this meager proficiency level in one month. And she still felt it wasn't good enough. Some just didn't have the knack for it and some loathed the rovers for all the shame and frustration they'd shown in front of others while trying to master these beasts.

Any other battle rover was effortless in comparison. Show a soldier the movements, then repeat over and over again until it became muscle memory. But the E-Quads had better response times than their riders. They took in data and adjusted for things that the human concentrating on their own movements couldn't see in time. Still, her forces had good formations, excellent results on obstacle courses, and great hit ratios from firing positions so she felt they were ready as they could be.

The thrill of the upcoming battle made it hard for her to sleep, but somehow she did. Awake an hour early, she cleaned her own rover one more time. It seemed to know her and turned to expose the flank exhaust that had some grunge stuck inside at a hard-to-see angle.

"Keep me safe today, Rover," she said with affection as she scraped the exhaust clean. She heard the clump of boots and turned.

"Bad news," the lieutenant said as he approached.

Jones snapped out a smart salute, which he returned distractedly.

"What bad news, sir? Weather says winds are not quite gale force topside today."

"No, not the weather." He rubbed the dust off his face shield. "Bravo Company had an E-Quad stolen a week ago and just now reported it. The miners have had time to see their capabilities and spread the word."

Sergeant Jones was dumbstruck. How could they not report this sooner? They've endangered everyone. "Sir, we've had three times the experience on our units as the miners would have with that one, so perhaps it isn't so bad after all."

"You're forgetting that most of these miners are real live engineers who built most of the equipment used to mine this damned rock."

Jones groaned. Damn and double damn indeed. "Did HQ change the battle plans when they found out?"

"No, but I have a really bad feeling about this one, Jonesy."

"She couldn't think of anything else to say, so she turned and ordered her troops onto their rovers and moved out. She put the most capable soldiers up front, and kept herself toward the middle as she called for full speed to the coordinates. The lieutenant came up the rear, holding on to the saddle grip for dear life, teeth barred in a death grin as his butt pounded in the saddle.

Before she knew it, they were ducking into tunnels, screaming battle cries and firing, flushing men and women from the mining tunnels assigned to them. Soon it was a chaos of shots ricocheting splinters of rock into the air and the eerie glow of lights from the E-Quad eye sensors as they careened through narrow spaces.

Jones pursued one miner as he dashed down a side exit and out into the open. He caught her by surprise by jumping on a crude imitation of her own E-Quad and speeding into the canyon beyond.

Damn, she thought, *If they've already replicated one in a week, how many more would there be?*

She urged Rover after him, marveling at how much easier his unit turned and climbed up the steep trails toward the windy plains above.

Where the hell was he going on that kludged-together rover, she wondered. *Waitaminute.* Was he actually going toward the collection point that their orders had them going to anyway? Was he onto them, or was this just the results of good intel and planning?

Her E-Quad surged and scrambled up the pathway, scattering small rocks off the steep path. She urged Rover on, leaning precariously forward and pressing her heels hard into its side, trying to get a clear shot of the man as he slung himself low along his rover's back.

A viscious wind gust attempted to scrape her from the trail as she charged up, slowly losing ground. *Damn and double damn.* Her heart raced as she clung harder to the E-Quad. Jones concentrated on balancing her weight and movements to make the rover's efforts more efficient. At least the miner had no weapon. Otherwise he would have fired by now. Getting up early had paid off on that account at least.

He crested the surface and disappeared from view. She galloped after, hoping that she was right about the weapons. She was the perfect target coming up out of the canyon. Heart in throat, she leaned low as they surged over the edge and was instantly knocked flat by the man's rover slamming into her full speed. They slid across the rocks and gravel, her tear-proof uniform saved her skin, but her left ankle snapped under the weight of the beast.

Rover was on its feet a second later, shielding her prone body precariously close to the edge as the miner circled his mount for another charge. An eerie sound filled the air as Rover used its mechanical warning alarms as a screaming equine challenge. It braced to defend its rider.

The miner pulled his unit to a stop, open-mouthed in surprise. He spit dirt. "None of ours have ever done *that*," he said.

The pain in her ankle made it hard to concentrate as she clawed around for her weapon. The laser was nowhere in sight. It must have gone over the edge when she was thrown. Her vision edged red as shock set in. Jones gritted her teeth and tried to stand, leaning against Rover for support.

Chaos came boiling up the ledge as the rebel miners drove what remained of her unit topside. Many she didn't recognize were among them. Bravo Company. And Charlie too. They'd all been overpowered. Set up.

The soldiers trudged sullenly, ignoring the yells and taunts of the miners riding their unit's E-quads who drove them upward into the thick swirling dust of topside. Some units bucked and skittered dangerously close to the edge as the men and women learned the commands that had taken the troops weeks of practice.

Rover stood firm, bracing and protecting her from the fierce wind gusts that threatened to topple her.

"Let it go. You've lost," the man said to her.

"I can't," she said. "Ankle's broken."

"Not my problem. Let it go."

She surprised him by swinging on board her mount, using the burst of adrenaline which coursed through her system. Sergeant Jones was not one to give in so easily. The instant she was on, she was urging Rover through the whirling dust of the windy plateau. She hung on for dear life, teeth clenched against the jarring pain of its gait. She had to make it to the prison ship and warn them. She'd need the soldiers on that craft as reinforcements.

A mile-wide tornado loomed out of the thick, blowing dust and debris. It spiraled jerkily toward her, almost taking her breath away in its suddenness and strength.

"Holy shit!" she screamed as she was jerked sideways from the force of Rover's course adjustment around the wobbling monster.

She couldn't hear the cries of despair behind her as her ragged soldiers were abandoned by the E-quad riders who dashed down the trail and into the safety of the caves below. Her attention had dwindled down to hanging on and staying conscious long enough to make it to the prison ship.

The miner she had initially pursued matched her speed as she angled toward the rendezvous point.

"Give up," he cried.

"Never," she said as she tried to steer Rover into him, hoping to trip his up, unable to do so with only one working foot.

"The Council granted us independence. We've laid charges on the landing point," he said as charged past her on his faster mount, forcing Rover around and away from it.

The tremendous explosion tossed her across Rover's neck and the E-Quad braced to a bone-jarring halt to save her from flipping over its head. Jones struggled to breathe, sure she now had broken ribs to add to her list of injuries.

"Will you surrender now?" His voice was mild, almost patronizing, as he grinned like an idiot.

She sucked air ineffectively, unable to answer.

"We've claimed all occupying troops and equipment as casualties of war. They granted us that if we can meet the delivery schedules they set. You aren't going anywhere, dear lady."

A year later, Jones found herself inspecting the newly designed E-Quads, marveling at their flexibility and intelligent programming. She was in charge of Zephyr's ground forces and was now a citizen of the dusty planet. Her ability to train both the rover units and the planetary defense troops who rode them had saved her life.

Jones was quietly satisfied that she was still a soldier and had attained a rank that would never have been possible working as a Council soldier anywhere else in the universe.

And she rode her original Rover, tweaking its instruments and joints, upgrading it as she went. It had, after all, saved her life.

ABOUT THE AUTHORS

Jack Mc Devitt
BLACK TO MOVE

Jack McDevitt has been described by Stephen King as "the logical heir to Isaac Asimov and Arthur C. Clarke." He is the author of twenty-two novels, eleven of which have been Nebula finalists, and more than eighty short stories. Seeker won the Nebula for best novel in 2007. In 2003, Omega received the John W. Campbell Memorial Award for best science fiction novel. He won the Georgia Writers' Association Lifetime Achievement Award in 2013. His first novel, The Hercules Text, won a special Philip K. Dick Award in 1986. He has received various other honors. Most recently, the International Astronomical Union named an asteroid for him.

A best-of collection of his stories is available in Cryptic, published by Subterranean Press.

McDevitt's most recent books are Coming Home, an Alex Benedict novel, and Thunderbird, both from Ace. Alex and his partner Chase Kolpath are antiquity dealers living in the far future. They specialize in solving historical mysteries. Another popular character has been Priscilla Hutchins, a starship captain during the tempestuous early years of interstellar flight. She is usually caught up with unexpected discoveries.

A Philadelphia native, McDevitt had a varied career before becoming a writer. He's been a naval officer, an English teacher, a customs officer, and a taxi driver. He has also conducted leadership and management seminars for the U.S. Customs Service. He is married to the former Maureen McAdams, and resides in Brunswick, Georgia, where he keeps a weather eye on hurricanes.

John C. Wright
PETER POWER ARMOR

John C. Wright is a retired attorney, newspaperman and newspaper editor, who was only once on the lam and forced to hide from the police who did not admire his newspaper.

In 1984, he graduated from St. John's College in Annapolis, home of the "Great Books" program. In 1987, he graduated from the College and William and Mary's Law School (going from the third oldest to the second oldest school in continuous use in the United States), and was admitted to the practice of law in three jurisdictions (New York, May 1989; Maryland December 1990; DC January 1994). His law practice was unsuccessful enough to drive him into bankruptcy soon thereafter. His stint as a newspaperman for the St. Mary's Today was more rewarding spiritually, but, alas, also a failure financially. He presently works (successfully) as a writer in Virginia, where he lives in fairy-tale-like happiness with his wife, the authoress L. Jagi Lamplighter, and their three children: Orville, Wilbur, and Just Wright.

John was recently the recipient of the very first Dragon Award for Best Science Fiction Book.

Jeffrey Lyman
COMPARTMENT ALPHA

Jeffrey Lyman is a mechanical engineer working in the New York area. In 2004 he attended the Odyssey Fantasy Writing Workshop for six weeks in New Hampshire. His first publication came in 2005, in the anthology *No Longer Dreams*, followed by a short story in the anthology *Bad-Ass Faeries*. Upcoming publications include a novella in the anthology *Blood and Devotion* and a short story in the anthology *Sails and Sorcery*, both by Fantasist Enterprises.

Lawrence M. Schoen
THRESHER

Lawrence M. Schoen holds a Ph.D. in cognitive psychology, with a special focus in psycholinguistics. He spent ten years as a college professor, and has done extensive research in the areas of human memory and language. His background in the study of behavior and the mind provide a principal metaphor for his fiction. He currently works as the director of research and chief compliance officer for a series of mental health and addiction treatment facilities. He's also one of the world's foremost authorities on the Klingon language, having championed the exploration of this constructed tongue and lectured on this unique topic throughout the world. Among other writing endeavors, he is currently expanding "Thresher" to novel length. He lives in Philadelphia with his wife, Valerie, who is neither a psychologist nor a speaker of Klingon.

Andy Remic
JUNKED

Andy Remic is a hard-hitting kick-ass military science fiction author with five novels in print. In his spare time he enjoys mountain climbing, sword fighting and hacking computer systems. He can kill a man with a single blow of his chainsaw, but prefers photographing woodland wildlife and biomod engineering. He is sometimes accused of nihilism.

Danielle Ackley-McPhail
FIRST LINE

Award-winning author and editor Danielle Ackley-McPhail has worked both sides of the publishing industry for longer than she cares to admit. In 2014 she joined forces with husband Mike McPhail and friend Greg Schauer to form her own publishing house, eSpec Books (www.especbooks.com).

Her published works include six novels, Yesterday's Dreams, Tomorrow's Memories, Today's Promise, The Halfling's Court, The Redcaps' Queen, and Baba Ali and the Clockwork Djinn, written with Day Al-Mohamed. She is also the author of the solo collections *A Legacy of Stars, Consigned to the Sea, Flash in the Can, and Transcendence, the non-fiction writers' guide, The Literary Handyman,* and is the senior editor of the *Bad-Ass Faeries* anthology series, *Gaslight & Grimm, Dragon's Lure,* and *In an Iron Cage.* Her short stories are included in numerous other anthologies and collections.

Danielle lives in New Jersey with husband and fellow writer, Mike McPhail and three extremely spoiled cats. She can be found on Facebook (Danielle Ackley-McPhail) and Twitter (DMcPhail, BadAssFaeries, eSpecBooks).

To learn more, visit www.sidhenadaire.com, www.especbooks.com or www.badassfaeries.com.

Charles E. Gannon
TO SPEC

Dr. Charles E. Gannon is a Distinguished Professor of English (St. Bonaventure U.) & Fulbright Senior Specialist (American Lit & Culture). He has had novellas in *Analog* and the *War World* series. His nonfiction book *Rumors of War and Infernal Machines* won the 2006 ALA Outstanding Text Award. He also worked as author and editor for GDW, and was a routine contributor to both the scientific/technical content and story-line in the award-winning games *Traveller*, and *2300 AD*. He has been awarded Fulbrights to England, Scotland, the Czech Republic, Slovakia, Netherlands, and worked eight years as scriptwriter/producer in NYC.

Bud Sparhawk
GLASS BOX

Bud Sparhawk's novel *Distant Seas* (Fantastic Books) is available from Amazon and other booksellers as trade paperback and eBook. He has a mass market paperback novel: *Vixen* (Cosmos) and two print collections: *Sam Boone : Front To Back* (Foxacre Press, 2001) and *Dancing with Dragons* (Wildside Press, 2008). He has three e-Novels available through Amazon and other channels.

Bud has been a three-time novella finalist for the Nebula award: *Primrose and Thorn* (Analog, May 1996), *Magic's Price* (Analog, March 2001), and *Clay's Pride* (Analog, July/August 2004). His work has appeared in two Year's Best anthologies: *Year's Best SF #11* (EOS), David Harwell-Editor) and *The Years Best Science Fiction, Fourteenth Annual Collection*, (St Martins Press, Garner Dozois – Editor.)

Bud's short stories have appeared frequently in Analog Fact/Fiction, less so in Asimov's, as well as in five Defending the Future and other anthologies, publications and audio books. He has put out several collections of some of his published works in ebook format. A complete bibliography can be found at: http://budsparhawk.com.

He also writes an occasional blog on the pain of writing at http://budsparhawk.blogspot.com.

C.J. Henderson
EVERYTHING'S BETTER WITH MONKEYS

CJ Henderson was the creator of the *Piers Knight, Jack Hagee,* and *Teddy London* series of novels, author of such diverse yet fabulously interesting titles as *The Field Guide to Monsters, Babys First Mythos, The Encyclopedia of Science Fiction Movies* and some fifty other books and novels. He has had hundreds of short stories published along with hundreds of comics and thousands of non-fiction pieces.

For more check out his website, www.cjhenderson.com. He passed away in 2014 from lymphoma.

James Chambers
MOTHER OF PEACE

James Chambers "writes stories that are paced fast enough to friction burn a reader's eyeballs," says Horror Reader.com. His tales of horror, fantasy, and science fiction have been published in *Bad-Ass Faeries, Breach the Hull, Crypto-Critters (Volume 1 and 2), Dark Furies, The Dead Walk, The Dead Walk Again, Hardboiled Cthulhu, Lin Carter's Anton Zarnak Supernatural Detective, No Longer Dreams, Sick: An Anthology of Illness, Weird Trails,* and *Warfear* as well as the magazines *Bare Bone, Cthulhu Sex,* and *Allen K's In-human.* His short story collection, with illustrator Jason Whitley, *The Midnight Hour: Saint Lawn Hill and Other Tales,* was published in 2005. His website is www.jameschambersonline.com.

Jeff Young
BLANKETS

Jeff Young is a bookseller first and a writer second, although he wouldn't mind a reversal of fortune.

He is an award winning author who contributed to the anthologies: *Writers of the Future v.26, By Any Means, Best Laid Plans, Dogs of War, In an*

Iron Cage, Fantastic Futures 13, Clockwork Chaos, TV Gods, The Society for the Preservation of C.J. Henderson and *Gaslight and Grimm.* Jeff's work was also published in the magazines eSteampunk, Realms, Cemetery Moon, Trail of Indiscretion, Realms Beyond, Carbon14 and Neuronet. He is also an editor with Fortress Publishing for their Drunken Comic Book Monkey line as well as the anthology TV Gods and the upcoming TV Gods : Summer Programming.

Jeff has helped run the Watch the Skies SF&F Reading Group of Harrisburg and Camp Hill for more than fifteen years. Finally, Jeff is also the proprietor of the online eBay and Etsy shops- Helm Haven, which produces Renaissance and Steampunk costume pieces.

Mike McPhail
SHEEPDOG

Author and graphic artist Mike McPhail is a member of the Military Writers Society of America. He is dedicated to helping his fellow service members (and those deserving civilians) in their efforts to become authors/editors/artists, as well as supporting related organizations in their efforts to help those "who have given their all for us." www.milscifi.com

He is best known as the editor and illustrator of the award-winning *Defending The Future* series of military science fiction anthologies, which just celebrated it's tenth anniversary. www.defendingthefuture.com

In 2014 he added the title of publisher, as the co-owner of eSpec Books LLC, Speculative Fiction Publishing. www.especbooks.com

Robert E. Waters
DEVIL DANCERS

Robert E Waters had been writing and publishing stories since 2003, with his first publication in Weird Tales. Since then, he has published over 30 stories in various print and on-line magazines and anthologies, including eSpec's *Weird Wild West* and the *Defending the Future* Mil SF anthology series. Robert is also a frequent contributor to Eric Flint's alternate history series, *1632/Ring of Fire*, with several stories published in the on-line *Grantville Gazette*, and most recently in Baen Book's *Ring of Fire IV* anthology. Robert's first novel, *The Wayward Eight: A Contract to Die For*, was released in 2014 under the Zmok imprint, and is a "weird wild west" adventure set in the Wild West Exodus gaming universe. Robert lives in Baltimore, Maryland with his wife Beth, their son Jason, and their cat Buzz. www.roberternestwaters.com.

John G. Hemry
DAWN S LAST LIGHT

John G. Hemry, writing as Jack Campbell, is the author of the best-selling Lost Fleet series. Under his own name, he's also the author of the 'JAG in space' series, the latest of which is *Against All Enemies*. His short fiction has appeared in places as varied as the latest *Chicks in Chainmail* anthology (*Turn the Other Chick*), and *Analog* magazine (which published his Nebula Award-nominated story *Small Moments in Time*). John's nonfiction has appeared in *Analog* and *Artemis* magazines as well as BenBella books on *Charmed*, *Star Wars*, and *Superman*. John is a retired US Navy officer who lives in Maryland with his wife (the incomparable S), and three great kids.

Brenda Cooper
Cracking the Sky

Brenda Cooper writes science fiction and fantasy novels and short stories, and sometimes, poetry. Her most recent novel is *Spear of Light*, from Pyr and her most recent story collection is *Cracking the Sky* from Fairwood Press. POST will be out from eSpec Books in late fall 2016. Brenda is a technology professional and a futurist, and publishes non-fiction on the environment and the future. Her non-fiction has appeared on Slate and Crosscut and her short fiction has appeared in Nature Magazine, among other venues.

See her website at www.brenda-cooper.com.

Brenda lives in the Pacific Northwest in a household with three people, three dogs, far more than three computers, and only one TV in it.

Nancy Jane Moore

Gambit

Nancy Jane Moore is the author of *The Weave*, a military science fiction novel published in 2015 by Aqueduct Press, along with several other books and numerous short stories and essays. A native Texan, she spent many years in Washington, DC, and now lives in Oakland, California. Moore has trained in martial arts since 1979 and holds a fourth degree black belt in Aikido. She is a member of the authors' co-op Book View Café, and blogs weekly at http://bookviewcafe.com/blog/. http://nancyjanemoore.com/

Maria V. Snyder

Godzilla Warfare

Meteorologist turned novelist, Maria's been writing fantasy and science fiction since she was bored at work and needed something creative to do. Over a dozen novels and multiple short stories later, Maria's learned a thing or three about writing. She's been on the New York Times bestseller list, won a half-dozen awards, and has earned her MA degree in Writing from Seton Hill University where she's been happily sharing her knowledge with the current crop of MFA students.

She also enjoys creating new worlds where horses and swords rule, 'cause let's face it, they're cool, although she's been known to trap her poor characters in a giant metal cube and let them figure out how to get out. Readers are welcome to check out her website for book excerpts, free short stories, maps, blog, and her schedule at http://www.MariaVSnyder.com.

Keith R.A. DeCandido

THE STONE OF THE FIRST
HIGH PONTIFF

Keith R.A. DeCandido is the international best-selling and award-winning author of about 45 novels, as well as a mess of short fiction, comic books, etc. He's probably best known for his media tie-in work, writing stories in the worlds of television (*Star Trek, Doctor Who*), games (*World of Warcraft, Dungeons & Dragons*), movies (*Serenity, Cars*), and comic books (*Spider-Man, X-Men*). He is also the author of the "Precinct" series of fantasy police procedurals, including *Dragon Precinct, Unicorn Precinct, Goblin Precinct, Gryphon Precinct, Tales from Dragon Precinct,* and a new comic book series. Other recent work includes *Leverage: The Zoo Job, Star Trek: The Klingon Art of War,* and *Ragnarok and Roll: Tales of Cassie Zukav, Weirdness Magnet.* Find out less, including links to his blog, Facebook, Twitter, and various and sundry podcasts, at DeCandido.net.

David Sherman
CHITTER CHITTER BANG BANG

David Sherman is the author or co-author of thirty-one novels, but only two previously-published short stories. His solo novels include nine about US Marines in Vietnam (he was one), the *DemonTech* fantasy series, and a vampire novel, *The Hunt*. With Dan Cragg, he has written the *Starfist* military science fiction series, its spinoff *Starfist: Force Recon*, and a Star Wars novel, *Jedi Trial*. His most recent novels are *The Hunt, The Junkyard Dogs,* and *Double Jeopardy*, the fourteenth in the *Starfist* series. He lives in South Florida, and invites readers to visit his website, www.novelier.com.

Judi Fleming
IRON HORSES

Judi Fleming works as a training specialist and instructional designer for the federal government in her day job and thus much of her writing is of the non-exciting technical sort. She is a graduate of Seton Hill University Writing Popular Fiction Master's Program.